SKIN PRIVILEGE

Karin Slaughter grew up in a small south Georgia town and has been writing short stories and novels since she was a child. She is the author of the Grant County series of international bestsellers *Blindsighted*, *Kisscut*, *A Faint Cold Fear*, *Indelible* and *Faithless*, and the bestselling stand-alone novel set in Atlanta, *Triptych*. She is also the editor of *Like A Charm*, a collaboration of British and American crime fiction writers. She lives in Atlanta.

Praise for Karin Slaughter

'Without doubt an accomplished, compelling and complex tale, with page-turning power aplenty'
Daily Express

'Confirms her at the summit of the school of writers specialising in forensic medicine and terror . . . Slaughter's characters talk in believable dialogue. She's excellent at portraying the undertones and claustrophobia of communities where everyone knows everyone else's business, and even better at creating an atmosphere of lurking evil'
The Times

'Slaughter deftly turns all assumptions on their head . . . Her ability to make you buy into one reality, then another, means that the surprises – and the violent scenes – keep coming'
Time Out

'A great read . . . crime fiction at its finest'
MICHAEL CONNELLY

'A fast-paced and unsettling story . . . A compelling and fluid read'
Daily Telegraph

'Criminally spectacular' *OK!*

KARIN SLAUGHTER

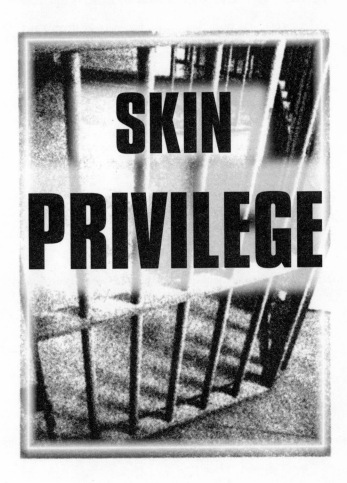

SKIN PRIVILEGE

C

Century · London

Published by Century 2007

2 4 6 8 10 9 7 5 3

First published in Great Britain in 2007 by
Century
Random House, 20 Vauxhall Bridge Road,
London SW1V 2SA

www.rbooks.co.uk

Addresses for companies within The Random House Group Limited
can be found at: www.randomhouse.co.uk

The Random House Group Limited Reg. No. No. 954009

A CIP catalogue record for this book
is available from the British Library

ISBN 9781844138593

The Random House Group Limited makes every effort to ensure that the
papers used in its books are made from trees that have been legally sourced
from well-managed and credibly certified forests. Our paper procurement
policy can be found at: www.randomhouse.co.uk/paper.htm

Mixed Sources
Product group from well-managed
forests and other controlled sources
www.fsc.org Cert no. TT-COC-2139
© 1996 Forest Stewardship Council
FSC

Printed and bound in Great Britain by
Clays Ltd, St Ives plc

For Susan

SKIN PRIVILEGE

PROLOGUE

WHAT HAD THEY GIVEN HER? What had the needle brought into her veins? She could barely keep her eyes open, but her ears were working almost too well. Under a sharp, piercing ring, she could hear a skip in the car's engine, the *thump-thump* as the tires rolled over uneven terrain. The man sitting beside her in the backseat spoke softly, almost like a lullaby you would sing to a child. There was something calming about his tone, and she found her head dropping down as he talked, only to jerk back up at Lena's curt, cutting responses.

Her shoulders ached from stretching her hands behind her back. Or maybe they didn't ache. Maybe she just thought they should, so her brain sent the message that they did. The ache was dull, a thud that throbbed along with her beating heart. She tried to focus on other things, like the conversation going on around her or where Lena was driving the car. Instead, she found herself spiraling back into her body, cocooning into every new sensation like a newborn rolling into a blanket.

The back of her legs were stinging from the leather, though she did not know why. It was cool out. There was a chill on the back of her neck. She remembered sitting in her father's Chevette on a long trip to Florida. There was no air-conditioning and it was the middle of August. All four windows were rolled down, but nothing would cut the heat. The radio crackled. There was no music, no station they could all agree on. In the front seat, her parents argued over the route, the cost of gas, whether or not they were speeding. Outside of Opelika, her mother told her father to pull over at the general store so they could buy frozen Cokes and orange crackers. They all winced as they moved to get out of the car, the skin on the back of their arms and legs sticking to the seats as if the heat had cooked their bodies to the vinyl.

She felt the car lurch as Lena put the gear into park. The engine was still humming, the soft purr vibrating in her ears.

There was someone else—not in the car, but in the distance. They were on the football field. She recognized the scoreboard, big letters screaming "GO MUSTANGS!"

Lena had turned around, was watching both of them. Beside her, the man shifted. He tucked the gun into the waistband of his jeans. He was wearing a ski mask, the kind you saw in horror films, where only the eyes and mouth were revealed. That was enough, though. She knew him, could almost say his name if her mouth would only move to let her.

The man said something about being thirsty, and Lena passed him a large Styrofoam cup. The white of the cup was intense, almost blinding. Out of nowhere, she felt a thirst in her throat like never before. The suggestion of water was enough to bring tears to her eyes.

Lena was looking at her, trying to say something without using her voice.

Suddenly, the man slid across the backseat, moved close enough so that she could feel the heat off his body, smell the subtle musk of his aftershave. She felt his hand go around the back of her neck, resting lightly on the nape. His fingers were soft, gentle. She concentrated on his voice, knew that what was being said was important, that she had to listen.

"You gonna leave?" the man asked Lena. "Or do you want to stay put and hear what I have to say?"

Lena had turned away from them, maybe had her hand on the door handle. She turned back now, saying, "Tell me."

"If I had wanted to kill you," he began, "you would already be dead. You know that."

"Yes."

"Your friend here..." He said something else, but his words were jumbled together so that by the time they reached her ears, they meant nothing. She could only look at Lena and judge from the other woman's reaction what her own should be.

Fear. She should be afraid.

"Don't hurt her," Lena begged. "She's got children. Her husband—"

"Yeah, it's sad. But you make your choices."

"You call that a choice?" Lena snapped. There was more, but all that came across was terror. The exchange continued, then she felt a sudden chill come over her. A familiar odor filled the car—heavy, pungent. She knew what it was. She'd smelled it before but her mind could not tell her when or where.

The door opened. The man slid out of the car and stood there, looking at her. He did not look sad or upset. He looked resigned. She had seen that look before. She knew him—knew the cold eyes behind the mask, the wet lips. She had known him all of her life.

What was the smell? She should remember this smell.

He murmured a few words. Something flashed in his hand—a silver cigarette lighter.

She understood now. Panic sent a flood of adrenaline to her brain, cutting through the fog, slashing right to her heart.

Lighter fluid. The cup had contained lighter fluid. He had poured it all over her body. She was soaked—dripping in it.

"No!" Lena screamed, lunging, fingers splayed.

The lighter dropped onto her lap, the flame igniting the liquid, the liquid burning her clothes. There was a horrible keening—it was coming from her own throat as she sat helplessly watching the flames lick up her body. Her arms jerked up, her toes and feet curled in like a baby's. She thought again of that long-ago trip to Florida, the exhausting heat, the sharp, unbearable rip of pain as her flesh cooked to the seat.

MONDAY AFTERNOON

CHAPTER 1

SARA LINTON LOOKED AT HER WATCH. The Seiko had been a gift from her grandmother on the day Sara graduated from high school. On Granny Em's own graduation day, she had been four months from marriage, a year and a half from bearing the first of her six children and thirty-eight years from losing her husband to cancer. Higher education was something Emma's father had seen as a waste of time and money, especially for a woman. Emma had not argued—she was raised during a time when children did not think to disagree with their parents—though she made sure that all four of her surviving children attended college.

"Wear this and think of me," Granny Em had said that day on the school campus as she closed the watch's silver bracelet around Sara's wrist. "You're going to do everything you ever dreamed of, and I want you to know that I will always be right there beside you."

As a student at Emory University, Sara had constantly looked at the watch, especially through advanced biochemistry, applied genetics, and human anatomy classes that seemed by law to be taught by the most boring, monosyllabic professors that could be found. In medical school, she had impatiently glanced at the watch on Saturday mornings as she stood outside the lab, waiting for the professor to come and unlock the door so she could finish her experiments. During her internship at Grady Hospital, she had stared blurry-eyed at its white face, trying to make out the hands, as she calculated how much longer she had left in thirty-six-hour shifts. At the Heartsdale Children's Clinic, she had closely followed the second hand as she pressed her fingers to a child's thin wrist, counting the beats of his heart as they ticked beneath his skin, seeking to discern if an "achy all-over" was a serious ailment or if it just meant the kid did not want to go to school that day.

For almost twenty years, Sara had worn the watch. The crystal had been replaced twice, the battery numerous times, and the bracelet once because Sara could not stomach the thought of cleaning out the dried blood of a woman who had died in her arms. Even at Granny Em's funeral, Sara had found herself touching the smooth bezel around the face, tears streaming down her own face at the realization that she could never again see her grandmother's quick, open smile or the sparkle in her eyes as she learned of her oldest granddaughter's latest accomplishment.

Now, looking at the watch, for the first time in her life Sara was glad her grandmother was not there with her, could not read the anger in Sara's eyes, know the humiliation that burned in her chest like an uncontrollable fire as she sat in a conference room being deposed in a malpractice suit filed by the parents of a dead patient. Everything Sara had ever worked for, every step she had taken that her grandmother could not, every accomplishment, every degree, was being rendered meaningless by a woman who was all but calling Sara a baby killer.

The lawyer leaned over the table, eyebrow raised, lip curled, as Sara glanced at the watch. "Dr. Linton, do you have a more pressing appointment?"

"No." Sara tried to keep her voice calm, to quell the fury that the lawyer had obviously been stoking for the last four hours. Sara knew that she was being manipulated, knew that the woman was trying to bait her, to get Sara to say something horrible that would forever be recorded by the little man leaning over the transcript machine in the corner. Knowing this did not stop Sara from reacting. As a matter of fact, the knowledge made her even angrier.

"I've been calling you Dr. Linton all this time." The lawyer glanced down at an open folder in front of her. "Is it Tolliver? I see that you remarried your ex-husband, Jeffrey Tolliver, six months ago."

"Linton is fine." Under the table, Sara was shaking her foot so hard that her shoe was about to fall off. She crossed her arms over her chest. There was a sharp pain in her jaw from clenching her teeth. She shouldn't be here. She should be at home right now, reading a book or talking on the phone to her sister. She should be going over patient files or sorting through old medical journals she never seemed to have time to catch up on.

She should be trusted.

"So," the lawyer continued. The woman had given her name at the start of the deposition, but Sara couldn't remember it. All she had been able to concentrate on at the time was the look on Beckey Powell's face. Jimmy's mother. The woman whose hand Sara had held so many times, the friend she had comforted, the person with whom she had spent countless hours on the phone, trying to put into simple English the medical jargon the oncologists in Atlanta were feeding the mother to explain why her twelve-year-old son was going to die.

From the moment they'd entered the room, Beckey had glared at Sara as if she were a murderer. The boy's father, a man Sara had gone to school with, had not even been able to look her in the eye.

"Dr. Tolliver?" the lawyer pressed.

"Linton," Sara corrected, and the woman smiled, just as she did every time she scored a point against Sara. This happened so often that Sara was tempted to ask the lawyer if she suffered from some unusually petty form of Tourette's.

"On the morning of the seventeenth—this was the day after Easter— you got lab results from the cell blast you'd ordered performed on James Powell. Is that correct?"

James. She made him sound so adult. To Sara, he would always be the six-year-old she had met all those years ago, the little boy who liked playing with his plastic dinosaurs and eating the occasional crayon. He'd been so proud when he told her that he was called Jimmy, just like his dad.

"Dr. Tolliver?"

Buddy Conford, one of Sara's lawyers, finally spoke up. "Let's cut the crap, honey."

"Honey?" the lawyer echoed. She had one of those husky, low voices most men found irresistible. Sara could tell Buddy fell into this category, just as she could tell that the fact the man found his opponent desirable heightened his sense of competitiveness.

Buddy smiled, his own point made. "You know her name."

"Please instruct your client to answer the question, Mr. Conford."

"Yes," Sara said, before they could exchange any more barbs. She had found that lawyers could be quite verbose at three-hundred-fifty dollars an hour. They would parse the meaning of the word "parse" if the clock was ticking. And Sara had two lawyers: Melinda Stiles was counsel for Global Medical Indemnity, an insurance company to whom Sara had paid almost three and a half million dollars over the course of her medical career. Buddy Conford was Sara's personal lawyer, whom she'd hired to protect her from the insurance company. The fine print in all of Global's malpractice policies stipulated limited liability on the part of the company when a patient's injury was a direct result of a doctor's willful negligence. Buddy was here to make sure that did not happen.

"Dr. Linton? The morning of the seventeenth?"

"Yes," Sara answered. "According to my notes, that's when I got the lab results."

Sharon, Sara remembered. The lawyer was Sharon Connor. Such an innocuous name for such a horrible person.

"And what did the lab results reveal to you?"

"That more than likely, Jimmy had acute myeloblastic leukemia."

"And the prognosis?"

"That's out of my realm. I'm not an oncologist."

"No. You referred the Powells to an oncologist, a friend of yours from college, a Dr. William Harris in Atlanta?"

"Yes." Poor Bill. He was named in the lawsuit, too, had been forced to hire his own attorney, was battling with his own insurance company.

"But you *are* a doctor?"

Sara took a deep breath. She had been instructed by Buddy to only answer questions, not pointed comments. God knew she was paying him enough for his advice. She might as well start taking it.

"And surely as a *doctor* you know what acute myeloblastic leukemia is?"

"It's a group of malignant disorders characterized by the replacement of normal bone marrow with abnormal cells."

Connor smiled, rattling off, "And it begins as a single somatic hematopoietic progenitor that transforms to a cell incapable of normal differentiation?"

"The cell loses apoptosis."

Another smile, another point scored. "And this disease has a fifty percent survival rate."

Sara held her tongue, waiting for the ax to fall.

"And timing is critical for treatment, is that correct? In such a disease—a disease that literally turns the body's cells against themselves, turns off apoptosis, according to you, which is the normal genetic process of cell death—timing is critical."

Forty-eight hours would not have saved the boy's life, but Sara was not going to utter those words, have them transcribed into a legal document and later thrown in her face with all the callousness Sharon Connor could muster.

The lawyer shuffled through some papers as if she needed to find her notes. "And you attended Emory Medical School. As you so graciously corrected me earlier, you didn't just graduate in the top ten percent, you graduated sixth in your class."

Buddy sounded bored with the woman's antics. "We've already established Dr. Linton's credentials."

"I'm just trying to put it all together," the woman countered. She held up one of the pages, her eyes scanning the words. Finally, she put it down. "And, Dr. Linton, you got this information—this lab result that was almost certainly a death sentence—the morning of the seventeenth, and yet you chose not to share the information with the Powells until two days later. And that was because...?"

Sara had never heard so many sentences starting with the word "and." She imagined grammar wasn't high up on the curriculum at whatever school had churned out the vicious lawyer.

Still, she answered, "They were at Disney World for Jimmy's birthday. I wanted them to enjoy their vacation, what I thought might be their last vacation as a family for some time. I made the decision to not tell them until they came back."

"They came back the evening of the seventeenth, yet you did not tell them until the morning of the nineteenth, two days later."

Sara opened her mouth to respond, but the woman talked over her.

"And it didn't occur to you that they could return for immediate treatment and perhaps save their child's life?" It was clear she didn't expect an answer. "I would imagine that, given the choice, the Powells would rather have their son alive today instead of empty photographs of him standing around the Magic Kingdom." She slid the picture in question across the table. It glided neatly past Beckey and Jim Powell, past Sara's two lawyers, and stopped a few inches from where Sara was sitting.

She shouldn't have looked, but she did.

Young Jimmy stood leaning against his father, both of them wearing Mickey Mouse ears and holding sparklers as a parade of Snow
White's dwarfs marched behind them. Even in the photo, you could tell
the boy was sick. Dark circles rimmed his eyes and he was so thin that
his frail little arm looked like a piece of string.

They had come back from vacation a day early because Jimmy had
wanted to be home. Sara did not know why the Powells had not called
her at the clinic, brought in Jimmy that day so she could check on him.
Maybe his parents had known even without the test, even without
the final diagnosis, that their days of having a normal, healthy child
were over. Maybe they had just wanted to keep him to themselves one
more day. He had been such a wonderful boy—kind, smart, cheerful—
everything a parent could hope for. And now he was gone.

Sara felt tears well into her eyes, and bit her lip so hard that the tears
fell from pain instead of grief.

Buddy snatched away the picture, irritated. He slid it back to Sharon
Connor. "You can practice your opening statement in front of your
mirror at home, sweetheart."

Connor's mouth twisted into a smirk as she took back the photograph. She was living proof that the theory that women were nurturing
caretakers was utter bullshit. Sara half-expected to see rotting flesh between her teeth.

The woman said, "Dr. Linton, on this particular date, the date you
got James's lab results, did anything else happen that stood out for you?"

A prickling went up Sara's spine, a spark of warning that she could
not suppress. "Yes."

"And could you tell us what that was?"

"I found a woman who had been murdered in the bathroom of our
local diner."

"Raped and murdered. Is that correct?"

"Yes."

"That brings us to your part-time job as coroner for the county. I
believe your husband—then ex-husband, when this rape and murder
occurred—is chief of police for the county. Both of you work closely
together when cases arise."

Sara waited for more, but the woman had obviously just wanted to
get that on the record.

"Counselor?" Buddy asked.

"One moment, please," the lawyer murmured, picking up a thick folder and leafing through the pages.

Sara looked down at her hands to give herself something to do. Pisiform, triquetrum, hamate, capitate, trapezoid, trapezium, lunate, scaphoid . . . She listed all the bones in her hand, then started on the ligaments, trying to distract herself, willing herself not to walk into the trap the lawyer was so skillfully setting.

While Sara was in her residency at Grady, headhunters had pursued her so relentlessly that she had stopped answering her phone. Partnerships. Six-figure salaries with year-end bonuses. Surgical privileges at any hospital she chose. Personal assistants, lab support, full secretarial staff, even her own parking space. They had offered her everything, and yet in the end, she had decided to return home to Grant, to practice medicine for considerably less money and even less respect, because she thought it was important for doctors to serve rural communities.

Was part of it vanity, too? Sara had seen herself as a role model for the girls in town. Most of them had only ever seen a male doctor. The only women in authority were nurses, teachers, and mothers. Her first five years at the Heartsdale Children's Clinic, Sara had spent at least half of her time convincing young patients—and frequently their mothers— that she had, in fact, graduated medical school. No one believed a woman could be smart enough, *good* enough, to reach such a position. Even when Sara bought the clinic from her retiring partner, people had still been skeptical. It had taken years to carve herself a place of respect in the community.

All for this.

Sharon Connor finally looked up from her papers. She frowned. "Dr. Linton, you yourself were raped. Isn't that correct?"

Sara felt all of the saliva in her mouth dry up. Her throat tightened and her flesh turned hot as she struggled with an unwelcome shame that she had not felt since the last time a lawyer had deposed her about being raped. Just like then, Sara's vision tunneled and blurred in such a way that she saw nothing, just heard the words ringing in her ears.

Buddy shot to his feet, arguing something, stabbing his finger at the lawyer, at the Powells. Beside him, Melinda Stiles from the Global Medical Indemnity said nothing. Buddy had told Sara this would happen, that Stiles would sit silently by, letting opposing counsel tear into

Sara, speaking only when she thought Global might be exposed. Another woman, another failed role model.

"And I want that on the goddamn record!" Buddy finished, pushing his chair away from the table as he sat down.

"Noted," Connor said. "Dr. Linton?"

Sara's vision cleared. She heard a *whoosh* in her ears, as if she had
been swimming underwater and suddenly pushed herself to the surface.

"Dr. Linton?" Connor repeated. She kept using the title, making it
sound like something vile instead of a position Sara had worked for all
of her life.

Sara looked at Buddy, and he shrugged as he shook his head, indicating there was nothing he could do. He had predicted that the deposition would be nothing more than a fishing expedition with Sara's life as
bait.

Connor said, "Doctor, would you like a few minutes to collect your
emotions? I know that your rape is a hard thing for you to talk about."
She indicated the thick file on the table in front of her. It had to be the
trial transcript from Sara's case. The woman had read everything, knew
every disgusting detail. "From what I gathered, your assault was very,
very brutal."

Sara cleared her throat, willed her voice to not just work but to be
strong, fearless. "Yes, it was."

Connor's tone turned almost conciliatory. "I used to work at the
district attorney's office in Baton Rouge. I can honestly say in my twelve
years as a prosecutor, I never saw anything as brutal, as sadistic, as what
you experienced."

Buddy snapped, "Sweetheart, you wanna quit with the crocodile
tears and get to the question?"

The lawyer hesitated for just a second then continued, "For the
record, Dr. Linton was raped in the bathroom of Grady Hospital,
where she was working as an emergency room intern. Apparently, the
perpetrator accessed the women's room through the drop ceiling. Dr.
Linton was in one of the stalls when he literally dropped down on her."

"Noted," Buddy said. "You got a question in there, or do you just
like giving speeches?"

"Dr. Linton, the fact that you were brutally raped figured greatly
into your decision to return to Grant County, did it not?"

"There were other reasons."

"But would you say that the rape was your primary reason?"

"I would say that it was one of many reasons that figured into my decision to return."

"Is this going somewhere?" Buddy asked. The lawyers exchanged words again, and Sara reached for the pitcher of water on the table, poured herself a glass with hands she willed to be steady.

She felt rather than saw Beckey Powell stir, and wondered if the woman was feeling guilty, seeing Sara as a human being again instead of a monster. Sara hoped so. She hoped Beckey tossed and turned in her bed tonight, realized that no matter how much she and her lawyer vilified Sara, nothing would bring back her son. Nothing would change the fact that Sara had done everything she could for Jimmy.

"Dr. Linton?" Connor continued. "I imagine in light of the brutal rape you experienced, it was quite an emotional ordeal to walk into that bathroom and discover a woman who herself had been sexually assaulted. Especially as it was almost ten years to the date that you were raped."

Buddy snapped, "Is that a question?"

"Dr. Linton, you and your ex-husband—I'm sorry, *husband*—you both are trying to adopt a child now, aren't you? Because as a consequence to this brutal rape you experienced, you cannot have children of your own?"

Beckey's reaction was unmistakable. For the first time since this had started, Sara really looked at the woman. She saw a softening in Beckey's eyes, a stirring of joy for a friend, but the emotion vanished as swiftly as it had come, and Sara could almost read the rebuke that cancelled it: You have no right to mother a child when you killed my son.

Connor held up a familiar-looking document, stating, "Doctor, you and your husband, Jeffrey Tolliver, filed papers for adoption with the state of Georgia three months ago. Isn't that correct?"

Sara tried to remember what they had put on the adoption application, what they had said during the state-mandated parenting classes that had taken up every free minute of their time over the last few months. What incriminating evidence would the lawyer wring out of the endless, seemingly innocuous process? Jeffrey's high blood pressure? Sara's need for reading glasses? "Yes."

Connor shuffled through some more papers, saying, "Just a moment, please."

The room was tiny, airless. There were no windows, no paintings on the wall to stare at. A dying palm tree stood in the corner, the leaves drooping and sad. Nothing good would come of any of this. No pound of flesh would bring back a child. No verdict of innocence would restore a reputation.

Sara looked down at her hand. Dorsal metacarpal ligaments, dorsal carpometacarpal ligaments, dorsal intercarpal ligaments...

Sara had visited Jimmy the week before he died, held his frail little hand for hours as he haltingly talked about football and skateboarding and all the things he missed. Sara had been able to see it then, that look of death in his eyes. The look was the mirror opposite of the hope she had seen in Beckey Powell's, even though the woman had heard the prognosis, had agreed to stop treatment so as not to prolong Jimmy's suffering. It was that hope that kept Jimmy from letting go, that fear that every child has of disappointing his mother.

Sara had taken Beckey to the cafeteria, sitting in a quiet corner with the bewildered woman and holding her hand just as she had held Jimmy's moments before. She'd described to Beckey how it would happen, how death would claim her son. His feet would get cold, then his hands, as circulation slowed. His lips would turn blue. His breathing would become irregular, but that shouldn't be taken as a sign of distress. He would have difficulty swallowing. He might lose control of his bladder. His thoughts would wander, but Beckey had to keep talking to him, engaging him, because he would still be there. He would still be her Jimmy until the very last second. It was her job to be there at every step, then—the hardest part—to let him go on without her.

She had to be strong enough to let Jimmy go.

Connor cleared her throat and waited for Sara's attention. "You never charged the Powells for the lab tests and subsequent office visits after you made James's diagnosis," she said. "Why is that, Dr. Linton?"

"I didn't, in fact, make a firm diagnosis," Sara corrected, trying to get her focus back. "I could only tell them what I suspected and refer them to an oncologist."

"Your college friend, Dr. William Harris," the lawyer supplied. "And you didn't bill the Powells for any of the lab work or any subsequent visits following the referral."

"I don't handle billing."

"But you do direct your office staff, do you not?" Connor paused. "Do I need to remind you that you're under oath?"

Sara bit back the sharp answer that wanted to come.

"According to the deposition of your office manager, Nelly Morgan, you directed her to write off as a loss the almost two thousand dollars the Powells owed you. True?"

"Yes."

"Why is that, Dr. Linton?"

"Because I knew that they were facing what could be crippling medical costs for Jimmy's treatment. I didn't want to add to the pile of creditors I knew that they would have." Sara stared at Beckey, though the woman would not meet her gaze. "That's what this is about, isn't it? Lab bills. Hospital bills. Radiologists. Pharmacies. You must owe a fortune."

Connor reminded, "Dr. Linton, you're here to answer my questions, not ask your own."

Sara leaned toward the Powells, tried to connect with them, make them see reason. "Don't you know it won't get him back? None of this will get Jimmy back."

"Mr. Conford, please instruct your client—"

"Do you know what I gave up to practice here? Do you know how many years I spent—"

"Dr. Linton, do not address my clients."

"This is the reason why you had to go to Atlanta to find a specialist," Sara told them. "These lawsuits are why the hospital closed down, why there are only five doctors within a hundred miles of here who can afford to practice medicine."

They would not look up at her, would not respond.

Sara sat back in her chair, spent. This couldn't just be about money. Beckey and Jimmy wanted something more, an explanation for why their son died. The sad fact was that there was no explanation. People died—children died—and sometimes, there was no one to blame, nothing that could stop it. All this lawsuit meant was that a year from now, maybe five years, another child would be sick, another family would be stricken, and no one would be able to afford to help them.

No one would be there to hold their hand, to explain what was happening.

"Dr. Linton," Connor continued. "As to your failure to bill the Powells for the lab work and office visits: isn't it a fact that you felt guilty for Jimmy's death?"

She knew the answer Buddy wanted her to give the question, knew that even Melinda Stiles, the silent advocate for Global Medical Indemnity, wanted her to deny this.

"Dr. Linton?" Connor insisted. "Didn't you feel guilty?"

Sara closed her eyes, could see Jimmy lying in that hospital bed, talking to her about skateboarding. She could still feel the cold touch of his fingers in hers as he patiently explained to her the difference between a heelflip and an ollie.

Interphalangeal joints. Metacarpophalangeal joint. Capsule, distal, radioulnar joints...

"Dr. Linton?"

"Yes," she finally admitted, tears flowing freely now. "Yes. I felt guilty."

◆

SARA DROVE THROUGH DOWNTOWN Heartsdale, the speedometer on her BMW 335ci barely reaching twenty-five. She passed the five-and-dime, the dress shop, the hardware store. At Burgess's Cleaners, she stopped in the middle of the empty street, debating whether or not to drive on.

Ahead of her, the gates of the Grant Institute of Technology stood open. Students walked down the main drive dressed as goblins and superheroes. Halloween had come and gone the night before, but the Grant Tech students tended to stretch every holiday into a weeklong affair. Sara had not even bothered to buy candy this year. She knew that no parent would be sending their kid to knock on her door. Since the malpractice suit had been filed, the whole town had ostracized her. Even patients she had treated for years, people she had genuinely helped, avoided her gaze at the supermarket or the drugstore. Considering the atmosphere, Sara felt it would not have been wise to don her usual witch's costume and go to the church party as she had for the last sixteen years. Sara had been born and raised in Grant County. She knew that this was a town that burned witches.

She had spent eight and a half hours in the deposition, every aspect of her life being raked over the coals. Over a hundred parents had signed releases so that their children's medical charts could be combed through by Sharon Connor, most of them hoping that at the end of the day there would be some money in it for them. Melinda Stiles, who had turned surprisingly helpful once the room had emptied of witnesses, explained that this was fairly common. A malpractice suit turned patients into vultures, she explained, and more would start circling as the Powell case proceeded. Global Medical Indemnity would run the numbers, weigh the losses against the strength of Sara's defense, and then decide whether or not they would settle.

In which case, all of this—the humiliation, the degradation—would be for nothing.

One of the college students in the street screamed and Sara startled, letting her foot slip off the brake. It was just a young man wearing a Chiquita Banana costume, including blue Capri pants and a yellow tie-top that showed a hairy, round belly. It was always the burly ones who dressed up as women the first chance they got. Would Jimmy Powell have been that sort of silly young man? If he had lived, would he have developed his father's stooped posture and thin frame or his mother's rounded face and cheery disposition? Sara knew he'd had Beckey's quick wit, her love of practical jokes and bad puns. Anything else would be forever unknown.

Sara took a left into the clinic parking lot. Her clinic parking lot, the one she had bought from Dr. Barney all those years ago, working part-time as coroner so that she could afford the deal. The sign was faded, the steps needed a new coat of paint and the side door stuck on warm days, but it was hers. All hers.

She got out of the car and used her key to open the front door. Last week, she had closed the clinic, furious at the parents who had signed releases in hopes of cashing in, furious at her town for betraying her. They saw Sara as nothing more than a cash machine, as if she was merely a conduit through which to access the millions of dollars sitting in the insurance company's coffers. No one saw the consequences of this smash-and-grab, the fact that malpractice premiums would go up, doctors would go out of business, and healthcare, which was already unaffordable for many, would soon be unobtainable for most. No one cared about the lives they destroyed on their way to becoming million-aires.

Let them think about it while they drove an hour and a half over to Rollings, the closest town with a pediatrician.

Sara left the lights off as she walked through the clinic's front lobby. Despite the chill October air, the building was warm, and she took off her suit jacket and laid it on the front counter as she walked to the bath-room.

The water was freezing cold straight out of the faucet, and Sara leaned down to splash her face, to try to get rid of the grime that was clinging to her skin. She wanted a long bath, a glass of wine, but these were things that she would have to go home to find and right now, she didn't want to go home. She wanted to be alone, to regain her sense of self. At the same time, she wanted to be with her parents, who were at this moment somewhere in Kansas, exactly halfway in their long-planned quest to drive across America. Tessa, her sister, was in Atlanta, finally putting her college degree to use as she counseled homeless people. And Jeffrey . . . Jeffrey was at home, waiting for Sara to return from the deposition, to tell him everything that had happened. She wanted to be with him the most, and yet she didn't want to see him at all.

She stared at her reflection in the mirror, realizing with a shock that she did not recognize herself. Her hair was pulled back so tightly that she was surprised she hadn't developed a stress fracture. Carefully, she reached up and loosened the band, wincing from the pain as roots were yanked out. Her starched white shirt showed water spots, but Sara did not care. She felt ridiculous in the suit, which was probably the most expensive outfit she'd ever owned. Buddy had insisted she have the black cloth sharply tailored to her body so that during the deposition, she looked like a rich doctor instead of a small-town plumber's daughter turned pediatrician. She could be herself in the courtroom, Buddy had told her. Sara could show Sharon Connor her real side when it would do the most damage.

Sara hated this duplicity, hated having to transform herself into a masculine-looking, arrogant bitch as part of her defense strategy. Her entire career, she had resisted quashing her femininity in order to fit into the boys' club of medicine. And now one lawsuit had turned her into everything she despised.

"You okay?"

Jeffrey stood in the doorway. He was wearing a charcoal-colored suit with a dark blue shirt and tie. His cell phone was clipped to one side of his belt, his paddle holster to the other.

"I thought you were at home."

"I dropped off my car at the shop. You mind giving me a ride home?"

She nodded, resting her shoulder against the wall.

"Here." He held up a daisy he had probably picked from the overgrown yard. "Brought you this."

Sara took the flower, which was little more than a weed, and put it on the edge of the sink.

"Wanna talk about it?"

She moved the daisy, lining it up perpendicular to the faucet. "No."

"Do you want to be alone?"

"Yes. No." Quickly, she closed the distance between them, wrapping her arms around his shoulders, burying her face in his neck. "It was so horrible," she whispered. "My God, it was just so awful."

"It's going to be fine," he soothed, rubbing her back with his hand. "Don't let them get to you, Sara. Don't let them shake your confidence."

She pressed into him, needing the reassurance of his body against hers. He'd been at work all day, and he smelled like the squad room—that odd mixture of gun oil, burned coffee, and sweat. With her family scattered, Jeffrey was the only constant in her life, the one person who was there to help pick up the pieces. If she thought about it, this had been true for the last sixteen years. Even when Sara had divorced him, even when she had spent most of her days trying to think of anything but Jeffrey, in the back of her mind, he was always there.

She brushed her lips against his neck, softly, slowly until his skin responded. She smoothed her hands down his back to his waist, pulled him closer in such a way that there was no mistaking her meaning.

He looked surprised, but when she kissed him on the mouth, he responded in equal measure. At the moment, Sara didn't so much want sex as the intimacy that came with it. It was, at least, the one thing she knew she was capable of doing right.

Jeffrey was the first to pull away. "Let's go home, okay?" He tucked a strand of hair behind her ear. "I'll cook supper and we'll lay on the couch and..."

She kissed him again, biting his lip, pressing closer. He had never needed much coaxing, but as his hand slid to the zipper on her skirt, Sara's mind wandered to thoughts of home: the pile of laundry that needed to be folded, the leaking faucet in the guest bathroom, the torn shelf liner in the kitchen.

Just the thought of taking off her panty hose was overwhelming.

He pulled away again, a half-smile on his lips. "Come on," he said, taking her by the hand and leading her out of the bathroom. "I'll drive you home."

They were halfway across the lobby when his cell phone started to ring. He offered a shrug to Sara, as if he needed her permission to answer the phone.

"Go ahead," she relented, knowing whoever it was would just call back—or worse, come find him. "Answer it."

He still seemed reluctant, but took the phone off its clip anyway. She saw him frown as he looked at the caller ID, then answered, "Tolliver."

Sara leaned back against the front counter, hugging her arms to her waist as she tried to read his expression. She had been a cop's wife far too long to think that there was any such thing as a simple phone call.

"Where is she now?" Jeffrey demanded. He nodded, his shoulders tensing as he listened to the caller. "All right," he said, looking at his watch. "I can be there in three hours."

He ended the call, squeezing the phone so hard in his hand that Sara thought it might break. "Lena," he said brusquely, just as Sara was about to ask him what was going on. Lena Adams was a detective on his squad, a woman who made a habit of getting herself into bad situations and dragging Jeffrey along with her. Just the sound of her name brought a sense of dread.

Sara said, "I thought she was on vacation."

"There was an explosion," Jeffrey answered. "She's in the hospital."

"Is she okay?"

"No," he told her, shaking his head as if he could not believe what he had heard. "She's been arrested."

THREE DAYS EARLIER

CHAPTER 2

LENA KEPT ONE HAND on the steering wheel as she scrolled through radio stations with the other. She cringed at the vacuous girls screeching from the speakers; when had stupidity become a marketable talent? She gave up when she hit the country music channels. There was a six-disc changer in the trunk, but she was sick of each and every song on each and every disc. Desperate, she reached into the floor of the backseat, groping for a loose CD. She fished out three empty jewel cases in a row, cursing more loudly with each one. She was about to give up when the tips of her fingers brushed a cassette tape underneath her seat.

Her Celica was around eight years old and still had a tape player, but Lena had no idea what this particular cassette contained, or how it had even ended up in her car. Still, she popped it into the dash and waited. No music came, and she turned up the knob, wondering if the tape was blank or had been damaged by last summer's scorching heat. She turned it up further and nearly had a heart attack when the opening drumbeats of Joan Jett's "Bad Reputation" filled the car.

Sibyl. Her twin sister had made this tape two weeks before she had died. Lena could remember listening to this exact song nearly six years ago as she sped down the highway, heading back to Grant County from a drop-off she'd made at the Georgia Bureau of Investigation's lab in Macon. The drive had been much like the one she was making today: a straight shot down a kudzu-lined interstate, the few cars on the road whizzing by eighteen-wheelers and mobile homes that were being transported to waiting families. Meanwhile, her sister was back in Grant County, being tortured and murdered by a sadist while Lena sang with Joan Jett at the top of her lungs.

She popped out the tape and turned off the radio.

Six years. It didn't seem like so much time had passed, but then again, it felt like an eternity. Lena was just now getting to the point where her dead twin was not the first thing she thought about when she woke up in the morning. It usually wasn't until later in the day when she saw something funny or heard a crazy story at work that she thought about Sibyl, made a mental note to tell her sister, then realized a split second later that Sibyl was no longer there to hear it.

Lena had always thought of Sibyl as her only family. Their mother had died thirteen days after giving birth. Their father, a cop, had been shot dead by a man he'd pulled over on a speeding violation. He'd never even known his young wife was pregnant. As there were no other relatives to speak of, Hank Norton, their mother's brother, had raised the two girls. Lena had never thought of her uncle as family. Hank had been a junkie during her childhood and a sober, self-righteous asshole during her teen years. Lena thought of him as more like a warden, somebody who made the rules and held all of the power. From the beginning, Lena had only wanted to break out.

She pushed in the cassette tape again, twisted the knob to lower the sound to a low, angry growl.

I don't give a damn about my bad reputation...

The sisters had sung this as teenagers, their anthem against Reece, the backwater town they lived in until they were old enough to get the hell out. With their dark complexions and exotic looks that came courtesy of their Mexican-American grandmother, neither one of them had been particularly popular. Other kids were cruel, and Lena's strategy was to take them on one by one while Sibyl kept to her studies, working hard to get the scholarships she needed to continue her education. After high school, Lena had spun her wheels for a while then entered the police academy, where Jeffrey Tolliver plucked her from a group of recruits and offered her a job. Sibyl had already taken a professorship at the Grant Institute of Technology, which made the decision to accept the job that much easier.

Lena found herself thinking about her first weeks in Grant County. After Reece, Heartsdale had seemed like a major metropolis. Even Avondale and Madison, the other cities that comprised Grant, were impressive to her small-town eyes. Most of the kids Lena had gone to school with had never traveled outside the state of Georgia. Their parents worked twelve-hour days at the tire plant or drew unemployment so they could sit around and drink. Vacations were for the wealthy—people who could afford to miss a couple of days of work and still pay the electric bill.

Hank owned a bar on the outskirts of Reece, and once he had stopped injecting the profits into his veins, Sibyl and Lena had lived a fairly comfortable life compared to their neighbors. Sure, the roof on their house was bowed and a 1963 Chevy truck had been on blocks in the backyard for as long as she could remember, but they always had food on the table and each year when school came around, Hank drove the girls into Augusta and bought them new clothes.

Lena should have been grateful, but she was not.

Sibyl had been eight when Hank, on a drunken bender, had slammed his car into her. Lena had been using an old tennis ball to play catch with her sister. She overthrew, and when Sibyl ran into the driveway and leaned down to pick up the ball, the bumper of Hank's reversing car had caught her in the temple. There hadn't even been much blood—just a thin cut following the line of her skull—but the damage was done. Sibyl hadn't been able to see anything after that, and no matter how many Alcoholics Anonymous meetings Hank attended or how supportive he tried to be, in the back of her mind, Lena always saw his car hitting her sister, the surprised look on Sibyl's face as she crumpled to the ground.

Yet, here Lena was, using up one of her valuable vacation days to go check on the old bastard. Hank hadn't telephoned in two weeks, which was strange. Even though she seldom returned his calls, he still left messages every other day. The last time she had seen her uncle was three months ago, when he'd driven to Grant County—uninvited—to help her move. She was renting Jeffrey's house after he'd found out his previous tenants, a couple of girls from the college, were using the place as their own personal bordello. Hank had said maybe a handful of words to her as he moved boxes, and Lena had been just as chatty. As he was leaving, guilt had forced her to suggest dinner at the new rib place up the street, but he was climbing into his beat-up old Mercedes, making his excuses, before she got the words out of her mouth.

She should have known then something was wrong. Hank never passed up an opportunity to spend time with her, no matter how painful that time was. That he had driven straight back to Reece should have been a clue. She was a detective, for chrissakes. She should notice when things were out of the ordinary.

She also shouldn't have let two whole weeks pass without calling to check on him.

In the end, it was Charlotte, one of Hank's neighbors, who called to tell Lena that she needed to come down and see about her uncle.

"He's in a bad way," the woman had said. When Lena tried to press her, Charlotte had mumbled something about one of her kids needing her and hung up the phone.

Lena felt her spine straighten as she drove into the Reece city limits. God, she hated this town. At least in Grant, she fit in. Here, however, she would always be the orphan, the troublemaker, Hank Norton's niece—no, not Sibyl, Lena, the bad one.

She passed three churches in rapid succession. There was a big billboard by the baseball field that read, "Today's Forecast: Jesus Reigns!"

"Christ," she murmured, taking a left onto Kanuga Road, her body on autopilot as she coasted through the back streets that led to Hank's house.

Classes weren't out for another hour, but there were enough cars leaving the high school to cause a traffic jam. Lena slowed, hearing the muffled strains of competing radio stations as souped-up muscle cars stripped their tires on the asphalt.

A guy in a blue Mustang, the old kind that drove like a truck and had a metal dashboard that could decapitate you if you hit the right tree, pulled up in the lane beside her. Lena turned her head and saw a teenage kid openly staring at her. Gold chains around his neck sparkled in the afternoon sun and his ginger-red hair was spiked with so much gel that he looked more like something you'd find at the bottom of the ocean than in a small Southern town. Oblivious to how stupid he looked, his head bobbed with the rap music pounding out of his car stereo and he gave her a suggestive wink. Lena looked away, thinking she'd like to see his spoiled white ass dropped off in the middle of downtown Atlanta on a Friday night. He'd be too busy pissing his pants to appreciate the gangsta life.

She turned off at the next street, taking the long way to Hank's, wanting to get away from the kids and traffic. Hank was probably fine. Lena knew one thing she shared with her uncle was a tendency toward moodiness. Hank was probably just in a dark place. He'd probably be angry to find her on his doorstep, invading his space. She wouldn't blame him.

A white Cadillac Escalade was parked in the driveway behind Hank's old Mercedes. Lena pulled her Celica close to the curb and turned off the ignition, wondering who was visiting. Hank might be hosting an AA meeting; in which case, she hoped the Escalade's driver was the last to leave instead of the first to show up. Her uncle was just as hooked on self-help bullshit as he had been addicted to speed and alcohol. She had known Hank to drive six hours straight to hear a particular speaker, attend a particular meeting, only to turn around and drive another six hours back so that he could open the bar for the early afternoon drunks.

She studied the house, thinking that the only thing that had changed about her childhood home was its state of decay. The roof was more bowed, the paint on the clapboard peeling so badly that a thin strip of white flecks made a chalk line around the house. Even the mailbox had seen better days. Someone had obviously taken a bat to the thing, but Hank, being his usual handy self, had duct-taped it back onto the rotting wood post.

Lena palmed her keys as she got out of the car. Her hamstrings were tight from the long drive, and she bent at the waist to stretch out her legs.

A gunshot cracked the air, and Lena bolted up, reaching for her gun, realizing that her Glock was in her glove compartment at the same time she processed that the gunshot was just the front door slamming shut.

The slammer was a stocky, bald man with arms the size of cannons and an attitude she could read from twenty paces. A large sheath containing a hunting knife was on his right hip and a thick metal chain dangled from his belt loop to his wallet in his back left pocket. He trotted down the rickety front stairs, counting a wad of money he held in his meaty hands.

He looked up, saw Lena, and gave a dismissive snort before climbing into the white Cadillac. The SUV's twenty-two-inch wheels kicked up dust as he backed out of the driveway and swung out into the street beside her Celica. The Escalade was about a yard longer than her car and at least two feet wider. The roof was so high she couldn't see over the top. The side windows were heavily tinted, but the front ones were rolled down, and she could clearly see the driver.

He'd stopped close enough to crowd her between the two cars, his beady eyes staring a hole into her. Time slowed, and she saw that he was older than she'd thought, that his shaved head was not a fashion statement but a complement to the large red swastika tattooed on his bare upper arm. Coarse black hair grew in a goatee and mustache around his mouth, but she could still see the sneer on his fat, wet lips.

Lena had been a cop long enough to know a con, and the driver had been a con long enough to know that she was a cop. Neither one of them was about to back down, but he won the standoff by shaking his head, as if to say, "What a fucking waste." His wifebeater shirt showed rippling muscles as he shifted into gear and peeled off.

Lena was left standing in his wake. *Five, six, seven...* she counted the seconds, standing her ground in the middle of the road as she waited for the Cadillac to make the turn, taking her out of sight of the guy's rearview mirrors.

Once the car was gone, she went around to the passenger's side of the Celica and found the six-inch folding knife she kept under the seat. She slipped this into her back pocket, then got her Glock out of the glove compartment. She checked the safety on the gun and clipped the holster to her belt. Lena did not want to meet the man again, especially unarmed.

Walking toward the house, she wouldn't let her mind consider the reasons why such a person would be at her uncle's house. You didn't drive a car like that in a town like Reece by working at the tire factory. You sure as shit didn't leave somebody's house flashing a wad of money unless you knew that no one was going to try to take it off you.

Her hands were shaking as she walked toward the house. The doorjamb had splintered from being slammed so hard, or maybe from being kicked open. Pieces of rotting wood and rusting metal jutted into the air near the knob, and Lena used the toe of her shoe to push open the door.

"Hank?" she called, fighting the urge to draw her weapon. The man in the Escalade was gone, but his presence still lingered. Something bad had happened here. Maybe something bad was still going on.

Being a cop had given Lena a healthy respect for her instinct. You learned to listen to your gut when you were a rookie. It wasn't something that could be taught at the academy. Either you paid attention to the hairs sticking up on the back of your neck or you got shot in the chest on your first call by some whacked-out drug addict who thought the aliens were trying to get him.

Lena pulled the Glock, pointed it at the floor. "Hank?"

No answer.

She stepped carefully through the house, unable to tell if the place had been tossed or if Hank just hadn't bothered to straighten up in a while. There was an unpleasant odor in the air, something chemical, like burned plastic, mixed with the usual reek of cigarettes from Hank's chain-smoking and chicken grease from the takeout he got every night. Newspapers were scattered on the living room couch. Lena leaned down, checked the dates. Most were over a month old.

Cautiously, she walked down the hallway, weapon still drawn. Lena and Sibyl's bedroom door stood open, the beds neatly made. Hank's room was another matter. The sheets were bunched up at the bottom like someone had suffered a fever dream and an unpleasant brown stain radiated from the center of the bare mattress. The bathroom was filthy. Mold blackened the grout, pieces of wet plaster hung from the ceiling.

She stood outside the closed kitchen door, Glock at the ready. "Hank?"

No answer.

The hinges creaked as she pushed open the swinging door.

Hank was slumped in a chair at the kitchen table. AA pamphlets were stacked hundreds deep in front of him, right beside a closed metal lockbox that Lena instantly recognized from her childhood.

His kit.

Junkies loved their routines almost as much as they loved their drugs. A certain type of needle, a particular vein...they had a habit for their habits, an M.O. they followed that was almost as hard to break as the addiction. Thump the bag, tap out the powder, flick the lighter, lick your lips, wait for the powder to turn to liquid, the liquid to boil. And then came the needle. Sometimes thinking about the rush was enough to get them halfway there.

Hank's drug kit was a metal lockbox, dark blue with chipped paint that showed the gray primer underneath. He kept the key in his sock drawer, something even a seven-year-old girl could figure out. Though the box was shut now, Lena could see the contents as clearly as if the lid was open: hypodermics, tin foil, torch lighter, filters broken off from cigarettes. She knew the spoon he used to heat the powder as well as she knew the back of her hand. Tarnished silver, the ornate handle bent into a loop that you could wrap around your index finger. Hank had caught her with it once and spanked the skin off her ass. Whether this was because Lena was messing with his stuff or because he wanted her to stay clean, she still did not know.

She was leaning against the kitchen counter, gun still in her hand, when Hank finally stirred. Milky eyes looked up at her, but she could tell he couldn't focus, couldn't see, didn't care. Drool slid out of his open mouth. He hadn't put in his teeth, hadn't bathed or combed his hair in what looked like weeks. His shirtsleeves were rolled up and she saw the tiny scars that needles had left so many years ago mingling with new punctures—ulcerous, gaping holes—where the drain cleaner or talcum powder or whatever the hell had been used to cut the shit he was putting into his veins had set up an infection.

The gun raised up into the air. She felt outside herself, as if the weapon was not connected to her hand, as if it wasn't her finger on the trigger, and her own voice saying, "Who the fuck was that man?"

Hank's mouth opened, and she saw the dark red gums where his teeth had been, teeth that had rotted in his mouth because the drugs had eaten him from the inside out.

"Tell me!" she demanded, shoving the Glock in his face.

His tongue lolled outside his mouth as he struggled to speak. She had to use both hands to keep the gun steady, keep it from going off in her hands. Minutes passed, maybe hours. Lena didn't know; she was incapable of keeping time, figuring out if she was in the present or somehow trapped in the past, back thirty years ago when she was just a scared kid wondering why her uncle's grin was so wide when blood was streaming from his nose, his ears. She felt her skin prickling from the heat inside the house. The odor coming off Hank was unbearable. She remembered that smell from her childhood, knew he wouldn't take care of himself, didn't want to bathe because the layer of grime on his skin clogged his pores and helped hold in the drug longer.

Lena forced her hands to put the gun down on the counter, keeping her back to him as she tried to stop the memories that came flooding back: Hank passed out in the yard, children's services coming to the front door to take them away. Sibyl crying, Lena screaming. Even now, hot tears slid down her cheeks, and she was suddenly that little girl again, that helpless, powerless little girl whose only hope in life was a useless fucking junkie.

She swung around, slapping him so hard that he fell into a heap on the floor.

"Get up!" she shouted, kicking him. "Get the fuck up!"

He groaned, curling into a ball, and she was reminded that even in a weakened state, the body did what it could to protect itself. She wanted to pummel him with her fists. She wanted to beat his face until no one would recognize him. How many nights had she lain awake, crying her eyes out as she waited for him to finally come home? How many mornings had she found him facedown in his own vomit? How many strangers had stayed the night—nasty, vile men with their leering smiles and fat, prodding fingers—while Hank remained oblivious to anything but chasing his high?

"Was that your dealer?" Lena demanded, feeling a wave of nausea building in her stomach. "Was that your connection?"

He whispered something, blood spraying in a fine mist on the filthy linoleum.

"Who?" she screamed, leaning over his curled body, wanting to hear his words, to get the dealer's name. She would track him down, take him into the woods, and put a bullet in his skull. "Who was that man?"

"He was..." Hank wheezed.

"Give me his name," Lena ordered, kneeling beside him, her fists clenched so tight that her fingernails were cutting into her palms. "Tell me who he is, you stupid fucker."

His head turned up, and she saw him struggling to focus. When his eyelids began to flutter closed, she grabbed his greasy yellow hair in her fist, yanked his head up so he had no choice but to look at her.

"Who is he?" she repeated.

"The man..."

"Who?" Lena said. "Who is he?"

"He's the one," Hank mumbled, his eyes closing as if the effort of keeping them open was just too much. Still, he finished, "He killed your mother."

MONDAY EVENING

CHAPTER 3

FROM THE MOMENT JAMES OGLETHORPE first set foot in Georgia, men had been trying to chop up the state into their own perfect little pieces. The first attempt came in 1741, when the Trustees decided to split the land into two colonies: Savannah and Frederica. When Georgia became a royal colony and adopted the Church of England as their official religion, the territory was sectioned into eight parishes. After the Revolutionary War, Creek and Cherokee land in the south was taken for white expansion, then later more Cherokee land was claimed in the north.

By the mid-1800s, no Indian territory remained, so the good ol' boys decided to start subdividing existing counties. Once 1877 rolled around, there were 137 counties in Georgia—so many little pockets of political power that the state constitution was amended to stop the overdevelopment, then amended again in 1945 to close loopholes that had allowed the creation of 16 counties in between. The final number allowed was 159, each with its own representative in the state assembly, its own county seat, its own tax base, schools, judges, political systems, and its own locally elected sheriff.

Jeffrey did not know much about Elawah County, other than that its founders had obviously borrowed the name from the Indians they had kicked out for the land. Night had come by the time he and Sara reached the town limits, and from what they could see, the place was not much to write home about. Lena was hardly the type to sit down and chat about her childhood, and Jeffrey understood why as he drove through Reece, Elawah's county seat. Even the dark of night could not obscure the town's depressing bleakness.

Jeffrey had studied American history at Auburn University, but you wouldn't find it written in any textbook that there were some places in the south that still had not recovered from Reconstruction. Running water, indoor plumbing, basic necessities that other Americans took for granted, were considered luxuries to people living on the wrong side of Reece's tracks. Jeffrey's hometown of Sylacauga, Alabama, had been poor, but not this kind of poor. Reece was the sort of festering wound that was only exposed when some kind of natural disaster yanked off the scab.

"Up here on the left," Sara said, reading the directions Jeffrey had gotten from the sheriff.

Jeffrey took the turn, glancing at Sara as a streetlight illuminated the car's interior. She had changed into jeans and a sweater, but her face was still drawn. He wasn't sure if this was because of the malpractice deposition or because of the situation with Lena. He had been surprised when Sara had volunteered to come. She was certainly no fan of Lena's. While the two women had managed to keep their exchanges civil over the years, some of the worst arguments Jeffrey and Sara had had in recent memory were over the young detective—Lena's stubbornness, her quick temper, what Sara saw as the other woman's casual disregard for her own safety and Jeffrey saw as the makings of a damn good cop.

Part of Sara's bad opinion was Jeffrey's fault. At home, he only talked about Lena in the context of her screwups. He'd never had a conversation with Sara about the things Lena did well: the way she could work an interrogation or the fact that sometimes she actually learned from her mistakes. Having made colossal mistakes of his own early on in the job, Jeffrey was more forgiving. Truthfully, Lena reminded him a lot of himself when he was her age. Maybe Sara felt the same way; she wasn't exactly a big fan of the Jeffrey Tolliver she'd known ten years ago.

If Jeffrey had to guess, he'd say that Sara's offer to tag along came because she hadn't wanted to be by herself. Or maybe she'd just wanted to get the hell out of town. Jeffrey wasn't too pleased with how the citizens of Grant County were treating his wife right now, either. For the last two months, he'd been keeping a running list in his head of people who would never have a speeding ticket fixed for them again.

"Up here," she said, pointing to a side street that looked like a dead end.

"You sure?"

Sara scanned the directions again. "It says take a right at the barbe-cue joint."

He slowed the car as he blindly reached overhead, looking for a way to turn on the interior lights.

"Here," she said, pressing a button near the rearview mirror. Sara's BMW was like butter on the road, but all the bells and whistles made Jeffrey's head hurt.

He took the directions from her, holding them up to the light.

She said, "It's not like I can't read your handwriting. You have the penmanship of a first grade teacher."

He pointed to the satellite navigation screen on the dash, which had read, "No data available for this position" for the last half hour. "How much extra did you pay for this thing?"

"What does that have to do with your handwriting?"

He didn't answer as he looked at his notes. He'd clearly written "right at barbecue joint."

Jeffrey handed the sheet of paper back to Sara and took the right. He drove slowly, the car's tires dipping into one pothole after another. He was about to turn around when Sara spotted a familiar blue road sign with an H on it. Farther up ahead, they could see the bright lights of a parking lot, and beyond this, what could only be the hospital.

"Fifth Avenue," Sara read off the street sign. She didn't say any-thing more as he pulled into the parking lot.

The Elawah County Medical Center was across from a Dunkin' Donuts and a Kentucky Fried Chicken, both closed this time of night. The hospital building was an architect's nightmare. Part poured con-crete, part cinder block, and yet another part brick, the two-story struc-ture looked like a mangy dog that had been kicked to the curb. The few vehicles scattered around the parking lot were mostly trucks, mud caked around their wheel wells from a recent rain. NASCAR stickers and Jesus fish dotted the chrome bumpers. They had driven almost three hours straight to get here, but there was no mistaking they were still in a small Southern town.

Jeffrey took an empty space right by the emergency room entrance. He didn't get out of the car, didn't turn off the ignition. He just sat there, thinking about what little information he'd been given. Lena had been involved in an explosion. She was being treated at the hospital. She had been arrested.

What has she done now?

Those were Sara's words—Sara, who couldn't understand why Jeffrey had stood by Lena all these years, who didn't know what it was like to grow up with no one rooting for you, no one thinking you'd end up doing anything but making your parents' own stupid mistakes. If that were the case, Jeffrey would die a worthless drunk like his old man and Lena would—he didn't know what would happen to Lena. Her only saving grace was that she had rejected Hank Norton as a role model. As for the rest of the people in Lena's life, Jeffrey had only met one of them, an ex-boyfriend, ex-felon, ex-neo-Nazi whose sorry ass Jeffrey had happily hauled back to prison.

"Hey," Sara said, softly. "You okay?"

"Yeah." He turned to her. "Listen, I know how you feel about Lena, but—"

"Keep it to myself?" she interrupted. He studied her face, trying to figure out if she was annoyed or angered by the request. Neither emotion seemed to register, and she actually managed a smile. "Let's just get this over with and go home."

"Good plan." He turned off the ignition and got out of the car. The smell of cigarette smoke wafted through the air, and Jeffrey could see a couple of paramedics leaning against an ambulance, shooting the shit as they waited for their next call. One of them tossed Jeffrey a wave and he nodded back as he walked around to open Sara's door.

Jeffrey warned, "I'm not sure how this is going to go."

"I can wait in the car," she offered. "I don't want to get in your way."

"You're not going to get in my way," he answered, though the thought had occurred to him. He opened the back door and took out his suit jacket. "You can examine her. Make sure she's okay."

Sara hesitated. He knew what she was thinking, that she hadn't felt much like a doctor lately, that with the lawsuit hanging over her head, she didn't quite trust her instincts anymore. "I'm not really—"

Jeffrey didn't press her. "It's okay," he said. "Come on."

The glass doors slid open as they walked into the emergency department. Inside, the waiting room was empty but for an elderly man in a wheelchair and a younger woman sitting in a chair beside him. They were both wearing surgical masks, eyes trained on the television hanging from the ceiling. Jeffrey was reminded of the health warnings he'd been seeing on the news lately about yet another new strain of flu that was going to kill them all. The receptionist behind the front counter wasn't wearing a mask, but he guessed from the sour look on her face as they approached that any germ floating around would be too frightened to go near her.

He opened his mouth to speak, but the woman cut him off, slapping down a clipboard on the counter and saying, "Fill these out. Follow the yellow line to the business office to work out a payment plan, then come back here. We're running about two hours behind right now, so if you're not here for a good reason, you might as well go home and try to sleep it off."

Jeffrey pulled out his badge and placed it on the counter beside the clipboard. "I'm here to see Sheriff Valentine."

The woman ran her tongue along her bottom teeth, making it look as if she had a pinch of snuff there. Finally, she gave a noisy sigh, pulled back the clipboard and turned toward her computer, where a couple of clicks brought up a hand of solitaire she'd obviously been playing.

Jeffrey looked at Sara, as if she could decipher the goings-on of the hospital. She shrugged, and he was thinking they'd been given the brush-off when the receptionist heaved another heavy sigh, then said, "Follow the green line to the elevator, take it to the third floor, then follow the blue line to the nurses' station. They might know what you're talking about."

He looked down. There were five painted lines under their feet. Two led down a hallway, one led toward the elevator, and the last one, a red line, led to the exit, which was less than ten feet behind him.

Jeffrey picked up his badge and tucked it back into his pocket. He let Sara walk ahead of him toward the elevator. As if by magic, the doors slid open on their approach. The floor of the car was reddish-pink from dirt, and the faint odor of Pine-Sol and vomit filled the air.

Sara stopped. "Maybe we could take the stairs?"

"What about the blue line?" Jeffrey asked, only half-joking.

She shrugged and got on. He followed suit, pressing the three button, noticing that there was a two but not a one. They both stood there, waiting for the doors to close. Nothing happened, so he pressed the three button again. Still, nothing happened. He pressed the two button and the doors closed. Above them, machinery whirred, and the elevator moved upward.

Sara said, "I really shouldn't be here."

He hated that she felt so out of place. "I want you here." He tried to sound more convincing. "I need you here."

"You don't," she insisted, "but I appreciate the lie."

"Sara—"

She turned around, studying the notice board screwed to the back of the elevator. "Meth is Death!" one of the posters warned, showing before and after photos of a beautiful blonde teenager who, after a scant year on meth, turned into a soulless crone with no teeth and festering wounds erupting from her once perfect skin. A number at the bottom was scribbled over, a crude drawing of a joint obscuring the last two digits. Another poster outlining the steps to performing CPR took up most of the remaining space. This one was vandalized with the usual graffiti you found in spaces like this: dirty limericks, phone numbers for loose women, and messages for various people to go fuck themselves.

Finally, the elevator doors groaned open and a bell dinged. A dimly lit hallway greeted them, and Jeffrey guessed the lights had been turned off so that patients could sleep. The emergency exit sign across from the elevator gave off a warm red glow, pointing toward a doorway at the very end of the hall. Jeffrey glanced around, holding the elevator doors open, wondering if they were on the wrong floor.

"There's the stripe," Sara whispered, indicating the single blue line on the floor. Jeffrey saw that it went to the right, past the emergency stairway and around the corner. He looked up the hall to the left, but all he could see were more patients' rooms and another exit sign.

They followed the painted line to the nurses' station. He realized as soon as they got there that the hallway circled around and that they could have just as easily taken a left and gotten to the same place.

"This is why people hate hospitals," Jeffrey told Sara, keeping his voice low. "If they can't make you feel sicker, they drive you crazy."

Sara rolled her eyes, and Jeffrey remembered the first time he'd told Sara that he hated hospitals. Her response had been almost automatic: "*Everybody* hates hospitals."

The nurses' station was oblong, open at both ends, and packed to the gills with charts and colored sheets of paper. There was one desk with a lamp casting a harsh light over the blotter. A newspaper was folded to the crossword, some of the squares filled in. Jeffrey guessed from the half-eaten pack of crackers beside an open can of Diet Coke that whoever had been sitting there must've been called away mid-snack.

Sara leaned against the wall, arms folded over her chest. "The nurse must be making rounds."

"I guess we'll wait here."

"We could find Lena on our own."

"I don't think the sheriff would appreciate that."

She gave him a curious look, as if she was surprised that he cared.

He was about to respond when he heard a toilet flush behind him. "Guess the nurse just finished her rounds."

They both waited, Sara leaning against the wall, Jeffrey pacing, reading the signs that had been taped to some of the patients' doors. "No Water." "No Solids." "No Unattended Toilet."

Christ, they knew how to bring you low in these places.

He heard water running from the bathroom faucet, then the familiar squeak of a paper-towel dispenser. Seconds later, the door opened and a gray-haired man in a uniform came out. He did a double take when he saw Jeffrey. "Chief Tolliver?"

"Jeffrey," he offered, walking over to shake the man's hand. He realized a second too late that he wasn't talking to the sheriff. The insignia on the dark brown and taupe uniform identified the man as a deputy. "This is my wife, Dr. Sara Linton."

"Donald Cook." The man shook Jeffrey's hand, nodding at Sara. He had a loud, booming voice, and didn't seem to be worried if he woke up any of the patients. "Sorry if I kept y'all waiting."

Jeffrey got straight to the point. "How's my detective doing?"

"No trouble at all," Cook answered. "She's been quiet as a mouse."

In a different situation, Jeffrey would have made some joke about mistaken identity. "Was she burned? Your sheriff said there was some kind of explosion—"

"She's got smoke inhalation, some cuts and scrapes. Doc says she'll heal up fine."

Jeffrey waited for Sara to press the man about Lena's condition, but she just stood there, listening. This wasn't like her. The hospital was Sara's element. He'd expected her to at least ask for Lena's chart or try to find the doctor in charge.

Then again, Sara didn't usually tag along when he was working. Jeffrey guessed she was trying not to interfere. He asked the deputy, "Can you tell me what happened?"

"Best talk to Jake about that." The man made his way behind the counter and fell back into the desk chair with a groan. He picked up the phone, saying, "Sorry I can't offer y'all a seat." He slipped on a pair of reading glasses so he could make out the numbers on the telephone. "They had a junkie in here last night who puked all over the chairs. Easier to just throw them out and order some new ones."

"No problem," Jeffrey said, tucking his hands into his pockets, trying to resist the urge to resume pacing. Though Sara seemed to be keeping her own counsel, he could see that she was just as surprised by the situation as Jeffrey. Lena's armed guard was a joke. The deputy should be sitting outside her room, not eating crackers and taking a crap when the mood suited him. Sara had been right. Jeffrey should've looked for Lena on his own instead of attempting to play the diplomat.

Cook unnecessarily held up his hand for silence, saying into the phone, "Jake? He's here. Yeah, brought a doctor with him." He nodded, then hung up, telling Jeffrey, "Jake said he's just pulling into the parking lot. Went home to get some supper. We figured it'd take a little longer for you to get here."

"What was she arrested for?" When the man didn't answer, Jeffrey gave him some options. "Property damage? Criminal neglect?"

Cook's lips turned up in a grin. "Not exactly."

Jeffrey knew what a "not exactly" meant—they had charged her with something small in order to buy time to figure out how to charge her with something big. He glanced back at Sara, feeling pulled in two different directions. Bringing Sara here was probably not one of his brighter ideas. Everything about the hospital was likely reminding her of the malpractice suit, the fact that somewhere back in Grant County her professional and private lives were being raked over the coals.

With some effort, Jeffrey shifted his focus back to Lena. "Can we go ahead and see her?"

"Might not be a good idea," Cook said, sliding a cracker out of the pack. Jeffrey felt his stomach rumble and realized he'd missed supper. Cook must have heard it because he offered, "You want one?" Jeffrey shook his head, and the man held the pack toward Sara, who shook her head, too.

Cook sat back, chewing his cracker. He raised his eyebrows at Jeffrey. "Bad situation."

Jeffrey knew that he was being played by the old man. Cook was probably bored out of his mind doing babysitting duty. Tossing Jeffrey a bone and seeing if he'd fetch was obviously more entertaining than doing the crossword. What the deputy didn't count on was that the dog might bite. Jeffrey looked at his watch, thinking he had wasted enough time. He could get his chain pulled in the comfort of his own home.

He told the deputy, "I'd really like to see her."

"That explosion was deliberately set." Cook's tone was a warning.

Jeffrey heard Sara shift behind him. "That so?" he asked.

"Yep."

He couldn't help himself. "You think my detective started it?"

"Like I said—"

"Talk to Jake."

"Right," Cook said, crumbs dropping onto his uniform as he chewed the cracker. Out of nowhere, he announced, "I worked with Calvin Adams."

Jeffrey guessed he meant Lena's father.

"Good man, Cal," Cook continued. "Took two in the head on a traffic stop. Liked to killed me when it happened."

Jeffrey didn't respond, but he knew all too well the feeling of losing a fellow cop. It was a loss that haunted you every day of your life—harder, maybe, than losing a family member or a spouse.

Cook was still leaning back in his chair, fingers laced over his belly. "You took me for the sheriff, huh?"

"Sorry?" Jeffrey asked. His mind had been wandering. "Yeah," he answered, realizing what the man had said. "My mistake."

"I've been wearing this uniform going on forty years," Cook proudly stated. "Finally threw my hat into the ring for the sheriff's job. Lost it to Jake." Jeffrey knew that the sheriff's office was an elected position. He said a silent prayer of thanks that he didn't have to campaign every two years to keep his job. It was a good position if you could get it. The sheriff's pension and benefits were some of the best in law enforcement.

Cook said, "Jake Valentine," with a chuckle. "Sounds like some kind of soap opera star. Boy ain't been off his mama's tit more than three years."

Jeffrey wasn't in the mood to gossip about the sheriff. He wanted to know more about the explosion, whether it was deliberately set, who else was hurt, and what in the hell Lena had to do with any of it. He knew Cook wasn't about to offer up answers on a silver platter, so he asked, "Do you know Hank Norton?"

"Sure I do. No-good piece of shit is what he is."

Jeffrey realized that he was relieved to hear the man talking about Lena's uncle in the present tense. He asked, "Has Hank been in trouble?"

"Caught somebody passing meth at his place three weeks ago. We closed it down, but Norton was so wasted I doubt he even noticed."

"I thought he was sober now."

"I thought my wife was a virgin when I married her." Cook blanched, remembering Sara. "Sorry, ma'am." He leaned his elbow on the desk, directed his words toward Jeffrey. "Lookit, Norton's been a junkie from the word go. Must've started when he was around sixteen, seventeen. You don't stay away from that kind of thing for very long."

"Speed, right?"

"So the story goes."

The elevator dinged, and Jeffrey heard the metallic whir of the doors sliding open. Two sets of footsteps echoed up the hall. The pair was having an animated conversation in hushed tones. As they drew closer, Jeffrey saw that one of them was a nurse. The other had to be Sheriff Jake Valentine.

The young nurse seemed to be hanging on the sheriff's every word as he described an elaborate scuffle he'd had with a drunk driver. Cook had been right about Valentine. The man looked about eighteen if he was a day. He was so tall and lanky that the gunbelt around his waist was pulled to the last hole, the end flopping out of the buckle like a tongue. A smattering of facial hair over his upper lip seemed to imply a mustache and the wet spot on the crown of his head suggested a cow-lick he'd tried to tame before coming to the hospital. He was at least two inches taller than Jeffrey, but the stoop in his shoulders and the turtle-like bend in his neck blew the advantage. Jeffrey imagined that his mother had spent every day of his young life telling the boy to mind his posture.

"Jake!" the nurse shrieked, punching him on the arm.

Cook made a groaning noise, indicating he'd heard the drunk driver story the sheriff was telling one too many times. He said, "Jake, that chief's here to see you."

Valentine seemed surprised to find Jeffrey standing in front of the nurses' station. Jeffrey wondered at the act. Even if Cook hadn't made the phone call, the hallway wasn't that dark.

"Jake Valentine," the sheriff offered, shooting out his hand.

"Tolliver." Jeffrey returned the gesture. Despite Valentine's slight appearance, the young man gave him a firm handshake. "This is my wife, Dr. Sara Linton."

Sara shook the man's hand and managed a forced smile.

The nurse went behind the counter and Valentine's demeanor changed to solemn as if a switch had been flipped. He told Jeffrey and Sara, "Sorry to be meeting y'all under these circumstances."

"Can you tell us what happened?"

Valentine indicated his deputy. "I figured Don here filled you in."

"Thought I'd leave you the pleasure," Cook returned, giving Jeffrey a wink.

"Darla," Valentine said, meaning the nurse, "mind if we step into your office?"

"Suit yourself," she answered, thumbing through a patient's chart. "Lemme know if y'all need anything."

"Actually," Jeffrey said, "I'd really like to know how my detective is doing. Lena Adams?"

"She's fine," the nurse replied. "Just got some smoke in her chest. Give her a few days and she'll be good as new."

"Good," Valentine said, as if he'd been the one to ask the question. "Up this way." He stepped back, indicating that Jeffrey and Sara should precede him.

Sara offered, "I can stay here if—"

"That's okay," Jeffrey interrupted. Considering how quiet Sara was being, he wasn't crazy about leaving her alone right now.

He let Sara take the lead up the hallway, trying not to be too obvious about checking the names of the patients on each door they passed.

Valentine spoke in a harsh whisper as they walked. "We found her at the high school last night. I live across the street. I could see the flames from my living room."

Jeffrey slowed his pace, wanting the younger man to catch up instead of nipping at his heels like a puppy.

Valentine continued, "We think it was a Cadillac Escalade. No plates or registration on it, so we're having trouble tracking it down. Parked right in the middle of the football field. Fire chief says there's obvious signs of an accelerant, probably gasoline."

"Wait a minute." Jeffrey stopped him, trying for clarity. He'd been told that there was an explosion and that Lena had been hurt. Jeffrey had assumed this had taken place in a building. "The Cadillac was torched? That's what exploded?"

"Right." Valentine nodded. Still keeping his voice low, he explained, "The car was sitting smack-dab on the fifty-yard line. I've never seen anything burn so hot in my life. They're gonna have a devil of a time getting an ID on the body. Fred Bart, that's our coroner, says the heat was so intense it shattered the teeth."

Sara had stopped a few feet away. "There was a body in the Escalade?"

"Yes, ma'am, in the backseat," the sheriff confirmed.

Sara pressed her lips together, looked at the floor. She didn't seem surprised or even shocked by the news. Jeffrey knew what she was thinking. It had finally happened. Through stubbornness or blatant disregard, Lena's actions had finally led to someone's death.

Valentine misinterpreted her silence for confusion. "I'm not telling this right, am I? I'm sorry, I just assumed Don—"

Jeffrey told him, "Don said he'd let you explain."

"Right." Valentine nodded again, but in a way that gave the impression that he didn't quite believe what Jeffrey was telling him. "Let's just go in here," he said, indicating a closed door.

Jeffrey turned around, sure the man was joking. They were standing in front of a linen closet.

"Give us some privacy," the sheriff offered, though as far as Jeffrey could tell, no one was around.

Sara crossed her arms over her chest. She looked at the closet with obvious trepidation.

Jeffrey asked, "Are you sure this is necessary?"

"This way we won't have to worry about waking anybody up." Valentine reached past him and opened the door. "After you."

Jeffrey was annoyed at the cloak-and-dagger, but he was willing to play along with the sheriff for now. The most important thing right now was figuring out what kind of mess Lena had gotten herself into. He felt around for the switch and turned on the light. Rows of sheets were stacked on the right, towels on the left. The remaining space was about eight feet deep and three feet wide. There were cells at the county jail that were larger than this.

Sara obviously wanted to stay outside, but he indicated she should go in ahead of him. Jeffrey followed and Valentine brought up the rear, closing the door. The closet got even smaller.

"So," the sheriff began, flashing a smile. He was talking in a normal voice now, and he leaned against one of the shelves, acting as if they were just a group of pals chatting before a football game. "About eleven o'clock last night I was sitting around watching the TV and I see these flames shooting up over by the high school. First thing I do is call the fire department, thinking the building's on fire again—we've had some kids try it before but the sprinklers stopped them in their tracks, which is a good thing because the fire department's all volunteer and it like to took forever to get them all there. Anyway, I got dressed and walked over to the school to see what was going on. It was faster to walk. Like I told you, I live right across the street."

The story was so embellished Jeffrey wondered how many times it had been repeated. He tried to get to the important part. "So you saw the car burning on the field?"

"Right," Valentine confirmed. "Last night was dark as pitch, but the flames were high, and I could see somebody sitting on the bleachers. I walked over, thinking it'd be some stupid kid gone out for a joyride, and I see Miss Adams—your detective. She was sitting on the bottom bleacher, soot and stuff all over her. Had her foot propped up on a gas can."

"Was she burned?"

"Nah, but she was beat something awful," the man answered. "Bruised down the side of her face like she'd been punched, blood coming out of her mouth, wheezing something horrible. Me, I've never seen anything like that before, but maybe I've been watching too many Lifetime movies with the wife, because the first thing that pops into my mind is, 'this woman just torched her husband.' You know, like he'd hauled off and hit her one too many times and she just snapped"—he snapped his fingers—"and so I sat beside her, tried to get her to talk."

Jeffrey asked, "What did she say?"

"Nothing," the man admitted. "I tried every trick I could think of to draw her out, but she wouldn't speak."

Jeffrey could imagine what Lena's reaction would have been to Valentine's various "tricks." The man was lucky she hadn't laughed in his face.

Valentine continued, "Wasn't until this morning when we did a search of the school parking lot and found her Celica that we got her name. I found her badge in the glove compartment and figured, hey—what's it hurt to give 'em a call?"

Jeffrey skipped over the fact that the sheriff had waited until daylight to search the parking lot. "She wasn't carrying any ID on her?"

"No, sir. Didn't find anything on her except a tube of ChapStick—the license was in the Celica and the badge was in the glove box like I told you. Nothing else in her pockets, nothing hidden in her…" His voice trailed off, and he blushed as he finished, "places."

"No weapon?" In addition to her Glock, Lena sometimes carried a large folding knife in her back pocket, but Jeffrey wasn't going to share that with the sheriff right now.

"No, sir. No weapons of any kind."

"Was anyone else injured or on the scene?"

"Nope. Just the victim in the Caddy and her on the bleachers."

"Did she have gasoline on her? Any kind of accelerant on her shoes or clothes?"

"Nope. But the gasoline can was empty."

"Did she have matches or a lighter?"

"Nothing except the ChapStick, and I cranked it all the way up to make sure what it was and it was ChapStick all the way through."

"Were her fingerprints on the gas can?"

"Can't really tell. It's an old can—lots of rust. We sent it to the GBI lab in Macon, but I can guess you're familiar with their time frame."

Jeffrey nodded. Unless a case had high priority, the lab probably wouldn't have time to process the gas can for at least six months.

He tried to be polite with his next question. "No offense, but what did you charge her with?"

"Not much," Valentine admitted. "I'm gonna shoot straight with you, Chief, what with us both being on the job and all. We don't have a lot on her, but I think you'll agree the circumstances are pretty suspicious, plus with her not helping us out by answering any questions."

Jeffrey had to admit that with a noncompliant person found at the scene of a homicide, he probably would have done the same thing. He repeated, "What did you charge her with?"

Valentine had the grace to look embarrassed as he counted off on his fingers, "Obstruction of justice. Impeding an investigation. Failure to produce identification when asked."

Jeffrey nodded again. He could see Lena doing all of that. Hell, he couldn't count on his own hands the number of times she'd impeded investigations back in Grant County—and those had been cases she was working on.

He asked, "Has she been arraigned?"

"The judge came over to the hospital this morning."

Jeffrey did a quick count of the money he had in his checking account. His paycheck wasn't due for another week. He would have to wait for the bank to open in the morning so that he could move the money from his savings and take out the cash from an ATM machine. He asked, "Where do I post bail?"

"Bail was denied."

Jeffrey tried to hide his shock, but then he figured out very quickly how this had probably worked. The sheriff was new to the job, but he'd managed to get a judge in his pocket. Still, Jeffrey tried to make the man see logic. "You think she's a flight risk? She was born here. She has ties to the community. She's been a distinguished officer on my force for over a decade."

"I understand that."

"You can't put a cop in jail. They'll tear her to pieces."

"She's not in the jail," Valentine reminded Jeffrey. "She's in the hospital."

"All I can tell you is you better have a damn good reason why you're keeping her in custody." Jeffrey could play this game, too. He'd been on the job a lot longer than Jake Valentine. Fuck the local yokels. Jeffrey had *state* judges in his pocket.

Apparently, Valentine wasn't as stupid as he looked. "I had nothing to do with that, Chief. I'll swear on a stack of Bibles. Not my fault she wouldn't plead."

"What does that mean?"

"It means what I said before. Your detective's not making a peep."

Jeffrey finally understood. "She hasn't said *anything* since you found her on the field?"

"No, sir. Not one word. Didn't ask for a drink of water or try to find out how her medical condition was doing or when she was gonna get out of here. She wouldn't talk to her court-appointed lawyer, wouldn't answer the judge when he asked if she was guilty or not guilty. She just laid there in the bed staring at the ceiling. Avery was so annoyed—Avery is the judge—that he denied bond and ordered a psych evaluation."

Jeffrey felt his mind reeling. Lena could certainly be obstinate, but her silence made no sense. Someone had died in that fire. How could she sit there watching the car burn?

Sara finally spoke. "Maybe her throat was damaged during—"

"Doc said there's no medical reason she can't talk," Valentine interrupted. "Problem is, she won't even make the effort."

Jeffrey still could not see the logic behind Lena's silence. "What did the shrink say?"

"She wouldn't talk to him, either," the sheriff answered. "Far as I know, she hasn't said one dang thing this whole time. Just lays there staring at the ceiling. I even tried to get Darla to draw her out. Nothing."

"Could be post-traumatic stress? Shock?" Jeffrey suggested.

Valentine looked as dubious as Jeffrey felt.

"Did you tell her I was coming?"

"Nope. Thought it'd be best to let her sit and stew for a while."

Jeffrey tried to put himself in the other man's shoes, to look at the case from all angles. "Do you have an ID on the corpse?"

"The car was too hot to tow off the field until this afternoon."

"Has your coroner seen this kind of thing before?" Jeffrey asked. The burned corpse was crucial; the body was the only thing that might offer an explanation of what had happened on that football field. In Georgia, the job of county medical examiner was an elected position usually held by the local funeral director or anyone else who wasn't afraid to touch a dead body. The fact that Sara, a medical doctor, had taken the job in Grant County was very rare. There was no telling who the local body handler was.

Valentine offered, "Fred Bart's a good man. He'll let me know anything he finds. I gotta say he wasn't too optimistic. Body like that—it's hard to even say whether it's a man or a woman, let alone how they died." He shrugged, gave a goofy smile. "What am I saying? I'm sure you know how this works."

Valentine hadn't exactly answered the question. Jeffrey tried to tread lightly as he fished for Bart's qualifications. "Sara's the coroner back home. She's a pediatrician, too."

"Oh." Valentine shifted away from the shelves, flashed a smile at Sara. "That's nice. My wife's a schoolteacher. All she does is correct my grammar and tell me to sit up straight."

Jeffrey had more questions, but something told him Valentine wouldn't answer them. "What made you call me?"

"Common sense," Valentine answered. He had seemed ready to leave it at that, but then he added, "I'll be straight with you, Chief. Your detective's just a little thing. Doesn't seem like she'd hurt a fly. I can't see her doing this. There's gotta be something more to the story. I figured if I couldn't get it out of her, maybe you could." He paused. "At the very least, you can save us a lot of time and money if you'd find out who's in that car."

Jeffrey doubted he would prove to be any help, but he said, "All right. Let me see her."

Again, Valentine let Jeffrey and Sara go first. Sadly, Jeffrey guessed this was more because the younger man's parents had always told him to respect his elders than out of any deference to rank.

As they walked toward Lena's room, Jeffrey tried to process what the sheriff had just told them. The facts were simple. Lena had been found at a crime scene where a car was torched and a body was burned beyond recognition. Why was she on the football field? What connection did she have to the dead person? Who had caused the explosion? He heard Sara's earlier question echo in his mind: *What has she done now?*

Despite Valentine's newness to the job, Jeffrey could not fault the man on the arrest. Based on the circumstances, Jeffrey would've arrested Lena, too. She was an obvious suspect, and her silence wasn't helping matters. Not that Lena had ever fostered a reputation for being helpful.

He could still remember the first time he'd seen her. She was in the police academy gymnasium, hanging halfway up the climbing rope, determined to make it to the top even though she was sweating so hard that her hands could barely keep their grip. No one else was around— this was something Lena was doing on her own time—and Jeffrey had watched her trying and failing to reach the top of the rope for nearly half an hour before he went to the commandant's office and asked for her file.

The mayors of the three cities that comprised Grant County had brought in Jeffrey as police chief to shake things up, to help force the department into the twenty-first century. Lena was the first non-secretarial woman hire in the town's history. Jeffrey had pinned everything on her, determined he had made the right choice even when sometimes the facts said otherwise. When Frank Wallace, his most senior detective, had announced a few weeks ago that he was finally going to take retirement at the end of the year, Jeffrey had taken the news in his stride, thinking Lena was ready to tackle some added responsibilities. Had he been wrong about her? In the nearly fifteen years that he'd known her, had Lena been living some kind of lie?

There had to be a reason for all this. Every crime had an explanation, a motivation. Jeffrey just had to find it. The sheriff was right about one thing. Lena was not a cold-blooded killer.

"Here we go." Valentine indicated a closed door, and Jeffrey could plainly see Lena's name on the sign. She was at the back end of the hall in a corner room. If Jeffrey and Sara hadn't followed that stupid blue stripe off the elevator, they would've found Lena without having to go through Cook.

Jeffrey suggested, "Maybe Sara and I should go in alone." If Lena was going to talk, it certainly wouldn't be in front of the man who had arrested her.

"Well…" Valentine began, scratching his chin. He took his time mulling it over. Down the hall, they heard the elevator doors ding. Probably Cook going out for more crackers.

"Let's just go inside," Jeffrey insisted, tired of waiting for the sheriff.

Like the hallway, the room was deep in shadow. Lena lay in bed just as Valentine had described: on her back, motionless. Velcro bands attached her wrists to the bed rails. Her hands hung limply, fingers brushing the mattress. Her eyes were closed, but Jeffrey did not know if she was sleeping or biding her time. She was just as battered-looking as the young sheriff had said. Blood crusted her bottom lip. The skin was scraped off down the side of her cheek. The dark bruises on her face must have stopped them from trying to wipe off the blood and soot; she looked filthy, beaten down.

Jeffrey felt speechless. He was glad when Sara stepped forward, asking, "Lena?"

Lena's head snapped around in surprise, eyes widening as she saw Jeffrey and Sara in the room. She bolted up in bed, jerking against the restraints as if she felt cornered, threatened. The bedsheets tangled around her feet as she pushed against the mattress, backing as far away from them as she could.

"No," Lena whispered. "You can't be here. No."

"Well, now." The sheriff's sloppy grin indicated that he was pleased with himself. "I knew you could talk."

"No," Lena repeated, ignoring everyone in the room but Sara. Her voice was venomous. "Get out. Get out now."

Jeffrey tried, "Lena—"

All her hatred seemed to focus on Sara. "Are you stupid? I said get the fuck out of here! Go!"

Sara's mouth opened in surprise. Jeffrey felt a white-hot fury spark inside him, and he spoke through clenched teeth when he ordered, "Lena, back off."

"Get out!" she screamed, jerking against the restraints. "Get her out of here!" she begged the sheriff. "I'll tell you whatever you want. Just get her *out*!"

Valentine seemed at a loss. He indicated the door with a nod of his head. "Maybe she should—"

"No," Sara insisted. She spoke so quietly that Jeffrey wasn't sure she'd actually said the word until she turned to the two men, asking, "Could you give us a moment alone?" She asked Jeffrey, "Please?"

Sara did not wait for an answer. She slipped Lena's chart out of the holder at the foot of the bed and studied it as she waited for them to leave. Jeffrey could tell she was forcing herself to do this, that if she could snap her fingers, she would've been anywhere but here. He just wasn't sure why she wanted to stay.

For the first time since he'd entered the room, Lena spoke directly to Jeffrey. "Get your fucking wife out of my face. I don't want her here."

He locked eyes with her, willing the young woman to understand that there would be lasting consequences for her words. Jeffrey could put up with a lot of bullshit, but he would be damned if an officer on his force would get away with trashing his wife.

Sara looked up from Lena's chart. "It's okay. Just give us a few minutes."

Despite his better judgment, Jeffrey managed, "We'll wait in the hall." He went to the door and held it open for the sheriff. Valentine stared at Lena for a few seconds, undecided. Finally, he shook his head, making it clear he wasn't happy with his choice, and walked out of the room.

In the hallway, Jeffrey let the door close behind him, then stood in front of it—not exactly blocking the way but close enough.

"So." Valentine rested his hand on the butt of his gun. He obviously was itching to go back into the room. "That what you expected to happen?"

Of all the scenarios Jeffrey had considered, this had not been one of them. He asked Valentine, "Where's Lena's uncle? Hank Norton?"

Valentine was staring at the door as if he wanted to bust through it. Jeffrey pressed, "He's Lena's next of kin. Didn't you contact him?"

Valentine nodded. "Wasn't there."

There were muffled sounds through the door, but no yelling that Jeffrey could hear. He indicated to the sheriff that they should walk up the hallway a bit. "You went by Hank's house?"

Valentine stayed where he was. "I can't find him anywhere. I went to his house last night, then again this morning. His bar's been closed. There was something happened a few weeks ago—"

"Cook told me about that."

"Yeah," Valentine said, a suspicious look crossing his face. The man obviously did not trust his deputy. Jeffrey wondered how they got any work done. The force had to be a small one, with probably no more than five deputies in all. Parking Donald Cook at the hospital was one way of keeping his enemy at arm's length, but Jeffrey was going to take a wild guess and say that the old-timer had a lot more friends in uniform than his young boss.

Jeffrey asked, "Any idea who it might be in the Caddy?"

"There are no missing persons that we know of. No reports on any suspicious characters hanging around. No Escalades reported missing. It's a puzzle."

At least he hadn't been sitting on his hands all night. "What about Hank Norton?"

"He drives a Mercedes that's probably older than I am."

"No." Jeffrey shook his head. "Do you think maybe it's his body in the car?"

Valentine shrugged. "All's I know is a DNA test is gonna blow half my wad for the quarter."

His budgetary concerns were valid, but Jeffrey wondered again why Valentine wasn't more eager to nail down the victim's identity. Maybe he already had some idea, but he wasn't yet willing to share the information.

"I know you said there weren't any accelerants on her clothes, but did forensics find anything on her shoes?"

Valentine took his time answering. "She was wearing those what-do-you-call-its, with the short heel."

"Pumps?" Jeffrey asked, thinking it was odd that Lena was wearing anything dressier than tennis shoes on her day off.

"Right, pumps. My wife wears those shoes hippies and lesbians wear.

You know, with the cork? I don't know what they're called, but she swears by them."

Jeffrey tried to get him back on subject. "Did they find anything on the shoes?"

"Just soot, dirt, the usual. Didn't seem like there was any need to send them to the lab." Valentine tilted up his chin, asked, "You think I should?"

Jeffrey shrugged. Though, if it was up to Jeffrey, he'd spend money on identifying the victim before worrying about Lena's shoes, but that hadn't been the sheriff's question. "Up to you."

Around the corner, he heard the elevator ding again. Jeffrey tried to think of something to keep them out in the hallway a little longer, wanting to give Sara as much time as he could. "Where's one?"

"What's that?"

"The elevator," he said. "The buttons only go to two and three. Where's the first floor?"

"Basement," Valentine told him. "Crazy, ain't it?"

"How do you get down there?"

"You have to use the stairs or go around the back of the building."

Jeffrey wondered how many fatalities the county coroner dealt with. "You got many bodies down there?"

"Bodies?" He looked shocked, then gave a chuckle as he explained, "Our morgue's over near the impound lot. The basement's for the laundry room, storage, that kind of stuff."

"That's strange," Jeffrey said, grasping at straws. "Why the impound lot?"

Valentine shrugged, glanced at his watch, then the door.

Jeffrey tried, "Is she going to need therapy or anything? Medication?"

"What, for the fire?" Valentine shook his head. "Nah. Doc says she'll be fine in a few days."

"What about your usual suspects?"

"What does that mean?"

"Your bad guys," Jeffrey clarified. "Persons of interest."

Valentine shook his head. "You got me on that one, Chief."

"Well," Jeffrey began, once again trying not to sound too condescending, "when something bad happens in my town, like a car gets stolen or somebody swipes a television, I've got a pretty good idea who might be behind it."

"Oh." Valentine nodded. "Yeah, I got you. Only, we don't get many cars being blown up on the football field here."

Jeffrey chose to ignore his sarcasm. "Any arsonists?"

"That's a big-city crime."

"Apparently not."

Valentine scratched his chin. "I figure whoever did this was trying to send a message."

"What kind of message?"

"Your detective's the only one who can answer that. Speaking of which," he said, nodding toward the door. "I think your wife's had enough time alone with her."

Jeffrey could only hope that was the case. He followed Valentine back into the room. Sara was leaning against the wall outside the bathroom. The bed was empty, the soft restraints hanging from the rails. The shower was running.

Sara explained, "I talked her into cleaning up."

"She talk back?" Valentine wanted to know.

Sara shook her head, and Jeffrey could see that she was telling the truth.

"Not much help then," Valentine said, obviously annoyed. He glanced at his watch, then at the bathroom door. "How long she been in there?"

"Not long."

He tried the doorknob, but it was locked. "Jesus, lady, you didn't think it'd be smart to go in there with her?"

Sara opened her mouth to answer, but Jeffrey cut her off, telling the man, "Watch your tone."

Valentine ignored him, knocking hard on the door. "Miss Adams? I need you to open this door now." He slipped his radio out of his belt. "Cook, you there? Come in." There was no answer, and the sheriff pressed his shoulder into the door, trying to pop it open.

For the second time that night, Sara's lips parted, but she did not speak.

"Cook?" Valentine tried the radio again. There was no answer, and he banged his fist on the bathroom door. "Miss Adams, you've got to the count of three to open this door."

The radio crackled. In a slow drawl, Don Cook asked, "What is it, Jake?"

"Find the passkey for the bathroom and get your ass in here!" Valentine barked. He tucked the radio back in its holster and put his shoulder to the door again. "Miss Adams," he tried again. "Lookit, just come out and everything will be fine."

Jeffrey asked Sara, "Does she have anything sharp in there?"

Valentine turned around, waiting for her answer.

Sara shook her head. "I don't think so."

Valentine asked, "Would she try to hurt herself?"

"I have no idea," Sara returned, her words clipped. "I'm not her doctor."

"Shit," Valentine hissed. He banged on the door again. "Miss Adams."

"Oh, no..." Sara's voice was so low and the banging was so loud that Valentine obviously didn't hear her.

"What's—" Jeffrey looked up, his question caught in his throat. He knew exactly what had happened on the other side of that door.

Cook came into the room, a key in his hand. "What's going on?"

Valentine snatched the key from him and slid it into the locked door. Steam from the shower filled the room. He strode inside and yanked back the curtain. The tub was empty.

"Motherfuck," Valentine cursed. Above the toilet, a ceiling tile had been pushed back, exposing a narrow crawl space. "Goddammit!" he screamed, kicking the wall. He told Cook, "Search the hospital top to bottom. Call backup now." Cook left, and Valentine looked right at Sara, saying, "You bitch."

Jeffrey grabbed the man by the collar and slammed him against the wall. "You ever talk to my wife like that again and we're gonna have a real problem. You hear me?" Valentine tried to get away, but Jeffrey tightened his grip. "You hear me?"

Valentine went limp like a kitten who'd been grabbed by the scruff of the neck. "She let my prisoner escape."

Jeffrey didn't let himself look at Sara, because he knew that she was thinking the same thing he was. Lena had tricked her. There was no getting around it.

He let the man go.

"Asshole." Valentine jerked his shirt back into place, scowling. He shoved past Jeffrey as he went into the hallway. Jeffrey followed him around the corner and into the next room. The bed was empty, obviously unused. "She let my prisoner escape," Valentine snarled. "I can't fucking believe I stood out in that hall letting you jerk me around while your wife was in there letting her escape."

"Sara's not a part of this."

"Why don't you do yourself a favor, buddy?" Valentine challenged. "You get that wife of yours, and you get back into your car, and you get the fuck out of my town."

Jeffrey didn't need to be asked politely. He turned without a word and went to find Sara.

She was still in Lena's room, stricken. "How could I have been so stupid? How could I—"

He took her by the elbow, leading her out of the room. "We don't need to talk about that right now."

"I shouldn't have been here in the first place."

Jeffrey led her into the hallway. The rent-a-cops had been called in, all two of them. Both men looked older than Don Cook and just as fit for duty.

Valentine started barking orders in between screaming into his radio for more backup. "I want her found *now*!"

Jeffrey pressed the button for the elevator. He glanced down the hall, figuring Lena's escape. Obviously, she had pushed back the tile over the toilet and used the crawl space over the drop ceiling to access the bathroom on the other side. Then, she had probably sneaked down the stairs to the basement. The elevator opened onto the emergency room, though even if she'd taken that route, he doubted she would've caused much of a stir. The receptionist probably wouldn't have even looked up from her game of cards on the computer.

The elevator doors slid open. Jeffrey pressed his hand to Sara's back, urging her to get on. Valentine and one of the hospital cops trotted past the elevator as the doors closed, probably on their way to search the basement.

Jeffrey pressed the button for the second floor, wondering again why the car didn't go down to the first floor. Maybe there was a freight elevator Valentine had failed to mention. Lena could've used that to get downstairs, but then what? The laundry would have sheets and towels. There was probably a staff lounge, maybe lockers for the cleaning staff. She could find clothes, cash. Jeffrey figured she had taken what she needed and gotten out of the hospital as soon as possible.

"How could I be so stupid?" Sara repeated, shaking her head. Tears were in her eyes. He had seen her angry countless times, but there was nothing so savage as the anger she could direct toward herself.

He instructed, "Tell me exactly what she said."

"Just the same stuff—that we had to leave. She barely even looked at me." She brushed away a tear with the back of her hand, her face white with fury. "I'm so sorry," she told him. "This is all my fault."

"I was standing out in the hallway," Jeffrey tried. "She used me, too."

"Not like..." Sara shook her head, unable to finish the sentence. "I unstrapped her, Jeffrey. I'm the one who let her go."

"Did she ask you to release her?"

"No—yes. Not directly. She said she felt dirty, that she was covered in dirt, and I just walked over and took off the straps. I didn't think twice about it. I even helped her out of the bed."

He tried to press gently. "Did she say anything else?"

"She apologized to me." Sara laughed at her own stupidity. "She was acting so scared. Her hands were shaking, her voice kept catching. I've never seen her so upset—not since Sibyl died. I fell for it completely. God, I'm such an idiot."

Jeffrey wrapped his hand around her shoulder, not knowing how to comfort her. He was so furious at Lena right now that he could barely think.

Sara said, "A drop ceiling. Of all the people who should know you can climb over a drop ceiling..."

He knew what had happened to her all those years ago at Grady Hospital, that her attacker had dropped down from the bathroom ceiling. If Lena had put a knife in his back, Sara had just unwittingly twisted it. He told her, "It's not your fault, Sara. You're not a cop."

"Then why am I here?" she demanded fiercely. "I should have stayed in the damn car. I should've just stayed home where I belong."

The elevator doors slid open. Two more sheriff's deputies were running through the lobby toward the stairs.

"Let's just get out of here," he told her, taking her by the arm. They were at the sliding doors when Valentine called to them.

"Hold on there," he said, jogging to catch up. He was out of breath, probably from running up and down the stairs. He held out his hand, palm up. "Give me the keys to your car."

Had Sara not been there, Jeffrey would have told the man to go fuck himself. As it was, he silently tossed him the keys, wanting to get this over with as soon as possible.

Valentine saw the BMW logo on the keyfob and gave Jeffrey the kind of look you'd give a whore on the street. Cops didn't drive BMWs, at least not where Jake Valentine came from.

"It's my wife's," Jeffrey told him. Sara had worked her ass off to be able to drive that car. As far as he was concerned, she could drive a Rolls-Royce if she wanted to.

Valentine pressed the button on the keyfob and the locks snicked up. Suddenly, he stopped. "Laundry room," he said, glaring at Jeffrey. "You asked what was on the bottom floor."

"I was making small talk."

"Don't bullshit me."

Sara said, "I'll be over here," walking toward one of the benches in front of the entrance.

Valentine gave him another nasty look before going to the car. Jeffrey knew the man wouldn't find anything there. Even if Lena had seen the BMW in the parking lot, there was no way to jimmy the door locks or open the trunk without the key. Breaking a window wouldn't do any good, either. One of the car's safety features was that if you engaged the central locking system from the outside, nothing could be opened from the inside. Jeffrey had actually been trapped inside the car once when Sara accidentally hit the lock button as she ran into the house to catch the ringing telephone. If the sunroof hadn't been open so he could crawl out, Jeffrey would've been stuck in the car for hours.

The sheriff could clearly see the empty seats and floorboards through the windows, but he still opened the door to make sure, taking off his hat, peering inside like he might catch Lena hiding under the center console. He walked around to the back of the car and popped the trunk. Except for Sara's first-aid kit and a couple of grocery bags to be recycled at the store, it was empty.

Valentine slammed the trunk closed. He told Jeffrey, "Guess I'd look like an even bigger jackass if I put out an APB on a fugitive wanted for 'failure to show identification.'"

"That's a fair assumption." The sheriff was already on thin ice with the charges he'd trumped up against Lena. He had to tread carefully now. They both knew that any mistakes he made at this point could end up ruining whatever case he might eventually build against her.

"Well." Valentine glanced around the parking lot. "That's Darla's Jeep. The red Chevy belongs to the maintenance crew, the Bronco is George's, and that's Bitty's Ranger over in the corner; she's been here since Thursday when she drove herself in with a pain in her side and it turned out to be appendicitis."

He had accounted for all the cars in the lot, but Jeffrey had to ask, "Where's your cruiser?"

Valentine laughed, but not out of amusement. "Don's got his best fishing pole in the trunk, so that was his first concern. Both our cars are out back. We're getting staff downstairs to check their lockers, see if anything is missing. I had somebody go over to Hank's to see if she shows up there." He tossed the key back to Jeffrey. "I reckon between your wife wasting my time and you jacking me around in the hallway, she could have up to a twenty-minute head start on me."

Jeffrey wasn't going to argue the finer points, such as Valentine pulling some kind of power move by making them all go into the linen closet. "At least."

"Lemme ask you something. Does it bother you that you just aided an escape?"

His tone had turned nasty in the blink of an eye. Jeffrey pushed away from the car, answering, "Not much."

"That's how you old cops work, isn't it?" Valentine was obviously furious. "Always stick together, no matter what laws you break. Gotta protect the brotherhood, huh?" His voice got louder with each word. "I wouldn't be surprised if you and ol' Don hatched this one up together. Pull your dirty tricks to make the new guy look like a fool."

Jeffrey warned, "You wanna be real careful what you say to me, Jake."

"I could arrest her," Valentine said, gesturing to Sara with an angry wave of his hand. "I *should* arrest her."

He had Jeffrey's full attention now. "We both know that's not gonna happen."

"Yeah? Well, this is." Valentine swung his fist—literally. His arm flew out roundhouse style instead of punching straight from his shoulder. This gave Jeffrey plenty of time to block the hit and slam his fist into the other man's gut. A whoosh of air came from Valentine's mouth as he doubled over. He would've fallen to his knees if Jeffrey hadn't caught him.

"God," the sheriff groaned, clutching his stomach. "Jesus..."

Sara stood from the bench. Jeffrey shook his head, telling her to stay put. He told Valentine, "Stand up straight."

Valentine struggled, his knees not working.

Jeffrey pulled him up by his collar until the other man was looking at him. "Just breathe," he said, feeling like he was talking to a child. "It'll pass."

"Let go of me." Valentine pushed Jeffrey away, but he still sagged against the car for support. "Goddamn, you're stronger than you look."

Jeffrey held out his hand to Sara, letting her know it was okay. "Where'd you learn to swing like that?"

"I grew up with four older sisters," he managed. Which explained why he hit like a girl. "Dammit. I shouldn't have done that. I shouldn't have hit you."

Jeffrey didn't point out that the man hadn't actually managed to hit him. He changed his position to stand between Valentine and Sara, telling the man, "Listen real careful, Jake. I already warned you once. You ever threaten with my wife again and I will beat you into the ground. We clear on that?"

Valentine coughed, then nodded.

"Can you stand up?"

"I think so."

Jeffrey waited for him to move away from the car.

"I'm sorry," Valentine told him. "I've got a short fuse."

"No shit."

The sheriff asked, "You gonna tell me if she contacts you?"

Jeffrey was caught short by the question, which would explain the truthful answer he gave. "I don't know."

Valentine stared at him, then nodded again. "Thanks for being honest."

Jeffrey watched Valentine stumble toward the front doors. The glass slid open and he went inside. Sara was still standing by the bench, and Jeffrey motioned her over.

"What was that about?" she asked.

"I'll explain later. Let's get out of here."

He made to open her door, but she said, "I've got it," and climbed in.

Jeffrey was walking around to the driver's side when a white sedan sped through the parking lot and screeched to a halt in the empty space next to him. Seconds later, a burly, bald man got out of the car. He was wearing a flannel shirt with the sleeves ripped off and a pair of jeans that looked splattered with oil. A heavy metal chain went from the front of his pants to his back. On his left hip was one of the largest hunting knives Jeffrey had ever seen.

While Jeffrey watched, the man took out the knife and placed it on the car seat, obviously knowing he wasn't allowed to bring the weapon into the hospital. Not that he looked as if he needed the weapon. If Jeffrey had to guess, he would say the guy weighed well over two hundred fifty pounds and that most of that was muscle.

The sedan shook when he slammed the door. Deep scratches cut across his face as if he'd gotten into a fight with a tiger and lost. He stared at Jeffrey, challenging, "What the fuck you lookin' at?"

Jeffrey pushed back his jacket, put his hand on his hip. His gun was tucked under the front seat of Sara's car, but the con didn't know that. "Don't make this a problem."

"Fuck you with your fucking problem," the man barked, heading toward the ER.

Through the glass doors, Jeffrey saw Jake Valentine leaning over the desk, talking to the receptionist. They both looked up when the man entered the waiting room. Valentine glanced at Jeffrey, but the sheriff was too far away to read his expression. He said something to the thug, holding out his hand, palm down, as if to calm him. Words were exchanged, then the man turned around and stalked back out. As he passed Jeffrey, he muttered, "Cocksucker," but Jeffrey wasn't sure who was being insulted.

Valentine came out of the hospital as the white car backed up, jumped the curb, and sped off.

Jeffrey glanced into the car, checking on Sara. He asked Valentine, "Friend of yours?"

"Local drug dealer who wanted to see one of his boys," Valentine explained. "I told him to come back during visiting hours."

Jeffrey gave him a close look, wondering if the man was lying. The exchange had looked a bit more heated than a denied visiting request, but then again the knife-carrying thug didn't strike Jeffrey as someone who liked to be told no.

"Here," Jeffrey said, reaching into his back pocket and pulling out a couple of business cards. He wrote something on the back of the top card, then thumbed to the next one to give to the sheriff. "My cell number is on the bottom. Call me if you find my detective."

Valentine gave the card a wary glance before taking it.

Jeffrey pocketed the rest of the cards. He got into the BMW and pulled out of the parking lot. Neither he nor Sara had much to say as he followed the route they had taken into town. Valentine was wrong about the twenty-minute lead. Jeffrey figured Lena had fifteen, tops. He asked the questions that the sheriff was probably asking himself right now: Where would Lena go? Who could she turn to?

Him. Lena had always come to Jeffrey when she had a problem, whether she needed something as small as a ride into work or as big as taking care of her asshole white supremacist boyfriend. This time was different, though. This time she had gone too far. Valentine was right about one thing: on purpose or not, Sara had aided Lena's escape. Lena was a cop; she knew the law better than most lawyers. She'd known exactly what she was dropping Sara into and she hadn't cared.

In the quiet of the car, Sara asked, "What now?"

"We go back home." He could feel her looking at him, trying to figure out if he was serious. "I mean it, Sara. This is it."

"You're just going to leave Lena down here to rot?"

"After what she said to you? What she *did* to you?" He shook his head, his mind made up. "It's over. I don't care what happens to her."

"Did you see her reaction when we walked into that room?"

"I heard what she said." He felt his anger spark back up at the memory. "There's no choice here, Sara. She used you. I'm not going to help her."

"I've never seen her so afraid. She's usually completely in control of herself."

He snorted at the idea. "Maybe with you."

"You're right. She never shows me her weak side. It's always this act, this posturing about how tough and invincible she is." Sara insisted, "That wasn't an act back there, Jeffrey. Maybe later, but when she saw us in her room, she was absolutely terrified."

"Then why not talk to me? Or at least to you? She had you alone. She knew you weren't going to run off and tell the sheriff anything. Why didn't she confide in you?"

"Because she's scared."

"Then she should've just shut up and left you out of it."

Sara spoke carefully. "I appreciate that you're taking up for me, but just think about it for a minute: Lena knew that if she hurt me, you would do exactly what you're doing right now. She didn't want *me* to leave town, Jeffrey. She wanted *you* to."

Jeffrey gripped the steering wheel, not wanting to admit that Sara could be right. "Since when did you start taking up for Lena Adams?"

"Since…" Sara's voice trailed off. "Since I saw her scared enough to risk everything in order to get you away from this town."

He saw the scene again, the way Lena had reacted. Sara was right: Lena wasn't faking her fear. She hadn't looked Jeffrey in the eye because she knew that he was probably the only person in the world who knew when she was lying.

Sara said, "I've seen her in a lot of bad situations, but I've never seen her terrified like that."

Jeffrey let her words hang between them as over and over, he replayed Lena's response in his mind, trying to figure out what it had to do with the dead body in the torched Cadillac.

Sara told him, "She said that I should be afraid."

"Did she say why?"

"She went into this pity thing about how everything she touches turns to crap. I thought she was feeling sorry for herself, but now I think she realized what she was doing wasn't working, so she decided to try something else." Sara shook her head. "She's terrified, Jeffrey— so terrified that she's willing to cut you out of her life if she has to. You're the only constant she's ever had. What's so horrible that she's willing to lose you?"

"Did you ever think maybe she's right?" he responded, not wanting to answer her question. "Maybe it's a good idea that I don't get involved."

She gave something like a laugh. "You're not going to leave this alone."

"You sound pretty sure about that."

"Seven-eight-zero, A-B-N." She paused, as if she expected an answer. "Isn't that what you wrote on the back of the card—the license plate number from the white car?"

Jeffrey took out the card, checked the number on the back. 780 ABN. As usual, Sara had perfect recall. He glanced at his wife. She was staring out the window, keeping her thoughts to herself. He knew that she was no longer regretting the fact that she'd come to the hospital with him. She was regretting that *he* was there, that Lena had yet again managed to pull Jeffrey into something dangerous.

Sara was a cop's wife, and she had absorbed a cop's mistrust of coincidence. The thug in the white sedan had shown up less than thirty minutes after Lena's escape. Even from where she sat in the BMW, the tattoo on the man's arm must have stood out to Sara like a neon sign.

It's hard not to notice a bloodred, four-inch swastika.

TUESDAY MORNING

CHAPTER 4

SARA PACED AROUND THE MOTEL ROOM with the phone tucked up against her ear, the cord limiting her movement like a leash on a dog. Both Sara and Jeffrey had been relieved when they had seen the "vacancy" sign outside the Home Sweet Home Motel as they drove out of Reece last night, but Sara had regretted their decision to stay the moment Jeffrey had opened the door. The place was almost from a parallel universe, the kind of dump that Sara thought only existed in B movies and Raymond Chandler novels. Just thinking about the dank shag carpet in the bathroom was enough to bring a shudder of revulsion. Making matters worse, neither Jeffrey's nor Sara's cell phone could get a signal in the motel. Sara had used all the alcohol swabs she could find in the first-aid kit from her car before she could even think about using the phone.

"What did you say?" her mother asked. She was somewhere in Kansas. Her parents were only two weeks into their road trip and already Sara could tell that Cathy was desperate to return home.

"I said that Daddy's not that bad," Sara answered, thinking it was a rare day indeed that she felt compelled to defend her father. Cathy and Eddie Linton had been married for over forty years, yet Sara had guessed from the beginning that their dream vacation together was a big mistake. The fact was, her parents did not spend much time in each other's company, let alone stuck in a confined space. Her father was always at work or fooling around in the garage, while her mother usually had some meeting to attend, a rally to organize, or a church group that took her away from home for hours on end. Their independence was the secret to their happy marriage. The thought of them both trapped in the thirty-seven-foot Winnebago they had purchased for their two month-long trek across America was enough to give Sara a headache.

"I just never realized how irritating he can be," her mother insisted. She was obviously in the kitchen of the RV; Sara could hear cabinets opening and closing. "How hard is it to hook up to a waste trap? The man is a plumber, for the love of God." She gave a heavy sigh. "Two hours, Sara. It took him two whole hours."

Sara held her tongue, though her mother had a point. On the other hand, her father was probably dragging out the chore in order to prolong his life.

"Are you listening to a word I'm saying?"

"Yes, Mama," Sara lied. She was wearing thick socks, but she used her big toe to prod a green M&M that seemed to be stuck in the carpet by the window. "Two hours."

Her mother was silent for a moment, then said, "Tell me what happened."

Sara gave up on the M&M when her sock kept getting stuck to the candy. She resumed pacing. "I told you what happened. I let her escape. I might as well have opened the door for her and driven her to the airport."

"Not that," Cathy insisted. "You know what I'm talking about."

It was Sara's turn to sigh. She was almost glad she'd made a fool of herself last night at the hospital because Lena's rapid departure had given Sara a new thing to toss and turn over when she was supposed to be sleeping. Now, her mother's question brought the malpractice suit firmly back into her consciousness.

Sara told her, "I would say their strategy is to claim that because I was attacked ten years ago, I was too distracted to tell the Powells that Jimmy had leukemia, and that he died because I waited an extra day."

"That's the most ridiculous thing I've ever heard."

"Their lawyer can be pretty persuasive." Sara thought about the lawyer, her Tourette's-like crocodile smile. "She even had me convinced."

Another cabinet was opened and closed. "I can't believe that another woman would do this to you," Cathy said. "It's disgusting. This is why women will never get ahead: other women are constantly cutting them off at the knees."

Sara held her tongue, not in the mood for one of her mother's feminist lectures.

Cathy offered, "I can come home if you need me."

Sara nearly dropped the phone. "No. I'm fine, really. Don't ruin your vacation because of—"

"Shit," her mother hissed; it was rare that an expletive crossed her lips. "I have to go. Your father just set himself on fire."

"Mama?" Sara pressed the phone to her ear, but her mother had already hung up.

Sara held the phone in her hand, wondering if she should call back, deciding that if something had been really wrong, her mother would have sounded less annoyed. Finally, she returned the phone to the cradle and went over to the large plate glass window looking out into the motel parking lot. Sara had kept the drapes closed most of the morning, thinking sitting alone in the dark room was less bleak than staring out into the empty lot. Now, she opened the polyester drapes a few inches, letting in a thin ray of light.

The table and set of white plastic lawn chairs by the window seemed perfect companions to the dismal view. Sara adjusted the threadbare towel she'd draped over one of the chairs and sat down. Exhaustion overwhelmed her, but the thought of getting back into bed, sliding between the rough, yellowing sheets, was too much to bear.

She had walked across the street earlier in the morning to buy coffee and ended up purchasing some Comet with bleach additive and a sponge that smelled like it had already been used. Her thought had been to tidy the room, or at least make the bathroom less disgusting, but every time she thought about taking the supplies in hand and actually using them, Sara found that she didn't have the energy. What's more, if she was going to clean anything, it should be her own home.

She tried to list the chores she could be doing back in Grant County right now: folding the laundry piled on the bed in the spare room, fixing the leak in the bathroom sink, taking the dogs for a walk around the lake. Of course, the reality was that Sara had done none of these tasks in the weeks since she'd closed the clinic. For the most part, she'd sat around the house brooding about the lawsuit. When her sister called from Atlanta, Sara had talked about the lawsuit. When Jeffrey got home from work, she had talked about the lawsuit. She had become so obsessed with discussing the suit that finally, her mother had snapped, "For the love of God, Sara, *do* something. Even patients in mental homes have to weave baskets."

Unfortunately, getting out of the house only exacerbated the problem. Whether Sara was at the grocery store or picking up Jeffrey's suits from the cleaners or even raking leaves in the front yard, she had felt people's eyes on her. Not just that, but she'd felt their disapproval. The few times she'd talked to anyone, the conversations had been brief if not downright cold. Sara hadn't told anyone about these exchanges—not Jeffrey, not her family—but she had found herself sinking deeper and deeper into depression with each encounter.

And now, courtesy of Lena Adams, Sara had one more failure to add to her list. How could she have been so easily tricked? How could she have been so utterly idiotic? All night, Sara had tried to parse each moment of her time with Lena, picking apart the seconds, trying to see how she could have acted differently, how she could have changed the outcome. Nothing came to mind except her own glaring stupidity.

Lena had been up on her knees in bed, the restraints keeping her from moving any farther away. As soon as Jeffrey and the sheriff left, she relaxed, her arms going limp.

Sara had studied her, noticed the way the other woman's chest shook with every exhale of breath. "What's going on, Lena? Why are you so afraid?"

"You have to get out of here. Both of you." Her voice was quiet, ominous. When she looked up, her eyes seemed to glow with terror. "You have to get Jeffrey out of here."

Sara felt her heart stop. "Why? Is he in danger?"

Lena did not answer. Instead, she looked down at her hands, the tangled sheets. "Everyone, everything I touch—it all turns to shit. You have to get away from me."

"Do you really think we're going to abandon you?" Sara had said "we," but they both knew that she meant Jeffrey. "Someone died in that car, Lena. Tell me what happened to you."

She shook her head, resigned.

"Lena, talk to me."

Again, no answer came. That must have been when Lena had decided her course of action, that if she could not control Sara, she could at least use her.

"I'm so dirty," she'd said, her tone of voice indicating the filth was more than skin-deep. "I feel so dirty." She'd looked up at Sara. Tears wet her eyes, and though her voice was more restrained, her hands still shook in her lap. "I need to wash off. I have to wash off."

Sara hadn't even thought about it. She'd walked over to the side of the bed and unstrapped the Velcro restraints. "You're going to be okay," she'd promised. "You need to trust me, or I can get Jeffrey—"

"No," Lena begged. "Just...I just need to wash off. Let me..." Her lips trembled. All the fight seemed to be drained out of her. She slid to the edge of the bed, tried to stand on shaky legs. Sara put her arm around the other woman's waist, helped her gain her footing.

Lena had really acted the part, Sara thought. A decided frailty had marked her every move. Nothing about her actions suggested she was capable of climbing on a toilet and pulling herself up into a drop ceiling, let alone eluding a manhunt.

Sara had been completely fooled, walking alongside Lena across the room, keeping her arm out a few inches from the other woman's back in case her support was needed. It was an automatic gesture, the sort of thing you learned your first week as a resident. Sara had escorted her all the way to the bathroom, shuffling her feet to match Lena's slow gait.

What Sara had been thinking as they walked was that Lena was not a whiner. She was the type of person who would rather bleed to death than admit she had been cut. Sara found herself wondering if maybe the doctors had misdiagnosed Lena, that she should look at the chest X-rays, find a stethoscope, review the drugs that had been administered, run some fluids, do some blood work. Was there brain damage, some kind of shock from the explosion? Had Lena fallen? Hit her head? Had she lost consciousness? Smoke inhalation was deadly, claiming more victims than fire alone. Secondary infections, fluid in the lungs, tissue damage—all sorts of possibilities were flashing through Sara's mind, and she'd realized that without warning, she was thinking like a doctor again. For the first time in months, she felt useful.

Then Lena had stopped her at the door to the bathroom, holding up her hand so that Sara would get the message that she needed privacy. Then, just before shutting the door, Lena had turned to Sara. "I'm so sorry," she'd said, her apology seeming so genuine that Sara could not believe this was the same woman who had been almost hysterical with fear and hatred five minutes earlier. "I'm so, so sorry."

"It's all right," Sara had assured her, smiling, letting Lena know that she was no longer alone in this. "We can talk about it later, okay? We'll get Jeffrey in here and we'll all figure out what to do."

Lena had nodded, probably not trusting her voice.

"I'll wait out here for you."

And Sara *had* waited, standing outside the door, grinning like a fool, thinking about how much she was going to *help* Lena. Meanwhile, Lena was probably bolting down the stairs, laughing at how easy Sara had made her escape.

Now, sitting at the plastic table in the dreary motel room, Sara felt her face redden with humiliation.

"Stupid," she said, standing up before the chair sucked out what little life was left in her.

Cathy was right. Sara needed to do something. She picked up the Comet and the odd-smelling sponge she'd bought at the convenience store and headed toward the bathroom. For some reason, the sink was outside the door, a long counter that was burned at the edges where people had rested their cigarettes while they—what?—brushed their teeth?

It didn't bear thinking about.

Sara sprinkled some Comet into the sink and started scrubbing, trying not to take any more chrome off the plastic drain in the process. She put some muscle into it, cutting through years of grime as if her life depended on it.

Pride before the fall, she thought. All those years of being the teacher's pet—the best student in the class, the highest grades, the best accolades, and the brightest future—for what? Emory University had accepted her before she graduated from high school. The medical college had practically rolled out the red carpet, offering enough financial aid for her father to easily make up the difference. Thousands of people a year applied for the limited number of residencies at Grady Hospital. Sara hadn't even had a fallback. She knew she was going to get into the program. She was so damn sure of her own abilities, her own intelligence, that she had never in her life thought she would not succeed at anything she set her mind to.

Except for stopping a one-hundred-ten-pound college dropout from escaping the Elawah County Medical Center.

"Stupid," Sara repeated. She gave up on the sink and went into the bathroom. She started on the toilet, using the scrub brush mounted on the wall to clean the bowl, trying not to wonder what had turned the bristles dark gray. As she got down on her knees beside the bathtub, Sara remembered her mother showing her years ago how to clean a bathroom—how much cleaner to use, how to gently scrub the porcelain with a sponge.

Sara sat back on her heels, thinking that one day, maybe soon, she would show her own child how to clean the tub or vacuum the living room. Jeffrey would have to explain how to sort laundry because Sara was forever pulling pink-streaked, formerly white socks out of the dryer. She could take the kid to the grocery store, at least. Jeffrey thought a frozen dinner was a well-balanced meal, which might explain why his blood pressure had to be controlled with medication.

A thought came to Sara like a knife in her chest. What if she ran into Beckey Powell at the grocery store? What if Sara was standing in the meat section, holding her child's hand, and Beckey walked up? How would Sara explain to her new son or daughter why Beckey Powell hated her? How would she explain why the whole town believed that her incompetence had led to the death of a child?

Sara wiped her forehead with the back of her hand, eyes watering from the overwhelming stench of bleach in the tiny bathroom. She wished that Jeffrey was there to keep her mind from going to such dark places. Since filing the adoption papers, they'd started playing what-if games. "What if we get a boy who hates football?" "What if we have a girl who loves pink and wants her hair braided?"

Sara imagined games were the last thing on her husband's mind at the moment. A dead person had been in that SUV and Lena was somehow entangled in that death. After meeting Jake Valentine, Jeffrey did not trust the local force to solve this crime without leaping to the easiest conclusion and pinning it all on Lena. He had left early this morning to plot strategy with Nick Shelton, a friend of his who worked for the Georgia Bureau of Investigation. Sara had not been invited to tag along.

She leaned back over the tub, rinsing the Comet, then sprinkling more powder to start the process again. The sponge was just about to give up the ghost, but Sara would not stop until the job was done. She folded the sponge in two and used the edge to attack the black ring around the periphery that probably dated back to the seventies.

Sara muttered a curse under her breath, wishing again that she was back home. At least in Grant County, she could stay out of Jeffrey's way and let him do his job. Here, all she could do was make sure he had a clean place to put his toothbrush. Overnight, she had turned into a glorified housewife, and for what? So that Lena could laugh her way out of town?

Sara knew that Jeffrey bent the rules sometimes. If he had been by himself last night, Jeffrey would have taken the empty nurses' station as an invitation to find Lena on his own. If he had walked into that hospital room alone, Lena might have opened up to him. She might have told him why she needed to get out of there instead of breaking out. She sure as hell wouldn't have tried to use Jeffrey in order to make her escape; she respected him too much.

Unlike Sara.

Cathy had said that women were their own worst enemies. Was Sara Lena's enemy? She didn't think so. It was true that Sara had never understood the bond between her husband and the thirty-five-year-old detective, but Sara wasn't stupid enough to be jealous. Barring the fact that Lena was as far from Jeffrey's type as you could get without going outside the species, their relationship was too much like that of an older brother and errant young sister to cause Sara concern.

Maybe the dislike came from Lena making such bad choices for herself. After her sister, Sibyl, had died, Lena had fallen into a deep depression. She even managed to get herself temporarily suspended from the force. That was when she'd started seeing Ethan Green. That was when Lena had lost all of Sara's sympathy.

As a doctor, Sara should have understood the process. Grief can lead to depression, depression can lead to chemical changes in the body that make it impossible to crawl out of the spiral without some help, be it pharmacological or therapeutic or both. God knew that over the last few months, Sara was more than intimate with the dangers of depression. Still, her personal experience did not help her understand why Lena had turned to Ethan.

Sara had read the women's journals, knew the statistics, studied the causal relationships. Depression can lead to vulnerabilities. Vulnerabilities attract predators. It was like a shark sensing blood in the water. Just because a woman gave the outward appearance of being strong, that did not preclude her from becoming a victim of domestic violence. In some cases, it made her more likely to fall victim; you could only keep up that tough act for so many hours before it all fell apart.

Sara knew this in her brain. She accepted that some women—smart women—got mixed up with the wrong person, ended up making compromise after compromise until there was nothing left but to sit there and take it. But, still, the fact that Lena's twenty-four-year-old boyfriend had abused her—not just abused her, but beaten her to a bloody pulp—was something that Sara could not get past.

It was as if Lena had been obsessed with the man, like she could not get him out of her system. Maybe if Ethan had been a drug, Sara would have better understood the addiction. Heroin, meth, opium…that would explain Lena's devotion, her inability to get through the day without a hit. The brainwashing would have made more sense if she had been in a cult, but there was nothing for Lena to fall back on but her own damaged personality. She had a good job, her own money, her own support structure. She had a gun and a badge, for chrissakes. Ethan was a paroled violent offender. Lena could have arrested him at any time. As a police officer, she was bound by law to report any case of domestic violence, even if she herself was the victim.

And yet she had left it up to Jeffrey. Lena was the one who had tipped him off that Ethan was carrying a gun in his backpack. Jeffrey refused to discuss it with Sara anymore, but she was certain that Lena had planted the gun, that the only way she had been able to get rid of her abuser was this coward's way. Ethan had ten years hard time hanging over his head. Lena had hidden the gun, then called in Jeffrey to do her dirty work.

And of course, Jeffrey had come running.

But wasn't that why Sara loved Jeffrey? Because he refused to give up on people, no matter how beyond reach they seemed? Sara was hardly one to talk about women making stupid mistakes with men. She had married Jeffrey twice, leaving him the first time after coming home to find him in bed with another woman. Jeffrey had changed in the years since their divorce, though. He had grown up. He had worked to get Sara back, to regain her trust and mend their relationship. She loved this new Jeffrey with such passion that it scared her sometimes.

Was that what had driven Lena to stand by Ethan no matter how many times he beat her? Had she felt the same lovesickness as Sara, the same lurch in her stomach when they were apart? Had she made such a fool of herself over him that she could not let go?

Sara dropped the scraps of the sponge into the wastebasket and rinsed the tub again. Jeffrey would be shocked when he got back from his meeting. She could not remember the last time she had cleaned her own bathroom so thoroughly. Sara hated most domestic chores and did them only because in a town as small as Heartsdale, her mother would find out if she hired a maid. Cathy's belief was that chores built character, and paying other people, especially women, to do them showed what sort of character you really were. Sara's belief was that her mother's Puritan work ethic had gone round the bend. There was a reason Sara had graduated from high school a year ahead of her class. When she was growing up, her mother thought that homework was the only valid excuse for getting out of cleaning duty.

She washed the cleaner off her hands, her mind going back to Lena and wishing that Ethan Green could be washed out of all their lives just as easily. Sara had seen Ethan only once—seen his body. The tattoos must have taken hours to ink onto his skin. There were at least ten that Sara had counted, but the one she could never put out of her mind was the large black swastika over his heart. What made a man embrace such hatred? What did it say about Lena that she could be with such a man, want him, make love to him, and not be repulsed by the hateful symbol on his body?

Last night, sitting in the car outside the hospital, Sara had seen the way the skinhead in the white sedan had looked at Jeffrey, the recognition that Jeffrey was a cop, his callous disregard for what that means. She had also seen the red swastika on the man's arm and felt a sudden sickening fear when Jeffrey made it obvious that he was not intimidated, would not back down. Now, she felt sick just thinking about it.

The phone rang and Sara's heart jumped. She ran into the other room and picked up the receiver. "Hello?" She waited, listening to static on the line, the sound of someone breathing. "Hello?" she repeated, then, for no reason, "Lena?"

There was a soft click, then the quiet of a dead line.

Sara returned the phone to its cradle, shivering. She looked at her watch, then checked it against the alarm clock on the bedside table. Jeffrey had left almost two hours ago to meet with Nick Shelton. He had told her he'd call on his way back, but there was no telling when that would be.

She saw a takeout menu on the table, the notes she had scrawled on the back. Sara picked up the menu, tried to decipher her own handwriting.

Jeffrey had left Sara an assignment. She loved him for trying to make her feel useful, but the fact was a monkey could've performed the task. After her coffee run to the convenience store, she had called Frank Wallace, Jeffrey's second in command, and asked him to track down the license plate from the white sedan they had seen at the hospital last night. Even Frank had sounded puzzled when he'd heard Sara's request. He had played along, though, typing the plate into the computer, humming under his breath. Sara had known Frank for as long as she'd been alive—he was a poker buddy of her father's—but she had felt uncomfortable talking to him on the phone, mostly because they both knew that she had no business doing policework.

Frank had the registration in under a minute. Sara had scrambled for something to write on and found the takeout menu in one of the bedside drawers. A corporation named Whitey's Feed & Seed owned the Chevy Malibu.

So, the Nazi in the white sedan had a sense of humor.

Sara had rung off with Frank and decided to take some initiative— something a monkey surely could not do—and run down the articles of incorporation for Whitey's Feed & Seed. After spending almost twenty minutes on hold with the secretary of state's office, she knew a man named Joseph Smith was listed as CEO and president of Whitey's Feed & Seed. Going on the assumption that this was a valid name and not some allusion to the founder of the Mormon Church, Sara called directory services. There were over three hundred listings for the name of Joseph Smith in the state of Georgia. Oddly enough, none of them lived in or around the Elawah area.

Frank's computer search had yielded a post office box as the address for the vehicle's registration, but the woman at the secretary of state's office had given Sara a local address, 339 Third Avenue. If Reece was like every other small town in the world, it was laid out on a grid pattern. The Elawah County Medical Center was on Fifth Avenue. Sara knew that the hospital was less than a ten-minute drive from the motel, which meant that Third Avenue had to be within a few miles.

Sara stared at the menu, her scribbled letters crisscrossing the dessert selections. She'd talked to her mother, cleaned the bathroom, refolded all the clothes in their suitcase and left three messages on her sister's cell phone to please call before boredom atrophied her mind. Short of sweeping the motel parking lot, there really was nothing else left for her to do.

A motorcycle revved outside, the pipes so loud that the plate glass window rattled. Sara looked out the slit in the curtains, but she could only see the back of the bike as it pulled onto the main road. Overhead, the sky was turning dark, but she guessed that any rain was at least a few hours away.

Sara tore off the address she'd written on the menu and wrote Jeffrey a note on the entrée section. She had seen some local maps at the convenience store when she'd walked over earlier that morning. Third Avenue had to be close by.

She snatched the motel key off the table and left the room before she could stop herself.

LENA

CHAPTER 5

"TELL US ABOUT OUR MOTHER," Lena and Sibyl begged Hank, almost as soon as they could talk. They were desperate for information about the woman who had died giving birth to them. Hank would always protest—he had a bar to run or a meeting to attend—but eventually he would settle down and recall a summer picnic or a trip to see long-lost relatives. There was always something that happened—a stranger on the side of the road that their mother helped, a relative she nursed back to good health. Angela the Angel always put others ahead of herself. Angela happily gave her life so that her twin daughters would live. Angela was looking down on Sibyl and Lena from heaven.

Even to a child's ears, the stories were unbelievable fairy tales full of goodness and light, but Lena and Sibyl had never tired of hearing about their mother's generosity, her open, loving heart. Sibyl had tried to emulate their mother, to be the sort of person who only saw good in others. For Lena's part, Angela Adams had been the invisible yardstick, the woman she would never meet and never measure up to.

And now Hank was telling Lena that her mother had not died in childbirth but had been killed by a drug dealer. Not just any drug dealer—Hank's drug dealer.

One of the first things Lena could remember Hank telling them about their mother was that Angela had been unequivocal on the subject of drugs and alcohol. After years of watching her older brother slowly dig his own grave, she had finally cut him out of her life and vowed never to let him back in. Hank had not cared at the time. He was twenty-six years old. He didn't want family or sex or money or cars. All he was interested in was finding his next high.

According to Hank, the first promise that Angela extracted from her husband, Calvin Adams, was that he would never go out drinking with his fellow officers. Calvin adhered to this—they were very much in love—and seldom touched a drop; certainly, he never drank in front of his young wife. Of course, no one would ever know how long that would have lasted. The couple shared only three months of wedded bliss before Cal pulled over his last speeding violation. The driver shot him twice in the face and drove off, never to be seen again. Lena's father was dead before his body hit the ground.

Angela's first sign that she was pregnant came at her husband's funeral. Not normally one to be weak-kneed or emotional, she passed out at Calvin's gravesite. Seven months later, she went into the hospital to give birth to twin girls and never came out. Septicemia is rare, but deadly. It took two weeks for the infection to overtake the new mother's systems, shutting down her vital organs one by one until, finally, a decision had to be made to take her off life support. Hank Norton, Angela's closest living relative, had made the decision.

It was, Hank often said, the most difficult thing he had ever done in his life.

It was, evidently, all a lie.

Angela Norton had been a petite woman, very plain looking until she smiled, then there was no way you could not notice her. She had the dark coloring of her Mexican-American mother, unlike her brother, who was pasty as a jar of buttermilk. Another quality Hank did not share with his sister was her extreme devoutness, courtesy of their mother's Catholicism. Angela was passionate about helping people while Hank was passionate about helping himself.

As an adult, Lena knew that every good story has its darkness and light, and now she could see that Hank had always painted himself in the blackest of hues.

Angela Norton had met Calvin Adams at a church fair. He'd been working the raffle for the sheriff's department and despite the fact that gambling was a sin, she wanted her chance to win the basket of baked goods being offered as prize. Angela was a shy girl, just a teenager when she met the dashing young deputy. She was bright and funny, and just about the kindest, most caring person to walk the face of the earth.

Angela and Hank's mother had died at a young age. Car accident. She had no other relatives, and her husband, career military, had been killed in Vietnam when the children were little. Cal was an only child. Both parents had died when he was in his early twenties. He had no other relations in town, no cousins or aunts or uncles that anyone knew of. No family for Lena or Sibyl to visit.

Calvin Adams cut a dashing figure. A bit of a nerd in high school, people had been surprised when he signed up with the sheriff's department. He had turned into a good cop, though—firm, but fair. Always willing to listen to both sides of an argument. He wore the gun and badge with pride but never lorded it over anybody. Angela and Calvin were in love, very much in love, and what happened to them was tragic.

After watching his sister take her last breath, Hank had taken the newborn Lena and Sibyl from the hospital because he would not leave his own flesh and blood to be raised by the state. Woefully unprepared that first night, he had improvised cribs by lining two dresser drawers with sheets and pillows, nestling his young charges in for the night as he went around his house and systematically destroyed any traces of alcohol.

He often claimed that night was his "turning point," that looking down and seeing those two helpless baby girls tucked into his sock drawers, knowing that he was the only thing standing between them and the hairy-chinned woman from children's social services, had given him the strength to turn his back on an old friend.

This was the history Lena had been told. These were the lies she had been spoon-fed all of her life. She could remember rainy afternoons with Sibyl, playing games with Hank's stories. They acted out the tragedy of their parents' short lives, always taking turns being Angela, the best, the kindest, one. Oh, how their parents loved each other. Oh, how they would have loved to hold their twin daughters in their arms. Things would have been different, so very, very different, had they lived.

Or would they?

Hank often claimed that he gave up his addictions the night that he brought his nieces home from the hospital, but Lena had lived through it. She knew the truth. Eight years passed before he really gave it all up. Eight years of weeklong benders and parties that lasted for days and the police sniffing around, and lies...nothing but lies.

She had lived in this house, seen it with her own eyes: all those years and yet she had never suspected that a drug addict would tell her anything but the truth about her own mother and father. Why would he lie about what had happened? What did he have to gain by all those lies?

Lena dried her hair with a towel as she sat on the edge of her bed. She had changed into one of Hank's old dress shirts so that she could get in the shower with him and scrape off some of his filth. He was so thin that she could feel his bones through the rubber kitchen gloves she wore to clean him. What looked like rope burns circled his wrists and ankles, but she knew he had probably caused the damage himself, picking the skin with his fingernails, peeling it away like an orange.

Meth mites. Speed bumps. Crank bugs. There were all kinds of names for the phenomenon that caused meth users to pick, scrape, and dig at their own skin. As part of the police outreach program, Jeffrey taught a drug course at the high school twice a year. Lena could clearly remember the first time she'd been forced to tag along. She'd felt her heart race as she'd heard Jeffrey talk about the chemistry behind the sickness, give an explanation for the self-mutilation she'd seen.

Meth causes the body temperature to rise, which in turn causes the skin to sweat. When the sweat evaporates, it removes the protective oil coating the dermis. This process irritates the nerve endings and makes the addict feel as if something is crawling under his skin. He will do anything to stop the sensation, use any instrument he can find to relieve his suffering.

Lena had once watched Hank take an ice pick to his arm, scratching it repeatedly back and forth until the skin split open like a sack of sugar. Just now, she had seen the scar in the bathroom, the thick rope of flesh that had been sewn back together. There were so many marks on his body, so many painful reminders of what he had been willing to do to himself just to get high.

And still, in all those years, Hank had never, ever been this bad.

Why? Why had he gone back to that life after fighting so hard to leave it? What had made Hank embrace the very thing he despised? There had to be a reason. There had to be a trigger that made him take that first shot.

Was it the drug dealer? Was Hank buying drugs from the man who had killed Lena's mother?

Lena finished drying her hair. She sat up, looking at herself in the mirror over the dresser. Dark curls sprung around her head, water still dripping at the nape. How could she be back in this place again? How could she be back in this room, on this bed, drying her hair after yet again hosing off caked shit from her uncle's emaciated body?

She was an adult now. She had a job, her own home. She wasn't under Hank's thumb anymore, dependent upon him for anything.

So, why was she still here?

"Lee?" Hank stood in the doorway, tattered robe wrapped around his body.

Her voice was trapped somewhere in her throat, but she managed, "I can't talk to you right now."

He obviously didn't care. "I want you to go home. Just forget what I said. Just go home and get on with your life."

"Did that man shoot my father?"

Hank looked over her shoulder. Lena knew there was a Rick Springfield poster behind her, a remnant from her teenage years.

"Tell me the truth," she insisted. "Tell me how they really died."

"Your father was shot. You know that, Lee. I showed you the newspaper article. You and your sister both."

She remembered this, but how could she trust him? How could she even trust her own memory after all this time?

She asked, "What about my mother? You said he killed my mother."

His throat worked as he swallowed. "Losing your daddy killed her, is what I meant." He scratched his neck, his chin. "It wasn't the man you saw what shot him, but people like him. Bad people you need to stay away from."

"You're lying," she said, never more sure of anything in her life.

He started picking at a sore by his ear. She knew he would start twitching soon, needing the drug.

"When did it start?" she asked. "When did you get hooked again?"

"It don't matter."

"Then tell me why," she said, aware that she was almost begging. "Why would you go back to this, Hank? You worked so hard to—"

"It don't matter."

"You're an old man," she told him. "You won't be able to fight it this time. You might as well go ahead and pick out a coffin."

"Just put me in a hole," he said. "That's where I belong."

"Am I supposed to feel sorry for you?"

"You're supposed to leave," he shot back, sounding for a moment like the old Hank again, the one who laid down the rules, said my way or the highway.

"I'm not going until you tell me the truth," Lena told him. "I won't leave until you tell me why you're doing this to yourself."

"Go back to Grant. Go back to your job and your friends and just forget me."

She stood from the bed, gripping the towel in her hand. "I mean it, Hank. I won't leave here until you tell me the truth."

He couldn't look at her. Finally, he said, "There ain't no truth to tell. Your mama and daddy died. There's nothing you can do to change that."

"I deserve to know what happened."

He pressed his lips together, shaking his head as he turned to leave. Lena grabbed his arm to stop him. "Tell me what happened to my mother. Tell me who killed her."

"I killed her!" he yelled, trying to pull away. "You wanna know who killed your mama? Me. It was *me*! Now go on home and let the dead stay buried."

She felt his skin slide under her fingers, knew that she was pressing a broken needle deeper into his flesh. She tried to let go but he clamped his hand over hers, held her in place.

Tears wet his eyes and his expression softened, as if for just a moment he could see past his need. "You and your sister were the light of my life. Don't ever forget that."

Lena jerked her hand away. There was a tiny sliver of dried blood just below his jugular where he must have taken a hit while she was drying her hair.

She cleared her throat, tried to speak past the lump that had formed there. "If you puncture an artery—"

"Yeah." He seemed resigned.

"Your neck will swell up," she continued. "You'll suffocate."

"Go home, Lee."

"Hank—"

"I know what will happen," he told her. "I don't want you to be here when it does."

✦

IN THE TWENTY YEARS since Lena had last set foot in the Elawah County Library, the only thing that had changed was the addition of a lone computer desk crammed up against the back wall between romance and general fiction. Even the lame Halloween decorations looked the same: the purple papier-mâché skeletons with their orange top hats, the black cats with glittery tails, the cauldrons of witches' brew. The only thing missing was the plastic pumpkin filled with candy corn that usually sat on the information desk. Lena guessed from the current clientele that the librarian didn't feel they were worth treating. The woman seemed to spend most of her time riding up and down in the freight elevator with her rolling cart and a sour expression that was scarier than any Halloween costume.

Sibyl had spent hours in the library when they were kids. She had been the good student, the one who whiled away her time catching up on homework or reading the latest science magazines Miss Nancy, the former librarian, ordered in Braille especially for her. Lena was the one who moped around, complaining under her breath, until Hank finally picked them up to go home. He used the library as a babysitting facility, making the girls stay there until he could get away from the bar and take them home.

Now, Lena regretted her youthful insolence, her lack of interest in how the library worked. Even blind, Sibyl would have been able to figure out the microfiche machine. Lena couldn't manage to thread the damn thing. She'd scrolled out two rolls of filmed newspaper archives like a kitten with toilet paper by the time the librarian came up from the basement again. Her look of perpetual disapproval went up a notch when she spotted Lena.

"Lemme have that before you break it," the woman ordered, snatching the film away from Lena. With her gaudy jewelry, loud voice, and bad attitude, she was certainly no Miss Nancy. From the smell of her—a sickly sweet perfume which did little to mask the stench of cigarettes—Lena guessed the woman was spending her time down in the basement smoking and hiding from the kids.

That was another thing that had not changed—downstairs was strictly off-limits to patrons. The library building had originally been the town's city hall until the government outgrew it. Built in the 1950s, the structure had all the modern touches, from a sunken concrete seating area you could smack your head open on to a bomb shelter in the basement. Lena had sneaked down there once and been very disappointed to find old voting registers and property deeds instead of the pornographic books and dead bodies that rumors suggested might be hidden in the library's bowels. The only things that pointed to the windowless room's former identity were a couple of metal bunk beds

crammed into the corner and floor-to-ceiling shelves packed with cans
of water and Dinty Moore beef stew.

Lena imagined the whole place reeked of unfiltered Camels now,
courtesy of the bitchiest librarian to walk the face of the earth.

"I don't know why you want this," the woman snapped, holding
up the microfiche. "Do you even know what you're looking for?"

"I want a particular date," Lena told her, trying to sound patient.
"July 16, 1970."

"Whatever," the woman mumbled in a way that made Lena think
she hadn't been listening. She seemed more intent on rolling the films
back tight enough to fit into their canisters. The key to the elevator was
on a springy chain around her wrist and it kept hitting the metal table-
top with annoying, regular clinks.

Lena sat back, giving the librarian more room, trying not to let
her impatience show. She finally stood up to avoid a jutting elbow and
let the woman have her seat. When Lena was a kid, libraries were silent
places—Miss Nancy had made sure of that. She had something she
called her "six-inch voice," which meant you spoke low enough so that
only someone six inches away could hear you. There was no running or
roughhousing allowed on Miss Nancy's watch, and she certainly would
not have cursed like a sailor as she struggled to thread the microfiche
machine.

There was a group of teenagers behind Lena. They were sitting at a
table, books splayed out in front of them, but she hadn't seen one of
them doing anything but giggling since she'd walked through the front
door. One of the girls saw her and quickly looked down at the book in
her hands, but Lena's eye had caught something else.

The library was small, with about sixteen rows of shelves evenly
spaced down the center. Lena walked past each row, trying to find the
slender figure she'd seen lurking behind the table of kids.

She found Charlotte Warren in the children's section. Obviously,
Charlotte hadn't wanted to be seen. She had her nose tucked into a
copy of *Pippi Longstocking* when Lena said, "Hey."

"Oh, Lee," Charlotte said, her voice going up in mock surprise, as if
she hadn't been the one who called Lena on the phone and told her to
come down and check on Hank.

Lena told her, "I found Hank."

Charlotte shelved the book, taking her time, lining up the spine with the neighboring paperbacks. With her mousy blonde hair and soft voice, Charlotte Warren had been destined from childhood to fill the role of stereotypical American mother, relying on Oprah and Martha Stewart to validate her existence.

Lena asked, "How long has he been like that?"

"I guess about a month now."

"He's been hitting it pretty hard."

"That's why I called."

"Who's selling to him?"

"Oh." Charlotte looked away, pushing her thick glasses back in place. "I don't know anything about that, Lee. I just saw him one day and he didn't look good and I thought that you'd want to know."

"I don't know what I can do," Lena admitted. "He's hell-bent on killing himself."

"He's been real depressed since Sibyl..." Charlotte didn't need to finish the sentence. They both knew what she meant. She fidgeted with a gold cross she wore on a chain around her neck. "I wanted to come to her funeral, but the kids were in school, and I just..." She let her voice trail off again. "You still a cop?"

"Yeah," Lena answered. "You still a teacher?"

Charlotte's smile wavered. "Going on my sixteenth year."

"That's good." Lena tried to think of something else to say. "Sibyl loved teaching."

"I'm married now. Did you know?" Lena shook her head and Charlotte supplied, "I've got three kids and Larry, my husband, he's such a great dad. He takes extra shifts at the factory so the kids can have everything they need. He goes to all the ball games and the school plays and the band concerts. He's a really good man, Lee. I lucked out."

"Sounds like it."

"You seeing anybody?"

"No." Lena had answered too harshly. She felt a warm rush of heat come into her cheeks.

Charlotte glanced over Lena's shoulder as if she was afraid someone would overhear them. "I've got to get my girl home, and..." She laughed, but it sounded more like a sob. "Gosh, you just look so much like her." She put her hand to Lena's cheek, let it linger for just a moment too long. Tears came into her eyes, and her lip trembled as she fought back her emotions.

"Charlotte—"

Charlotte took Lena's hand, squeezed it hard. "Take care of Hank, Lee. Sibby would've wanted you to look after him."

Lena watched her walk over to one of the kids sitting at the table. Though Charlotte was a couple of years older than Lena and Sibyl, she had been Sibyl's closest friend. From early childhood until high school, the two were inseparable. They had spent hours together in Sibyl's room, gone to the movies together, even driven down to Florida together every spring break. They had lost touch when Sibyl moved away to go to college, but friendships like that never really went away.

Charlotte was right about one thing. Sibyl would have wanted Lena to take care of Hank. She had loved him like a father. It would have killed her all over again to know he was living like this. But what if she had found out that Hank had lied to them all those years? How would Sibyl have felt about him then?

"It's set up," the librarian barked from across the room. She tossed a wave at the microfiche machine like she was finished with it.

"Thank you," Lena returned, though the woman was already jamming her key into the lock to open the elevator and make her escape.

Lena walked back over to the machine. There were other, better ways to go about this. She could call Jeffrey. She could ask him to search the police database for her mother's name. She could go down to the sheriff's office and ask for her father's murder book. She could track down Hank's dealer and put a gun to his head, tell him if he ever so much as talks to her uncle again, she'll splatter his brains all over his shiny, white car.

The dealer was the problem. Jeffrey would want to know why Lena was running her mother's name. Worse, he would probably want to help out. She couldn't very well tell him that her uncle was back on meth and had said some crazy things she wanted to check out. Jeffrey would be on his way to Reece before she could hang up the phone.

Talking to the Elawah sheriff might bring some unwelcome attention as well. Hank was using pretty heavily; he might even be under surveillance. Even without that, over thirty years had passed since Calvin Adams had been murdered. All his case files had probably been lost or destroyed by now.

She had to use the tools that were available to her, and the library was the best place to start. Hank had lied to her about so many things that Lena didn't trust anything anymore. She had to start from the be-

ginning and work her way toward the truth. Maybe when she got a
little more information, knew better where she stood, she could go to
Jeffrey and elicit his help. She had worked with him long enough to
know the questions he would ask. What she had to do now was try
to find some of the answers.

Lena took a seat at the machine and scanned the front page of the
Elawah Herald.

LOCAL DEPUTY SLAIN

Lena sat on the edge of her chair as she read the story word for
word. She couldn't recall the article Hank had shown her when she was
a child, but this seemed to be it. All the details were there: Speeding
stop. Dead at the scene. No suspects.

So, at least Hank hadn't lied about that.

Lena adjusted the knobs on the machine and scrolled down, over-
shooting the next edition, then slowly winding her way back. The
Herald was a weekly paper, not more than fifteen or twenty pages long,
and her father's shooting was the biggest news in town. Each subsequent front page for the next month carried the story, basically regurgi-
tating the same details over and over again. Shot twice in the head. No
suspects found.

She pressed the fast-forward button, hoping that she wouldn't have
to change the film to find the week of her mother's death. She scrolled
into 1971, slowing around the first week of March. She scanned the
obituaries for her mother's name, then skipped to the next week's paper,
then the next. She was about to give up when she saw a photograph on
the front page of the September 19 edition.

Hank had only one photograph of their mother. It was a Polaroid,
the colors unnaturally bright. Angela Norton was seventeen or eighteen. She stood on an anonymous beach somewhere in Florida, wearing
a modest one-piece white-and-blue checkered bathing suit with a large
bow around the waist. Her hair was piled on her head and she stood
with her hands at her side, palms down, striking a pose. This had been a
time when teenagers wanted to look older, more mature, and Lena had
always liked the expression on her mother's face: the pursed lips and serious eyes, the streak of blue eye shadow and the dark, Cleopatra-like
eyeliner placing the young woman firmly on the precipice of the sexual
revolution.

For Lena and Sibyl's sixth birthday, Hank had hired an artist from out of town to do a likeness of Angela's face. The oil painting hung in the living room over the couch. It had been such a staple of Lena's life that she barely even looked at it anymore.

She looked at the photograph of her mother in the paper, though. Angela Adams, nee Norton, sat in an old rocking chair Lena recognized from Hank's house. A baby was in either arm, their bodies swaddled in blankets.

Above her, the headline read, THE GRIEVING WIDOW AND HER TWINS.

TUESDAY MORNING

CHAPTER 6

JEFFREY SAT IN A BACK BOOTH at the City Diner listening to the messages on his cell phone. The coffee here was the hi-test kind, and when the waitress came over to fill his cup again, he smiled and waved her away, thinking if he drank any more of the black tar his head would vibrate off his neck. He was already hearing a buzzing in his ears and this, combined with the pouring rain outside, was making him feel like he had stuck his head in a hornet's nest.

He pressed the three button on his cell phone, fast-forwarding through the Heartsdale mayor's message asking him to get to the bottom of a group of vandals who were kicking over trashcans on his street, an act that to the mayor's thinking was one of the first signs of lawless thugs taking over the city.

Jeffrey closed the phone after the last message, which was from a vinyl-siding salesman wanting to talk to him about exciting distribution opportunities. There was nothing from Sara and she wasn't answering the phone at the motel. He hoped that she was taking a long bath, then thought about the grime he had seen at the bottom of the tub last night and hoped instead that she'd stepped outside to get some air. He was worried about her. She had been much too quiet, even before Lena had run rings around her. The many times he'd woken up in the middle of the night, he'd found her wide awake, curled into a ball, her back to him.

He hated leaving her alone this morning, especially in that disgusting room. Frankly, he hated exposing her to the seedy underbelly that, until last night, she hadn't known existed. The place was what Jeffrey thought of as a jerk-stop motel, the sort of establishment that catered to truck drivers, whores, and the more than occasional cheating spouse. Jeffrey had spent more than a few evenings in such motels with more than a few women, so he recognized the signs. Even a fool would figure something was going on as soon as he checked in. The clerk behind the front desk had asked Jeffrey how many hours he needed the room.

Jeffrey had parked the BMW in full view of the street in case Lena was looking for him. Though, for all he knew, Lena was halfway to Mexico by now. Part of him hoped she stayed there. He was angry at Lena for not trusting him, even angrier with her for duping Sara, and furious with himself for letting it all happen in the first place.

Sara was right about one thing—Lena had been terrified last night. She'd obviously felt that short of getting Jeffrey to leave, her best option was escape. The question remained: why did she want to get rid of Jeffrey? What could be so bad that she'd refuse his help? The person in the Escalade had been killed. Still, in the cold light of day, Jeffrey couldn't think of anything—not even murder—that would make him turn completely against her. There had to be an explanation, a reason for her involvement in this death. Lena always played it close to the bone, but she had never willfully jeopardized anyone but herself.

And, still, he could not help but wonder if it was Hank Norton's body in the back of the burned Escalade. On the way to the diner this morning, Jeffrey had called the station back in Grant County and gotten Hank's address off Lena's personnel file. He had tried the phone number she'd given, but no one picked up. Surprisingly, the satellite navigation in Sara's car had actually recognized the address. Jeffrey had taken this as a sign that he should drive by and see if Hank Norton was home. The place looked abandoned, but Jeffrey assumed that was because it hadn't been painted or repaired in the last thirty years. He would've gotten out of his car and checked for himself, but there had been an Elawah County Sheriff's Department cruiser parked right across the street. The man had given him a wave as Jeffrey drove by.

If Hank was in the back of the Escalade, that might explain why Lena had run. No matter the bad blood between them, if someone had killed her uncle, she would hunt him down like an animal. If she had killed him herself...Jeffrey had stopped there, not letting his thoughts take him down that dark road. After almost two decades of knowing Lena, he should have a better idea right now about whether or not she was one of the good guys.

Last night at the hospital, she'd had her chance to ask for his help and voted with her feet. Obviously, she wanted to go it alone. Obviously, Jeffrey wasn't going to let her do it. There was still the matter of her being a detective on his force who was involved in a violent crime. She had left that hospital because she was running from something—something she desperately did not want Jeffrey to know about. Whether she was involved in the explosion or had set it herself, Jeffrey was going to figure out what had happened. Jake Valentine couldn't find his ass in an ass-storm. If Lena was going to be extricated from this mess, it was all down to Jeffrey.

Of course, this would have been a lot easier if he had any idea what the hell was going on.

After he drove past Hank's house, Jeffrey had called the Georgia Department of Corrections to make sure Ethan Green was still locked up. They had assured Jeffrey that Ethan was still behind bars, but as nice as the woman on the phone had sounded, Jeffrey didn't quite trust the information she had pulled up on her computer. He had called Coastal State Prison himself and spoken directly to the warden. It was a relief to hear from the man that Ethan was still a resident of the state penal system, but Jeffrey was not stupid enough to dismiss the con from his list of possibilities.

Though he claimed to be reformed, Ethan Green had been a skinhead since childhood. He was raised in a skinhead family and had been arrested along with his skinhead friends. Jeffrey had seen the black swastikas and disgusting images the young man had etched into his skin. There was no way Ethan hadn't realigned himself with his boys the minute he'd walked back into prison. The only way for animals like that to survive was to live in packs. The only question was how far was Ethan's reach outside the prison walls? The man at the hospital last night had sported a red swastika on his arm. Was he somehow connected to Ethan? Had the imprisoned skinhead sent one of his boys to get to Lena? That might explain her fear. But, would it explain why she would refuse Jeffrey's help?

He looked at his watch, wondering why Nick Shelton was late. The

Georgia Bureau of Investigation's southeastern field rep was a busy man. They had chosen the diner as a halfway point for both of them — far enough from Reece to avoid prying eyes and close enough to Macon so that Nick wasn't out of the office too long. Jeffrey had been cryptic on the phone last night as he arranged to meet the man, but he was hoping Nick could fill in some blanks on Jake Valentine and what was going on under the new sheriff's watch. Nick worked on cases that crossed county lines, and Elawah was in his district. If anyone could tell Jeffrey whether or not skinheads were operating in town, Nick Shelton could. The GBI agent took pride in bringing down the bad guys, and despite his tendency toward the flamboyant, he was a damn good cop.

He was also late by almost an hour.

Jeffrey picked up his cell phone and thumbed to the number for the motel. Before he'd left, Jeffrey had asked Sara to get in touch with Frank Wallace back in Grant County, but they both knew that this was just an excuse for Jeffrey to call in later and check up on her. Jeffrey very seriously doubted knowing who the white sedan was registered to would open any earth-shattering leads. It was the kind of base-covering work that Jeffrey usually assigned to junior officers.

Jeffrey was listening to the phone ring, his chest feeling tight as each one passed unanswered, when Sara finally picked up.

"Jeff?"

"You sound out of breath," he told her, relieved to hear her voice.

"I went for a walk," she told him, then started to explain why. When she got to the part about buying a map, he found himself squeezing the phone so hard that it nearly popped out of his hand.

"So," she continued, obviously excited by her little stroll. "It was just a vacant lot, but still, I thought I could go to the county courthouse and see whose name is on the property deed. What do you think?"

Jeffrey couldn't speak. Tracking down the registration from the relative safety of the motel room was one thing. Walking into what could have been a den of skinheads — or worse — was quite another.

"Hello?" Sara said. "Are you still there?"

Jeffrey cleared his throat, trying to keep his tone steady and not go with his gut reaction to demand what the hell she thought she was doing. "I'm here."

"I was saying that I can go to the courthouse—"

He stopped her dead in her tracks. "I need you to stay in the room,

Sara. Don't go to the courthouse. Don't make any more phone calls. Just stay in the goddamn room and keep out of trouble."

She was the one who was quiet this time.

He spoke through gritted teeth. "I can't do my job and worry about you at the same time."

She let some time pass before answering. "Okay."

He could tell from the way she'd said the word that she was angry, but there was nothing he could do about that right now. "Promise me you'll stay there until I get back."

Again, there was the hesitation. Suddenly, he realized he was wrong. Sara wasn't angry. She was disappointed with herself because *he* was angry. He could almost hear her thoughts, knew that she was berating herself for doing one more stupid thing.

"I know you were just trying to help out, but, Sara, Jesus, the thought of you traipsing out on your own like that…this isn't Grant County. You didn't grow up here. These people don't know you. It's not safe, Sara. Do you understand what I mean?"

"Yes."

"Baby…" He shook his head, words failing him. "Please, just stay in the room. I'll get back as soon as I can."

"No," she told him. "Do your job. You're right. I'll stay here."

Now he felt like a complete asshole. He looked out the diner window. Nick Shelton was getting out of his Chevy pickup.

"It's not your fault," he told her. "Listen, Nick just pulled up."

"Okay," she said. "I'll see you when you get here."

She didn't slam down the phone, but Jeffrey wished she had. Sara wasn't compliant. She was headstrong and arrogant and demanding— all the things a man could want in a woman. Over the last few months, he had watched her go from a fighter to someone who just rolled with the punches. Jeffrey wanted her to be angry again. He wanted her to tell him to fuck off, that she knew what she was doing and he should be grateful she was wasting her time down here helping him out when she could be back home tending to patients. He wanted her to scream at him, to rail against the Powells and all the other bastards who were trying to keep her down.

He wanted his brilliant, beautiful wife back.

"Hey, Chief." Nick Shelton came through the front door of the diner, rain flattening his long brown hair to his skull. "Sorry I'm late."

Jeffrey stood up, shaking the other man's hand. "No problem."

"Raining like a pisser out there." Nick called over to the waitress, "You got some fresh coffee for me, darlin'?"

She gave him a big smile. "Sure do."

"Leave me a little room at the top, will you? Maybe this much?" He held his thumb and forefinger about an inch apart.

"Be right back." She giggled, giving him a wink. Jeffrey had barely gotten a "good morning" from the woman, but he gathered Nick, with his tight jeans and the heavy gold chain around his neck, was more her type.

The GBI man watched the waitress leave, giving her wide bottom an appreciative smile. "Might get me some fries with that shake."

Jeffrey tried to steer the conversation away from the waitress. "How you been doing, Nick?"

"Working like a dog, is how." He picked at the napkin dispenser on the table, shredding the first few. "State cut my budget in half for god-damn Homeland Security. We got gangs and drugs and murderers run-ning around here faster than clam chowder through my grandma but the feds are making us shoot our wad on fighting damn terrorists who couldn't even find Elawah or Grant County on the map. Hell, they don't even need to make the trip. Give us a few more years and we'll all kill each other on our own."

Jeffrey had never had a conversation with Nick that didn't involve some kind of complaint, but he tried not to fuel it with his own. "Sorry to hear you're having a hard time, Nick."

"Bob Burg's working some consultancy job up north making twenty times more than the state ever paid him."

Jeffrey felt himself getting pulled in. Bob Burg had been Nick's counterpart, handling counties that ran along southeastern Georgia. "What happened?"

Nick used the shredded napkins to wipe the rain off his face, saying, "I guess they figured all that time I wasted popping home to sleep and change my underwear could be put to better use. They kicked him out and gave me his territory."

"They fired Bob?"

" 'Merged the offices to streamline the operation,' " Nick quoted in a businesslike drone. "Bunch of dumb-ass pencil-pushing motherfuck-ers, and don't even get me started on them cash bonuses they've been handing out to the higher-ups to thank them for all this kissing up and kicking down." He sat up as the waitress came back. "Why, thank you, darlin'. You did it up perfect." He gave her a wink and the woman giggled again before sashaying off.

Nick continued, "I can't blame Bob for being pissed off, but he left a freakin' mess for me to clean up. Paperwork missing, files incomplete."

"I'm sorry to hear that."

Nick shrugged, brushing it off. He asked, "How's Sara doing?"

"She's good," Jeffrey lied, trying to fight the sadness he felt.

Nick gave him a sharp glance over the coffee cup. "Heard you and her's already made some friends in town."

"That got around fast."

"It's not every day that a crack squad loses a prisoner." He gave Jeffrey a wink. "And gets gut-punched for their trouble."

Jeffrey felt a grin on his face. "He was asking for it."

"I have no doubt."

"Tell me what you know about Jake Valentine."

Nick grabbed the sugar dispenser off the table. "Jake Valentine," he echoed, giving the name a jaunty ring. "Ol' buddy Jake was a deputy for maybe two days before he ran for office." He kept pouring the sugar as he talked. "There was this old coot, Don Cook, wanted the job, but people in town were sick of the codgers sitting on their asses, collecting their paychecks, while the rest of the town was going to hell in a handbasket."

"Meth?" Jeffrey guessed. There wasn't a town in America that wasn't being slowly crippled by the scourge of methamphetamine. It was cheap to buy, cheaper to make, and almost impossible to quit. The drug ruined the life of anyone it touched, including some law enforcement officers who had unwittingly walked into booby-trapped labs.

"Meth," Nick confirmed, finally finished with the sugar. He grabbed the creamer, saying, "Jake's a little wet behind the ears, but he's a good kid."

"He didn't look old enough to drive a car."

"That's true, but he's willing to learn, which is more than you can say for most everybody you meet. I guarantee you, if he can hang on to the job long enough for his balls to drop, he's gonna make a good sheriff."

"He doesn't seem to have much support from his deputies."

"Maybe one or two will bug out on him, but only when the chips are down." He added, "Don Cook's not as powerful as he thinks he is."

"What about Jake's predecessor?"

"Al Pfeiffer. He was a good guy, but nothing says it's time to retire like a firebomb thrown through your front window."

Jeffrey was sure he'd heard wrong. "What?"

Nick nodded, pouring cream into the cup until the liquid touched the rim. "They firebombed his house. Wife and grandkid barely got out. The old man suffered third-degree burns on his face and arms. Lost one of his fingers. Never made a case because nobody would talk: no witnesses, no crime scene evidence, no nothing. Happened in broad daylight on a Sunday afternoon. Take that as a warning, Chief. These boys don't fuck around. They're making too much money."

"Skinheads?" Jeffrey asked.

"Guessed it again, Chief." Nick gave him a careful look. "Something tells me you've played this game before."

Jeffrey knew it was his turn to share. "I saw this guy outside the Elawah hospital last night—tough-looking con. He had a big red swastika tattooed on his arm."

"That old thing." Nick waved his hand like an old lady fielding gossip. "It's used by the Skin Brothers. Now, there's an interesting bunch of Nazis. Started in the prisons back in the late fifties. Integration on the outside, segregation on the inside. All them white boys running the cell blocks didn't like the black guys coming in and they made it known every way they could." Nick leaned forward, kept his voice low. "In the 1950s, you had maybe sixty-five, seventy percent white in all the federal and state prisons, basically in line with the white population on the outside, right?"

"Right."

"Now, it's upside down. You got maybe a sixty-forty, eighty-twenty mix in some prisons. The whites are the minorities, the blacks and Hispanics are the majority."

"So, in come the gangs."

"Crips, Bloods, the Boyz, Tiny Raskals, MS-13, Nazi Low Riders."

Jeffrey said, "Which brings us back to meth again."

"That kind of quick money to be made, there's always gonna be some kind of war going on, some asshole wanting to swing his dick around. Whites on whites, blacks on blacks, all that matters anymore is the green. You got the Aryans telling the Low Riders what to do, the Low Riders telling the Aryans to fuck off, the purists telling them both they're selling out the white race...long story short, whoever's in charge better be looking over his shoulder all the time."

"Who uses the black swastika?"

"Just about all of 'em but the Skin Brothers." He anticipated Jeffrey's next question. "And never the twain shall meet. You put a Skin Brother in with, say, a Low Rider, they see their tats, you might as well put two tomcats in a cardboard box. Only one of 'em's gonna come out alive."

"You positive about that?"

"Their feud goes so far back nobody even remembers how it got started. Part of the oath they take when they jump in is to kill any motherfucker playing for the other team. Red or black, you get that tattoo, you better be damn sure it's for life. You'll see peace in the Middle East before those two get together."

Jeffrey breathed a little easier. Whatever was going on in Reece, he could take Ethan Green out of the equation for the moment.

Nick leaned back, cupping his coffee in his hands. "You hear about that case with the Hells Angels out on the West Coast?"

Jeffrey shook his head.

"Let me tell you, them're some violent motherfuckers. Been inside most of their adult lives, no hope of getting out, they'll cut you just as soon as look at you. The feds are trying to go after them with the RICO statutes, saying they're the same as organized crime. They had to bolt the bastards to the floor during the trial. One of 'em was already in for stabbing his lawyer with an ink pen. These guys got nothing to lose; just biding their time at the old SuperMax, waiting for their number to come up. They know they're never gonna see the light of day without a set of bars casting a shadow through it and they don't care how many bodies they leave in their wake."

Jeffrey felt his blood turning cold in his veins. "Let's go back to the Skin Brothers."

"Technically, it's the Brotherhood of the True White Skin, but that don't flow off the tongue near as well."

"Tell me more about them."

"For the last five, maybe ten, years, it's been run by two brothers, Carl and Jerry Fitzpatrick. Carl's in prison and Jerry lives out on a zillion-dollar compound with the rest of the family. Thinks he's some kind of preacher for the Way of Whitey."

"True believer?"

"Sadistic true believer," Nick amended. "You don't cross Jerry. He takes care of the stray lambs himself—tracks them down and shatters their little legs so the rest of the flock knows they better keep on the path. You got grown men, mean-as-fuck skinheads with twenty kills under their belt, who piss their pants at the thought of Jerry coming after them."

"He's never been caught?"

"Oh, he's been charged plenty, but nothing sticks. Witnesses tend to change their minds when their fingernails are pulled off and their children go missing."

"Where's the compound?"

"Up in a little town called Keene, New Hampshire."

"Why is it always a relief when these guys are Yankees?"

Nick pretended surprise, clutching his hand to his chest. "Racists in the liberal North? How dare you, sir."

"Shocking," Jeffrey agreed, wondering not for the first time why the rest of America wanted to believe racism only happened south of the Mason-Dixon. It was as if Watts and Harlem, the cases of Rodney King and Abner Louima, were startling anomalies on their respective coasts.

Nick continued, "The FBI has the Fitzpatrick brothers on their watch list, but I'm not sure what kind of priority they've been given. All this anti-immigration shit that's been stirring up has been like free PR for the neo-Nazi groups. Suddenly, saying we should close our borders and kick out the people with the funny-sounding names doesn't sound like extremist rhetoric anymore."

"Good thing we let the Fitzpatricks slip in first," Jeffrey commented. "What's the brother in prison for?"

"Shooting two cops."

"New Hampshire have the death penalty?"

"Just for this very thing," Nick said. "Only problem is, they've set their age limit at seventeen. Carl was two weeks shy of his seventeenth birthday when he pulled the trigger. Life in prison without the chance of parole. Smart boy, our Carl. He met the right people on the cell block, made some good contacts, worked his way up in the group, and—as these things happen—beat his boss to death with a dumbbell and took over the organization. Real upwardly mobile guy."

Jeffrey tried not to think about the two cops that had been shot, how their families, their children, had coped with the loss all these years. "So, how do the Fitzpatricks pay their bills?"

"They're real heavy into meth. Like, super-heavy, kill-your-mama heavy. The Fitzpatricks control everything going in and out of the Southeast corridor, from Florida on up. Some of those boys are billionaires. Only catch is, they're dead before they reach the age of thirty."

Jeffrey already knew this. "And?"

Nick added more sugar to his coffee as he spoke. "They say they've got skin privilege, that being white means they're better than everybody else, that they should be in control. They view it as a special ordination from God." The waitress walked by and Nick gave her another wink. He turned back to Jeffrey, asking, "You like your history, right?"

"Well enough."

"Then let me tell you this story," Nick began. "The Skin Brothers got started by a World War II vet, an Army National Guardsman from out West by the name of Jeremiah Todd. Claimed he was with one of the infantry divisions that helped liberate Dachau." Nick tried the coffee again, then started back with the cream. Jeffrey suppressed the urge to throw the cup across the room as Nick continued, "Todd gets back from Germany and starts telling everybody it's all been overblown, that the press is just making a big deal out of nothing. He was there and saw it with his own eyes, and it was just a bunch of Jews stirring up trouble, trying to bring down America."

Jeffrey felt disgust welling up into his gut. "He was a Holocaust denier?"

"Right."

"Where does the red swastika come in?"

"Before Hitler came along—no shitting you—Todd's National Guard unit had a red swastika on their badges."

Jeffrey provided, "It was a Native American symbol for luck."

"Yep," Nick confirmed. "A lot of the southern and western divisions had Native American call signs. Of course, come the war, the Guard made them change it, but it was on Jeremiah Todd's division uniforms up until the early thirties. You know how those military boys are. They don't let go of tradition without a fight."

"How did Todd end up in prison?"

"Liquor store, convenience store. Some kind of holdup with a gun or a knife or whatever. I don't know the details. Suffice it to say, the fucker ended up inside the same stupid way they all do."

"I take it he's dead?"

"Shanked in the food hall over an extra bread roll about twenty years ago," Nick supplied. "But obviously there were some believers left over. They passed on the gospel, all the way up to New Hampshire, it seems. Prisons are seeing a big-time resurgence of these gangs, especially the white pride assholes. First thing you have to do when you get inside is declare yourself, pick a side for protection so you don't get shanked by the brothers or raped by the Aryans or beat by the brownskins. And it don't stop at the prison gate. Some gangbanger fucks them up on the inside, they reach out to the guy's family on the outside. Like I said, most of 'em ain't got nothing to lose. What's the worst that can happen? They get another life sentence tacked on to the six they already have? The SuperMax only gives them an hour outside a week instead of two? They know they're never getting out, so what does it matter?"

"And they're running drugs on the outside, too?"

"Inside and out," Nick said. "Somebody's gotta pay for Armageddon, and these guys sure as shit ain't gonna make the money digging ditches." He sipped some more coffee before asking, "How does Lena tie into this?"

"I have no idea," Jeffrey admitted.

"I would've like to've seen Jake's face when he realized she'd run out on him."

"He wasn't smiling, I can tell you that."

"You figure out why she legged it?"

Jeffrey shook his head. "You think after all these years I've figured out why the hell she does anything?"

Nick gave an appreciative chuckle. "She always was a pistol."

Jeffrey wasn't up for discussing Lena's finer qualities. "How come you know so much about this group?"

"Remember Amanda Wagner?"

Jeffrey had met the hostage negotiator a few years ago when the GBI had been called into Grant to handle a situation gone bad. He asked, "What does this have to do with tactical?"

"Nothing. Wagner's got some new team she's put together to deal with violent crimes that cross county lines—some kind of quick response unit that's supposed to cut through the red tape, ha-ha-ha. These guys, the Skin Brothers, they've been causing a lot of problems up north; Cherokee, Rabun, Whitfield. She had all the field reps come into Atlanta a few months ago to give us the lowdown, let us know the signs to watch out for."

"What are the signs?"

"The red swastika, mostly. They run meth out of these small towns like it's freaking IBM, straight up the drug corridor through Atlanta, New York, New England, and on up to Canada. We don't even know how many people are in the organization. Estimates run from a couple hundred to a couple thousand." He paused, shaking his head. "It's the same old story: they go after the teenage boys who feel misunderstood and isolated and they give them a family to be a part of, a belief system to explain why the fact that they're white hasn't saved them from being poor. They pump them full of hate and put a gun in their hand. You've seen it for yourself, Chief. These kids go in and out of jail, in and out, until they get popped for something major, and then the next thing you know, they're king of cell block nine, raking in money on the inside, giving orders to their soldiers on the outside. Hell, look at Carl Fitzpatrick. You think he'd have this much power on the outside?"

Jeffrey suddenly felt an overwhelming tiredness. He wasn't even certain this was connected to Lena. All that he had was a gut feeling, and right now, his gut was telling him that no good would come of getting involved with this group. "Are you going to tell Amanda they're operating in Elawah now?"

"Hell, she's the one who told me," he answered. "Thing is, you know as well as I do that the GBI can't come onto an investigation until the locals directly ask for help."

Jeffrey knew Nick was telling the truth, just like he knew the GBI sometimes made sure it was well-prepared in anticipation of a town asking them to step in. "Have you gathered any information on the group operating out of Elawah?"

"Not much," Nick admitted. "Seems to be a tight structure. Some of these gangs, you know exactly who's running the show because the bastard in charge wants you to know. They don't become gangsters so they can hide behind their mama's skirts. They wanna be out in the open, playing the big man, seeing the fear in people's eyes when they drive down the street."

"But not in Elawah?"

"Not in Elawah, and not with the Brotherhood," Nick confirmed. "How the Fitzpatricks work is, they get a handful of key people in town and if there's a problem, they send in out-of-state help to take care of it. That way, nobody gets their hands dirty and nobody knows who to rat on if they get caught. They're real serious about this Armageddon shit. Jesus is gonna come and wipe out darkie and Carl and Jerry Fitzpatrick are gonna inherit the earth."

Jeffrey felt his uneasiness grow. It was always the true believers who felt they had nothing to lose. Christ, what had Lena gotten herself mixed up in?

Nick told him, "There's a couple or three henchmen in Elawah doing the dirty work. Don't ask me their names because I've got no idea. We've kind of poked around, but everything ran cold. Whoever's running them is keeping himself to himself. Playing the Wizard of Oz behind the curtain. That's how the organization works. It's not about flash or showing your piece or banging the ho's, it's about money and control."

Jeffrey sat back in the booth, watching Nick add more sugar to his coffee. "What about the sheriff?"

"Valentine?" Nick shook his head. "No way Jake's running this. It's too sophisticated. Somebody with a lot of patience and a lot of control is pulling the strings."

He meant someone older, more mature. "Cook?"

"I'd buy Cook taking some cash to look the other way, but being a part of it?" Nick shook his head again. "Might be, but I'd be surprised."

"Pfeiffer, then? Maybe he got greedy and that's why they threw the firebomb?"

"That'd make sense if there'd been a vacuum. You know how it is— take out the guy and all the cockroaches scramble to take his place. There wasn't a scramble. Matter of fact, you trace back the purity levels and they actually spiked after Pfeiffer left."

Jeffrey knew that drug agencies tracked their effectiveness through the purity of the drugs on the street. The weaker the mixture, the better they were doing at shutting down the supply line. The higher the concentration, the more likely it was that the bad guys were winning the game.

Jeffrey asked, "How much money do you think's involved here?"

"Just in Elawah?"

Jeffrey nodded.

"Shit, hoss, more money than you or me's ever gonna see in our lives unless it's in the evidence lockup. They just did that bust up in Atlanta, right? Caught two guys driving a U-Haul packed to the rafters with crystal meth. Paper says the street value's upwards of three hundred million."

Jeffrey could not even fathom that kind of money. "The sheriff before—Pfeiffer. Why didn't he call in the GBI?"

"You'll have to ask him yourself." Nick reached into his back pocket and pulled out a piece of damp notebook paper. "When you told me you were in Reece, I assumed you might have some questions I couldn't answer. Sorry it got wet," he apologized, unfolding the page. "Old guy lives a far piece out, so you're gonna need a good map. I'll let you borrow mine if you promise to get it back to me."

Jeffrey scanned the address, noted that the town was at least four hours away from Reece. "He doesn't have a phone?"

"He's so far off the grid I'd be surprised if he's got electricity."

Jeffrey looked again at the piece of paper Nick was offering him. Elawah wasn't his county. These weren't his people. Jake Valentine hadn't said word one about needing any help, and even if the man had, it wasn't Jeffrey's job to bail him out. He was here to help Lena, not take on a bunch of skinheads. The problem was, he didn't have much else to go on. Short of following up on Sara's idea and going to the county courthouse to look up the property deed, there was nothing else Jeffrey could think to do.

Sara. He couldn't leave her alone in the motel room while he drove to within spitting distance of the Florida border. Of course, she might make the trip look a little less official. Nick mentioned that Pfeiffer had a wife. Sara could help get the woman out of the way while Jeffrey asked the man some hard questions.

Nick was still holding out the paper. He asked, "What's it gonna be, hoss?"

Jeffrey hesitated again, thinking about the terror in Lena's voice as she'd told Sara to get out of town. He wasn't fooling anyone, especially himself. "I'm going to need to borrow your map."

LENA

CHAPTER 7

THE HOME SWEET HOME MOTEL on the outskirts of Reece had been Lena's only option the night before. The two-story cinder block building looked like a slasher movie set out of the sixties. Even as a kid, she'd thought of it as the Whore Hotel, the kind of place where people who didn't want to get to know each other too well met to fuck. At the age of sixteen, Lena had pretended to lose her virginity here. The guy, Ben Carver, was thirty-two, which was about the only thing she'd found attractive about him. He was dull and stupid to the point of being possibly retarded, and she'd been on the verge of breaking up with him until Hank had found out they were seeing each other. Hank forbade her to see Ben again, and the next night, Lena had found herself flat on her back at the Whore Hotel.

She wouldn't say it was the most boring three minutes of her life, but it came close. It was safe to say that when Ben didn't call her the next day, she was far from heartbroken. Lena had been too terrified to think about anything but her fear of being pregnant. Ben had said he would use a condom, but she had been too embarrassed to check. Lena had been completely powerless when it came to protecting herself. The only pharmacist in town refused to fill prescriptions for birth control pills. As far as she knew, the pharmacy was still owned by the same man today. She bet the bastard had no problem selling Viagra to unmarried men at ten bucks a pop.

Not that birth control pills were a hundred percent effective. There was always that less than one percent chance, that one time when the pill failed and the condom broke, and then before you knew it, you were sitting on a hard plastic chair at a clinic in Atlanta, waiting for your name to be called.

Lena could still remember everything about that day—the texture of the chairs, the posters hanging on the walls. Hank had waited outside, mumbling to himself, pacing the parking lot. He hadn't agreed with Lena's decision, but in his fucked-up Hank way, he had supported her through the whole thing. "I'm not in any position to cast judgment," he'd told her. "We all make mistakes."

Was it a mistake, though? Most everybody was quick to say that abortion was okay in cases of rape, as if the fact that the woman didn't enjoy the sex negated any squeamishness they might have about the procedure. Lena's relationship with Ethan was a lot of things: tumultuous, violent, brutal...but then sometimes it could be tender, loving, almost affectionate. The truth was that most of the time, she had willingly had sex with him. Most of the time, she had put her hands on his body, welcomed him into her bed. Could she trace back the conception of their mistake to a specific night, a specific time, and say whether or not it had been consensual or the other kind? Could she separate what it felt like to be beaten by him from the way it felt to be loved by him?

Could she really say that their baby had been a mistake?

Lena sat up in bed, not wanting to think about it anymore.

She made her way to the sink area and took her toothbrush out of her bag; she had not wanted to leave it by the sink last night. God only knew what people got up to on the cracked, plastic basin. The room was even more disgusting than she remembered; the carpet cupped the soles of her shoes as she walked across it and the sheets on the bed were so nasty that she had slept in her clothes. She had basically lay there all night, falling in and out of sleep, startling at any noise, afraid that the creepy night manager would use his passkey and try to catch her off guard. This was just the kind of place where that sort of thing happened.

She had slept with her gun by her hand.

The photograph from the newspaper was seared into her brain, and when she wasn't worrying about being raped and killed, she worried about her mother, the lies she and Sibyl had been told. It was clear now that Angela Adams had not died after two weeks spent lying comatose in the hospital. She had lived at least six months past Lena and Sibyl's birth. On the day the picture had been taken for the newspaper, she had held them in her arms, posing for the photographer as she told the reporter that she thought it was a travesty that her husband's murder had gone unsolved. "I loved Calvin more than my own life," she had told the reporter. "He should be here now being a father to these precious little babies."

Her words were much more saccharine than Lena would have liked, but the sentiment hit home. Her mother had loved them. She had been devastated by the loss of their father. She had held them in her arms.

Lena walked around the room as she brushed her teeth. When had Angela really died? And how? Hank had said that the thug leaving his house was the man who had killed Angela Adams. The drugs had let down Hank's guard, and she was certain that he had been telling the truth, or at least the truth as he saw it.

But did Hank mean the man had actually, physically killed her mother? He was certainly old enough to have been around when Calvin Adams was shot and killed. Had the thug been the one who ordered the hit on Calvin all those years ago, leaving Angela with no husband and two twin daughters to raise on her own? Had it been too much for Angela to bear? Had suicide seemed like the only way to make the pain stop? Lena could understand the draw. There had been many times in her life when she had considered the option herself.

Suicide might explain why Hank had lied about the timing, the mode, of Angela's death. He didn't want the girls to be burdened with the legacy of their mother's suicide. Lena could understand—if not forgive—that. At least there was some kind of logic to the lies.

If her mother had killed herself, it would also make sense that Hank was trying to do the same. Lena had seen it many times as a cop: suicides ran in families. Without a doubt, if Hank maintained his present lifestyle, he would be dead before the month was out. Whatever he was doing to himself, it was completely and entirely deliberate. Lena had never thought of Hank as anything but a survivor. You didn't shoot junk into your veins for twenty years and still keep breathing if you had a death wish. You didn't suddenly stop hanging on to your life by your fingernails unless someone gave you a damn good reason to let go.

Lena spat into the sink, then used a bottle of water to rinse her mouth.

Hank had always been careful, as if he could distinguish himself between being a user and an abuser. For all his blackouts and open sores, he was careful about one thing. If speed was Hank's religion, he prayed at the altar of his veins. This was where the dope entered his system, and he was rigorous about making sure he took care of them. He never cooked with the same needle he injected with because the spoon or cotton could kink the tip and leave a bigger scar. He always used new needles, fresh alcohol swabs, and vitamin E to keep the tracks down. He didn't smoke before he shot up because that made the veins harder to find, the needle less likely to hit at the right spot.

Sure, there were times when his need overcame his logic; the track marks scarring his forearms, the way he sometimes lost feeling in his hands and feet because the veins couldn't get enough blood to his extremities, betrayed that fact. But, as drug addicts went, he had always been fairly careful.

Until now.

Lena turned on the water in the shower, then changed her mind, thinking she would feel even more filthy if she stepped her bare feet into the soiled, gray bathtub. She checked the lock on the door, then quickly took off her clothes, changing into a fresh pair of underwear and slipping back into her jeans from the day before. She found a T-shirt in her bag and kept her eyes on the door as she put it on.

Hank wouldn't talk to her. He had made that clear yesterday. Whatever his reasons, she knew that he was stubborn—as stubborn as she was. No matter what she said, how much she begged or beat him, he wouldn't talk until he was damn good and ready. The way he looked yesterday, unless a miracle happened, he would more than likely take his secrets to his grave.

Lena caught her reflection in the mirror over the dresser. It was tilted down toward the bed, spidery lines meant to give the appearance of lace framing the corners. She didn't see Sibyl anymore when she looked in the mirror. Sibyl would forever be trapped in a particular time that would never allow her to move on. She wouldn't have tiny lines around her eyes or the faint trace of a scar on her left temple. Her hair wouldn't get those few streaks of gray Lena had found in the bathroom mirror last week and, much to her shame, had plucked out with a pair of tweezers. Even if she'd lived, Sibyl would never have gotten that hard look to her eyes, that flat, cold stare that sent out a challenge to the world.

Sibyl would never know that their mother had lived however long—at least long enough to hold them. She would never know that just as Lena had always predicted, Hank had finally given in to his addiction. Nor would she stand at his graveside, cursing him for his weakness.

Hank was going to die. Lena knew there was no way he could pull himself out of his current condition without some kind of medical intervention. Yet, every time she thought about him, she didn't see the Hank from the last twenty-five years, the one who dutifully attended his AA meetings and ran to Lena's side whenever she called him. She saw the addict of her childhood, the speed freak who chose the needle over his nieces. When Lena thought of his state of decline, she felt the rage only a child can feel toward a parent: you are all I have in the world and you are abandoning me for a drug that will destroy us all.

That's what addicts didn't see. They weren't just screwing up their own lives, they were screwing up the lives of everyone around them. There were some nights of Lena's childhood when she had actually kneeled on the side of her bed and prayed that Hank would finally mess up, that the needle would go to far, the drug would be too potent, and he would finally die. She had envisioned adoption, a mother and father to take care of her and Sibyl, a clean place to live, order in their lives, food on the table that didn't come out of a can. Seeing Hank now, knowing the state he was in, Lena could not help but recall those sleepless nights.

And part of her—a very big part—said to let him die.

Lena sat on the bed as she tied her sneakers. Thinking about Hank wasn't going to get her anywhere but back in bed feeling sorry for herself. She wasn't sure what she was going to do today, but her top priority was getting out of this dingy room. The library's microfiche archives didn't go past 1971. The newspaper office was based out of the back room of an insurance company, so Lena didn't have much hope that they kept old issues. Still, she would try to get in touch with the weekly's editor, a man whose full-time job was picking up roadkill off the interstate.

Lena supposed she could find her mother's death certificate through the proper state office, but she would need Angela's Social Security number, place of birth, or at the very least her last known address in order to help her narrow the search. She knew both her mother's and father's birth dates from her own birth certificate, but beyond that, there was nothing. The hospital might have kept a billing address or other pertinent information, but she would need a warrant to get that information. She had thought about trying the county courthouse, but according to the message on their phone, they were closed while asbestos tiles in the floor were being removed.

Since the motel was right next door to Hank's bar, Lena decided she might as well start there. Technically, the Hut was not in Reece's city limits. Like a lot of small towns all over America, Elawah was a dry county. If you wanted to buy liquor, you had to cross the county lines into Seskatoga, which explained why the Elawah sheriff's department spent most of its weekends scraping teenagers off the road that led out of town.

Lena opened the door to her room and immediately closed her eyes, her retinas screaming at the sudden light. She blinked several times to regain her vision, staring at the floor of the concrete balcony. Just to the left of her foot, she saw a small, red X chalked onto the ground, maybe three inches square.

She knelt down, running her fingers along the red mark, wondering if it had been there when she checked in last night. It had been dark, but the ancient sign outside the motel cast enough light to see by. But, Lena hadn't been looking at the ground as she walked into the room. She'd been concentrating on the basics: bringing in her bag, finding her toothbrush, falling in to bed.

Lena looked at the tips of her fingers, saw that the chalk had transferred to her skin. The chalk mark didn't mean anything except that the maid didn't clean much. Judging by the state of Lena's room, the woman wasn't exactly thorough.

Still, Lena glanced around as she stood back up. No one jumped out at her, and she went to the balcony and scanned the parking lot. Except for a motorcycle parked in the handicap space, her Celica was the only vehicle there.

She looked back at the ground. An X. Not a swastika, not a cross. Just a red X to mark the spot.

Lena wiped her hand on her pants as she strolled across the balcony toward the stairs. She kept her eyes on the ground, looking for other marks, trying to see if any of the other rooms had been singled out. There was nothing out of the ordinary, just cigarette butts, trash, and a few leaves, though the closest tree to the motel was about twenty feet away in the forest that ran behind the building.

She stopped in the front office to get a cup of coffee. There was a box of change by the pot, requesting fifty cents for each cup. Lena dropped a dollar in the box and stood looking into the parking lot as she poured herself a cup.

"Nice morning," a man said. She turned toward the front counter and saw that it wasn't a man, but a teenager—the redheaded would-be gangsta she had seen in the Mustang outside the school yesterday.

She said, "Shouldn't you be in school?"

"Work release," he told her, leaning against the wall behind the counter. His T-shirt was so big the shoulders lapped around his elbows. He had a belly on him, but she could tell from his large hands and feet that he would lose that in the next few years as he grew into his body. He would still have that carrot-colored hair, though, and those freckles would never go away.

"I'm Rod," he told her. "You want some Halloween candy?"

"No." Lena remembered the decorations from the library. Halloween was two nights away. She hadn't even remembered what day it was.

He asked, "Are you a cop?"

So much for being undercover. "What makes you say that?"

"You talk like a cop."

She tasted the coffee and tried not to gag. "How do you know what a cop talks like?"

"I've seen it on TV."

Lena fished her change out of the honor box. "You shouldn't believe everything you see on TV."

"Junior watches it all night," he said, probably meaning the clerk who had stared at Lena when she checked in last night as if she was the first woman he'd seen in his life. "He's got porn tapes he keeps under the couch. Mr. Barnes doesn't know. He's the owner." The kid gave her a big grin. "You can watch some of them if you want."

"Wait for that." She started to leave, but changed her mind, thinking she might as well try. "Hey." The kid was still leaning against the wall, waiting. "I saw a man the other day," she began, resting her coffee cup on the door handle, trying to appear disinterested. "He had a swastika on his arm."

The kid stood away from the wall. His voice went up three octaves. "A swastika like Hitler?"

"Yeah."

"Cool."

"You think that's cool?"

"Well, yeah. I mean, no, it's obviously, like, wrong." He leaned back against the wall. "I just meant it as in good for him for, you know, like not being ashamed." He lowered his voice. "There are some people in this town who have some white sheets in their closet."

"Like who?"

"Well..." The kid realized he had an angle to work. "Why don't we go back in the office and we can talk?"

"Why don't you call me when you get some fuzz on your peaches?" Lena moved to push the door open just as a woman was walking in.

"Christ," the woman hissed as Lena's coffee spilled down the front of her shirt. She was older, her salt-and-pepper hair pulled up into a blue bandanna. She was trim, too—about Lena's height—and pissed as hell. "Watch where you're fucking going."

"Sorry," Lena apologized, but the woman still scowled as if Lena had done it on purpose.

"Just fuck off," the woman barked, pushing past Lena and going into the office. She slammed the door so hard that the pictures hanging on the wall rattled.

Lena asked the kid behind the counter, "What's her problem?"

"She's the maid."

That explained why the motel was a rat's best friend. "She always that pleasant?"

The carrot shrugged, still smarting from Lena's brush-off. "Better you than me."

Lena left the building, feeling bad for the woman, thinking she'd probably be pissed if she had to work at this dump, too. It was one thing to work a crap job when you were young, but the lady had to at least be pushing sixty. She should be retiring to Florida, not cleaning motel rooms for pocket change.

Lena walked across the parking lot, wishing she'd put on a jacket before heading out but not wanting to go back into the miserable room to fetch one. The sun was already busy burning off the fog, and she knew that in a couple of hours, she'd be glad she was in short sleeves.

She dumped the rest of her coffee into a storm drain as she crossed the street, glancing down to see if it ate through the concrete. There was a Stop 'n' Save catty-corner to the hotel, just opposite Hank's bar. She tossed her empty cup into the trash as she walked into the general store, which was little more than a front for selling cheap beer. She had sneaked out of Hank's house many a night to hang out behind the store with the other bad kids from high school.

Inside the store, the air-conditioning was already on full blast in anticipation of the coming heat. Lena walked past the coffee machine and grabbed herself a Coke. As she paid, she had the vague feeling that she knew the woman working behind the counter, probably from high school, but neither one of them was particularly interested in starting up a conversation. Lena dropped her extra pennies into the cup and headed back out the way she had come.

She stood on the sidewalk, waiting for the traffic to clear. The motel was directly across the street, and she saw that some creative vandals had broken the lights in the sign so that at night "Home Sweet Home" would turn into, "Ho eet me." What else had the vandals done to the motel? Were they the ones who had scratched the red X in front of Lena's door? The mark was bothering her. She wondered how long it had been there and if someone was trying to send her a message. Whatever it meant, she wasn't getting it. Still, she looked around as she waited for a truck to pass, her skin tingling, her gut telling her that she was being watched.

As casually as she could, Lena glanced over her shoulder. The woman behind the counter at the convenience store was staring out the window.

Candy, Lena suddenly remembered. That was her name. They had called her "Corny" because someone had said that she walked like she had a corncob stuck up her butt.

There were times that Lena thought she wouldn't take all the money in the world to be back in high school.

The traffic cleared and she popped open the Coke as she started to cross the street, wondering how in the hell Hank's shitty bar had managed to help put Sibyl through college and bail out Lena more times than she wanted to admit. The Hut was a three o'clock bar, the kind where everyone started to look good around three in the morning. Desperation hovered like a black cloud over the place, and she suppressed a shiver as she got closer to the building.

The bar didn't even have a sign out front; everybody knew what it was. The roof was thatched on the front, but what looked like a case of mange had set in around fifteen years ago and Hank hadn't bothered to fix it. Tiki torches with orange and red lightbulbs banked the front door, which was painted to look as if it had been fashioned from grass. The exterior walls were decorated in a similar theme, but the paint was so faded you couldn't tell what you were looking at unless someone gave you a clue. There were windows all along the front, but they had been painted black so long ago that they had taken on the appearance of rotten wood.

The yellow ATF tape across the door was the only thing that looked new. Hank hadn't told her the bar had been closed. There were only two reasons to explain the Bureau of Alcohol, Tobacco and Firearms paying a visit to the Hut: either Hank had been caught selling liquor to underage patrons or he'd been caught dealing drugs.

Lena tried the door, but it was locked. She put her hand on top of the jamb and felt for the spare, but it wasn't in its usual place.

She gave up and walked around the side of the building. She didn't need to get inside the bar anyway. Hank's office, which bore a closer resemblance to an outhouse, was tucked behind the bar on the edge of a slow-running stream.

Lena tried the shed door just in case, but it was locked, too. Hank must have locked it himself; there was no sign of ATF tape on the shack. The federal boys probably hadn't bothered to get a warrant for the shed. The drug trafficking going on inside the bar would've been enough to make the headlines.

She put down her can of Coke and pushed her hands against the small window tucked high on the creek side, but it would not budge. A rock helped, and the untempered glass shattered into a million pieces, some of it falling into the open mouth of her soda can. Lena found a stick and used it to knock away the broken glass. Still, she didn't like the idea of climbing blind through the window. What's more, it was high up, probably too high to get to without a ladder. She had done stupider things, but at the moment, Lena was hard-pressed to remember what.

Out of frustration, she kicked the wall, mad at herself and this idiotic situation. The board made a hollow sound, and she kicked it harder until the wood splintered. A few more kicks created a nice hole in the shack. She cringed as she reached in and pulled out the pink insulation, sneezing from the dust, wondering if she was inhaling asbestos. There were black flakes of mold and excrement from animals that she didn't want to think about, but she pulled out enough fiberglass to expose the backside of the paneling that lined the inside office. She used her foot again, kicking out the plywood, which made a cracking sound as it pulled away from the rusted penny nails holding it to the studs.

A few minutes later, Lena was inside Hank's office.

She brushed off her jeans as she looked around, trying to find the light switch. She pushed away a spiderweb, then realized that it was actually the cord for the overhead light. Lena tugged the string and the bare bulb flickered on, then made a loud pop as it blew.

Lena cursed again. She had a flashlight in her car, but she didn't want to go back and get it. Instead, she used the light coming in through the broken window to look for the spare bulbs Hank always kept in his desk. He had wired the office himself using a hundred-foot extension cord he'd snaked through a piece of metal pipe and plugged in at the bar. This was not the first time the light had blown. She found the pack of bulbs in the bottom drawer and changed the light, trying not to think about what her hands might find in the dark. Her feet crunched on the broken glass as she twisted the bulb, the socket making a dry, crackling sound as she tried to get the right angle. Finally, the light came on and the sudden heat from the bulb made her jerk back her hand.

She wasn't just being paranoid. Hank had almost electrocuted himself a couple of times trying to change the bulb.

Lena looked around the airless room, which was wallpapered with posters from beer and liquor companies. Half-naked women stared back at her, most of them fellating bottles they held in their hands. White cartons stuffed with paperwork that dated back to the bar's grand opening were stacked against the back wall, leaving about ten square feet for a desk and two chairs. Piles of receipts were in shoe-boxes scattered around the desk.

Six years ago, Lena had sat in one of those stupid plastic chairs across from Hank, drinking so much Jack Daniel's that she made herself sick, as she tried to work up the courage to tell him that Sibyl was dead.

Was that when he had started using again? Had the news that his beloved girl, his favorite niece, was dead, been what had finally thrown him over the edge?

Or had it started six months ago when Hank had taken Lena to the abortion clinic? He had stood outside the building, chain-smoking cigarettes, listening to angry protestors with their disgusting signs screaming about hell and damnation, condemning Lena and everybody else in the clinic to hell for their sins.

Had she done this to him? Had Lena's actions helped put the needle back in his arm?

The guy with the red swastika had helped, too—she was certain of it. Lena had to find the man, to figure out who he was working for. Guys like that were muscle. There was a brain somewhere, and once Lena found that brain, she would burn his fucking house down with him inside.

Lena sat in Hank's chair, the springs squeaking like an old barn door. The top drawer to his desk was locked, and she took her folding knife out of her back pocket and flicked open the blade from the white pearl handle. The lock jimmied open easily enough. In the drawer, she found Hank's business checkbook, a couple of free coupons to Harrah's casino up in the mountains, and his spare set of keys to the bar. The larger drawers contained files that seemed mostly to do with the running of the business. Liquor distributors, payroll, taxes, and insurance. She flipped back through the checkbook and saw the last balance was dated three weeks ago. At the time, he had around six thousand dollars in the bank.

What date had the bar been closed down? She would have to find out from the sheriff's office. She wondered if that old fart Al Pfeiffer was still running the show and had to smile at the thought of going into his office, flashing her gold shield in the fucker's face. Pfeiffer had a neat trick where he pulled over young girls for speeding and frisked them to within an inch of their ovaries. He had pulled over Lena once and taken a few liberties before she had figured out what was going on and slammed her knee into his groin. Pfeiffer had thrown her into jail without charging her or giving her a phone call. She had sat in the cell for six hours before Hank had come down to the station to file a missing persons report.

His face. God, she could still see Hank's face. There was this split second when he saw her coming out of the jail when his eyes filled with tears and his mouth opened, letting out this yelp-like sound when he realized that she was okay. Just as quickly, his mouth had closed into an angry frown, and he had cuffed her on the back of the head, asking her what the hell she was doing getting herself into trouble, who the hell she thought she was sassing the police. He hadn't wanted to hear her story. Pfeiffer was one of his AA buddies and Hank thanked the man for not formally charging her.

Still, his face...

Lena had seen that same transformation so many times now that she'd come to think of Hank in almost schizophrenic terms. One second, the loving guardian who would do anything for her, the next second the angry disciplinarian threatening to beat her to within an inch of her life.

And now the drug addict—back to that old role again, waiting for the curtain to finally come down.

She put her elbows on the desk and dropped her head into her hands. The shack was like a kiln, and she felt sweat rolling down her back and into the waist of her jeans. Still, she sat there, heat engulfing her body, the water in the creek a constant murmur as she thought about Hank, the way he had looked in the shower, the hard words he had used when he told her to leave.

There had to be an explanation for his disintegration. Did the bar's closing send him into a spiral? Was that what had finally pushed him back into his old ways? Lena looked around the cramped office, trying to put herself in Hank's mind. He had no love for this place. He had always seen the Hut as a way to make money and nothing else. There was almost a perverse pleasure he got from being a recovering alcoholic and having the strength to be around liquor all day without imbibing. Had it been a crutch all these years?

She pushed herself back from the desk, her shoe sliding on a piece of paper. Lena reached down to pick it up, her hand freezing midair as she stared at the light blue notepaper on the concrete floor. The handwriting was a perfect cursive, the kind they used to teach in school back when it mattered. The words were easy to read from this distance, but still, she picked up the paper and sat back in the chair so she could study it. She had to read through the page two more times before the words started to make sense.

Lena rummaged through the desk, looking for the rest of the letter. She moved the shoeboxes and found three more pages underneath, then a few more that had fallen behind the desk. When she put them together, Lena found that there was not just one but three letters, all dated within the last two months. She read through them, feeling like she was reading someone's diary. The notes were banal in parts, listing details of shopping for groceries and picking up the kids after school. Some of it was intensely personal, the kinds of things you shared only with a close friend.

Finished, Lena pressed her palm flat against the stack of letters, fingers splayed out, as if she could divine their true meaning.

How had she been so blind?

TUESDAY AFTERNOON

CHAPTER 8

AL PFEIFFER LIVED AS FAR from Elawah County as you could get and still be in the state of Georgia. Dug Rut was a border town on the edge of the Okefenokee Swamp, which meant that the trip would take Jeffrey and Sara into a primitive wetland known mostly for its alligators and mosquitoes, both of which could kill a man. In high school, Jeffrey and two of his friends had planned to take a few weeks during their summer vacation and explore the swamp, but that was the same year that *Deliverance* came out, and even though the movie was filmed in the north Georgia mountains, it was enough to turn any man off the idea of canoeing.

Still, Jeffrey remembered a little bit about the wetlands from his reading. He knew that the headwaters of the Suwannee and the Saint Marys rivers were located in the swamp, each eventually draining to the Gulf of Mexico and the Atlantic Ocean, respectively. Hundreds of endangered birds and mammals resided in the protected wildlife refuge and the plant life was of the sort you would expect to see in a science-fiction film. The place was as cut off as it was remote, and families tended to live and die there without seeing the rest of the world. Back in the early 1900s, there were folks living in the swamp who still had not yet heard that the Civil War was over. Not much changed in their lives when they got the news.

The ride down was a quiet one. Sara hadn't had much to say when Jeffrey got back to the motel. Oddly, she had cleaned the bathroom, something she seldom did at home unless she was pissed at Jeffrey or knew that her mother was coming over. She had actually seemed proud about bringing a shine to the crappy fixtures. For Jeffrey's part, he had stared at the tub while he was taking a leak, fighting the urge to redirect the stream and mess up Sara's handiwork. If he'd wanted a wife who took pleasure out of cleaning a toilet, he would've married his high school sweetheart back in Alabama.

Sara had listened politely as Jeffrey had relayed the details he'd gotten from Nick about the Brotherhood, the meth business running up the eastern seaboard, the possibility that Elawah might be a stop along the cartel's railroad. She'd nodded, but not offered her opinion on anything. She hadn't asked him what he'd hoped to accomplish by talking to Al Pfeiffer or how any of this tied in to Lena. Part of him had hoped she would. Jeffrey wasn't sure how to answer those questions himself. Talking it out with Sara might have helped him understand.

Two hours into the trip, Jeffrey wasn't even sure he was still in Georgia. Kudzu and knotty pines gave way to sand and palm trees. When he rolled down his window, he caught a whiff of the briny coast mixing with the pungent odor of shit that told him he was downwind from a paper company. An hour later, he followed a back route cutting into the state, toward the little bit of Georgia that fingered into Florida along the Saint Marys. By then, he could barely see the road. The car's windshield was caked with all manner of streaks from the bugs that had flown into the glass, some of them as big as his fist.

Jeffrey was about to pull over and look at the map Nick had given him when he noticed all the usual signs that indicated you were getting close to the border between two southern states: hot boiled peanuts, fresh produce, fireworks, totally topless/XXX-rated girls. Sara said she needed to use the restroom, so he pulled over at the rest stop on the Florida side. Jeffrey got out of the car to check his bearings, then got back in the car because in the full heat of the sun, it was almost too painful to be outside. He tried to think back to when he was a kid and the first week of November meant wearing a jacket and hoping it would snow so you wouldn't have to go to school.

In the car, Jeffrey turned on the ignition and ratcheted up the air-conditioning, letting the cold, artificial breeze blow on his face. He spread the map on his lap again and traced his route, squinting to read Nick's handwriting where the GBI agent had noted streets and landmarks that the original cartographer had either failed to notice or considered inconsequential. Still, Nick had never been to visit Al Pfeiffer and the map only gave detailed directions to Dug Rut, not to Pfeiffer's house. There was just the street address to go by: 8 West Road Six. It was a good start, but Jeffrey would need better directions than that.

Sara got back into the car. She handed him a bottle of water.

"Thanks."

"You're welcome."

He stared at her, trying to think of something to say.

She indicated the map. "Do you know where you're going?"

"I'll need to stop at a gas station closer in to town and see if they can give me better directions."

"Okay." She slipped on her seat belt, clicked it into the buckle.

Jeffrey waited, but she didn't say anything else. He gave her the map. She folded it up as he reversed the car out of the space.

Jeffrey merged back onto the highway and followed the signs to Dug Rut. Less than a mile off the main road, he understood where the town had gotten its name. The land was obviously part of the canal system they'd built in the early 1900s in an attempt to drain the swamp. New York's Central Park had suffered this same fate, but the Okefenokee had proved to be too difficult to destroy. The handful of swamps left in America were probably some of the few remaining places on the continent where a man could live wholly sustained by the land, whether it was for food, shelter, medicine, or some of the cleanest drinking water on earth. Jeffrey wondered how long it would be before they were all completely destroyed.

Downtown Dug Rut wasn't much to write home about. There was a bar and a post office, but not much more than that. The tiny strip of storefronts lining Main Street were all closed. The owners hadn't even bothered to put rental signs in the windows. There was something sad about the place, and as Jeffrey coasted through a stop sign, he was starting to give up hope of finding a gas station.

He did a U-turn in the middle of the street and turned back toward the post office. Sara didn't move to get out when he parked in front of the building, so he nudged her, saying, "You don't think I'm going to ask for directions, do you? They'll take away my man card."

She gave him a tight smile and got out of the car.

Jeffrey watched her make her way toward the building. Her jeans were baggy in the back, and he realized that she had lost more weight. He didn't like it. Sara had always been lean, but she was too thin now.

When he made love to her, he could feel her ribs scraping against his chest. Her hips were disappearing, the curve of her waist cinching too tight. From the back, she could almost pass for a teenage boy.

Jeffrey took a deep breath and let it go slowly. Eight years ago, Sara had come home from work early to find Jeffrey in their bed with another woman. Not just in bed, but in action. The look on Sara's face— the betrayal, the hurt, the anger—had been the biggest wake-up call of his life, and Jeffrey had used every tactic he could think of to try and win her back. Just getting her to talk to him had been the biggest hurdle. Once she could speak to him without clenching her jaw, he had worked on getting her into bed. It hadn't been nearly as easy as the first time, but Jeffrey found that waking up with Sara next to him was even more rewarding. Six months ago, he had practically begged her to marry him. Hell, the truth was that he *had* begged her, even getting down on both knees at one point. Sara had taken her own sweet time, but finally she had said yes.

And now, it was almost like she was disappearing before his eyes.

Sara came out of the post office, and Jeffrey found himself looking at the map again instead of watching her walk toward him.

"They were very nice," Sara told him as she got into the car. She was holding a postal form where she'd written down some directions. "They said he's about three miles west of here."

"Why don't we just go to Florida?"

Jeffrey heard his words fill the empty space in the car, knew they had come out of his own mouth, but had no idea where the question had come from.

Sara smiled, shaking her head. Still, she suggested, "Drink margaritas on the beach?"

He felt himself smiling back. "Rub suntan oil all over your body."

"Then aloe when the sun burns off the top layer of my skin." Sara turned to him, still smiling. "You need to go left on Main Street."

"I'm serious about Florida."

"I'm serious about taking a left."

He reached out to her, tracing his fingers along her lips. "You're beautiful. Do you know that?"

She kissed his fingers, then put his hand back on the steering wheel. "Left," she repeated. "Then take a right onto a road called Kate's Way."

Jeffrey backed out of the space and turned onto Main Street. He slowed as they came to a gravel road, trying to read the handmade street sign. He did this at three roads before finding Kate's Way, a bumpy, one-lane path that looked as if it was seldom used. The scenery changed abruptly the farther they traveled. This part of Georgia was flat marshland, huge, big-bottomed cypress trees growing straight out of the tea-colored water. Spanish moss draped over the branches like lace and there was a constant sound of crickets, birds, frogs, and the occasional gator bellow that they could hear even with the car windows rolled up tight.

The curves in the road suggested they were following a creek that hadn't made it onto Nick's map. Jeffrey slowed the car to a meandering pace, careful not to speed lest he meet a car coming from the opposite direction. He imagined it would be a truck, and that the truck would contain a local who didn't cotton to someone being on his road, public right-of-way or not.

He didn't meet any such truck, and when Sara told him to take the next right turn onto yet another deserted-looking gravel road, Jeffrey made a joke about leaving breadcrumbs.

Two miles down, there was a large, rusted mailbox beside a dilapidated lane, and Jeffrey pulled over to check the number. The sign was so faded that neither one of them could read anything, but a quick scan of Sara's notes told them they were in the right place.

Jeffrey turned down the driveway, slowing to a stop to let a rabbit jump across the path. He went a few more feet, then slowed again for a couple of chickens. After the birds had taken their own sweet time moseying to the other side, Jeffrey accelerated, kicking up dust in his wake. He hadn't meant to draw so much attention to himself, but maybe it was wise to announce your presence to a man who had been firebombed out of his own home.

"Well," Sara said, surprised when she saw the house.

Jeffrey shared the feeling. Pfeiffer's spread was a little more grand than what Jeffrey would have imagined if he'd let himself sit down and think about it. The house was on a rise, thick green grass carpeting the lawn, a stone path leading down to the creek. Built in a mini-plantation style, two large white columns held up a second floor balcony. Large floor-to-ceiling windows let in the afternoon sun and opened for a crosswind on more temperate days. On the bottom floor, a wraparound porch completed the picture.

Jeffrey parked his car on the pad in front of the mansion.

"Nice digs," Sara commented.

"Why don't you stay in the car?" Jeffrey suggested. "I'll go make sure this is the right place."

She opened her mouth to say something, then changed her mind and gave him a nod instead.

As Jeffrey got out of the car, he could hear the buzz of an air-conditioning unit coming from the side of the house, its insistent whirring blocking out the crickets and birds, though the rushing white waters of the creek managed to compete with the fan. He glanced around, looking for power lines, guessing they were buried in the ground. That would've set Pfeiffer back a wad of cash. It was three times more expensive to bury lines than it was to string them across the sky. Jeffrey assumed the man had laid a phone line in the process and wondered how he'd managed to have a phone number that Nick Shelton couldn't trace. Maybe he had put it in his wife's name, or a family member's. Obviously, Al Pfeiffer had gone to some trouble to make sure he couldn't be contacted.

Jeffrey put his hand in his pocket, trying to use the casual gesture to hide his trepidation. He felt the keyfob and realized he'd left Sara without any air-conditioning and no way to roll down the windows. He glanced back at the BMW. Sara waved and he nodded back.

He continued up the path. The closer he got to the house, the more he could see that there was something too new about the place, a crisp whiteness to the vinyl siding, a too-clean look to the porch stairs, that gave lie to its plantation roots. Climbing the cement stairs, Jeffrey figured that the house had probably been constructed by a local builder who specialized in slinging up little Taras. This far out in the middle of nowhere, it couldn't have come cheap.

Between the sheriff's pension, disability for his injuries, and whatever he had socked away, Al Pfeiffer was obviously living comfortably. This was certainly not the kind of place Jeffrey would choose for his retirement, but the isolation had its benefits, especially when you were the type of person to open your front door with a shotgun in your hand.

"What do you want?"

Jeffrey's hand had been raised to knock when the front door was flung open. The shotgun was pointed squarely in his face, about two inches from his nose. Now that Jeffrey thought about it, he'd heard the quick *cha-chunk* of the pump being jerked, a shell being loaded into the chamber, as he'd lifted his hand in the air. He had been just a few seconds off from registering the sound, though, and those few seconds could have meant life and death if the man behind the gun hadn't been more careful. Or maybe the man was just terrified. His eyes kept darting over Jeffrey's shoulder, checking to see if he was alone.

Jeffrey still had his hand in his pocket. He found the keyfob and pressed the lock button, hoping to God the BMW was within reach of the signal.

"You got to the count of three before I blow off your head and ask questions later."

"Are you Al Pfeiffer?"

"Who the fuck else would I be?"

"I've got my—" Jeffrey slid his hand out of his pocket so he could reach for his badge. He stopped when the man moved closer, firmly pressing the barrel of the Remington under Jeffrey's right eye.

Saliva spit from Pfeiffer's mouth when he demanded, "You think I'm stupid, boy?"

Slowly, Jeffrey put both of his hands in the air. He wanted to look over his shoulder. Where was Sara? Was she safe? His heart was beating so hard in his chest that he could barely hear his own voice when he told the man, "I'm a cop."

The weapon held steady, but the fear in the man's eyes was unmistakable. "I know what you are."

"My wife is in the car. I don't want her to get hurt."

He glanced over Jeffrey's shoulder. "I don't give a fuck who's in that car. She gets out, that's the last thing you'll ever hear."

Jeffrey looked down the barrel of the shotgun at Al Pfeiffer, saw the way he struggled to keep the tremor out of his hands. He also saw the damage from the firebomb. Mottled skin slackened one side of his face, his left eye nearly closed from scarring. He was wearing a short-sleeved dress shirt, white and finely starched, the grotesque scarring on his arms showing where the flesh had been burned off the bone. There were tears in his eyes, but Jeffrey did not know if this was from pain or fear. This close up, it looked like a combination of both.

Jeffrey took a step back, away from the pressure of the barrel against his face. "I'm the chief of police for Grant County."

Pfeiffer held the shotgun steady at Jeffrey's chest. "I don't care if you're the fucking President of the United States. Get off my land."

"Why are you scared of another cop?"

"You wouldn't be here if you didn't already know the answer to that."

"I just want to talk."

"Do I look like I wanna talk to you?"

"I need to know—"

"You see this gun pointing at you, boy?" The man took a step closer, the barrel of the shotgun pressing hard into Jeffrey's chest. Pfeiffer was about half a foot shorter and twenty years older, but his voice was firm when he said, "You listenin' to me, boy?" He paused, but not for an answer. "I done told you I ain't got nothing to say to nobody. You hear? Nothing."

"I just—"

"You go back and tell them that, hear? You tell them Al Pfeiffer told you to fuck on off back to the hell you came from."

"If you could just—"

"You get off my property!" the old man screamed. "You get into that fancy car of yours and if you ever come back, I'll chop you up and throw you to the gators. You got that?"

Jeffrey knew better than to argue, especially since he was entirely confident that Al Pfeiffer was more than prepared to carry out his threat. "I got you."

"Now, get," Pfeiffer said, using the barrel to push Jeffrey away.

Jeffrey walked backward, not wanting to turn his back on the man until he absolutely had to. Fury was something he could handle, but fear made people irrational. Jeffrey didn't want to be in range of that shotgun if Al Pfeiffer decided letting Jeffrey go scot-free wasn't the right course of action.

Which, the moment Jeffrey turned around, is exactly what the man did.

The first shot must have been fired into the air, but it was loud enough to make Jeffrey hunch his shoulders. He heard Sara scream, then the second shot cracked the air. This one was a more direct warning, scattering the gravel about six inches from where Jeffrey stood. He scrambled to get out of the way, slipping on the loose stone, falling hard on his palms.

"Shit," he cursed, making himself stand. It wasn't going to be like this, not with him biting dirt while some madman played target practice. Jeffrey held up his hands in the air, yelling, "You're gonna have to shoot me in the back, if that's the kind of man you are."

The shotgun pumped again, loading another shell.

"No!" Sara screamed, pounding her fists against the window. "Jeffrey!"

He walked toward the car, hands in the air, this time leaving his back as a clear target. He stared at Sara. Her fists froze mid-strike, inches from the window. There was a valet key in the center console. She had to know that. He had told her when he put it there and she'd made some joke about having to drive to Atlanta before they'd find a valet to use it.

Sara's mouth moved. He read the words. "Hurry, hurry, hurry..."

An eternity seemed to pass as Jeffrey closed the twenty feet between himself and the car. His back felt white-hot, more from the bull's-eye painted on it than from the blazing sun.

While time had slowed down as he walked to the car, the clock started ticking as soon as he got behind the wheel. He fumbled with the keyfob, and Sara snatched it out of his hand, starting the car herself.

"Go," she begged. "Hurry."

He threw the car into reverse and punched his foot on the gas. A quick look showed him that Al Pfeiffer was still holding his stance, legs spread, back straight, shotgun pointed into the air. The bastard had a smug smile on his face as he watched the retreat. Jeffrey let off the gas a little as he reversed out of the driveway, letting the man know he shouldn't get too cocky just yet.

Jeffrey headed straight out the way they had come. The car bumped against the curve as he pulled back onto the main road. He chanced a look at Sara. She was clutching the door handle so hard that her knuckles had turned white.

As soon as they passed the post office, she told him, "Pull over."

Jeffrey slowed the car, afraid she was going to be sick.

"Pull over," she repeated, opening the door.

He slammed on the brakes. Sara didn't even wait for the car to stop before jumping out.

Jeffrey slid across the seats, following her. "Are you—"

She turned on him, slapping him square across the face. For a full ten seconds, Jeffrey was too stunned to react. She had never hit him, never so much as raised her hand.

He rubbed his face, felt the inside of his cheek with his tongue. "You wanna tell me what the hell that was about?"

Sara paced in front of him, cupping her hands over her mouth. He knew that she couldn't yell when she was this angry. Her words got caught in her throat and her tone went so low that she could barely make a sound.

"Sara—"

"You asshole," she whispered. "You stupid, arrogant *asshole*."

Jeffrey smiled because he knew that it would irritate the shit out of her. He had no idea what she was mad about, but he knew that if she slapped him again, there was going to be a real problem.

He glanced at the road as a green pickup truck drove by, slowing for the show. They hadn't seen another car since they'd entered Dug Rut. This was probably the biggest thing to hit town since the stop sign had been installed at the end of Main Street.

Sara waited for the truck to pass before asking, "Why did you slow down?"

"When did I—" He stopped. The driveway. He had slowed when he'd seen that smug look on Al Pfeiffer's face.

"You couldn't let him get the best of you, could you? You just had to slow down and goad him on." She shook her head, tears welling into her eyes. "You're just as bad as Lena. You play these games with people, these glorified pissing contests, like it's not a matter of life and death." She tapped her hand to her chest. "*My* life, Jeffrey. *Your* death."

Jeffrey tried to shrug it off. "His shots were wide. They were just a warning."

"Oh, you have no idea how consoling I find that."

"You can't let people like that know you're scared."

"*You* can't let people know you're scared," she corrected. "He had a gun, Jeffrey. A shotgun."

"We were out of range."

"Out of range?" she echoed, incredulous. She held up her finger to stop the words that were about to come out of his mouth. "You locked me in the car. He put that gun in your face and you locked me in the car."

"I was trying to protect you."

"Who was protecting *you*?" she demanded. "I'm not a child, Jeffrey. I'm not some scared little girl who needs her hand held to cross the street."

"And I am?"

She didn't answer. Her focus had shifted from Jeffrey to something over his shoulder. The green pickup was back, slowing down for another look. The windows were tinted, but as he turned, Jeffrey could make out two figures behind the dark glass as the truck rolled by. It occurred to Jeffrey that maybe the driver wasn't looking for a show. Maybe he was looking to finish what Al Pfeiffer had started.

He ordered, "Get in the car."

Sara didn't argue. She walked briskly toward the BMW and Jeffrey followed. He climbed behind the wheel and started the engine, not bothering to look for traffic as he pulled back onto the road. He glanced in the rearview mirror, watching the truck make another U-turn.

He told Sara, "They turned around."

She slipped on her seat belt, clicking it into place.

The BMW gave a slight jerk as he pressed the accelerator to the floor. The truck sped up as well. Sweat rolled down Jeffrey's back as he navigated the snaking road. Two minutes passed before the truck pulled off onto a dirt trail. Either the man had lost interest or he knew that there was no way he could take on the in-line six.

Or both Jeffrey and Sara were paranoid as hell.

"They're not following," he told her, though she had seen as much in the mirror on the visor.

She pressed her lips together, stared out the window.

He asked, "Are you all right?"

"Why did we come here?"

"What?"

"Why did we come here?" She was speaking in a regular tone of voice now, but he could tell he was still not off the hook. "Why did we have to come to this place?"

"I told you. I wanted to talk to Al Pfeiffer."

"To accomplish what?"

"To see why he left town."

"He left town because someone tried to kill him and his entire family."

Suddenly, Jeffrey found himself longing for her silence. "This is my job, Sara. I talk to people who don't want to talk to me."

"As far as I can recall, you've never been shot at by one of them before."

He let his lack of response concede the point.

She asked, "What does any of this have to do with Lena?"

"I don't know."

"How does this help find out who was in the Escalade or why they were killed?"

"I don't know that, either."

"Well," she said, rolling down the window a few inches, letting in some air. "You don't seem to know a lot of things."

Now the silence came. Jeffrey gladly welcomed it, staring ahead at the empty highway, counting off the mile markers. He found it difficult to swallow as he thought about the gravel spraying up, the gunshot ringing in his ears. Why had he slowed down the car? What primal instinct had made him take his foot off the gas, to push back at the man who had nearly pushed him into oblivion?

Pfeiffer had been carrying a Remington Wingmaster, the kind of shotgun used by most law enforcement officers. Jeffrey had lied when he'd told Sara that they were out of range when he took his foot off the gas. If Pfeiffer was a good shot, and his nearly fifty years toting a badge indicated he probably was, the man could have taken out Sara or Jeffrey with a twitch of his finger.

He had to get Sara out of here. She was right that he was like Lena, but they were alike because they were both cops. There were certain people in this world that you couldn't show your weak side to. As far as Jeffrey was concerned, Sara was his weak side. Her safety had been the first thought that came to his mind when he'd seen that shotgun. He had locked the doors because he didn't want her running to the house and getting her head blown off. He could not worry about his own safety so long as she was in jeopardy, and the only way to remedy the problem was to send Sara back to Grant County.

But, then, why had Jeffrey slowed the car? Why had he kept Sara in range of the shotgun just to prove a point? He could have gotten her killed.

At least half an hour of driving passed before his chest stopped feeling like a rubber band was around his heart, and it took another half hour for him to realize that the reason his hands were sticking to the wheel was because the side of his left palm had been ripped open on the gravel driveway.

Jeffrey coasted into the first gas station he saw.

Sara looked at the gas gauge on the dash as if to check up on him. That hadn't been why he'd stopped, but the needle was halfway down to the E, so Jeffrey decided he might as well fill up the tank. If Sara noticed the blood on his hands and the steering wheel, she didn't say anything.

Jeffrey's gun and holster were still tucked under his seat and he clipped them onto his belt as he got out of the car. He fumbled with the gas cap, fingers stiff from being wrapped around the steering wheel, and managed to get the nozzle in the tank before walking to the little convenience store. When he opened the glass door, he had to duck at the last minute to avoid a cowbell hanging from the jamb.

"Sorry about that," the clerk apologized, though the smirk on his face said watching unsuspecting customers get smacked in the head was one of his favorite pastimes. "Gotta move that thing one day."

Jeffrey glared at the young man as he made his way to the back of the store. Inside the bathroom, he looked at himself in the mirror, saw his hair was damp with sweat, that dirt had splattered his shirt when the gravel scattered. His hands were a mess and he used a paper towel to turn on the faucet so he wouldn't leave blood all over the fixture. The cold water stung like hellfire, but he kept his hands under the stream, trying to clean the debris out of his wounds.

"Jesus," he muttered, glancing into the mirror again. He shook his head, trying to think through what had happened. His intention had been to talk to Pfeiffer cop to cop, have a little off-the-record conversation about the situation in Elawah so that Jeffrey could figure out what exactly Lena had gotten herself into. Was he dealing with skinheads? Would Jake Valentine be any help? Could anybody left in the sheriff's department be trusted?

Pfeiffer had been firebombed out of town, so Jeffrey doubted seriously that the man wielded any true power. Smug attitude aside, the ex-sheriff had obviously been terrified to find Jeffrey at his front door. A cop was only afraid of another cop for one reason: corruption. The question was, who was crooked in Elawah's sheriff's department? Jeffrey wouldn't put Jake Valentine at the top of his list, but you never knew. And of course there was always Deputy Donald Cook, who Nick had easily pegged for taking something under the table. Cook certainly wasn't happy with his job. He'd made no attempt to hide the fact that he thought his boss was an idiot.

But all of this kept bringing him back to Sara's big question: what did any of it have to do with Lena?

Nothing. It was all a bunch of loose threads that may or may not tie together. Skinheads trafficked meth, Hank Norton used meth. Ethan

Green was a skinhead, the thug in the white sedan was a skinhead. Al Pfeiffer was terrified of cops, Lena had escaped from the cops.

Someone had died in Lena's presence. There had to be something out there that Jeffrey was missing, some piece of information that would pull it all together. There had to be a reason Lena had left that hospital without talking to him first. She could be ball-breakingly stubborn about so many things, but she was not stupid. There had to be a logical explanation.

Using one of the flimsy paper towels from the dispenser, Jeffrey washed his face as best he could, patting his neck and chest to clean off the dried blood. His hand was still throbbing, but he tried to ignore it as he walked back through the store.

"What's the damage?" Jeffrey asked, pulling out his county credit card.

"Sorry." The clerk pointed to a sign behind him that said, "In God we trust. All others pay cash."

"Right." Fortunately, Jeffrey had dropped by a cash machine before heading out of Grant County yesterday afternoon. He pointed to the first-aid packets behind the clerk. "Give me a couple packs of those aspirin, too."

"Thirty-eight fifty-three," the clerk told him, tossing the aspirin on the counter and taking the bills Jeffrey handed him. "Bad day?"

Jeffrey ripped open the pack with his teeth. "What do you think?"

The clerk bristled. "No need to take it out on me, buddy." He rang the sale and handed Jeffrey the change. "You take care, now."

"You, too," Jeffrey managed, ducking past the cowbell as he left the store.

In the car, Sara kept her own counsel. Jeffrey pulled back onto the road and followed the signs back to the highway.

The sun was finally setting as he managed to get to the interstate. The aspirin hadn't even touched his headache. Sara must have been exhausted. By the time they crossed into Elawah County, her head was tilted to her shoulder, and she was making that soft, clicking noise she always made when she slept.

Jeffrey took the unopened bottle of water she'd bought him at the rest stop and drank it down. There was some wisdom to the adage that you should be careful what you wish for. This morning, he'd been thinking it would be nice to see a flash of Sara's anger. Now, all that he could think was that it was a hell of a lot easier to love her when she was sleeping.

The sign outside the motel was barely doing its job when he pulled into the space in front of their room. Only seven letters were left to illuminate the entire parking lot. Jeffrey cut the engine as he surveyed their surroundings. A black Dodge Ram was parked a few spaces down from him. The flickering light in the hotel office told him that the manager was watching television. When Jeffrey had checked in, the boy had glanced up from the set with glassy eyes, so bored he could barely manage to blink. Jeffrey imagined there were worse jobs you could have. Working a convenience store where your biggest thrill came from whacking strangers in the head with a cowbell came to mind.

Jeffrey reached over and gently shook Sara awake. She squinted at the hotel, confused for a moment, then sat up, obviously remembering soon enough where they were and what had happened.

He couldn't keep himself from asking, "You okay?"

She nodded, opening the door, getting out of the car.

Jeffrey followed suit, stretching his back as he stood. His hand went to his holster when he heard a noise behind him.

"Sorry about that." Jake Valentine came out of the shadows, an open beer bottle in one hand, a small cooler in the other. He startled when he saw Jeffrey. "Something happen?"

"Just went for a drive," was the best that Jeffrey could come up with.

Sara walked toward the motel room, offering, "I'll leave you two alone."

"Uh, ma'am?" Valentine stopped her. "I just wanted to say I'm real sorry for what I said last night. Heat of the moment and all. I should've just held my tongue. I didn't mean what I said."

She nodded. "Thank you for apologizing."

If Valentine had been expecting a more grateful response, he was talking to the wrong woman. Jeffrey unlocked the door for her. Sara reached down and wrapped her hand around his wrist, letting it rest there for a few seconds. He felt pathetically grateful for the gesture and gave her the room key because it seemed like a symbolic thing to do. She smiled at him—genuinely smiled—and he felt the band that had been squeezing his chest for the last four hours loosen some more.

"Only be a minute," Valentine said, as if he was worried Jeffrey would follow Sara into the room.

Jeffrey was tempted, but as the door clicked shut, he asked Valentine, "What's going on, Jake? You find Lena?"

Valentine chuckled as he put the cooler on the ground and pulled out a fresh beer. Jeffrey saw four empties tucked into what was left of the ice. "Brought you one of these. Peace offering."

"Thanks," Jeffrey said, holding the cold bottle against his head. He'd driven at least ten hours today on about two hours of sleep. His muscles ached, his head throbbed and the last thing he wanted to be doing right now was talking to Jake Valentine.

Still, he walked toward the front of the motel, seeing if the sheriff would follow. The man obviously wanted something, and Jeffrey was going to make it as difficult as possible for the sheriff to ask for his favor. He could consider it payback for their little do-si-do in the linen closet last night.

A long tunnel ran behind the front office of the motel, giving access to either side. Jeffrey wasn't really hungry, but he knew he should try to eat something. He asked Valentine, "You got any money?"

Valentine pulled a handful of coins out of his pocket. Jeffrey took what he needed and fed it into the machine. He stared at the candy bars and crackers, trying to decide which was less likely to give him indigestion. He settled on SunChips and made the selection.

"I like those, too," Valentine offered.

Jeffrey held out the bag. "You want some?" Valentine shook his head and Jeffrey took a seat on one of the wooden benches opposite the vending machines. He ripped the bag open with his teeth and ate a few chips. They were stale.

Valentine just stood there watching him, obviously not knowing what to do. He looked even younger out of his uniform, his spaghetti build punctuated by the high-waisted jeans and overlarge polo shirt. The Georgia Bulldog red ball cap he was wearing wasn't helping much, either. It sat tilted slightly to the side on his narrow head. Even with the noticeable bulge from his ankle holster, he looked like a starter for the varsity basketball team.

If Jake Valentine was the secret drug kingpin of Elawah County, he was sure hiding it well.

"Nice night," Valentine murmured. "You and the wife out for a drive?"

Jeffrey opened the bottle with a twist, ignoring the pain shooting through his hand. He hated beer, but his head was hurting so bad he would've drunk poison to make it stop pounding.

Valentine said, "All jokes aside, still no sign of your detective."

Jeffrey wasn't surprised. Short of Lena knocking on the front door of the jail and asking to be let in, he doubted very seriously that she would be found. Jeffrey had asked Frank Wallace to keep an eye on her credit cards, but Jeffrey assumed nothing had come up or Frank would've called. He also asked the senior detective to keep an eye out in Heartsdale, but both men had agreed that it was highly unlikely Lena would show back up in Grant County.

Jeffrey stared at the abandoned building on the other side of the motel, a tin-roofed hovel that some enterprising soul had painted to look like a grass shack.

"Hank's place," Valentine volunteered, nodding toward the building. "Bartender was selling meth from behind the counter. ATF said a secret informer tipped 'em off. Told me this after the fact, mind you. First I heard about it was Junior, the night manager here, calling to ask me did I know Hank's bar was surrounded by sixty state police cars."

Jeffrey took another swig from the bottle. He could hear the trickle of a stream, the swaying of trees in the forest that backed onto the hotel and bar. He wanted to be home, floating on his back in the lake, the sound of Sara and her sister's laughter muffled by the cool water. He wanted to be in bed, lying on his back, with Sara's mouth on him.

Valentine cut through his thoughts. "I'm guessing you already knew about Hank's bar," he said. "Just like I'm guessing you're the one who cut the ATF tape on the back door."

"Good guess," Jeffrey said, though he had a feeling Lena had done the honors. So, she was looking for something. The cut tape was like a fingerprint. All it told you was that someone had been there. It didn't tell you when or why. Maybe she had gone there for money. Maybe she had been there last night while Jeffrey and Sara tried to sleep.

"Anyway..." Valentine stubbed his toe against the asphalt. "I was in the neighborhood and figured I'd just..."

Jeffrey gave a heavy sigh as he stood from the bench, too tired to let this play out slow. "I take it from the empty bottles in your cooler that you've been here a while. You're not in uniform, so you're trying to look like you're off duty, but the fact that a three-year-old could spot that ankle holster tells me you've either been watching too much TV or you've got something to be afraid of. My bet's on the last one."

Valentine chuckled, but Jeffrey could tell the younger man was shaken. He looked out at the parking lot, took a long pull from his beer.

Jeffrey tossed the empty SunChips bag into the trash. "Tell me about Al Pfeiffer."

"Al retired."

"Why?"

"Wanted to spend more time with his grandbabies."

"And less time on fire?"

Valentine's eyes narrowed. "Why're you interested in that old man?"

Jeffrey took a healthy mouthful of beer, trying not to shudder from the bitter taste. Not only did Valentine look like a teenager, he had the tastes of one. Jeffrey would've bet his pension the kid hadn't paid more than three bucks for the six-pack.

"Lookit," Valentine said. "I just wanted to let you know we've got the coroner coming in tomorrow."

Finally, the reason for his visit. "That so?"

"He's gonna look at the body from the Escalade, let us know what he thinks happened."

"Sounds like a good plan."

"You mentioned before about your wife..." Valentine's voice trailed off. When he saw that Jeffrey wasn't going to help him, he added, "It just sounded to me like she's got a lot of experience."

Jeffrey could not believe what he was hearing. "She does."

"I'd be real grateful if you could have her come over, maybe look at the body, tell us what she sees."

Jeffrey tried to see the angles, to figure out why Valentine would make such a request. Nothing came to mind, and the beer wasn't helping. "I thought you said your guy was good."

"Oh, he is, but something like this...look, we'd pay her. We've still got some money left in the budget. Just tell me what her rate is."

Jeffrey knocked back the rest of the beer and immediately wished he had another, then he thought of his father and wished he hadn't drunk anything at all.

Valentine took his silence the wrong way. "I can get cash if—"

"Are they paying you off?"

"What's that?"

Jeffrey pressed his empty bottle into the man's chest. "Something's going on in your town and you're either a part of it or you're taking money to look the other way."

Valentine gave a forced laugh. "You sure those are my only options?"

Jeffrey warned him, "Listen, Barney Fife, I'm going to find out what's going on here one way or another, and I don't care whose toes I have to step on to do it."

"You gonna punch me again?"

Jeffrey thought back to Sara slapping him, how powerless she must have felt locked in the car. "I might."

Valentine leaned down to put Jeffrey's bottle in the cooler. When he straightened, he gave Jeffrey a lazy, half-smile like they were old friends. "You should come to my house for supper sometime."

Jeffrey walked back down the tunnel toward the parking lot. "Why would I want to do that?"

Valentine matched his stride. "I'll show you around, point out the little projects I've been working on." He flashed his goofy grin. "I'm a lot handier than I look."

"You going somewhere with this?"

"We're trying to build a deck out back. Every payday, we buy a couple of pieces of cedar for it. The wife figures it'll take a year before we've got everything we need, but we're real patient people. We're not like some folks who can just throw money around, raising mansions out of swampland. We just take our time and do it the right way."

He was talking about Al Pfeiffer. Jeffrey wondered if Valentine knew his old boss had been paid a visit today. Pfeiffer probably still had ties to the community, maybe came back to see friends. People would know where he was living. They would keep in touch.

Jeffrey was in front of the room. He pointed to the door. "This is my stop."

Valentine tipped his hat. "You enjoy your evening, Chief. Let me know what your wife says."

Jeffrey watched the man put the cooler in the passenger seat of his black truck, then walk around to the driver's side. He opened the door and tossed Jeffrey a wave before getting in. Once the truck pulled away, Jeffrey could see the desk clerk peering out the window. He felt the kid's eyes on him as he knocked on the door.

Sara wasn't exactly smiling when she opened the door, but she hadn't called him a stupid asshole in at least four hours, so maybe his luck had turned.

The room was as dank as it was depressing; exactly as Jeffrey had remembered it from the night before. Sara had already removed the dark, multi-patterned coverlet off the bed. He wondered how much DNA had been transferred in the process.

She asked, "What did our new best friend want?"

"For you to do the autopsy on the body."

"Why would he want that?"

"Good question," he replied, sitting on the bed. He thought better of it and lay down on his side, bunching the pillows up under his head, kicking off his shoes. "Add that to the long list of things I don't know."

She walked to the door and checked the lock, then turned out the lights. In the dark, the mattress shifted as she got into bed. Like Jeffrey, she didn't bother to take off her clothes. He waited for her to curl up beside him, but she didn't.

Sara had once told him that even when they were divorced, she'd still had nightmares about getting a phone call in the middle of the night. It was something even cops couldn't joke about, that fateful call that told your wife or girlfriend or lover that your number had finally come up. Some coked-out idiot or stupid drunk had pulled a knife, squeezed the trigger, and there was nothing your loved ones could do but pick up the phone, wait for the words.

She must have been thinking about that today when Al Pfeiffer pulled the trigger. She must have been terrified that she was going to be trapped in the car, unable to help him, watching him die.

"Jeff?" He wasn't sure what he expected Sara to say to him, but as usual, she managed to come up with something he could have never anticipated. "I was thinking about fixing the patio—maybe replacing some of those broken stones, making the wall a little higher so people can sit on it without their knees going up around their ears." She paused. "What do you think?"

He rolled over onto his back. A thin stream of light was coming in through the curtains and he could just make out her profile. "I think the last time you messed with concrete, we had to borrow your dad's jackhammer."

"The bag said it was self-leveling."

He smiled at the familiar excuse.

"I want to do the autopsy."

Jeffrey didn't know what to say. His initial response was to say no, but that was only because Jake Valentine had asked her to do it. "I don't know that it'll get us out of here any sooner."

Her silence told him she wasn't going to be easily swayed. Jeffrey tried to frame his next words carefully, offering, "I can ask Frank to drive down here and pick you up after you're finished."

"No," she told him. "I'm not going to leave you."

"What if I want you to?"

The phone started to ring before she could answer. Jeffrey leaned over her and picked up the receiver.

"Hello?"

"Why are you still there?"

Jeffrey sat up so fast that he jerked the phone off the bedside table. "Lena?"

"You can't be there," she said, her voice a raspy whisper. "Why are you still there?"

"Where are you?" he asked. "Let me come get you."

She started crying, sobs choking her words. "Why...?" she cried. "Why didn't they kill me instead?"

"Who?" he demanded, confused. "Who are you talking about?"

"Just go," she begged. "You have to go before they—"

"Who's they, Lena? Who's after you?" All he heard was the staccato of her breath. "Lena?" He pressed the phone to his ear. "Lena? Are you there? Where are you? Let me come get you."

The line went dead.

WEDNESDAY MORNING

CHAPTER 9

SARA USED HER THUMB to trace the pattern of dried blood on the BMW's steering wheel as she followed Jake Valentine's cruiser through downtown Reece. Shock or trauma or a combination of the two had managed to knock her out last night. She had slept more deeply than she had in months. Had Jake Valentine not banged on their door at seven-thirty this morning, she would probably still be in bed.

Up ahead in Valentine's car, she could see Jeffrey having an animated conversation with the sheriff. Sara hoped to God he was managing to get some information out of the man. Common sense told her this would not be the case. Jeffrey hadn't told Valentine about Lena's phone call last night because he knew the man would trace the number. For his part, Valentine wasn't offering any updates on the manhunt. This morning, when he'd seen the cuts on Jeffrey's face and hands in the daylight, all he'd said was, "Hate to see the other guy."

Sara hadn't even noticed until then how badly he'd been hurt. She had always taken care of Jeffrey's body. Over the years, she had disinfected his cuts, rubbed arnica gel into his bruises, bandaged sprained ankles and broken fingers. After impromptu football games, she had iced his knee so he could walk the next morning. Hours he spent fixing things around the house were rewarded with long back rubs and whatever else she could think of to help him relax. Even after the divorce, when Sara couldn't stand to be in the same room with him, she had rushed to the hospital when a stray round of buckshot had lodged in his leg.

She hadn't seen him cut open his hand yesterday. She had seen the shotgun being fired into the air, then the second warning shot, close enough to stop her heart beating in her chest. She had watched Jeffrey lurch forward, sliding on the gravel, but she hadn't thought to check him out, to look for cuts and abrasions. All she'd been able to focus on was the absolute terror she'd felt each time Al Pfeiffer pulled the trigger, and her white-hot fury when Jeffrey had slowed the car afterward.

His foot had come off the pedal. Sara had thought something was wrong with the car. She had looked down, panicked, to see what was wrong, and seen exactly why the car had slowed almost to a full stop. She had looked at Jeffrey then, the way his mouth twisted up at the corner as Al Pfeiffer gave him that look. God, that look. Sara had wanted to slap it off his face. They were just like a couple of boys on the playground seeing who could kick the most dirt in the other's face before a teacher came along. Lena was the same way—she didn't have a dick to swing around, but she could certainly kick up dirt with the best of them.

That was when Sara had finally realized why they had really trekked all the way down to the swamp, why Jeffrey was clutching at the slimmest lead to Lena's disappearance he could find. Sara had been the one standing outside the bathroom when Lena ran, but Jeffrey had been in the hallway. He had been less than ten feet from Lena, less than ten feet from stopping her escape.

Jeffrey had been duped, too, and his ego wouldn't let him get past it.

Last year, Sara had taken a ballistics course at the GBI academy in Macon. She had just dealt with two shooting cases at the morgue and she wanted to better equip herself for investigating gun-related crime. As part of the course, there had been a technical session at the firing range. The instructor had used different weapons and ammunition to shoot gel-filled dummies at various distances to give the students a better understanding of pattern and dispersal. The Remington Wingmaster was one of the most popular shotguns on the market, favored by police and bad guys alike. Using heavy density shot, the weapon dispersed sixty percent of its pellets into the target from a distance of sixty yards.

By Sara's estimation, when Jeffrey had slowed the car yesterday, they were approximately sixty yards from Al Pfeiffer.

He should be glad she lived long enough to slap him.

Up ahead, Valentine turned on his blinker. Sara followed the cruiser into the Elawah County impound lot. There were about fifty trucks in various states of destruction piled around the compound, front ends hanging off like loose teeth, back bumpers crumpled into tailgates. Knowing small towns, she guessed that most of the owners either did not have the money to get their trucks out of impound or they were still in jail waiting to be tried on drunk-driving charges. Basically, the county lot was a glorified insurance processing unit.

The sheriff's car bumped down a short gravel strip, then parked on a paved lot. Ahead, Sara saw a large metal building, about fifteen feet high by thirty feet square, and guessed that the car from the accident had been towed into the building for examination.

Not that what had happened to the Cadillac Escalade had been an accident. Sara tried to enter every case with an open mind as to cause, but it wasn't as if an SUV found burning in the middle of a football field could have gotten there by chance. Someone had parked it there, deliberately set it on fire, and walked away, leaving the body inside.

The question remained: was that someone Lena Adams?

Sara got out of her car. The smell of gasoline and oil mixed in the air with an undertone of car exhaust. No noise came from the shop. She guessed the mechanics were taking their morning break.

Jeffrey and Valentine walked toward the BMW. The sheriff kicked some mud off the wheel. "Looks like you've been off-roading, Chief."

Jeffrey told him, "I was down around the Okefenokee yesterday."

Valentine's eyebrows shot up. "That so?" he asked, making a show of scratching his chin. So much for peace and understanding being brokered on the drive over. He told Jeffrey, "I know some folks who moved down to the swamp a while back."

"Friends of yours?"

"Oh, I wouldn't say that." Seemingly out of the blue, the sheriff announced, " 'Land of the Trembling Ground.' "

Jeffrey was silent, so Sara asked, "I'm sorry?"

Valentine explained, "That's what the Indians called it. Okefenokee, Land of the Trembling Ground. Only about six percent of the swamp is on solid ground, see. The rest is just a couple of feet of felled vegetation riding on top of the water. You walk on it and it's like walking on a pool float, only a little bit easier." He tipped his hat down, blocking the sun out of his face. "You go down there, too, ma'am?"

"Yes, I had the pleasure."

"Lots of skeeters, gators, even some meat-eating plants." He chuckled at this last bit, as if it brought back a fond memory. "My daddy took me and my little brother there once when we were kids. Took us three days to paddle from the east to west side; liked to nearly killed us. Saw all kinds of crazy things." His eyes slid over Jeffrey's way, and his affable voice changed to a warning. "Dangerous place down there."

Jeffrey crossed his arms over his chest. "I guess for some it might be."

Yet again, Sara had managed to get downwind at a pissing contest. She clapped her hands together to break the standoff, telling Valentine, "Well, I suppose the body is inside?"

"Yes, ma'am," he said, indicating the office beside the building.

Sara walked toward the office, the two men following.

Valentine asked Sara, "How was the drive down to the swamp?"

"Fine, thank you."

He reached ahead of her to open the door. He chuckled to himself. "Say, you didn't happen to see Lena Adams down there thumbing a ride, did you?"

Sara forced a smile back on her face. "Afraid not."

Valentine smiled back as he opened the door. "Had to ask."

Instead of the filing cabinets and desks Sara had been expecting, they walked right into what could only be the morgue. A large stainless steel gurney was chocked to the concrete floor, an open, empty body bag lay on top. The sink and dissecting trays up against the wall were much like the ones back at the Grant morgue, but the freezer for body storage was a walk-in type used in larger restaurants. She didn't see a Dictaphone. Jeffrey would have to take notes on her findings.

"Not too shabby," Valentine interjected, though she could tell from the look on his face that he was slightly ashamed of the morgue's location. "Most of our autopsies are car wrecks, accidents, that kind of thing. We handle the load from Seskatoga, Ahlmira, and a couple of other counties. Having the morgue on site makes it easy to take them from one to the other."

"Of course," Sara said, feeling like she had just insulted the man when in fact the facilities were more than serviceable. She was lucky not to be stuck in the embalming room at the local funeral parlor. "Where's the Escalade?"

"Through here," he said, opening another door. A large, open warehouse was on the other side. Two desks and a row of filing cabinets were shoved into the corner. Tools lined the far wall. Six hydraulic lifts had cars on them, but no mechanics were in sight. Car parts were scattered around, crashed vehicles in various states of disassemble so that damage could be assessed, blame placed on the right head. Sitting in the middle of the warehouse was obviously the SUV. It was draped in a gray tarp, plastic spread underneath to protect the floor.

Valentine walked toward the Cadillac, explaining, "We towed it straight here once the metal cooled down. Being honest, all the fire department did was keep the field wet while they let the fire burn itself out. Not much left after that."

Sara reached into her pocket and pulled out a band to tie her hair into a ponytail. She asked Valentine, "Do you know the cause of fire?"

The sheriff shook his head. "Some kind of accelerant was used, but the kicker was the gas tank going off. They're not sure if it was rigged or not, but you can tell from the back of the car that the tank exploded. Must have been pretty full, from the looks of it."

Jeffrey asked, "Did you hear an explosion?"

Valentine looked thoughtful as he grabbed on to the tarp and started rolling it back. "Come to think of it, maybe I did. It's hard putting the pieces together after the fact."

"I guess so," Jeffrey said, in a way that made it sound like he thought the other man was lying. He stepped forward to help Valentine roll back the tarp.

Sara tuned out their conversation as she stood in front of the decimated Cadillac. The car was a shell of its former self. The tires had melted so that the frame sat on soot-blackened steel rims. Parts of the roof had been blown away but, surprisingly, some of the leather and the foam padding for the seats remained.

"Guess the cushions were treated or something," Valentine offered. "We can call in the shop guys to unbolt the frame when you're ready to move the body."

Sara looked into the backseat. Cutting the corpse away from the leather would take hours. It would be like separating pieces of wet toilet tissue.

Still, it had to be done.

She leaned into the car, assessing the victim. The body's frame was small, but that did not necessarily mean it belonged to a woman. It could be a teenage boy or a man with a build similar to Valentine's. No matter who it was, the death this human being had suffered had obviously been excruciating. The arms and legs were flexed in a pugilistic fashion, as if the victim had tried to fight off the flames. Heat-related fractures riddled what Sara could see of the bones. The left hand had been engulfed, completely eaten off by fire. The hair had been burned away, the flat orbs of the eyes left lidless in their sockets.

She asked, "Have you taken photographs?"

Valentine nodded and she leaned farther into the car, trying not to touch anything as she checked to see if the seat belt had been buckled. The actual belt had been burned away—part of it had melted into the flesh—but she saw the metal buckle firmly secured and assumed the passenger had been restrained.

Had the victim tried to get out, Sara wondered. What was it like to be trapped in the back of a burning SUV, flames licking up around you, as you struggled with the seat belt, scratched at the door handle, desperately trying to get out?

Horrifying, she decided. It must have been absolutely horrifying.

Several long seconds, perhaps a full minute, must have passed before the body gave up, the organs shut down. This was not counting the wait before the fire caught, before the gas tank exploded. There was no telling how many minutes ticked by as the victim waited for the inevitable.

Sara's lips parted as she went in for a closer look, trying not to inhale the distinctive odor of burned flesh.

Around seventy-five percent of the skin from the external surface of the body had been burned away. Most of the underlying muscles and ligature were scorched but not completely destroyed. The top of the head and the back of the skull were essentially charred off, and Sara could see shattered bits of teeth and the side of the tongue through a large hole in the left side of the victim's jaw. The jawbone was remarkably white, and she had to assume that the chunk of flesh covering it had been knocked away as the body was jarred during transport.

A patch of skin the size of a standard piece of paper was missing from the torso, and Sara could clearly see the chest wall and thoracic contents. The abdominal organs were likewise exposed, the liver sitting like a cooked piece of dark meat under the frayed strips of the stomach; it had obviously exploded from the intense heat. Sara imagined the tiny pieces of what looked like blackened cork dotting the outside of the small intestines would turn out to be the burned remains of the stomach contents.

What remained of the skin around the thighs had melted into the seat, sinew draping like Christmas tinsel down the legs. Crusty remnants of a pair of blue jeans and white underwear were still stuck in place where body fluids had leaked into the material then dried. The top of a white sock circled the left ankle. Though there was scant residual skin on both feet, a split piece of toenail remained on the right big toe. A square of chipped, pink nail polish showed. Sara leaned down, moved in closer. The area around the pubis had extensive damage, but she was fairly certain she was looking at a woman's genitalia.

She closed her eyes for just a second, unbelievably relieved that the victim was not Hank Norton. It gave her some hope that Lena's involvement in the crime did not run as deep as Jake Valentine believed.

"Sara?" Jeffrey asked. There was a slight edge to his voice. "You okay?"

"Yes," she told him, giving a slight shake of her head to answer the question that was obvious to everyone but the sheriff.

Valentine said, "Pretty bad, huh?"

Sara nodded. "Has your coroner seen the body?"

"Just a quick look-see on the field that night," Valentine supplied. "Fred says he's never seen anything like it. Worst case he's ever had. Oh—" He stopped abruptly, as if he'd just remembered something. "Once we get the body out, we'll give Fred a call and get him over to help with the X-rays. The machine's real temperamental. You might not want to try it on your own."

"Fred is your coroner?" Jeffrey asked.

"Yep," Valentine confirmed. "Fred Bart. He's in the middle of a root canal right now, but he said to just give him a call and he'll hop on over."

Sara must have looked confused because Valentine barked a laugh. "He's *doing* the root canal, not getting it. Fred's the only dentist in town. Does the coroner's job for fishing money, he says. Real nice guy, but he knows when to let an expert take over." Valentine offered a weak smile. "Which brings me to thanking you again for doing this, Dr. Linton. I know we haven't talked about fees yet, but I ran by the bank this morning."

He pulled out a wad of bills and Sara felt a blush working its way up her neck. She had assumed she was doing this as a favor. There was a difference between getting a check from Grant County and taking cash from Jake Valentine. The thought of money changing hands made her feel cheap.

Valentine counted out some twenties, explaining, "We usually pay Fred around two-fifty a pop, but I—" He stopped as the opening bars of "I Wish I Was in Dixie" chimed from his pants pocket. "Sorry about that," he apologized, fumbling with the money as he tried to locate his cell phone. He opened the phone with the usual hello, but didn't say much else as he listened. Only a few seconds passed before his mouth dropped open.

Abruptly, he told the caller, "I'll be right there," then ended the call.

Jeffrey exchanged a glance with Sara before asking the sheriff, "Something wrong?"

"I gotta go," Valentine told them, suddenly serious. "There's been a bad accident on the highway. Guy I went to school with slid under an eighteen-wheeler." He tucked the money back into his pocket, realized what he had done, and offered it to Sara.

"No," she told him, not taking the cash. "Thank you."

Valentine seemed too distracted to be surprised. He pocketed the money again. "You mind if I leave you to this?"

Sara let Jeffrey answer. "No problem. Is there anything I can do to help?"

"No," Valentine said, a little too quickly, his tone a little too high, as if he was afraid Jeffrey would offer to come along. He seemed to realize this and added, "Thank you, though," then made a hasty exit, almost jogging to the door.

Jeffrey said, "Well, at least we know why he wanted you to do the autopsy."

Sara looked at the body, calculated the time it would take to dissect the poor creature. "We'll be tied up here for most of the day."

"What's he trying to keep us away from, though?" They heard the sheriff's car start, wheels crunching on gravel. Jeffrey said, "Either that bastard's really sharp or really stupid. I can't figure which."

"Policemen aren't known for their stunning intelligence."

He cut his eyes at her. "You're feeling better."

Sara didn't know how to take the comment. Beyond his obvious sarcasm, the fact was that she *did* feel better. Whether it was from last night's heavy sleep or yesterday's outburst, she felt as if she had gotten some sense of herself back. She had walked into the morgue without any hesitation. Her assessment of the body had come like second nature. She had not second-guessed herself or worried about being told she was wrong or stupid or incompetent. She had simply done her job.

He said, "If I'd known it was going to help this much, I would've rustled up a dead body sooner."

She laughed because he probably had a point. "Some husband you are."

"I'm not going to apologize."

She knew he was talking about yesterday. She also knew from being with him for what seemed like the past million years that the world was not going to come to an end if they were annoyed with each other.

She told him, "I'm not going to apologize, either."

That settled, Jeffrey indicated the burned remains in the SUV. "So, it's not Hank."

"No, it's a woman."

"I guess that's a relief."

"Yes," she agreed. "But it raises the bigger question—"

He finished her sentence. "Who is she, and how is she connected to Lena?" He leaned over for a better look at the body. "What do you think?"

Sara gave him an honest answer. "I think I'd rather be home digging up the patio."

He glanced back at her. "It's not too late to back out."

"You know I can't do that."

"Did you see this?" he asked, pointing toward the neck. "What do you think it is?"

Sara was about to ask what he meant but as she turned the light caught the glint of a thin gold chain seared into the flesh. "A necklace of some kind. We really need X-rays."

"I could look up Fred Bart in the phone book and give him a call. Try to get an idea of when he's going to be here."

Sara knelt down beside the SUV so she could see how the seat was anchored. Fred Bart had obviously handled his share of auto accidents. If Jeffrey was right and Jake Valentine had thrown the autopsy to Sara in order to keep an eye on them, Bart would probably not be too eager to help out. She told Jeffrey, "We can go ahead and get her out before he comes."

"You're sure it's a woman?"

"Unless I've forgotten basic anatomy," she answered. "Jake didn't seem too curious about my findings."

Jeffrey shrugged.

"Am I imagining things, or did it seem like he didn't care one way or the other?" Jeffrey shrugged again, so she continued, "Or, maybe he already knows who this is? And if you shrug again—"

"I don't know, Sara. I can't tell you anything because I just don't know."

She stared at him, wondering why she kept forgetting how irritatingly stubborn he could be. Probably for the same reason he kept forgetting how persistent she was.

Sara turned her attention back to the car. "Can you look for a large wrench?" She studied the bolts holding down the seat more closely. "On second thought," she told him. "Look for a torch."

This was going to be a long day.

LENA

CHAPTER 10

LENA PULLED INTO THE TEACHERS' PARKING LOT at the high school, noticing that her eight-year-old Celica was the best car in the lot. She had once teased Sibyl about the fact that after spending a zillion years working on various college degrees, her professor's salary at Grant Tech had been just five thousand dollars more a year than what Lena made as a cop. Sibyl had pointed out that Lena ran the risk of getting shot for five thousand dollars less a year than a college professor made and it had stopped being so funny.

It was no secret that Lena hadn't exactly been a star student at Elawah High. She'd made straight Bs and Cs until high school, or more specifically, until puberty, then everything went downhill from there. She had flunked algebra twice, spending two summers making it up so she could graduate on time. The thought of quitting had never occurred to her, but she knew from Hank that the current dropout rate at Elawah was almost fifty percent. Not many kids saw the point in applied physics when they were pretty much going to end up at the tire plant slinging rubber anyway.

Charlotte Warren's husband worked at the plant. Of course, she wasn't Charlotte Warren anymore. Larry Gibson had graduated the same year as Charlotte. When Sibyl had left for college, the two had obviously started seeing each other. Three kids later and Larry was middle management at the tire plant while Charlotte bided her time teaching. They were well on their way to the American dream except for the fact that, according to the letters Lena had found in Hank's office, the woman was miserable.

"What is wrong with me?" Charlotte had written. "Why can't I be happy?"

Lena couldn't focus on Charlotte's marital misery now, though. She was here to find out information about Hank and what had caused him to slip back into his old ways. She needed to find out why he had lied to them and what had happened to her mother. Charlotte Warren might know his secrets. You didn't write about the kind of secrets Charlotte had revealed in her letters to a stranger. Though the last letter Lena found was dated over a month ago, Charlotte had pretty much poured out her heart to Hank. Lena was betting Hank had returned the favor. If she couldn't get answers from her uncle, then she would get them from his confidant.

There was no guard at the school's front entrance and Lena was able to walk right in. There was a directory of classrooms on the front wall and Lena found Charlotte Gibson's easily enough.

Like many rural schools, the building was a one-story structure with plenty of room to grow but no money to make it happen. Ten trailers, or "temporary classrooms" were stacked along the back of the building and overlooking the football field. Lena stood at the open back door and looked at the sorry trailers. They might be calling them temporary, but Lena knew that at least two of them dated from her time as a senior. Some of them were on poured concrete slabs but most of the classrooms were on stilts. Weeds shot up between empty soda cans and wadded-up sheets of paper that students had thrown underneath them. Rickety wooden stairs led to open doors and she wondered if the buildings were air-conditioned. They couldn't have been more than eight feet by fifteen and knowing the county, the school was packing kids in there like meat. No wonder the dropout rate was so high. Lena had been here for less than five minutes and she was already anxious to leave.

She walked along the concrete walkway that fronted the trailers, thinking it was strange that Charlotte had been slotted back behind the school. Surely she had enough seniority to warrant a real classroom inside the building. Then again, the woman was lucky to have her job. Judging from the letters Lena had found, Hank had been Charlotte's AA sponsor. Up until a year ago, it'd taken the woman a swig of gin just to get out of bed.

"Do you want to go see the principal?" a teacher's voice bellowed from an open door, and Lena cringed, remembering the many times teachers had asked her the same thing. Not that it was a question; if you got them mad enough to ask, you were pretty much going to the office anyway.

The trailer at the very end was Charlotte's, and it looked to be the worst of the lot. The bottom stair had rotted through and someone had placed cinder blocks on the ground to make up the step. The door was open, a screen door hanging crookedly from the jamb. Inside, Lena could see two long rows of desks facing the back of the trailer where Charlotte was bent over a stack of papers. No one else in the classroom.

Lena stood outside the door, watching Charlotte grade papers. Now that she was here, she did not know what to say to the woman. Lena felt as if she'd somehow violated Charlotte by reading her letters. Maybe she had. Charlotte's words were deeply personal, meant only for Hank. If the shoe were on the other foot, if Charlotte had read Lena's personal letters, Lena would have been furious.

Still, it was clear now that Charlotte knew more about Hank than she'd let on in the library. The two had obviously shared a deep friendship. God knew the woman could keep a secret. Lena was used to getting people to blab their darkest deeds, whether it was stealing a car or murdering a spouse. She had to think of this as an interview for a case rather than something that affected her personally. Jeffrey's words echoed in her ears: *Make the suspect comfortable, make some small talk, then make her tell the truth.*

Lena knocked on the screen door once before she realized it wasn't attached to anything. It started to fall to the side and she caught it, a shard of wood piercing the fleshy part of her palm.

"Shit," she hissed, letting the screen hit the ground.

"Splinter?" Charlotte asked. She had managed to cross the trailer while Lena wrestled with the door.

Lena sucked at her hand, nodding.

"Come on in," Charlotte offered. If she was surprised to see Lena, she didn't say so.

"Why do they have you stuck out here?" Lena asked, walking inside. Bright posters decorated the walls and the room was clean and orderly, but there was no hiding the fact that it was little more than a tin box baking in the sun. The floor was springy under her feet and someone had used a bright silver tape to try to seal up the single-paned windows.

Charlotte pulled the door to and turned on the air-conditioning unit hanging on the wall. She had to raise her voice over the hum of the machine when she offered, "You want me to look at your hand?"

Lena sat on the edge of Charlotte's desk and held out her hand.

"Not too bad," Charlotte appraised, squinting at the splinter. She was more relaxed in the classroom than she'd been in the library. She seemed like an adult here, as if she were in her element. "I can get that out with a needle if you—"

Lena jerked her hand back. "No, thanks. It'll work itself out."

Charlotte smiled, sitting in one of the student desks. "Still scared of needles?"

"Still scared of clowns?"

Charlotte laughed as if she'd forgotten her childhood terror. "You can get used to a lot of things."

Except having sex with your husband, Lena thought. She looked around the trailer, saw the water stains on the ceiling and felt the breeze from the poorly insulated windows. "Who'd you piss off?"

"Sue Kurylowicz." When Lena didn't react, she explained, "You'd remember her as Sue Swallows."

"Swallowin' Sue who used to blow guys behind the Stop 'n' Save?"

Charlotte laughed again; another thing she had forgotten. "Sue's the assistant principal now."

"Jesus Christ, no wonder this place is a sty."

"That's not Sue's fault," Charlotte defended. She indicated the room, the school. "You can't put pearls on a pig."

"She sure did blow plenty of 'em, though." Lena shook her head. "I can't believe she's your boss. God, that must suck."

"Oh, she's not that bad," Charlotte murmured, smoothing down her skirt with the palm of her hand. She was more like the Charlotte from the library now: quiet, subdued. "I know it doesn't look that way, but Sue's been a really good friend to me these last few years."

"Like Sibyl?"

She pressed her lips together. "No. Nothing like Sibyl."

Lena had caught the flash of fear in the other woman's eyes, and some of her resolve wavered. The desire to tread softly was new to her, but she tried to go with it, asking, "When did the bar close down?"

"I think it was two weeks ago," Charlotte answered. "I read about it in the paper. The bartender was selling meth along with shots, apparently."

"Deacon?" Lena asked, shaking her head as she said the name. Deacon Simms had worked for Hank going on thirty years now. He had a felony record and a surly attitude, which made him perfect for the bar but virtually unemployable anywhere else. Hank loved him like a brother.

Charlotte told her, "Deacon left a while back. This was some new guy."

Hank hadn't told her that Deacon was gone, but then he hadn't told Lena a lot of things. She knew the bartender had a temper—he was always clashing with Hank—but over the years, Deacon had thrown up his hands a million times and sworn he was never coming back. The longest he'd ever managed to stay away was for three days. He'd run into Hank at one of their AA meetings and all was forgiven.

Lena wondered if Charlotte had seen Deacon at any AA meetings. Of course, if Charlotte was anything like Hank, she wouldn't have told anyone if she'd seen the Pope himself there, munching on free cookies and drinking coffee. Still, she tried, "Do you know where Deacon went?"

"I haven't seen him around."

"There was this guy," Lena began. "I saw him outside Hank's house. He had a swastika tattooed on his arm."

"In plain sight?" Charlotte looked outraged. "That's disgusting. Who was it?"

"I was hoping you could tell me," Lena admitted. The guy was going to be harder to find than she'd thought. Lena was getting close to the point where, short of driving aimlessly around town looking for the thug, she was going to have to get some help. She just had to figure out how to ask Jeffrey for assistance without implicating Hank. It wasn't like Lena could call up her boss and ask him to help her track down her uncle's dealer.

"I'm sorry I can't help you," Charlotte said softly.

Lena shrugged off the apology. "Why do you think Hank's using again?"

"Who knows?" she answered, picking at an invisible spot on her skirt. "Maybe he's just tired of feeling things."

She sounded like someone who knew what she was talking about.

And, of course, Lena knew the truth behind her words. "I found your letters."

Charlotte laughed again, but this time there was no joy in the sound. She looked at her hands, then the floor—anything but Lena. "I suppose you read them?"

"I wish I hadn't," Lena admitted.

Charlotte let out a slow stream of air between her lips. "There were so many things I said in those letters. Things I've never told anyone."

"You tried to kill yourself."

She nodded and shrugged at the same time.

"Why?" Lena asked. "If you're so miserable here—"

"What, just leave?"

"Yeah."

"It's so easy for you," Charlotte began. "You don't have kids or a house you worked on making a home or a husband who loves you so much he's willing to give up everything or..." She stopped herself, reining in her emotions. "I love my husband. I really, really do. I can't tell you what my life would be without Larry. He's stood by me through all this crap I've dragged my family through. Even when I..." Her voice trailed off. "When I took those pills, he was there. He's the one who called the ambulance. He was the first one I saw when I woke up in the hospital. He took a leave of absence from work even though it cost him a promotion. He cleaned the house and fed the kids and did the shopping and at night he worked part-time at the God-awful motel so we could afford for me to keep seeing the therapist. He did everything while I laid up in bed feeling sorry for myself."

"Six years ago," Lena recalled from the letters. "When Sibyl died."

Charlotte gave a weak smile. "You know, it wasn't even about her. I mean, yes, of course I was devastated. She wasn't just dead, but the way she died just made it so much more awful." She stopped, collecting herself. "Sibby was so gentle, and for her to go that way..."

Lena didn't want to think about it, to remember the details. "I understand," she said. "You know I understand."

"It made me look at how my life had just happened without me even paying attention. Did that happen to you, Lee?"

Lena had never thought about it, but she guessed that it had.

"Suddenly, I was this grown-up married woman, driving a minivan and trying to coordinate picking up my kids from soccer practice between finding time to cook dinner and scheduling a date-night with my husband."

Lena felt claustrophobic just listening to the description, but she felt the need to say, "That doesn't sound so bad."

"Exactly," Charlotte agreed. "Here I was in this perfect life, and all I could think about was that if I had to go to one more church potluck or softball game, I was going to kill myself. And one morning, I woke up and decided to follow through."

"Does your husband know about Sibyl?"

"Larry knew we were close, but not anything more than that." She finally looked up at Lena. "I think it would destroy him if he knew. Not for the reason you're thinking, but because he knows... he knows something is missing and he tries so hard to..."

"Did you talk to your therapist about it?"

"The Christian therapist who's also the minister at our church?" Sarcasm clipped Charlotte's words. "Oh, yeah. We talked it out and he prayed for me and Jesus took it away like magic." Tears fell from her eyes. "It's my cross to bear, Lena. Make your bed and lie in it, right?"

"But, if you—"

She shook her head stubbornly. "If Larry found out, he would be devastated. I can't do that to him. You have to understand that I really, really love him. He could deal with just about anything—another man, even—but this, this is something he can't compete with, and it would just kill him."

Lena tried to tread carefully. "Does he need to compete with it?"

Charlotte gave her a sharp look. "You mean was it all just a *phase*?" Her bitter tone implied she'd heard this explanation before. "Being in love with someone, feeling connected with someone, like your heart is part of theirs, that's not a *phase*."

"I know," Lena said, because it sounded like what Charlotte needed to hear.

"I've been with other men, Lee. It's not like I just haven't met the right one."

"I'm sorry," Lena apologized. "I wasn't saying that."

Charlotte looked at her hands. Her wedding ring was a rock, glittering in the crappy trailer. A man didn't buy a woman a ring like that unless he was head over heels in love. She told Lena, "When Larry and

I first started dating, he knew that I was getting over someone. He just didn't know it was a woman."

Lena had been the sighted one, but she'd ended up being more blind than her sister. Sitting in Hank's shack of an office, reading Charlotte's deepest feelings, Lena had remembered all the times Sibyl had shut the door to their room, asking Lena to leave her and Charlotte alone so that they could study. Lena had never guessed exactly what they had been studying.

For years, Lena had blamed Sibyl's lesbianism on Nan Thomas, the woman she had been living with when she died. It had taken a long time for Lena to accept that her sister's sexuality was not going to change. Lena had even developed a kind of friendship with Nan. Somewhere in the back of her mind, though, Lena had still thought of Sibyl as some innocent who had unwittingly been plucked from the straight world. If it had started as far back as Charlotte Warren, then her whole notion of why Sibyl had changed was thrown out the window.

The truth was that Sibyl hadn't changed at all. She had always been that way, only Lena had been too stupid to see it.

Lena asked, "Does your husband know that you're in AA?"

"It's kind of hard to hide when you get suspended from your job for being drunk." She laughed, though there was nothing funny about what she was saying. "This was back when I was in the building instead of stuck out here in the trailer park. I fell flat on my face in full view of the newspaper staff. If it wasn't for Swallowin' Sue I would've lost my job." She smiled. "I guess you could argue that it was the middle of the year and it's nearly impossible to find anyone who's willing to teach anymore, but I like to think she let me continue teaching because she believes in me."

"You're acting like this is all some kind of joke."

"Oh, Lee. If I didn't laugh about it, I wouldn't be able to get out of bed in the morning."

"Why did you start drinking?"

"Because it was a slower, more socially acceptable way to kill myself." She added, "And it helped anesthetize me. I didn't want to feel anything."

"That's the same thing you just said about Hank."

"Yes. It is." Charlotte's throat worked. Now that she was looking at Lena, she couldn't seem to take her eyes off of her. "You're so much like Sibby, you know?"

Lena shook her head. "I don't look like her anymore."

"It's inside," Charlotte insisted, holding her hand to her chest. "Y'all were always the same inside, too."

Lena had to laugh. "Sibyl was nothing like me. I was in trouble all the time. They probably have a chair outside the principal's office named after me."

"She was just better at getting away with it," Charlotte countered. "Remember how she used to mouth off to Coach Hanson in biology class?"

Lena felt herself smiling. "She ran circles around him. He hated her guts."

"Remember that awful music she used to listen to? God, she had such a crush on Joan Jett."

"Was it Sibyl who—I mean, was she the one who—" Lena felt her face turning beet red. "Christ. Never mind."

"It was mutual," Charlotte supplied. "We were both studying on the bed. We had the window open and it started raining outside and I reached over to close it and one thing led to another and it just...happened."

Lena felt her stomach drop. Sibyl's bed was by the wall. They had made out on Lena's bed.

"Are you okay?"

Lena nodded, trying to block the image that came to her mind.

Charlotte took Lena's reaction the wrong way. "She never thought you would accept her."

"I didn't," Lena admitted, feeling a familiar sadness. "I do now, but I didn't when it mattered."

"She knew you loved her, Lee. She never doubted that." Charlotte stood and walked over to the window. "What's Nan like?"

"Nan?" Lena echoed. "How do you know about Nan?"

"She called me when Sibyl died."

"Oh." Lena felt ashamed for not making the call herself.

Charlotte seemed to pick up on this. "You had a lot going on, Lee. Don't worry."

"I should have let you know. You were..." Lena didn't know how to characterize Sibyl's relationship with Charlotte. "I should have called you."

"She sounds kind of snooty on the phone."

"Nan?" Lena shrugged. "Not really. Sometimes she gets

prickly, but she's okay most of the time. I lived with her for a while."

"Hank told me," Charlotte said. "We had a good laugh over that one."

Lena felt her stomach drop. "What else did Hank tell you about me?"

"That he was worried about you. That there was this guy you were seeing who was really bad, and he was worried you wouldn't get away from him." She paused, hesitating before adding, "That he went to Atlanta with you."

A lump came to Lena's throat. "Is that why he started using again? Because I..." Lena couldn't say the word, couldn't talk about what had happened at the women's clinic.

"Listen to me," Charlotte ordered, her tone sharp. She waited until Lena looked up. "You cannot make someone use drugs, just like you can't make them stop. You don't have that much power over Hank or anybody else. Hank started using again for his own reasons."

She sounded just like one of his AA pamphlets. "Did he tell you his reasons?"

Charlotte shook her head again. "Mostly, he just listened to me. I was so wrapped up in myself that I didn't see what was going on with him until it was too late."

"When did he start back?"

"I'd guess three months ago, maybe four or five if he started slow."

"Did he say anything in your meetings?"

"I can't tell you what he said in meetings, Lena. You know that." She held up her hands, as if to stop the next question. "I can tell you that two months ago he told me that he couldn't be my sponsor anymore. I was hurt, I didn't really question him like I should have because I was too busy feeling angry and rejected. Part of me was glad when he didn't show up at the next meeting or any of the ones after that. Sometimes, he'd drive over to the ones in Carterson and I just assumed he was going to those."

Carterson was about fifty miles away, not a long drive for someone like Hank, who liked to be on the open road.

Lena asked, "When did you realize he had stopped going to meetings?"

"A few week ago. I got over myself and asked a friend in Carterson to tell Hank I said hi and she told me she hadn't seen him in forever."

"Did you ever see a white SUV outside his house?"

"No." She added, "Larry and I go for walks after supper. We pass by Hank's almost every night. I've never seen anyone there. As a matter of fact, I wondered if you had come to get him. His car was in the driveway, but there were never any lights on except the usual one in the kitchen."

Hank always left the kitchen light on as a deterrent to thieves; not a good strategy if the entire neighborhood knew the trick.

Lena asked, "When did you last see him?"

"Four days ago—that's why I called you. He was outside trying to fix his mailbox. Somebody put a cherry bomb in it, probably one of those kids from a couple of streets over getting a head start on Halloween. Larry offered to help but Hank cursed at him, told us both to go away, so we did."

Lena mulled this over. "He's been holed up in his house for how many months and the only thing that got him outside was a broken mailbox?"

"He was so high, Lee. I'm surprised he could stand up on his own, let alone walk the twenty feet to his mailbox. His skin was awful. He obviously hadn't bathed in a while. A fool could see what he's doing."

"Which is?"

"Trying to end it."

Lena felt her voice catch. "End his life?"

Charlotte shrugged. "End his misery, maybe."

"What's changed? What happened that set him off?"

"I have no idea. That's the truth. My focus every day when I get up is not taking another drink. I'm an alcoholic. We're not known for our altruism."

Lena doubted that was the case with Charlotte. She pressed, "But you saw he was having problems two, maybe three months ago?"

"I don't know," Charlotte admitted. "Maybe I saw that he was depressed or preoccupied or acting differently, but all I cared about was me. School had started back and I was in this hellhole with kids snickering behind my back and teachers snickering in front of it. I was struggling to stay sober. My focus was on what would keep me on the right path." She held out her hands as if she were helpless. "By the time

I realized something was wrong with him, it was too late. He wouldn't talk to me, he wouldn't return my phone calls, he wouldn't answer the door. He just kept telling me to leave him alone and let him do what he wanted to do."

Lena was familiar with the refrain. "That's when you started writing him the letters?"

"Yes." She paused, lost in her own thoughts. "It was awkward at first, but then when he didn't write back it was almost freeing. I just wrote whatever I wanted. I've never done that before, just said what was on my mind."

"You talk a lot about Sibyl, what it was like when you were together." Some of the passages had been so hard to read that Lena had found herself staring out the window, lost in another time. Charlotte had managed to capture the essence of Sibyl: her good nature, her loving kindness. Even after Lena had finished reading the letters, the feelings had stuck with her, so that it was almost like Sibyl was alive again.

Charlotte said, "Hank is the only one who knew about her. Us. What we felt for each other, that it was love and not something grotesque." She leaned her back against the window, arms crossed low over her waist. "But you know what? A long time ago, he asked me what would've happened if Sibyl and I had made it work. I could have transferred to Georgia Tech, you know. They wouldn't have offered me a full ride like they did with Sibby but I was already in college, doing pretty well, making the honor roll. I was miserable living with my folks and having to drive back and forth to Milledgeville. I could've transferred and gotten a job in Atlanta or got student loans or something to make it happen, but I didn't."

"Why not?"

"I guess it scared me. Everything scared me back then. Atlanta's so big, so anonymous. I felt safe here. And it would've killed my parents."

"It was easier for us to leave home than it was for you," Lena tried. "Your folks were—"

"My folks would've never talked to me again if I'd followed her to Atlanta. They caught us together once. Did you know that?" Lena shook her head, shocked that Sibyl had never told her. "It was fall break of my sophomore year and Sibby was about to go off to Tech. My parents were supposed to be visiting my aunt Jeannie for the day but they got into a fight. They were always fighting back then. This was around the time mother found out he'd been screwing Mrs. Ford from the church for about the last five years." She laughed at the irony. "So, they came back early and found us . . . Well, you can imagine how they found us. They called Hank at the bar and made him come over right then to confront us. He was furious—but at them, not Sibyl. He said we were both adults and that it was none of their damn business."

" 'Let he who is without sin . . .' " Lena quoted. It was one of Hank's favorite verses. He was always throwing it out right before he told you that what you were doing was wrong.

Charlotte said, "Y'all were so lucky to have him."

Lena laughed. "Are you kidding me? I would've killed for your parents when I was growing up."

"You can have them."

"Okay," Lena allowed. "What they did then was bad, but they never accidentally locked you out of the house all night or forgot to feed you or left you alone with strangers and they sure as hell never got so drunk they ran over you with their car and—"

"What?"

"You know what Hank did."

Charlotte looked confused. "What did he do?"

"He blinded her. He took away Sibyl's sight. How can you—"

"Lena, that wasn't Hank."

Lena felt her heart stop mid-beat. "What are you talking about?"

Charlotte stood in front of her, still confused by Lena's reaction. "I was there that day."

"No, you weren't."

"You and me and Sibby were playing in the front yard with an old tennis ball I'd stolen from my brother. You threw the ball over Sibyl's head and she ran into the driveway and—"

"No," Lena insisted. "You weren't there." Even as she said the words, she could picture the day: throwing the ball over Sibyl's head, making her chase after it. And there was Charlotte Warren on the other side of the driveway, scooping up the ball and tossing it back to Lena. "No." Lena shook her head as if she could clear the memory. "You weren't there."

"I was, Lee. I saw the car backing up. I yelled, but she didn't stop. The bumper hit Sibyl's head. I saw her collapse in the driveway." As she spoke, Lena saw it happening again. Sibyl running into the driveway, Charlotte screaming. "There was just this thin line of blood." Charlotte traced her finger along her own temple, down her jaw, exactly where the blood had been on Sibyl. "You started sobbing, you were hysterical, and Hank came running out of the house and your mother just—"

"My mother?" Lena felt light-headed. She leaned back against the desk. "What are you talking about? My mother was there? She was there when Sibyl...?"

"Lee," Charlotte began, putting her hand on Lena's shoulder. "It wasn't Hank. Your mother was driving the car. She's the one who blinded Sibyl."

WEDNESDAY EVENING

CHAPTER 11

SARA LAY IN BED, trying not to think about what was living in the mattress underneath her body. The autopsy had taken ten brutal hours, and when they had finally gotten back to the motel, she had nearly cried at the sight of the filthy room. Sara knew there was a maid around here somewhere. Earlier this morning, she had seen the woman pushing around a large cart with all sorts of cleaners and a vacuum. Except for the bed being made, nothing else in the room had been touched. Sara hadn't exactly been expecting a thank-you note for scrubbing the bathroom, but the woman could have at least vacuumed the rug. The green M&M she had seen under the table yesterday morning was still nestled in the shag carpet.

Sara closed her eyes and listened to Jeffrey humming in the shower, the water slapping against the plastic tub. She had cleaned the cut on his hand using some disinfectant they'd found in the morgue, but he would have to bandage it on his own when he got out of the shower. She was too tired to do it herself, and frankly, part of her could not let go of her anger from yesterday afternoon. They had spent the entire day together, yet neither one of them had been willing to break the ice and talk about what had happened.

Jeffrey seemed fine with this, which only served to annoy Sara more. The situation made her feel like the prototypical bitchy sit-com wife who was always harping on her poor, misunderstood husband. She had always supported Jeffrey, even when she'd thought he was wrong, and it was unfair of him to let her be cast in the role of shrew.

On top of that, Sara still had a bad feeling about Elawah and whatever Lena had drawn them into. The autopsy she had performed that day only served to heighten that sense of dread. Over the years, Grant County had seen its share of violent deaths but Sara was hard-pressed to think of a more awful way to die than being burned alive. She was usually adept at separating the victim from the crime. If you were going to cut into a dead body, you couldn't think of it as a person anymore. You had to look at it as parts of a whole: circulatory, respiratory, tissue, organs, skeleton.

Still, as Sara worked on the woman, she'd found herself wondering about her life, the method of her death, the family she was leaving behind. Then, she began to wonder about the perpetrator. What kind of person could do this to another human being? Certainly not the kind of person she wanted Jeffrey talking to.

They had not waited for Fred Bart to come before starting the autopsy, which was a good thing considering the dentist had never showed. Removing the remains from the car had proven to be the easy part. Once the corpse was on the table, Sara found that the woman's body had been so ravaged by fire that the usual procedures could not be followed. There was no need for the Stryker saw since the back of the skull had fractured off in Sara's hand, allowing the brain to slip out like the pit of a ripe peach. There was no need for a Y-incision to open the torso when there was hardly any skin left to cut.

All but two of the ribs were fractured by the heat. The larynx and trachea were seared, the tongue cooked into the neck organs. The pleural surfaces of both lungs were charred, the air spaces consolidated with soot. Most of the skeletal musculature had a well-done appearance. The bone marrow was black.

The soot in the lungs proved the woman had lived long enough to inhale the smoke. Sara was certainly not an arson specialist, but she assumed that the gas tank explosion had been the result of a fire that started inside the car. The blast from the tank had gone up and out, mostly damaging the very rear of the SUV. The woman, even sitting in the backseat, would have been able to remove her seat belt, get out of the car, before the real damage started.

From all appearances, she had not been raped. Sara wondered why this came as a relief. Sara herself had been raped—brutally so, as a certain lawyer liked to point out. As awful as that experience had been, she imagined it was much more painful to be burned alive.

The thing that terrified Sara most was that the woman surely knew what was coming. There had been no obvious damage to the skull; no one had knocked her out before the fire was set. She had watched and waited as flames devoured her body.

The shower cut off, and Sara rolled over onto her stomach, wishing she'd thought to bring their pillows from home. She was wearing socks, sweatpants, and a long-sleeved shirt buttoned up to the collar, even though the room was stuffy from the heat and smelled of wet fried chicken. The remnants of a pizza they'd had delivered were on the plastic table, and she thought about getting another slice, but her body would not move. She would have asked Jeffrey, but earlier he had taken one look at the well-done ground beef topping and dry-heaved.

The bed shifted as he got in. She waited for him to turn off the light, to bunch up his pillow and arrange the blankets like he usually did before he settled down. He did none of this, asking instead, "You asleep?"

"Yes," she lied. "Did you put something on your hand?"

He didn't answer her question. "I shouldn't have slowed the car." He added, "Yesterday," as if she needed some clarification, then repeated, "I shouldn't have slowed the car."

Sara closed her eyes. "I shouldn't have slapped you," she answered, though as much as she tried, as shamed as she felt for resorting to violence, Sara couldn't bring herself to truly regret it.

Still, she rolled over, put her head on his chest. He gave a deep sigh, and she felt the last of her anger dissipate.

She said, "You smell like hotel soap."

"It could be worse," he pointed out, though thankfully didn't tell her how. "Did you call your mother?"

"She was taking a nap with Daddy." Sara added, "At six in the evening."

Jeffrey laughed, but Sara had never told him that she was twenty-two years old before she found out that her parents' ubiquitous Sunday afternoon "nap" excuse had been a cover for something far more illicit than sleeping. Nor did she tell him that her nineteen-year-old sister had been the one to inform her.

Jeffrey laced his hand through hers, suggesting, "Maybe soon we'll be taking naps."

A baby. Their baby.

He told her, "I checked the machine while you were doing your autopsy notes. The adoption agency didn't call."

"I checked it while you were in the shower."

"They'll call," he said. "I can feel it."

"Let's not talk about it," she told him. "I don't want to jinx it." The truth was that it could take years before a baby was available, though the fact that they had agreed to take a child up to the age of two and hadn't asked for a specific race or sex had definitely moved them up the list. The woman at the agency had said that it could be next year or it could be any day now. All they could do was wait—something neither Jeffrey nor Sara was very good at.

Jeffrey stroked her arm, then her side. His thumb slipped just under the waist of her pants, and he suggested, "Maybe we could take a nap right now."

She sat up on her elbow and looked him in the eye so that her answer would be loud and clear. "No part of my naked body is touching any part of this skanky motel room."

He gave her one of his sly grins. "Is this some kind of come-on?"

Sara let her head fall back to his chest, not wanting to give him the chance to change her mind. "Please tell me that what I did today is going to help you so we can get out of here."

"I don't know that I can do that," he admitted, stroking her arm again. "We still don't know who the victim is. If Lena had stuck around, we probably could've found a lawyer to get her out by now."

"Don't mention lawyers," she begged.

"We never did talk about that," he said. "How the deposition went. What the strategy is."

"It's okay," she said, but her voice caught in her throat. There hadn't been a message from Buddy Conford on the answering machine, either. This meant that Global Medical Indemnity was still trying to decide whether or not Sara's medical judgment was worth fighting for or to capitulate to Jimmy's grieving parents.

For once in her life, she willingly changed the subject back to Lena. "I'm just glad it wasn't Hank in that car."

"You and me both," he said, knowing better than anyone how easy it would be for the local cops to up Lena's charges to murder if the victim had been her uncle. "I still don't know how Jake thinks he's going to make a case without an ID. There has to be a motive. If he can't prove a connection between Lena and the victim, then game over."

"Not knowing the victim's name doesn't negate the fact that she's dead." Sara smoothed down the hairs on his chest so they wouldn't tickle her nose. "And Lena was at the scene. She had her foot on the gas can."

"They probably won't be able to get her prints off the can."

"That doesn't offer a resounding proof of innocence."

"They don't have a statement from her. She didn't say a word to anyone."

Sara thought to ask why he was giving Lena the benefit of the doubt when he would most certainly take her actions as an admission of guilt from anyone else, but she was too tired for the argument that would follow.

Jeffrey said, "I wish we could find Hank. He's got to know something."

"You're sure he's not at home? Hiding, maybe?"

"As far as I could tell, no one was there." He added, "Valentine has a car right across the street. I'm sure he knocked on the door when Lena went missing."

"Maybe you need to knock hard enough to open the door."

He laughed in surprise. "I think being married to a cop is finally starting to rub off on you."

"Then listen to me. I'm worried that Lena has done something to jeopardize Hank."

Jeffrey took his time responding. "Has it occurred to you that it could be the other way around?" She didn't answer, and he continued, "Hank's probably back on drugs. Maybe he pissed off his dealer. Maybe Lena came down to take care of things, only the dealer didn't want to be taken care of."

She looked up at him, resting her chin on her hand. "Go on."

"These guys don't like being fucked with," Jeffrey continued. "And they're not afraid of cops."

For the first time since they'd gotten here, Sara was finally hearing something logical. She could easily imagine Lena pissing off the wrong people, damn the consequences. The same pattern she had established with Ethan Green—provoking her skinhead lover until he retaliated with force—could be playing out again in Elawah County.

Jeffrey told Sara, "You didn't see Pfeiffer up close. He was terrified. Maybe he thought they had sent me to finish the job." He hesitated, as if he hadn't quite worked out the next bit. "It could be that the reason

Lena didn't want to talk to me the other night was because she didn't want to expose me to these people."

Sara put her head back down on Jeffrey's chest. She could not give the woman the benefit of the doubt, but she didn't want the ensuing argument that might come if she voiced her opinion. "Do you think the man we saw at the hospital could have been Hank's dealer?"

"Jake said the guy was a dealer."

"He also said that the guy was there to visit one of his boys in the hospital," Sara pointed out. "Jake had plenty of opportunity to tell you then and there that the man was supplying Hank and that Lena had gotten in the way."

"I wasn't exactly high on his list at the moment," Jeffrey reminded her. "To his thinking, you and I had just helped Lena escape from custody."

Sara didn't want to dwell on that point. "Do you think Hank might have helped her?"

He shrugged. "To get out of town, she would need a car, clothes, money. Lena could do that on her own or she could find help."

"I don't know if I buy Hank being capable of coordinating all that."

"He's an old man," Jeffrey allowed. "Then again, you don't get track marks on your arms like that from going to Sunday school."

He had a point. Actually, he had a lot of good points. She wondered why he hadn't been thinking like this yesterday. It would have saved both of them a hell of a lot of trouble, not to mention nearly eight hundred miles on her car.

She asked, "So, what's on the agenda for tomorrow?"

"Maybe knock real hard on Hank's door." He chuckled, obviously still pleased that Sara had come up with the idea. "Failing any response, I guess I'll find out a little more about Jake Valentine. I've got some contacts at the sheriff's academy over in Tifton. Hopefully, they can give me a better idea of the kind of cop he is. Then, I'm going to call Nick and get him to run a deep background check on Jake."

"You can't get Frank to do that from the station?"

"The GBI can go deeper than a look-see," he said, using the slang for the routine checks he could run at the police station. "It takes several days to pull a complete profile."

"Jake can't have a record or he wouldn't have made it through the Public Safety screening."

"I'm going to cross-reference him for known associates."

"Surely, they would've flagged his file if he was a known associate of a criminal."

"Depends on how he's known."

"And if he has some connections near your connections, and they find out you've been digging around about him?"

"I imagine he won't be too surprised to hear the news."

She reached for his hand, her fingers brushing his skin until they touched a sloppily applied Band-Aid. She curled her hand around his. "Do you think Jake is part of any of this?"

"Jake grew up here. He was only a deputy for a couple of years before he moved up. I think he knows everything that's going on in this town. Whether he's involved in it or just standing on the outside looking in is the question."

"When did you come up with all of this?"

She expected him to make a joke about his stunning brilliance or remarkable sleuthing abilities. Instead, he surprised her.

"That woman," he began, and she understood he meant the charred body they had worked on all day. "There's somebody out there who's missing her. They're either too scared to ask the sheriff for help, or they know that it's useless, that Jake can't or won't help them." She could hear the indignation in his voice. "If you can't trust the police to take care of you, to do their jobs the right way, then what's the point?" He paused, but she knew he wasn't expecting an answer. "It's not right, Sara. It's just not right."

Twenty-four hours ago, she had wanted to kill him, but now all that she could think was that she had never loved him so much as she did right now.

"Can you imagine how you'd feel if something like this happened in Grant County?"

Sara could not imagine such a violation. The first time she had met Jeffrey had been on the Grant County High School football field. She was team doctor, watching the game from the sidelines. Sara had turned around for some reason, looking up into the stands. That was when she'd seen Jeffrey with Clem Waters, the mayor. He loomed over the man, making Clem look like a dwarf. There was something about Jeffrey's presence that made it difficult for Sara to breathe. She had never told him this before, but her heart had stopped at the sight of him. When she saw him walk down onto the field, her knees had actually felt weak. If a player hadn't managed at that very moment to get the crap knocked out of him, she would have made an absolute fool of herself. As it was, she had only been a partial fool.

She wrapped her arms around him. "You wouldn't let it happen," she assured him. "Not in our town. Not ever."

He pressed his lips to the top of her head, then reached over and turned out the lamp on the bedside table. Sara settled back in, curling her body into his. She felt herself relax just as she felt him tense.

She asked, "What's wrong?"

"Do you smell something burning?"

"After today, that's all I smell."

"No." Jeffrey turned the lamp back on. "I mean it. Something's burning."

"I can't smell—"

He got out of bed and slipped on his jeans. Reluctantly, Sara sat up, knowing that he wouldn't go to sleep until he located the source of the smell. Considering the state of the hotel, she wouldn't be surprised if the electrical wiring was smoking.

He pulled back the drapes and checked the parking lot. "I can't see anything."

"I don't suppose that means you'll come back to bed?"

Jeffrey slipped on a T-shirt from the suitcase and opened the door. He stood there, letting the cold in, sniffing the air. "It's coming from outside."

She stood up. "I can smell it now."

They both put on their shoes before walking out into the parking lot. Sara pulled the sleeves of her sweatshirt down over her hands to fight the nighttime chill. Outside, the odor was more intense, like smoke from a roaring campfire. The sound of crackling was obvious, too, and they both followed the noise to a tunnel that ran along the back of the motel's front office.

There was a crowd of guests gathered at the end of the tunnel, all of them looking as if they were embarrassed to be seen here. Their fear of being caught by their neighbors and spouses could not compete with the desire to watch a spectacle. And spectacular the sight was: the building next to the motel was surrounded by flames, smoke wafting into the night sky.

As Jeffrey and Sara reached the front of the crowd, the windows blew out of the building with an earth-shaking explosion. Jeffrey put his arm around Sara, turning her away from the debris. There was another loud boom. The front door blew off and skittered across the parking lot.

Jeffrey had to raise his voice over the roar of the fire to ask, "Has anyone called nine-one-one?"

Someone from the crowd answered, "Twice."

Jeffrey told Sara, "That's Hank's bar."

"I hope no one is in there," she answered, shielding her eyes with her hand to block out the intense light. The flames seemed to be concentrated around the periphery of the building, as if someone had poured gasoline around the outside and lit a match. With the windows gone, the fire was working its way in, following the line of the studs and beams, dancing across the roof. If there were fire sprinklers in the building, they weren't working. Sara guessed the bar would be completely engulfed within the next five minutes.

There was a piercing noise, like a hurt animal or maybe a siren. Sara glanced down the road, expecting a fire truck, but there were only a couple of cars and a motorcycle driving slowly by.

"Lena," Jeffrey murmured, striding toward the building.

Through one of the broken windows, Sara saw a figure move to the middle of the bar. In the glowing light, she could tell that the person was looking at something in his hands.

"Hey, you!" Jeffrey had obviously realized what Sara had: that the person inside wasn't Lena after all, but a man with broad shoulders and a stocky build. He looked up when Jeffrey called again, but he made no move to leave.

Jeffrey turned back toward Sara. He nodded once, as if to say, "You know I have to do this," then ran toward the building.

"Jeffrey!" she called. It was too dangerous. The fire would reach the man in seconds. "Jeffrey!"

He jumped back as a wall of flames shot up in front of him, but would not give up. Ignoring Sara's pleas, he circled the building, looking for another way to reach the man.

"No," Sara whispered, helplessly watching Jeffrey dart into the burning building. Inside, the man's shirt was on fire now, but insanely he turned away from Jeffrey, disappearing farther into the building. Jeffrey chased after him, reaching out, then they both vanished.

"No," Sara repeated, waiting, watching the open doorway for Jeffrey. She circled, glass crunching under her shoes, scanning the building, looking through the gaping holes where windows used to be. She had gone halfway round the bar and was standing at the edge of the woods when there was a loud explosion, this one so intense that it knocked her to the ground.

Seconds passed. Her ears rang, her brain felt enveloped in static. Sara shook her head, debris falling from her hair. She pressed her hands into the packed dirt and sat up on her side. Flames shot up from the building. Her skin felt singed by the heat. She managed to get to her knees, but could not stand. Her mouth opened, but she could not speak.

"Sara!" Jeffrey came running out of the woods, sliding on the dirt as he dropped to his knees beside her. "Are you okay?" He put his hands on either side of her face. "Are you hurt?"

She put her hands over his. "I thought—"

The distinctive wail of a siren filled the air. This time, there was no mistaking that the noise came from a fire truck. The back wheels screeched as it pulled into the parking lot, an ambulance right behind it. The firemen scrambled like ants as they hooked up hoses and directed people away from the blazing building.

"Sara," Jeffrey repeated. "Talk to me. Are you hurt?"

She shook her head, collapsing against him, her arms so tight around his waist that she was surprised he could still breathe.

"You're okay," he told her, stroking back her hair. "You're okay."

Sara couldn't trust herself to open her mouth without sobbing. She felt numb, caught in a vacuum that muffled sound and sensation.

Jeffrey coughed, and she loosened her grip around him but did not let go.

She'd thought he was dead. For that split second, she'd seen her life without him, felt what it would be like to lose him.

"He ran into the woods," Jeffrey told her, as if she gave a damn about the man who'd lured him into the building. "He had something in his hands. I couldn't see what it was."

One of the paramedics knelt beside Sara, put his hand to her back. "Ma'am, are you okay?"

She managed to nod her head. Shock. She must be in shock.

The other paramedic asked, "Can you breathe? Do you need some oxygen?"

She had to clear her throat before she could tell him, "No." Obviously he did not believe her. He tried to put a mask over her mouth but she pushed him away.

Jeffrey looked worried. "Maybe you should—"

"I'm okay," she told them all, feeling foolish having so many people fuss over her. She pulled on Jeffrey's shirt, trying to stand. He practically lifted her off the ground, his arm around her waist. She put her hand over his to keep it there.

She told him, "I want to go back to the room." He didn't ask questions. He led her through the crowd, using his hand to push people aside and make a path. They were all staring, and Sara looked down at the ground, concentrating on putting one foot in front of the other, holding Jeffrey as closely as she could.

"Hold on, Chief." It was Jake Valentine.

"Not now," Jeffrey told him.

He took off his ball cap. "If you could just—"

"Not now," Jeffrey repeated, tightening his grip around Sara's waist. The lights from the snack machines were flickering as they walked by, the compressors buzzing like a hive. Sara hadn't closed the door properly when they'd left the room and Jeffrey slowly pushed it open with one hand. She could feel his body tense as he looked around, made sure no one was inside.

He tried not to make a big show of it, but he kept Sara behind him as he checked out the small room that held the toilet and the tub. Once he was certain they were alone, he turned on the faucet and took a rag off the towel rack.

"I want to know why he ran," Jeffrey said, wetting the cloth, his mind still on the man in the building.

Sara pushed herself up onto the countertop, feet dangling above the floor. Her senses were coming back. She could smell an acidic mix of smoke and sweat coming off Jeffrey's body. His shirt was wet with perspiration and soot.

He said, "I couldn't get a good look at him. Smoke was everywhere."

"Can you breathe okay?" she asked, the doctor part of her brain whirring to life. "Does your chest or throat hurt?"

He shook his head. "Come here." Carefully, he washed her face with the rag, saying, "There's a stream that runs behind the building, some kind of shack beside it. The guy tripped down the bank and fell into the water. I thought I'd catch him then, but he just disappeared." Jeffrey picked something out of Sara's hair and threw it into the trashcan. "I couldn't tell if he dropped what he was carrying. Whatever he had, he thought it was worth running into a burning building for." He

rinsed out the rag. She could see that it was spotted with dirt and wondered what her face looked like. He finished, "Then the building blew,
and I saw you go down."

She felt something cool on her cheeks and realized that she was
crying.

"Hey, now," Jeffrey said, wiping her tears. "You're okay."

Emotions came rushing in. Sara didn't give a damn about herself. "I
just ... you went into that building, and then the next thing I saw ... I
thought you were ..."

He gave her a curious smile, as if she was overreacting. "Come on,
babe. I'm fine."

She touched his face, tried to keep her hands from shaking. Sara
knew that Jeffrey was attracted to her toughness, her independence. She
couldn't be that person right now, couldn't let him think for a moment
that she could survive without him. "I don't know what I would do if
something happened to you."

"Come on." He tried to make a joke of it. "You'd have a line of
guys waiting to take my place."

Sara shook her head, unable to play along. "Don't say that."

"Maybe Nick Shelton would finally get his shot. Y'all could get
matching necklaces."

She kissed him, feeling grit on his lips. Sara didn't care. She opened
her mouth to him, wrapped her arms around his shoulders, her legs
around his hips, pulling him as close as possible. She wanted to feel
every part of his body, to know that he still belonged to her. Something
frantic took hold, and she tore the neck of his shirt trying to take it off.

"Hey—" He pulled back, that same curious smile on his face. "We're
okay, all right? We're fine."

We, he had said, but that had never been her concern. She could see
right through him—that his smile didn't really reach his eyes, that he
was talking too fast, that he was worried about something—too worried to tell her about it. She touched the tips of her fingers to his lips, let
them travel down his neck, his chest. When she scratched her fingernails down the front of his jeans, he finally stopped smiling.

"Don't ever leave me," she told him, unbuttoning his jeans, opening
the fly. It sounded like a threat, but she was speaking out of sheer terror
at the thought of her life without him. "Don't ever leave."

He was ready even before she wrapped her hand around him. His
tongue went deep into her mouth as he kissed her, long, firm strokes

that matched her own. Sara kissed back harder, used both hands to tease him until he jerked down her pants and spread her legs apart. She slid to the edge of the counter, putting her full weight onto him as he pushed inside of her. Again he tried to slow her down, but she gripped the counter with one hand and thrust against him, quickening his pace.

"Fuck…" he breathed, slamming her back against the mirror, kissing and biting her neck. She felt his teeth graze her breast, his hands gripping her ass as he pushed harder, deeper. Sara dug her fingernails into his back, knowing how close he was, wanting nothing more than for him to let go.

"You feel so good," she whispered putting her lips to his ear, letting him feel her breath. "So good…" She kept talking, coaxing him along with the words she knew would push him over the edge.

He gasped, the muscles along his back tensing like wire. Sara squeezed her eyes closed, focusing everything on the warm flowering at her center as his body shook with release. He slowed his pace and this time she let him, relishing each stroke, wishing she could hold him in forever.

He shuddered again as he finished, falling against her, his hands gripping the counter as if he needed help standing. She traced her fingernails lightly up and down his back. His skin was hot and sticky but still she wanted to feel every part of it. Sara kissed his shoulder, his neck, his face.

"Jesus," he panted. "I'm sorry I couldn't…" He shook his head. "Jesus."

Sara put her mouth to his, gave him a soft kiss. She could count on one hand the number of times Jeffrey had let himself finish before she did. She could also honestly say she had never felt closer to him in her life.

He was smiling again, that half-smile that could infuriate her and make her love him at the same time. "I bet you Nick couldn't do that."

She leaned her head back against the mirror, still not ready to make a game of this.

"You know what they say about short guys overcompensating."

She looked at him, saw that he needed her to play along. "Give me a little credit," she relented. "I think I can do better than Nick."

He smoothed back her hair. "Do you know that I have loved you pretty much since the first time I laid eyes on you?"

She laughed. "You had a hot date lined up the very same night."

"I did not."

She poked him in the ribs. "You had to call her to tell her you'd be late."

He brushed his lips across hers. "I love you, Sara."

She felt her throat tighten. She gave him her usual answer, her joking answer that had driven him crazy the first year they were together because she would never say the words back to him. "I know."

"You know what else?" he asked, tucking a strand of hair behind her ear. "You are a dirty, dirty girl." Sara felt herself blush crimson and he laughed out loud. "That, too, but I meant literally. Look in the mirror."

She turned and checked her reflection. He'd managed to wipe off most of the dirt from her face but she still looked as if she'd been hit by a truck.

He said, "I have to be honest. I don't like what you've done with your hair."

She turned back around. "You're not exactly the prize pig at the fair."

"Then why don't we finish this in the shower?" He glanced down, ran his hands up her thighs. "Or did you want to give me a chance to redeem myself right now?"

"You think you remember how?"

They both jumped as a loud banging shook the door.

Sara slid off the counter, pulling up her sweatpants and closing her shirt in one swift motion. Her heart was pounding like she was eighteen years old again, caught in the back of a Buick with a boy instead of an old married woman who had every right to be in a cheap motel with her husband.

There was more pounding on the door, almost like a hammer. Light streamed in at the top where the flimsy plywood bent from the impact. The plate glass window overlooking the parking lot made an ominous creaking sound.

Sara buttoned her shirt as Jeffrey tucked himself back into his jeans. "If that's Jake Valentine," he began, but didn't have time to finish his sentence. The window shattered, glass flying into the room, curtains billowing as a large object smashed onto the plastic table then fell to the floor.

Jeffrey had dropped to his knees, his arms covering his head. "What the—"

Wheels screeched on asphalt outside.

Sara's mouth opened in surprise. The object was a man. Someone had just thrown a man through their window.

Instinctively, she ran toward him but Jeffrey caught her hand, yanking her to the ground.

"Go into the bathroom," he ordered, reaching under the mattress and pulling out his gun. "Now."

Sara ran in a crouch as Jeffrey moved toward the door. He put his hand on the knob, tried the door, but it wouldn't budge.

He pressed his back to the door, then the wall, making his way to the window. Quickly, he looked out the window, scanning the parking lot, then kneeling back down under the ledge. He did this twice, and Sara held her breath each time, waiting for his head to be blown off.

Jeffrey glanced back at Sara. "Stay here," he told her, then jumped through the broken window.

Sara held her breath, ears straining for the sound of gunshot. She crawled on her knees toward the man, trying to see if he was alive. Glass was everywhere, and she picked around it, trying not to cut herself. She kept her head down as she pressed her fingers to his neck, but wasn't sure if what she felt was a pulse or her own shaking hands.

"Sara."

She screamed, ducking down at the same moment that she realized it was only Jeffrey.

"Whoever it was is gone." He used the butt of his gun to knock away some glass before climbing back through the window. "Is he dead?"

She finally looked at the man. He was on his left side facing the window. The white pearl handle of an expensive-looking folding knife stuck out of his back. A large shard of glass was fixed in his neck but there was only a trickle of blood, not the expected spurt generated from a beating heart. Still, she pressed her fingers to his carotid just to make sure.

She told Jeffrey, "Nothing."

He seemed almost relieved. "The door's been nailed shut."

Sara sat back on her knees, said a silent prayer of thanks that it was just a man thrown through the window and not a flaming ball of fire.

Jeffrey tilted the man's head, looked at his face. "I think it's the guy from the bar."

"It has to be," she told him. The man had obviously recently been in a fire. His eyes were open but the lashes were singed off. His close-cropped hair was covered in soot. His shirt was burned away in large patches, the flesh underneath showing first- and second-degree burns.

Jeffrey started to tear open the man's shirtsleeve.

"Don't," Sara told him, thinking there might be evidence on the shirt, but she saw Jeffrey's reason soon enough.

Tattooed onto the dead man's arm was a large red swastika.

LENA

CHAPTER 12

LENA SAT AT HANK'S KITCHEN TABLE, her back against the wall, waiting for him to come home. The clock over the stove ticked loudly, and Lena had to force herself not to match her breathing to the noise. The Mercedes was in the driveway, so he must have come home at some point, but he was nowhere to be found now. The house was empty, the shed and beat-up old pickup in the backyard were both vacant. She'd driven by the bar, called the hospital, even talked to some old coot at the sheriff's office who gave her the standard line about waiting twenty-four hours, but Hank had pretty much disappeared. His cell phone was on the kitchen table, the battery dead. The answering machine showed no messages. The blue metal box, his drug kit, was gone. There was no way Hank would go anywhere without his kit. He must have taken it with him, which meant he'd left the house of his own accord—but that didn't tell her where he had gone.

Lena didn't even know what she would do if and when he turned up. What would she say if he walked through the door right now? What could she possibly ask him? Four hours had passed since she'd talked to Charlotte at the school, but the passage of time had done nothing to give Lena any clarity.

Hank had not been driving the car.

Angela Adams had blinded her own daughter, then—what? Driven away? Left Hank to deal with the fallout, to shoulder the blame?

The one thing Lena had sworn she'd never forgive him for and the bastard hadn't even done it. All that anger she'd held against him for most of her life was still boiling up inside her, only now she had nowhere to direct it. Should she be mad at her mother, a woman she couldn't even remember meeting? What was so bad about Angela Adams that Hank would let people assume he blinded his own niece rather than let the girls know that she was alive? What had she done to all of them?

The fluorescent light over the kitchen sink bathed the room in a blue cast as the sun started to go down. Hank's AA pamphlets were still scattered on the table, strewn across the floor, stacked hundreds deep on the gas stove. The clock kept ticking, marking away the minutes, then another hour.

After the accident, Sibyl hadn't been able to remember running into the driveway, or even the fact that she'd been playing ball with Lena in the first place. At the time, the doctor said this was fairly normal with severe head trauma, that sometimes the memories never came back. The sisters had never really talked about it afterward. Maybe they had as children, but as time passed, Sibyl's blindness and the cause of it had just become an accepted thing between them. Talking about the accident would have been like talking about the sun rising every morning: a foregone conclusion.

Meanwhile, Lena had blamed Hank and Hank sure as hell hadn't done anything to disabuse her of the notion. Whenever she threw it in his face, he'd just tighten his jaw, stare somewhere over her shoulder, and wait for her to finish.

Charlotte Warren had to know more about this than she was letting on; she was three years older than Lena and Sibyl. Her memory was better, her shock less traumatic. Still, all the woman had revealed were the bare facts: the car had hit Sibyl, Hank had come running, and Angela had bolted, not stopping to see if Sibyl was okay, not bothering to explain what had happened. The police had arrived within minutes, then the ambulance. Charlotte's mother had taken her daughter home and told her to forget what had happened, that no good would come from talking about it.

According to Charlotte, she had taken her mother's words to heart. Even as her relationship with Sibyl developed into something more serious, Charlotte had assumed that there were some things that were just too awful, too painful, to talk about.

Had it been that simple, though? Had Charlotte and Sibyl really never talked about that day? Lena supposed it was feasible that if Sibyl wouldn't discuss the subject with her own sister, she wouldn't bring it up with Charlotte Warren, either. Sibyl had bristled at the thought of having anyone's pity. She had devoted her life to being as self-sufficient as a seeing person. She'd never given in to her disability or used it for personal gain. Maybe she hadn't talked about the accident because she hadn't wanted anyone to feel sorry for her.

So many secrets, so many people protecting Angela Adams, and no one willing to explain why.

Lena reached back over her head to the phone on the wall. The receiver was sticky in her hand, the buttons stuck with grime. She dialed Nan Thomas's number, thinking she'd ask Sibyl's lover exactly what her sister had known about that horrible day. Her heart was pounding by the time Nan's phone started to ring. Lena waited, counting off the rings until voice mail picked up.

She hung up, not leaving a message.

What if Sibyl had known it was their mother? No. She would have said something to Lena. There was no way she could have gone all those years without telling Lena that their mother had been alive years after Hank had told them she'd died, that they had been lied to.

Unless Sibyl was trying to protect Lena, too.

"Shit," Lena cursed, rubbing her eyes. She was tired, and sitting in Hank's house was somehow worse than being in her crappy motel room. It was certainly dirtier.

She stood up and walked toward the back door. Lena put her hand on the knob but didn't turn it. Instead, she dropped her hand and walked back toward the hall. She stopped in front of the bathroom, then turned back around and went into the kitchen. The chair's legs scraped across the wood floor but she was hardly worried about the finish.

Many years ago, Hank had run out of room to put all his shit. He'd gotten precut strips of plywood from the hardware store and made Lena hand them up through the attic opening one by one so he could nail them in place. Of course he'd had the wisdom to tackle this project in the middle of August, the hottest month of the year. When he'd come down out of the attic, the last piece of wood nailed in place, he'd passed out in the hallway from heatstroke.

The next day, he was back up in the attic, stacking boxes, moving stuff around. Lena was ten, maybe twelve at the time. Just a few years after Angela Adams had blinded Sibyl. What had Hank put up there? What papers had been hidden above her head all this time? He left so much shit lying around that the extra stuff in the attic hadn't even occurred to her until now.

Lena climbed onto the chair and pressed her hands against the access panel. It felt stuck, though not with paint. Something was on top, a box maybe, and Lena had to use her fist to punch up the panel and knock off the box. By the time she managed to slide the panel aside, her hand was throbbing, blood trickling from her knuckles. The stagnant air from the attic wafted down, but Lena didn't give herself time to think it through before reaching up into the open space, grabbing the beams on either side of the opening and pulling herself up.

The roof was pitched, but not enough to stand. She kept at a low crouch as she moved toward the light switch, knowing that long rusty nails from the shingles were jutting down, waiting to rip her scalp open. Even with the sun down, the attic was hot as hell. A bead of sweat rolled down her back. Knowing she was wasting her time, she flicked the light switch. Much to her amazement, the bulb came on, illuminating a small area of the cramped attic. A blown bulb and an empty pack were on the floor so she had to think Hank had been up here recently. There was no telling what he had been doing. Boxes were stacked everywhere, papers spilling out all over the place. Rat droppings dotted the plywood floor. She heard a squeaking sound as some kind of animal protested her invasion.

The smell hit her with sudden intensity, the overwhelming stench of death.

As a rookie cop, Lena had handled her share of calls from out-of-town sons and daughters who were wondering why Mom or Dad or Grandma wasn't picking up the phone. Generally, there was a very good reason, and the more senior officers considered it on-the-job training to send the rookies out to discover the bodies.

Once, Lena had found an old woman sitting in her recliner, dead as a doornail. An unfinished afghan and some knitting needles were in her lap, the TV chattering in the background. The woman smelled like urine and rotting meat. Lena had puked her guts out on the back porch before she'd radioed back to the station to tell them what she'd found.

Now, in the attic, she felt like puking again—not from stress, but from fear. She knew what a dead person smelled like, the way their body fluids seeped out, the gases escaped, as they decomposed. She knew the way their skin sank into the bones, that more likely than not they'd baked in their own shit as they'd waited for someone to find them.

A thought flashed into her head, one that wouldn't go away: had she found her mother? Had Angela Adams been up here all those years, her body rotting into the floorboards as Lena and Sibyl lived down below?

No. It wasn't possible. Too much time had passed. The odor would be gone. Hank would've moved it by now.

Lena felt her heart beating in her throat. Hank. She always thought of him last, even now. Tears sprang into her eyes. She reached up, steadying herself against a rafter. There was another noise in the attic, the sound of her own cries, like a siren winding down.

She saw it now on the opposite end of the attic: a pale foot sticking out from behind the boxes; a man's foot, the sparse spattering of hair around the ankle, the waxy sheen of death on the skin.

"No," Lena whispered, because that was all she could manage.

He had finally done it. He had climbed up here with his kit, taken that last needle, burned that last bag of powder, and killed himself. Just as he had told Lena he would do. Just as she had secretly hoped that he would do all those years ago.

She could leave right now. She could go back to Grant County. She could go to work on Monday, do her job, come home, have some dinner, maybe watch a movie on TV. She could call Nan and maybe go visit. They would drink beer and sit in the backyard and talk about Sibyl and maybe Lena would ask her sister's lover exactly what Sibyl had known. Or maybe she wouldn't. Maybe they would talk about the weather or some book Nan was reading that Lena couldn't begin to understand. Nan would ask about Hank and Lena would tell her that she hadn't heard from him in a while, didn't know what he was up to.

Lena crawled to him on her hands and knees. Her arms were trembling so badly that she had to stop halfway, steady herself, before she could go on. She was hearing things again, words in a small voice, like a little girl was saying them. "I'm sorry," she heard. "It's my fault...I should've never left you...I should've called an ambulance...I should've taken you to the hospital...I should've stopped you." Lena realized that the voice she heard was her own. She sobbed, gasping for air in the closed attic.

Lena reached up, shoved away the boxes so that they toppled to the side. She saw the naked man lying dead in front of her.

It wasn't Hank.

THURSDAY MORNING

CHAPTER 13

JEFFREY HAD NEVER LIKED sleeping in strange places. In his wilder days, he'd been loath to spend the entire evening with a woman, and not just because her husband might come home. He liked being able to get up in the middle of the night and know where the bathroom was. He liked knowing where the light switches were and which cabinet the glasses were in.

What he didn't like was waking up in Jake Valentine's house.

He had easily found the sheriff in the parking lot of Hank's bar next door, though there wasn't much the sheriff could do but watch the building burn. Jeffrey had found him standing beside one of his deputies, thumbs hooked into the waist of his blue jeans as he watched the last of the fire burn itself out. Valentine was still wearing his ankle holster and smelled a lot like the beer he'd been drinking with Jeffrey the night before. When Jeffrey had asked the man to follow him back to the motel, he hadn't asked questions.

"That's Boyd Gibson," Valentine had said when Jeffrey showed him the dead man lying on the floor of his and Sara's motel room. "I went to school with him."

Not, "How the hell did this dead guy get in your room?" or "Who stabbed him in the back?" Just, "Damn, his daddy's gonna be heartbroken."

Jeffrey supposed he should be thankful that Valentine had offered them his spare room for the night. Grant County was a long drive and

Sara had turned quiet again—too quiet for Jeffrey's liking. When he asked if she minded sleeping at the sheriff's house, she'd merely nodded, silently tucking her clothes into the suitcase she'd brought from home. She hadn't spoken during the quick drive to Valentine's house, either. When Jeffrey climbed into bed beside her, she'd put her head on his chest, wrapped her arm around him.

Jeffrey found himself listening to see if Sara was crying again. Sara very seldom cried, and when she did, he felt as if his heart was being squeezed in a vise. She wasn't crying, though. She was thinking. That much was obvious when she leaned up on her elbow, her tone telling him she'd made up her mind when she said, "I'm not leaving this place until you do."

He'd opened his mouth to argue the point, but she put her fingers to his lips, shushed him. "When I married you"—she allowed a smile—"at least this last time, I knew you were the kind of man who runs toward trouble instead of running away from it." She paused, her tone soft but firm. "I can't stop you from trying to save the world, but I won't abandon you while you're doing it."

He had felt like an absolute shit then—not because he still wanted her to go home, not because he'd put her in the line of fire, but because he had been lying to her face from the minute that dead body had been thrown into their room.

Jeffrey had seen the tattooed man on the floor, saw the dark, black blood flowering out from the pearl-handled folding knife in his back, and said nothing.

"I'm not leaving until you do," Sara had told him.

There wasn't anything else to say after that. He closed his eyes but sleep wouldn't come so he found himself listening to Sara's breathing. She was obviously restless, and after a while she turned on her side, then laid flat on her stomach. At least a full hour passed before her breathing finally slowed and she fell asleep.

Jeffrey got out of bed and dressed, even though there was nowhere for him to go. He desperately wanted to take a shower, but there was only one bathroom in the house and he didn't want to wake anyone up. He didn't want to prowl around Valentine's home, either, so he pulled up a metal folding chair and sat by the window looking out at the street. He adjusted the blinds just enough to see outside. Like the guest bedroom, the living room was on the street side of the house, and Jeffrey imagined the sheriff had been looking at much the same view as Jeffrey was now when he noticed the fire coming from the football field. It would've taken him less than five minutes to jog over to see what happened. At least that part of the sheriff's story checked out.

Despite the modest house, Valentine, or maybe his wife, seemed to be quite the gardener. Tiny landscaping lights lining the front yard illuminated their handiwork: fall plantings and grass that was mowed neat like a green blanket. There were so many things a man did to make a house a home, whether it was replacing a rotted soffit or painting the walls or hanging some ugly floral wallpaper in the bathroom that your wife had picked out. Not that Sara was partial to large floral patterns, but judging from the Laura-Ashley-gone-wild scheme throughout the house, Jeffrey was guessing Mrs. Valentine was.

He tried to think of all the changes he and Sara had made to their home over the years. The only ones that came to mind were more recent. Before the woman from the adoption agency came for a home visit, Sara had convinced Jeffrey to get on his hands and knees with her and look at the house the way a baby might. He'd played along, laughing until they'd found a nail sticking out from the kitchen cabinet under the sink. By the time he spotted a finger-sized gap between an electrical socket and the Sheetrock in the laundry room, he was ready to tear down the house and start again from scratch.

Jeffrey found himself wondering what Al Pfeiffer's house had looked like before the firebomb had been thrown through his window. What had Pfeiffer been thinking as he watched his home burn down? Or had the old sheriff been too consumed by his own injuries to take much notice of what he was losing? Jesus, had he heard them nailing his front door shut and known what was about to happen?

Jeffrey glanced back at Sara lying in bed. What had he gotten her into? Or, worse yet, what had Lena gotten them into? Just yesterday, he had been looking for ways to tie together all the threads. Tonight, the solution had come flying through his window with a big bow tied around it. The pearl-handled knife jutting out of Boyd Gibson's back belonged to Lena.

Jeffrey sighed, slouching back in the uncomfortable metal chair. He stared out the window again, watching the empty street. He must have dozed off, because the next thing he knew, a hint of light was slanting in through the window. A car pulled up outside. The driver got out and stumbled toward the house across the street, dropping his keys twice before he managed to open the front door. Less than a minute later, he came back out of the house and walked in a drunken diagonal back toward his car. Jeffrey was wondering if he should intervene when the man fell into the backseat. The front door of the house opened a crack, a woman poked out her head to check on the man, then shut the door again.

Sara stirred and Jeffrey turned around to see if she was awake. She was still on her stomach, arms and legs spread as she took advantage of his empty side of the bed. There was enough light now so that he could see her face. He hated arguing with her, couldn't function when they were mad at each other. Watching her in the morgue, the careful, respectful way she handled that poor woman's body, had reminded him of all the reasons he needed Sara in his life. She was the one person who could cut through all the bullshit and show him what was important. She was his conscience.

When Jeffrey had initially met Cathy and Eddie Linton, his first thought was that they just didn't make marriages like that anymore. Now, being with Sara, he understood that they did.

The floor creaked outside the bedroom door as someone walked past. The bathroom was at the end of the hall, separating the two bedrooms, and Jeffrey listened as the footsteps softened, shuffling across the tile. The door clicked closed.

Seeing the house last night, Jeffrey had found himself thinking there was no way Jake Valentine was on the take—not unless he had a secret mansion somewhere out in the woods. The place was definitely a fixer-upper. Fake pine paneling lined the living room and the kitchen cupboards were original to the house—not a good thing when you lived in a 1960s ranch. If Jake was taking money to look the other way, the sheriff sure wasn't spending it on himself.

The shower turned on. Jeffrey wondered if it was the sheriff or his wife. Myra Valentine wasn't exactly friendly with them last night, but not many wives would be glad to welcome two strangers into their home at one in the morning. She was a short woman, maybe five feet tall in her socks, the top of her head not quite reaching Jake's chest. What she lacked in height she made up for in girth. Jeffrey guessed she was at least a hundred pounds overweight. Standing side by side, the Valentines looked like the living embodiment of the number ten.

Like her husband, Myra hadn't asked a lot of questions. After the most basic introductions were made, she had hustled Jeffrey and Sara into the guest bedroom with the kind of efficiency you'd expect from a high school English teacher, fetching Sara a towel and washrag, briskly changing the bed so they would have fresh sheets to sleep on. When Jeffrey had volunteered to help, she'd given him a scowl that made him feel like he'd been caught passing a note in class.

The shower turned off. Noises came from the rest of the house. Pots and pans clattered together. A radio was switched on, the sound down low. In the bathroom, a hairdryer whirred. Sara didn't move. She had always been a heavy sleeper. She'd told him once that it came from her grueling internship, where catching sleep was a competitive sport. Two years ago, she'd slept through a hurricane while he'd anxiously stared out the windows, waiting for the oak tree in the front yard to come crashing down on the house.

Jeffrey stood up, stretching his arms over his head, feeling his spine creak as it tried to align itself to something other than the shape of a folding chair. There was a dull throb in his head and he could still smell smoke from last night's fire on his skin and hair. He could smell Sara mixed in there somewhere, too, and his body stirred at the thought. If he'd been just about anywhere else in the world but Jake Valentine's house, he would've climbed back in bed with her and done something about it.

Instead, he laid out some fresh clothes, putting them in a neat pile on the edge of the bed, so desperate for a shower that he could almost feel the warm water on his back. At the motel, Sara had just shoved everything into the suitcase. Now, Jeffrey folded her shirts, smoothed down her jeans so they wouldn't wrinkle.

The front door opened and closed and Jeffrey went to the window again, peered out through the blinds. He'd thought Jake Valentine was sneaking out, but he saw the gangly young man standing in the front yard, hands on his hips as he surveyed the street like the lord of the manor. The sheriff was wearing a ridiculously short red velour robe that stopped a few inches shy of his knees, and when he bent over to retrieve the morning paper, Jeffrey winced at the sight of the tighty whities cracking a smile.

Valentine tucked the paper under his arm as he walked over to the car parked in front of his house. He was wearing brown loafers and socks with the robe, and his footprints left their mark in the grass as he walked toward the neighbor's car. He checked the backseat where

Jeffrey assumed the drunk was still sleeping it off, then looked up and down the street again before heading back to the house.

Jeffrey closed the blinds, not wanting the light to wake up Sara. When he turned around he saw that he was too late.

She was on her side, watching him. "How'd you sleep?"

"Like a baby."

"Babies don't tend to sleep sitting up in metal chairs."

"High chairs?" He smiled at her dubious expression, sat beside her on the bed. "You okay?"

"I'm better," was all she allowed. "What're we doing?"

He took her hand. "You still sticking around?"

"Yep."

He wasn't happy about her staying, but he'd be stupid not to use her. "I was hoping you could tell us something about our drop-in visitor from last night."

"Boyd Gibson?" Sara sat up, leaned her back against the headboard. "Do you think Jake will ask me to do the autopsy?"

"I'd bet money on it," Jeffrey told her. Valentine would want to keep tabs on Sara and Jeffrey, and there was no better way to occupy their time than by sticking them at the morgue all day. What the sheriff probably wasn't planning on was that Jeffrey had no problem leaving Sara alone at the morgue.

She asked, "Do you want me to do the procedure?"

"Might as well," he answered. "Maybe something will turn up."

She lowered her voice to just above a whisper. "Like Lena's fingerprints on her knife?"

She could've kicked him in the face and he would've been less surprised.

Sara explained, "The handle is very distinctive. I've seen her with it before."

"I'm sorry," he apologized, knowing he should have told her hours ago. "I guess I didn't want to think about how it might have gotten there."

"I don't want a marriage where we keep things from each other. We did that one time before and it didn't work for either of us."

"You're right," he agreed, feeling even shittier since she was letting him off so easy. He felt the need to apologize again. "I'm really sorry."

She offered, "It could've been self-defense."

"Nice try," he said, giving a dry laugh. It was hard to make a case for self-defense when the victim had been stabbed in the back. "You think you'll get anything useful from the body?"

"You know I hate to make predictions," she prefaced. "But, from what I saw last night, it was pretty straightforward: knife in the back, blade through the heart, death probably instantaneous." She shrugged. "Does it really matter if he was hit in the head before he was killed, or what he had for his last meal?"

"What about a tox screen?"

"It'll take months to get results back, and even when we do, what can it tell us?"

"Nothing new," Jeffrey admitted. "We know he's a white supremacist by the tattoo. We know he was in the bar before it burned down because we saw him."

"Do you think he set the fire?"

Jeffrey shook his head. "It looked to me like the fire started from the outside. Besides, I'm certain he was looking for something in that bar when we saw him. He sure as hell didn't want to leave there without it."

"Drugs might explain his behavior."

"But not his motivation," Jeffrey pointed out. He tried to think through his day, pin down things he could do that would actually move them toward his goal, which was finding out what exactly Lena had stumbled into and trying to help her find her way out. "I want to go by Hank's house and see if I can find anything."

"Drop me off at the morgue first and I'll start the autopsy."

He had to try, "If you left here around one, you'd be back in Grant in time for supper."

"Or, I could find us another hotel to stay in," she countered. "I remember seeing a town with more than a bar and a post office about half an hour from here. Maybe they'll have something."

"You know I don't want you here. I mean, I do, but I—"

She shushed him. "I know."

The hallway floor squeaked, but this time, whoever it was didn't go into the bathroom.

Sara pulled her knees to her chest, straightened the blanket so it covered her, just as a light knock came at the door.

Jeffrey said, "Come in."

Jake Valentine smiled as he cracked open the door. "Sorry to disturb y'all." He had changed from his skimpy robe into his sheriff's uniform, a decided improvement, though he still looked as if he was wearing his daddy's clothes. "Myra's already gone off to school, but she left you some bacon and eggs on the stove if you want." His mouth went up in a quick smile, as if the thought of his wife cooking breakfast made him happy.

"Thank you," Sara told him. "That was very nice of her."

Valentine took off his hat and addressed Sara. "Anyway, ma'am, I was kind of hoping, you'd oblige us again today with the autopsy on Boyd. That's the man from last night. Boyd Gibson. I can get you cash if—"

"That's really unnecessary," she cut him off. "I'm glad to help out."

"That's great." Valentine twirled his hat between his hands. "I'll head over to Grover's now, pick him up and tote him to the morgue so he can make the formal ID."

Sara was never good at hiding her surprise. "You haven't told him about his son yet?"

Valentine stopped playing with his hat. "Grover does the second shift at the tire factory," he told her, as if that was an excuse. "I figured I'd let him finish his work, get some sleep, before I told him about Boyd."

Sara nodded, but her disapproval was evident. Especially in a small town, where rumors pretty much became gospel, a cop had to get to the family first to make sure they heard the truth rather than rampant speculation. It was bad enough when you had to tell a parent that their child was dead, but when you knew the victim, had actually spent time with the family, it made everything harder.

Sara volunteered, "Maybe you could take Jeffrey with you to tell the father. I'm sure Mr. Gibson will have some questions about how his son died, and Jeffrey was one of the last people to see him alive."

Valentine's mouth twisted to the side as he thought about her suggestion, more than likely trying to come up with a good reason to say no. "Uh, you don't need him to help you in the morgue today?"

Sara feigned surprise at the question. She shook her head, giving an innocent-sounding, "Not really."

Jeffrey offered, "You could interview me on the way there."

"Interview you for what?"

"About last night," Jeffrey clarified. "I'm assuming you'll need a statement from me about what happened. The bar burning down. The dead man being thrown through our window."

"Yeah," Valentine agreed. "Okay." He glanced at his watch. "We'd better get, then."

"Just give me ten minutes to take a quick shower," Jeffrey said, grabbing his clothes off the bed. "I'll be right with you."

✦

JEFFREY DIDN'T KNOW WHETHER it was just for his benefit, but Jake Valentine was a painfully careful driver. The man never met an intersection he didn't slow down for and he actually stopped at a green light on the outskirts of town, telling Jeffrey, "It turns red real fast." He liked to talk, and Jeffrey kept his own counsel, nodding to keep him going as they made the trip to tell Grover Gibson his son had been stabbed to death.

After half an hour of nonstop babbling, Valentine seemed to exhaust himself of talk of the weather and local anecdotes involving high school seniors pulling pranks during homecoming week. Not once had he brought up the reason for their trip, or speculated on who might have killed Boyd Gibson. Jeffrey knew that even Jake Valentine would've dusted the knife sticking out of Boyd's back for prints. He'd have to scan in anything he found and send it to the state lab for cross-referencing. Unless he put a rush on it, and that was seriously doubtful, he'd have something back in a few days.

Jeffrey asked, "You ever been in a situation like this before?"

"What's that?"

"Known a victim," Jeffrey answered. "This Boyd Gibson. You went to high school with him, you said."

"We ran in different crowds."

"You were with the jocks and he was with the stoners?"

"Oh, me." Valentine laughed. "My daddy's biggest disappointment was me not being able to handle a basketball." He glanced at Jeffrey. "Dad was all-state his last year at UGA. Scored thirty-seven points in the last half pretty much on his own. Me, I'm just good for changing lightbulbs and getting down boxes from the top shelf."

"What made you pick up the badge?"

"Oh." He waved his hand, dismissing the question. "Just thought it'd be something to do."

"Seems like a pretty dangerous job to take up on a whim, considering the last guy who had it was chased out of town."

"He landed on his feet."

"Sounds to me like he got when the gettin' was good."

Valentine gave Jeffrey a sharp look. "You telling me I should do the same?"

"I'm telling you this is a dangerous job for somebody who doesn't have his heart in it."

Valentine slowed his car for a turn onto a one-lane dirt road. "I might just surprise you, Chief."

"You know what surprises me?" Jeffrey asked, feeling the temperature drop in the car as they got out of the sun and drove down the tree-lined path. "It surprises me that you don't seem to have any questions."

"What kind of questions should I have?"

"Start with why my detective gave you the slip," Jeffrey began. "Who made Hank Norton disappear? Who got his bar closed down? Who's been setting fires? Who killed your buddy from high school?"

Valentine slowed the car to a stop. He put the car in park and turned toward Jeffrey. Two things occurred to Jeffrey. One was that they were in the middle of nowhere and the other was that Jake Valentine was the only one of them who was armed.

He felt a bead of sweat roll down his back.

Valentine rested his hand on the bottom curve of the steering wheel, his fingers inches from the gun on his belt. He said, "You look nervous, Chief."

"I want to know why you stopped."

"To answer your questions," he said. "Come on, let's go for a walk." He opened the door and got out. Jeffrey sat there, his heart beating hard enough to feel. The lane they were parked on was little more than packed dirt, dense forest on either side. No one knew they were out here but Sara, and there were a lot of excuses she could be told as to why Jeffrey never came back.

Valentine stood in the road a few feet in front of the car. He waved for Jeffrey to get out. "Come on, Chief."

Jeffrey opened the door. He'd left his gun in the back of Sara's car, locked in the trunk with their suitcase. He'd thought they were coming here to tell a man that his son was dead, not chase bad guys.

Valentine said, "It's getting cool out."

"Yeah," Jeffrey agreed. He felt the wind stir up as he got out of the car. He'd put on a light jacket over a long-sleeved T-shirt this morning but he didn't zip the jacket closed. He wanted the sheriff to think that Jeffrey wanted to be able to reach into the coat if he needed to.

Jeffrey closed the car door. The lane was covered in fall leaves, the trees bending over to block out the light. It would've been gorgeous if Jeffrey hadn't had the powerful suspicion that he'd been brought out here for some kind of ambush.

"This way." Valentine started strolling down the lane, slow enough for Jeffrey to catch up.

Jeffrey said, "I didn't plan on going for a walk."

"Pretty day for it, though. Might want to zip up your jacket."

"I'm fine," Jeffrey assured him.

Valentine reached up and tugged a bright orange leaf from an over-hanging branch. He twirled it in his fingers as he talked. "Good country folk live out here. Real simple people. Most of them, they just wanna go to work, come home to the wife and kids, maybe have enough money left over at the end of the week to get a couple of beers and watch the football game on TV."

Jeffrey kept his hands at his sides. There was a way you walked when you were carrying a gun, like you had brass ones swinging to your knees. "Grant County's not that much different."

"Guess not." Valentine let Jeffrey get a foot or so ahead of him. The move was subtle, but Jeffrey knew the other man was looking for the telltale bulge of a gun at his back.

Valentine said, "Most small towns are alike, I think. Politics and all that crap blurs things, but we all have the same goals whether we're in south Georgia or south France or Timbuktu. We want to feel safe. We want our kids to go to good schools and have the opportunities we didn't. We want to live our lives and feel like we've got some control over our destinies."

He was sounding like a different person now, the aw-shucks gestures and good-ol'-boy slang all but gone.

"What's this leading up to, Jake?"

He gave Jeffrey a lazy smile. "This way." He pointed to a small trail that cut through the woods.

"What's down there?"

"See for yourself."

This time, Valentine took the lead and Jeffrey followed, the hairs on the back of his neck prickling as they went deeper into the forest. The trail didn't appear to be well-used. The ground sloped downward and Jeffrey slowed his pace, putting some distance between himself and the sheriff. Valentine didn't seem to notice. He kept walking, still twirling the leaf. It wasn't until he reached a small clearing that he stopped, waiting for Jeffrey.

"Lookit this," Valentine said. He pointed to a sloped rock with a hole in it. A long section of white PVC pipe was propped up against the hole. A trickle of water fed into the pipe.

"It's a natural spring," Jeffrey said, more than a little surprised. He knelt down to check it out before he could think about what he was doing. He looked up at the sheriff, waited for the man to make his move.

"Here." Valentine offered his hand, helped Jeffrey stand. "The pipe goes down the hill here." He started walking, following the pipe's path. The woods started to clear and the trees thinned out as they made their way down the slope toward what looked like an abandoned shack. Jeffrey guessed they walked about fifty yards before they reached a huge plastic holding tank of springwater. Jeffrey could hear the water dripping into the tank, saw the larger plastic pipe feeding into a shack sitting in the middle of a clearing.

"Plumbing," Valentine told Jeffrey. "Springwater goes into the hookup at the house. Cold as a witch's tit if you wanna take a shower, but pretty damn smart, don't you think?"

"Yeah," Jeffrey agreed. He could see a beat-up Ford parked in front of the shack. A long wire ran from the roof to an electric pole. Except for the small satellite dish angled off the roof, he could be looking at a home circa the Great Depression.

Valentine said, "Just got electricity out here a few years ago. Liked to took forever for the county to do it. Grover had to do most of the work himself."

"This is where Boyd Gibson's father lives?"

"Course it is. Where'd you think I was taking you?" Valentine took off his hat and wiped his forehead with the back of his sleeve. He was sweating as bad as Jeffrey, and it suddenly occurred to him that Jake Valentine had been just as wary during their tense walk through the woods as Jeffrey had been.

Valentine pointed to a dilapidated wooden picnic table tucked back into the woods. It'd obviously been there for a while; kudzu had taken over. Valentine told Jeffrey, "Me and Boyd used to sit up there and smoke weed when we was kids. Skipped school all the time, always in trouble. Now, it was his brother, Larry, who was the jock. Me and Boyd were the stoners." He was quiet for a moment, seemed to be reflecting as he stared at the picnic table. "Boyd's old man hated my guts. Mind you, I wasn't crazy about him, either. He beat his wife to an early grave and then he started hauling off on his sons. Beat me once, too—blamed me for getting Boyd hooked and I think maybe he's right." He rubbed his jaw as if in memory of a punch. "Maybe I'm just fooling myself because I sure as hell drink too much, but with drugs I think that some folks can take it or leave it. I tried a little bit of everything: coke, speed, dope. It was nice, but then I met Myra and she didn't stand for that kind of thing so I just left it behind. Boyd couldn't do that. He got into meth real heavy, started shooting up, which was something I was always too chicken to do—needles scare the crap out of me. Once Boyd started putting that shit in his veins, he never looked back. You and Sara got kids?"

Jeffrey was taken aback by the sudden question. "We're trying."

"Myra says she won't bring a baby into this world without knowing he's gonna have a daddy."

Jeffrey and Sara had talked about the same thing many times. "It's dangerous work being a cop, but you can't put your life on hold because of it."

Valentine nodded, looking back at the picnic table. Jeffrey could see the beginnings of a bald spot on the crown of the man's head. That would explain why he wore a hat all the time. Jeffrey's father had been an asshole of the highest degree, but Jeffrey took comfort in the fact that his old man had died with a full head of hair.

Valentine said, "Myra and me, we knew each other in high school— well, the kind of way you know who the bad folks are and who the good folks are. Her family moved to town my sophomore year. Big city girl." He laughed at a private joke. "Myra was the good one, in case you need to be told. Real religious, loves the Lord. She was pretty surprised when I showed up at the same college as her, thought I was just some dumb pothead who'd end up slinging tires at the factory. I had to work my ass off to convince her I wasn't just some fool chasing a piece of tail." He chuckled again. "That was ten years ago, and she hasn't changed a bit. God, but she's pretty. Smart as a whip and don't mind putting me in my place, which I probably need more often than not. Now, I can't even imagine what my life was like without her. Miserable, I guess. Maybe I'd be in jail instead of running the place. Could've just as easily been me as Boyd thrown through your window last night."

Jeffrey crossed his arms, wondering if what he was hearing was the truth or some carefully planned story to get his defenses down. Valentine hadn't exactly been forthcoming over the last few days, and now he was laying down his life story like he was testifying at a tent revival.

Valentine leaned back on his heel, put his hat on his head. "You wanted to know who's been setting fires, who chased off Hank and got his place closed down?" He glanced back at the small house as if to make sure no one was listening. "Answer to both questions is Boyd Gibson. He was working the bar, slinging Bud Light with meth chasers, when the ATF came in. As far as who stabbed him, I've got me some ideas, but I'm gonna have to trust you a hell of a lot more before I tell you that."

"Did he torch the Escalade?"

"Wouldn't be surprised."

"Why did my detective run?"

"I gather she's as hardheaded and arrogant as her boss. I arrested her because I think she's involved in this up to her eyeballs. I'm gonna find her again, and I'll be goddamned if I let her slip away from me a second time."

Jeffrey spoke from experience. "You're fighting a losing battle."

"Yeah, well…" He shrugged. "We'll see about that."

"Who's in charge?" Jeffrey asked. "Who's running the skinheads?"

"If I could answer that, you and me probably would've never met." Valentine's sloppy grin came back. "Anyways, Chief, I guess I should warn you that the last time I saw Grover Gibson, he threatened to beat the shit out of me if I ever stepped foot on his property again."

Part of Jeffrey relished the idea of the young sheriff getting his ass kicked. "Maybe you should call some backup, then. I'm not really here in an official capacity."

"I figured as much when you got into my squad car without your gun." He gave Jeffrey a wink before heading toward the house, saying, "I hope that pretty wife of yours really is a doctor. I have a feeling I'm gonna need some stitches."

LENA

CHAPTER 14

DEACON SIMMS WAS ONE OF THOSE MEN who always looked old and out of step with the world, even when he was in his twenties. Lena supposed Deacon had considered himself a rebel, that when his gray braid slapped against his back as he drove his ancient Harley to the bar, he had thought he was making some kind of statement against society. He still looked every inch the Hells Angel he'd been in his younger days: Handlebar mustache. Confederate flag on the T-shirt stretching across his gut. Leather chaps over faded jeans.

Even in the 1970s, he had looked like someone caught in a time-warp, an old hippie whose slow speech and delayed reasoning proved that you didn't quit being a pothead no matter how many years ago you stopped lighting up. Like Hank, Deacon was wrapped up in AA and NA and any A that would have him. Unlike Hank—please God, hopefully unlike her uncle—Deacon was dead.

Now, leaning over the man's body in Hank's attic, Lena guessed Deacon had been beaten to death. His face looked more like a bruised plum, his sunken cheeks caked with dried blood. His lip had been broken open, the split cutting into his mustache so that it hung off like an actor's prop. Deacon must have lived for a while. Lena wasn't a doctor, but she had seen enough bodies at Sara Linton's morgue to know that you didn't bruise like that unless your heart was still pumping blood. If Lena had to guess again, she'd say that he'd been dead a week, maybe ten days. How long had he waited to die? Had the con with the swastika stuck him up there? Had Hank?

There were certain procedures to follow when you found a stiff. Lena had learned them all her second week at the police academy, when they taught the important stuff they didn't want to waste on the cadets who washed out in the first week.

First, you roped off the scene, then you made the phone calls. By law, the coroner had to pronounce that the person was dead, even if the body was so putrid the smell made your eyes sting. It was the coroner's job to decide whether the death was suspicious or not. Deacon Simms was what you'd call a no-brainer, an instant call to your chief who would then radio out homicide to take over. Next, forensic evidence had to be gathered, pictures taken, the area around the body vacuumed and fingertip-searched for any trace evidence that might have been left by the killer. Only after that would they remove the body for autopsy and go over their findings in order to track the killer.

In the case of Hank's attic, someone would point out the way the rat turds and dust were disturbed in a large swath from the access panel to Deacon's final resting place and conclude that he'd been dragged there. Maybe they would notice the boxes stacked in front of the body and assume that he'd been hidden there, left to die. Certainly, they would see the deep cuts on his palms and forearms and say that he had tried to defend himself from someone who was wielding a very sharp knife. The fact of his missing clothes would indicate that there had been something on said clothes that the killer felt might lead back to him. Or maybe the doer got some kind of sick twist out of beating a sixty-year-old man to death and leaving him naked up in an attic to die.

The most disturbing part was the trophy—the patch of skin that had been removed right above Deacon's left nipple. Blood surrounded the area, but the wound had not been fatal. It was just the skin the killer had wanted, a two-inch by two-inch square that had been expertly peeled from the body. The faded tattoos surrounding the missing flesh offered some clue as to what had been drawn on the removed section. Before his death, Lena had never seen Deacon without his shirt on, but she was more than familiar with the scenes adorning his chest. Deacon was Hells Angels, the original hate-mongers.

Someone had carved off his swastika.

The only good thing the missing skin told her was that Hank had not been involved in Deacon's death. The two had argued just about every day of their lives together, but Hank would never have hurt the only person in the world who could be called his friend. No matter what dark places Lena had let her mind go to over the past few days, she knew now without a shadow of a doubt that Hank would never intentionally harm anyone but himself. He was not a murderer.

The thought brought Lena to an obvious question: what had Hank been doing while someone had beaten Deacon to death and left him in the attic to die?

She had to find Hank. The local police would assume Hank had something to do with Deacon's murder. They would see a desperate drug addict and a violent death and leap to the obvious conclusion. Even Jeffrey would have a hard time believing Hank was innocent. He'd want to know how many days had passed with Hank living in the house and Deacon lying dead right above him. He'd want something more concrete than a missing piece of skin to prove Hank's innocence. Lena couldn't give him any of that. The fact that Hank was missing sure didn't do much to help matters. You only bolted if you had something to hide.

Or maybe Hank was hiding from someone. Maybe he was hiding from Lena.

She crawled back across the attic on her hands and knees, then dropped down onto the kitchen chair. Lena reached around the access panel and moved the box back in place. When she was finished, she found a rag in the bathroom and wiped the trim around the panel's opening so that her dirty fingerprints didn't show. She put the chair back in the kitchen, turned off all the lights but the one over the kitchen sink, then locked the door behind her.

She felt like a criminal as she drove her Celica through town. Hell, she *was* a criminal. Not only had she failed to report Deacon's death, she'd hidden the body, wiped off her fingerprints. She could just imagine sitting in Al Pfeiffer's office, the old fart leering at her as she told him what had happened. Al would find Hank. He'd bring him in and have him up on murder charges before Lena could even open the phone book and look for a lawyer.

Some of the outside lights were on at the bar as Lena pulled up, but there were no other cars in the lot. She assumed the lights were on timers, but then saw the rigged cords where Hank had strung together some cheap solar panels. The bulbs were a pale, fading orange and she doubted they would stay on for much longer. She leaned over and got the flashlight out of the glove compartment before getting out of the car.

Tape with the logo of the Bureau of Alcohol, Tobacco and Firearms still crisscrossed the front door. Lena checked the seal with her flashlight to make sure it hadn't been broken before heading to the back of the building. She felt the hair on the back of her neck go up as she crossed out of the semi-lit parking lot and walked along the dirt path that led to Hank's office. Considering the week she was having, she didn't think her paranoia an unhealthy emotion.

She had tried to cover the hole she'd kicked in the wall of Hank's office with a couple of trashcans from the bar. Unless you knew what you were looking for, the damage wasn't as obvious as she'd thought. She glanced over her shoulder, shined her light toward the woods, before pushing aside the trashcans and going into the office.

Inside, the shack looked exactly as she'd left it. She couldn't decide if it was a good thing or a bad thing that Hank hadn't been back. Deacon Simms was dead. Other than Charlotte Warren, Hank didn't have any friends he could turn to. There was no couch he could crash on, no spare room he could hole up in.

The checkbook was still open on his desk. She sat down in the chair and went back through the register. As far as she could remember, everything was the same as when she'd found Charlotte's letters. Still, Lena flipped through the checks, making sure none were missing. Next, she went through the desk again, this time looking for anything that might connect to Deacon Simms. All she found was Hank's spare set of keys under a beat-up old copy of *I Am the Cheese.*

Lena pocketed the keys and flipped through the book, which bore the stamp of the Elawah County Library on the spine. Glued on the back of the cover was a paper pocket with a checkout slip tucked inside. "Lena Adams" was scribbled on the strip where she'd signed out the book a billion years ago. She'd needed it for an English paper. Lena had loved the book but blown off the assignment. When the teacher had called Hank to let him know, Lena had lied, told him she'd lost the book. In addition to tanning her hide, Hank had made her pay for the book out of her allowance.

And the asshole had kept it this entire time.

Lena tossed the book onto the desk, accidentally knocking over a stack of receipts. She was scooping them up, trying to put them back in a pile, when she saw the telephone underneath. The phone was old, the kind they started making shortly after getting rid of the rotary dial. Lena reached behind it and followed the cord under the desk, looking for the answering machine. She guessed that as with the electric supply, Hank hadn't bothered to pay the phone company to get service all the way out to the shack. The galvanized pipe with the extension cord that led back to the bar was about two inches round—there was plenty of space for a long telephone extension cord.

She tucked the checkbook under her arm and knelt down to leave the shack through the hole. There wasn't anything worth stealing in the office, but she moved the trashcans back in front of the hole.

The back door of the bar was padlocked, but that had been Hank's doing, not the drug agents. As with the front door, ATF had stuck their usual tape across the jamb but she easily cut the seal with one of the keys. Lena matched the Kryptonite key to the padlock, then a smaller Yale key to the deadbolt. The metal door groaned as it opened, the pungent odor of stale smoke and beer spilling into the night air.

The soles of her shoes snicked across the rubber fatigue mats as she walked through the kitchen. Something ran over her foot and she stood stock still, hoping that it was just a rat then hoping that it was alone. She used her flashlight to find the light switch, her mind conjuring a host of rabid rodents eager to attack. There was a noise in the corner that she chose to ignore as she walked to the front of the bar.

Lena coughed, her lungs not quite used to the stale smoke and lack of oxygen. She turned on the light switches as she walked through, one of them triggering the jukebox into starting up in the middle of a song. Trash was scattered everywhere and she saw the sheen of spilled drinks that had left sticky spots on the linoleum. It didn't take a detective to read this scene. The cops had come in, cleared everybody out, made their arrests, and turned off the lights on their way out.

Suddenly, Lena remembered something. She knelt down behind the bar and rapped the floor with the back of her knuckles, straining to hear over the jukebox. She finally found what she was looking for and took out her knife to pry up a tile. Underneath, she saw a cigar box cradled between the joists. Hank's hidden stash. Lena opened the box; there was about two thousand dollars in it. She hesitated, feeling suddenly like a thief. This was Hank's money. Was it stealing from him if she took it so he couldn't buy dope?

She stood on the top of the bar and tucked the money behind a bottle of scotch that was so cheap the coloring had turned to sediment in the bottom. She jumped down and returned the empty cigar box to its hiding place. Some country crooner Lena didn't recognize was just dipping into a ballad as she pressed her heel into the tile, snapping it back in place. She felt better now, like she had done something to help Hank instead of contributing to his demise.

The telephone was behind the bar under the cash register, just where it always was. The answering machine beside it read twelve calls. Lena pressed play, and figured that the most recent calls came first when her own voice said, "Hank, it's Lee. Where are you?" She was shocked at her tone as it echoed in the bar, the anger that radiated from every word. Did she always sound this hateful when she called him? Lena shook her head: another thing she couldn't think about right now.

The next call was from Nan, Sibyl's lover. Her words were kinder but her message was clear, "I haven't heard from you in a few days and I was getting worried. Please let me know if you're doing all right."

Message ten came on, a staticky silence Lena was about to fast-forward through when she heard the beginning of an automated message that made her stomach knot.

Georgia, like just about every state in the union, used an electronic system to handle calls from prison inmates. A computerized voice announced the prison from which the call originated and advised the listener to be sure they understood the charges before they pressed a button to okay the call. Then, every two minutes, the same automated voice came on the line to remind the recipient that he or she was talking to an inmate in a state prison. The exorbitant charges helped pay for listening software to monitor inmate calls as well as protect unsuspecting strangers from getting a twenty-dollar bill for a two-minute call.

The recording was pretty standard, first announcing the origin of the call, then allowing a three-second spot for the inmate to say his name. Over the years, for various cases, Lena had listened to some of the inmate calls coming out of the Grant County jail. It was amazing what the perps could fit into the short bursts the three seconds allowed. They seldom said their names—it was more like the world's fastest opportunity to beg somebody to talk to you. They ranged from, "Mama, I love you, please talk to me," to her personal favorite, "I'm gonna kill you, bitch," from a man who kept insisting to the judge that he posed no threat to his wife.

Hank's machine played the fifth message, a duplicate to the four that preceded it. "This is a collect call from an inmate in Coastal State Prison. Press one if you wish to talk to inmate—"

Lena put her hand on the bar to hold herself up. She let the machine play, her throat feeling as if she had swallowed glass.

Five times the same message played, five times she heard his voice. She could not stop herself. She listened to the next one, then the next. All of them were the same. All played that hard, emotionless voice that seemed to echo the computer's own.

The number one flashed on the machine as the final message played.

"This is a collect phone call from an inmate at Coastal State Prison. Press one if you wish to talk to inmate—" Lena held her breath, hoping it would be different this time, that this was all some kind of sick joke.

It was not.

The speaker captured his voice perfectly, playing his slow, sure cadence as he enunciated each word.

"Ethan Green."

Lena ripped out the machine and threw it against the wall.

THURSDAY MORNING

CHAPTER 15

BACK IN GRANT COUNTY, Sara had a helper, or diener, who performed the less glamorous tasks relating to autopsy. Carlos catalogued all the surgical tools, kept up with the samples, took the X-rays, cleaned up the substantial mess, and basically made Sara's job far easier just by being in the room. He took notes, weighed organs, and—most important—performed a duty known as "running the gut," which meant standing over a sink and cleaning out the bowels so the contents could be examined and weighed. The task was as odious as it sounded, and handing it off to someone else was a gift from heaven.

The word "diener" was German for "servant," but Sara had always thought of Carlos as her assistant, a vital part of her job. If she'd ever doubted his value, not having him around to help was a harsh reminder. Even Jeffrey doing his best yesterday was better than going it alone. From the minute she'd opened the freezer and seen Boyd Gibson lying facedown on a gurney, Sara had known her day was going to be as long as it was difficult.

At five-foot-eleven, Sara was hardly dainty, but she nearly threw out her back maneuvering Gibson onto the metal gurney. The dead man's body was solid as a brick, comprised of as much muscle as fat. He was thickly built, what her father would have called a fireplug, but through a process of pushing and pulling she managed to get him out of the body bag and onto the table without dislodging the knife from his back.

After taking X-rays to document the position of the knife, Sara took the body back to the main room of the morgue, where she measured for weight and height. Next, she started on the man's shoes and clothes. The sneakers were loosely tied, probably a year old. His jeans and underwear were newer, but not by much. She found his wallet with most of the usual contents chained to one of his belt loops. A leather sheath was attached to his belt, the hand tooling matching the design on the bone handle of the knife it held. The artwork wouldn't have been Sara's first choice: a hunting scene with two hounds chasing pheasant out of the woods.

After checking to make sure the hole in the shirt lined up with the hole in Gibson's back, she carefully cut off the shirt, photographing her actions as much as she could. Considering the antiquated autopsy suite, Sara was surprised by the sophistication of the digital camera. Jeffrey had taken the photographs yesterday, but she was quickly becoming adept at using the many features. The macro zoom was better than the one she had at home, and the large LCD on the back let her scroll through the pictures to make sure she'd gotten exactly what she wanted.

She took a few shots of the clothes lying on the paper she'd spread out on the counter, then examined the material for trace evidence. Other than dirt and a few hairs that looked to belong to the victim, Sara found nothing remarkable on Boyd Gibson's clothes. Likewise, his New Balance sneakers were muddy but seemingly innocuous. Still, she carefully bagged and catalogued every item, taking particular care to record the contents of the man's wallet: a driver's license for Boyd Carroll Gibson, aged thirty-seven, one Delta SkyMiles American Express card, one Bank of Elawah Visa card, two snapshots of what looked to be bluetick hounds sitting by a stream and five dollars in cash. Either Boyd Gibson was an exceptionally neat man or someone had screened the contents of his wallet. Sara made a note to mention this to Jeffrey.

She picked up the camera again and photographed the nude body, zooming in around the knife—Lena's knife. When Sara had first seen the weapon last night, she'd known instantly who it belonged to. The look on Jeffrey's face had confirmed the belief. She could tell then that he didn't want to share the information, didn't want to admit that Lena was more than a passive spectator in this mess they had gotten themselves into.

And what about Hank? It would have taken two people to swing Boyd Gibson through the motel window. Sara had only met Lena's uncle a few times, but from her recollection, Hank Norton was a slight man, and not very tall. If he wasn't Lena's accomplice, then who was? There was no way Lena had managed to do this alone.

Or maybe she hadn't done this at all. Just because the knife belonged to Lena did not mean that she had been the one to stab the man. Sara had to keep an open mind. She couldn't go into the autopsy with preconceived notions or she'd blind herself to other possibilities.

Sara leaned over Gibson's body, going in for a tighter shot of the stab wound. She frowned, noticing a discrepancy between the size of the blade and the size of the wound. The handle of Lena's knife was almost exactly perpendicular to the body—traveling slightly upward and perhaps a few inches to the left, suggesting a right-handed killer, who'd come from behind and stabbed into the heart. Yet, the elongated shape of the wound indicated that the knife had gone in at an angle from an extremely superior position. Lena was right-handed, but she was roughly five feet four inches tall. Either the knife had been bumped in transport or Lena had stood on a ladder to stab him.

Knowing the Elawah sheriff's office, Sara would have bet half her paycheck that the knife had been bumped during transport. She made a note to ask Jake Valentine about this. The inconsistency was just the type of detail a defense lawyer longed for. Sara would have to be very specific how she described the wound in her notes in case this ever ended up in court. Otherwise, she would be torn apart on cross-examination.

Then again, the deposition Sara had given in the malpractice suit had pretty much proved that no matter how thorough you were, no matter how carefully you prepared yourself, there was always some greedy jackal of a lawyer out there who could twist your words to suit their cause.

Sara muttered a few expletives in the name of lawyers before she continued the external examination.

She found a few cuts and scrapes on the palms that most likely came from sliding down the bank of the creek outside Hank's bar. The burn marks on the man's arms were unremarkable and certainly survivable barring a radical infection. The singed hair would have grown back in a few months, the eyelashes in a few weeks. Surprisingly, Gibson had only one tattoo, the ugly red swastika Jeffrey had pointed out the night before. Usually these guys were as marked up as a bathroom wall. Sara used one hand to press a small metal ruler against the tattoo and with the other held the camera as she documented the size and detail.

She stopped, putting down the camera to make more notes, wishing not for the first time that Jeffrey were there to help speed along the process. They had developed a rhythm yesterday, and she found herself wanting him there if only to share her observations on the body. Gibson had a series of old scars crisscrossing his back that made Sara think that at some point he'd been whipped with a belt or something similar. There was a long, white scar down the side of his right thigh that appeared to be from an open fracture.

The timer on the X-ray developer buzzed, indicating the films were ready, and Sara studied them on the ancient light box hanging by the door. Dark lines told the story: signs of an old spiral fracture in the left forearm, as well as long ago posterior, lateral breaks in the ribs. The skull showed long-healed fractures across the suture line. Indications of a long bone shaft fracture dated back at least ten years. If Sara had to guess, she'd say that Boyd Gibson had been severely abused as a child.

She turned back to the body, unable to keep herself from feeling sorry for the man. How many postmortem X-rays had she seen in Grant County exactly like this? It was very seldom she came across a dead criminal whose body did not reveal some sign of childhood abuse. As a pediatrician, she had to wonder about the people in Boyd Gibson's early years. How had he hidden such abuse from his teachers, his doctor, his pastor? How many times had Gibson's mother or father made an excuse about clumsiness or boyhood exuberance to cover for broken bones and concussions? How many adults had ignored the evidence before their eyes and believed them?

While childhood abuse certainly didn't excuse the man's adult actions, Sara could not help but wonder whether Boyd Gibson would have ended up on her table if he'd had a happy childhood.

Of course, there were plenty of people out there in the world who had suffered worse than this and they didn't turn into Nazi drug dealers. Or end up killing them.

Had Lena done this horrible thing? Had she stabbed this man in the back? Sara couldn't see it for the same reason she couldn't see Lena burning someone alive. The woman had a temper, true, but if Lena Adams killed someone, she would be looking them in the eyes when she did it.

Hardly a defense, but the truth was often awkward.

Sara turned her focus to the murder weapon. She could tell from the powder marks on the pearl handle that Jake Valentine had already dusted it for prints. From the looks of it, nothing had been lifted. Lena would have known to use gloves, to wipe down the weapon. Was that when the knife had dislodged, as she cleaned the handle of her prints?

Sara zoomed the camera in close to see if there were any minute ridge marks the Elawah sheriff's department had missed. Her eyes blurred as the handle came into sharp detail, and she glanced away for a second to clear her vision.

"Wait a minute," she said to no one in particular. In looking away, she had seen something else. Three small, round bruises were on the back of the dead man's arm. Someone very strong had grabbed Gibson hard enough to leave a mark. Sara could tell from the color that the bruise had happened immediately prior to Gibson's death.

She pressed the ruler underneath the bruises and took photos from several angles. Then, just to make sure, she went back over the body inch by inch, searching for other marks she might have missed.

Satisfied that she'd done all she could, Sara removed her gloves and reviewed her notes, making sure that she could read her writing and that nothing could be misinterpreted. From the moment Sara entered an autopsy suite, she always kept it in the back of her mind that everything she did would eventually be reviewed at trial. On the heels of the malpractice deposition, she felt doubly paranoid.

She kept coming back to the knife, not because it was Lena's—a fact that she blatantly left out of her notes—but because the wound still troubled her.

Sara took off her reading glasses and rubbed her eyes. Unlike the day before, the adjacent garage was in full swing, air compressors buzzing on and off, exhaust fumes seeping into the morgue. She wasn't happy that the garage odors were so overwhelming, not just because it was giving her a headache but because an autopsy was more than about what you saw. Certain smells from the body could point to anything from diabetes to poisoning.

Sara slipped on her safety goggles and a fresh pair of latex gloves as she walked to the table in the middle of the room. Using a large bore needle, she took central blood and urine samples and labeled them accordingly. With her foot, she pushed over a small step stool so that she would have enough height to stand over the body. Once she was in place, Sara braced her right hand against Gibson's back and wrapped her left around the handle of the knife. She was about to pull out the knife when someone knocked on the door.

"Hello?" a man asked, walking into the room without being invited. He saw Sara, hand still on the knife, and gave a low whistle. "Hope you're taking that out and not putting it in."

Sara dropped her hands. "Can I help you?"

The man gave a quick, ferret-like smile that showed a straight line of small, square teeth. He held out his hand, then thought better of it. "Fred Bart," he said. "You've been doing my job."

Sara got down off the step stool. She was at least a foot taller than the man, and there was something about him that instantly rubbed her the wrong way. Still, she apologized, "I'm sorry. I was asked by the sheriff to—"

He barked a loud laugh. "Just pulling your leg, sweetheart. Don't worry about it."

Growing up in the South, Sara had often been called sweetheart or darlin' or even baby. Her grandfather called her princess and the mailman called her peanut, but somehow they managed to do it in an endearing rather than derogatory way; she even signed Christmas and birthday cards to them using the familiar names. That being said, there was a fine line between the kind of men who could get away with this sort of thing and the kind who could not. Fred Bart, with his cheap, too-tight suit and mirror-finish loafers, fell squarely into the latter category.

"Nice to meet you," Sara told him, making an effort to be polite. "I was in the process of ..." She let her voice trail off as Bart picked up her notes. "I'm not finished with those."

"That's okay, darlin'. I think I can figure them out." He started reading, and Sara fought the urge to rip the pages from his hands. Instead, she put her hands on her hips and waited, focusing a laser beam of hate at the top of his balding head. The remaining tufts of hair over his ears had an unnatural appearance, and after a long period of study, she decided he was an advocate of Grecian formula.

Bart was at least a decade older than Sara if not more, the kind of guy who never forgave the world for the fact that he'd started losing his hair in his twenties. She got the feeling he was the type who blamed other people for a lot of things he found wrong with himself. She glanced down at his hands, checking for a wedding ring, glad to find at least there wasn't a woman out there who was having to put up with the busybody know-it-all.

When he was finally finished checking her notes, he gave her a quick smile and dropped the pages back where he'd found them. She expected at least a snarky comment about her penmanship, but all he said was, "Need help with any of this?"

"I think I can handle it."

Bart took a pair of gloves out of the box. He slipped them on as he said, "I can at least help you with getting that knife out. Don't know if you've ever run into anything like this, but they tend to stick the longer you wait."

"I can manage, thank you," Sara told him, unable to find a way to tell the dentist she knew what she was doing without tearing his head from his neck and tossing it out the window like a soccer ball.

"No problem at all," he answered, standing on the stool Sara had just vacated. He put both hands on the knife, then gave her a questioning look. When she did not move, he told her, "Can't do this without you holding him down, sweetheart."

She was suddenly aware of the fact that she was standing with her hands on her hips and her mouth pursed, looking exactly like the stereotype of a man-hating feminist bitch that Fred Bart probably kept in his mind to explain why his excessive charms didn't work on a woman.

Sara pressed her hands against the corpse's back and Bart pulled the knife. She noticed how easily the flesh relinquished the blade.

Apparently, Bart noticed, too. "Not so bad," he said, dropping the knife onto the tray beside the body. "Find any fingerprints?"

"You'd have to ask the sheriff. I'm just doing the procedure."

"Might want to take your own," he suggested, snapping off the latex gloves. "In my experience, little buddy Jake ain't exactly up on his forensic techniques." He tossed the gloves into the wastecan and took out a pack of cigarettes.

"I'd prefer you didn't smoke in here."

He put the cigarette in his mouth, let it dangle as he talked. "You one of those smoking Nazis?"

Sara wondered at his word choice considering the red swastika on the victim's arm. "I would just prefer you didn't smoke," she replied evenly.

He flashed another smile, made a show of taking the cigarette out of his mouth and putting it back in the pack—just for her. "So, what'd you find? Anything interesting?"

Sara picked up the camera to document the wound. "Not yet."

"You're a pediatrician, right?"

"That's right." She felt the need to add, "I'm also a medical examiner."

"Didn't think people could afford to be doctors anymore." Bart gave a dry laugh, and Sara didn't know if she was just being sensitive or if the man knew about the malpractice suit. He would've had to do some digging to find that out; she was probably just being paranoid. After what she'd been through over the last few days, Sara figured she had an excuse.

Bart walked around the body, stopped at the tattoo. "Figures," he said. "I got one of these bastards here last month. Took out a telephone pole out on Highway 16. Sideswiped a family in a minivan while he was at it." He glanced up quickly. "Family made it. Just bumps and bruises."

Sara realized she might be able to get some information from him if she tread carefully. "Are skinheads a problem around here?"

Bart shrugged. "Meth's the big problem, and skinheads come with it. Good luck for me, though." Sara must have looked confused, because he clarified, "I'm a dentist. I thought for sure Jake would've told you that." He crossed his arms, the shoulders of his cheap suit riding up to his ears. "Ten years ago, I'd be lucky if I got one root canal a month. Now, I do two, maybe three, a week. Get them from all over the county, sometimes into the next. Crowns, bridges, veneers. It's boom-time."

Sara had seen what meth could do to a person's mouth. Most heavy users lost their teeth within the first year.

"Big business," Bart said. "But I'd trade it all in if I never had to see another kid hooked on that shit." His face reddened. "Sorry for my language, ma'am."

Sara didn't know if it was his apology or his obvious concern, but she felt herself not hating him so much.

Bart said, "Let me help you turn the body."

Sara was still reluctant to accept his offer, but she had to admit she wasn't relishing maneuvering Gibson over on the table. She took a few more photographs, then waited for Bart to glove up again. He took the head and shoulders and Sara took the feet. It gave her some amount of pleasure to watch the dentist struggle under the weight as they rolled Gibson onto his back. It also gave her pause, because if the two of them were having trouble just flipping the body on the table, it must have taken some pretty strong men to toss him through a window.

She said, "Big guy, huh?"

Bart shrugged his shoulders, but she could see a bead of sweat roll down his cheek. "I've seen worse."

"I can imagine."

She saw his eyes flash as he registered the comment, probably wondering if she was being condescending. Sara kept him wondering, all but batting her eyelashes when she said, "Thanks so much for lending me some of your muscle."

Instinctively, he reached for his cigarettes, then stopped himself. "I see you figured out Bertha." He pointed to the X-rays. "I keep asking the county to replace that thing and they keep telling me no."

"It serves its purpose," Sara allowed. If you watched enough television, you would assume that all police departments were at the cutting edge of forensic technology. In reality, no lab in the country could afford the billions of dollars of equipment you saw being used on an average Thursday night drama. What little equipment the state had was in high demand, and sometimes it took up to a year to get an analysis back.

Bart was still studying Boyd Gibson's X-rays. He gave a low whistle. "Not much of a childhood." He traced a faint line along the clavicle. "Nasty break."

"Did you know him?"

Bart turned around, and for the first time since he'd come into the room, he seemed to be really looking at her. "Yeah," he said, his tone filled with sadness. "His mama used to bring him in. She was always torn up." He indicated his face, and Sara realized he was indicating abuse. "Never saw it in Boyd or his brother—he's got an older brother—but I called the sheriff plenty of times about Ella. That was her name." He turned his back to Sara as he looked at the films again, or maybe he just didn't want her to see him upset. "She was a great lady. Quiet, respectful, good cook. Everything you'd want in a wife. I guess some men can't be happy with that. Grover sure as hell wasn't."

Sara waited to make sure he was finished speaking before asking, "What did the sheriff do when you reported it?"

"This was back when Al was in charge," Bart said, turning back around. "Al was a good man, but you couldn't press charges back then without the wife on board to testify, and Ella wasn't going to say a word against Grover. Not that she had any love left for him, but she knew what he would do to the boys, and it wasn't like she could go out and get a job to support all of them."

"Is she still with him?"

"No," he said, looking down at his feet. "Cancer took her when Boyd was about ten, maybe eleven. I didn't see him much after that. Grover wasn't gonna waste his drinking money on having their teeth cleaned." He pointed to the corpse. "Course, I've seen him plenty lately."

"How's that?"

Bart directed his gaze toward Gibson's forearms, where track marks scarred the flesh. They were fairly healed, at least four to six months old. Gibson was also heavy, and meth users tended to be extremely thin.

She said, "He doesn't look as if he's been using lately."

"Yeah, he got cleaned up for a while." Bart shrugged. "Lots of 'em clean up for a month, sometimes a year. Then something happens and they're back on the needle quick as you please."

"Is that what happened to Boyd?"

Bart didn't exactly answer her question. "He came in about six weeks ago. He didn't have the money for the work, but I set up a payment schedule for him. He was in awful pain. His whole mouth was infected. Would've lost the rest of his teeth if I hadn't done something."

"I saw the bridge," Sara said, indicating the dental film. She hadn't yet examined Gibson's mouth.

Bart looked at the X-ray. "Not as bad as it could've been." He gave a quick smile. "You must see that kind of thing a lot more than me."

"What's that?"

"Indigents." He pronounced the word sharply, but Sara could not tell if she was meant to infer derision or pity. "They come in and you know they can't afford it but you can't turn them away because that's not why you went to school."

Sara nodded and shrugged at the same time, not knowing what else to say. She was hardly going to have a protracted discussion about the dismal state of healthcare with this man.

"Well." Bart glanced at his watch as if he had just remembered an appointment. "Anyway, I just wanted to drop by and make sure you were making yourself at home. Let me know if you need anything, all right?"

"Thank you," Sara said, and she really meant it until he flashed one of his ferret smiles.

"You take care now, darlin'. Wouldn't want you to get mixed up in any of this."

She felt her own smile tighten on her face. "Thank you," she repeated, but Fred Bart had already left.

Sara looked back at the dead man lying on the table as if he might offer some wry comment about what had just happened. Of course he did not. Sara took off her gloves as she walked back over to her notes. She found the right page and recorded that Fred Bart had assisted with the removal of the knife. She also noted that the knife had easily slipped from the wound. Bart was right about one thing; usually the blades stuck, whether from dried blood or tissue that stiffened around the metal.

She pushed this to the back of her mind as she continued the external examination, photographing the healed scars that indicated needle use, making note of a few scratches on the front of the shin. Gibson's mouth was already open and the bridge spanning the gap where his front teeth should have been popped out easily. Though she didn't want to, Sara had to admit that Bart did good work. The gums were almost completely healed and there didn't seem to be any indication that the bridge had fit awkwardly.

Sara checked the time, wondering what was taking Jeffrey and Jake Valentine so long. They were supposed to bring Boyd Gibson's father in to identify the body but that had been a good two hours ago. Technically, Jake had already positively identified Boyd Gibson, but she knew from experience that the family generally needed to see the victim in order to get some closure.

She called Jeffrey's cell phone but he didn't pick up. She left a message for him, but after twenty minutes passed without him returning her call, she decided to go ahead with the internal examination. She could always cover the body when Gibson's father arrived to spare him the more graphic aspects of his son's death.

She regloved and returned to the table, where she picked up a scalpel and began the Y-incision. Because there was a Dictaphone over the autopsy table that she used back in Grant, Sara could not stop her mind from doing a running narration of every movement she made, so that when she opened the rib cage or examined the pleura, she heard a little voice in her head echoing the motions.

She followed the penetration path of the stab wound to the heart, finding just as she'd predicted. The blade had pierced the left posterior thoracic wall and exited the anterior, causing almost immediate death. She stopped here, making some more notes, taking photographs and measuring the blade's path, then doing her own drawing of exactly what she'd found.

Even without the stab wound, the heart was in bad shape. Enlarged from the extra weight on Gibson's frame, the major arteries were already showing signs of disease. Had the knife not killed him, his bad health habits would have ensured he didn't live into a comfortable old age.

Though she had obvious cause of death, Sara continued the autopsy in minute detail, carefully weighing and dissecting the organs, taking tissue samples. Boyd Gibson's last meal had been similar to the one Jeffrey and Sara had shared: pizza. He preferred pepperoni from the looks of it, but he'd chosen to eat a healthy salad to balance it out. Maybe he had smoked while he ate. Judging from the coloring and the enlarged air spaces in his lungs, Gibson had been a heavy smoker. Considering this, Sara thought it odd that he hadn't had cigarettes in his pockets.

She made a note of this, took more photographs and did so many drawings that her hand cramped. Unfortunately, her devotion to detail was only punishing herself. By the time the clock hands ticked past noon, her feet were killing her and her back felt as if it had been bent into a shepherd's hook.

And, honestly, Sara had never been an artist. Her drawings looked like the class project of a psychopathic kindergartener.

She covered the body and sat down, every vertebrae in her neck popping as she looked up at the ceiling in hopes of counteracting the fact that she had been looking straight down for the last two hours. She was just starting to let herself worry about Jeffrey when she heard a car pull up outside.

Jake Valentine opened the door, knocking at the same time. "Sorry we're late," he told her, a sloppy grin on his face. He had a piece of toilet tissue shoved up his nose. The bridge was swollen, the fingertips of a bruise spreading under his left eye.

Sara stood in alarm. "Where's Jeffrey?"

Before she had finished the question, he came in behind Valentine, shutting the door.

"Slight altercation," Jeffrey explained. He shared the same sloppy grin as the sheriff, as if they'd just had a great deal of fun together.

"What kind of altercation?" Sara felt like she was talking to two naughty children, and Jeffrey's burst of laughter did nothing to disabuse her of the notion.

Valentine laughed, too, though she could tell from the tears in his eyes that it hurt to do so. He told her, "Grover wasn't exactly happy to see me."

Jeffrey explained, "He punched Jake in the face as soon as he opened the door."

Sara noticed that he was using the sheriff's first name now. Only two cops could bond over one of them getting their face punched.

Valentine told Sara, "Lucky thing you told me to bring him along this morning. You'd probably have me on that table right now if he hadn't been there."

"Shit," Jeffrey replied. "Probably be both of us if you hadn't tripped the old fool."

Sara resisted the urge to roll her eyes. "I take it Mr. Gibson is not coming in to do the formal identification?"

Valentine explained, "He wasn't too broke up about losing his son. They weren't exactly close." He shrugged, allowing a hint of seriousness to enter his voice. "Maybe when he sobers up, it'll hit him."

Jeffrey turned serious as well, telling Sara, "He was out of control. We cuffed him, took him to the station, so he could sleep it off. Not the first time he's been there, from the looks of it."

"No," Valentine agreed. "Probably won't be the last, either."

"I took several photographs of his face," Sara offered. "You can show those to his father. It might make things easier."

Jeffrey asked Sara, "Did you find anything?"

"Not really." She picked up the murder weapon and placed it on a sheet of brown paper so that she could photograph it. This was the first time Sara had really examined the full blade and handle. Looking at it now, she noticed two things about the knife: the blade was thin, maybe half an inch wide, and it was at least four inches long. Most important, unlike the majority of folding knives Sara had seen, there was no serration. The blade was smooth on one side and sharp on the other.

Valentine's cell phone rang, the opening bars of "Dixie" filling the room. He checked the caller ID, then told them, "If y'all could excuse me for a minute?"

Sara waited until the door closed before picking up the camera and scrolling through the photographs.

Jeffrey asked, "Did you call the hospitals to see if Lena or Hank have been admitted?"

"There are three within a fifty mile radius," she told him, scanning through the photos. "No sign at any of them."

"I guess that's good," he said, though she could tell he was disappointed. If Lena had been tucked up in a hospital last night, there was no way she could have been out killing Boyd Gibson.

Sara found the photo she wanted. "This should make you feel better."

"What's that?"

"Look at the wound," she said, finding the series of close-ups she'd taken. "It's jagged at the bottom and jagged at the top. I knew something wasn't right."

Jeffrey looked at the knife on the table, then back at the camera's LCD. He obviously knew where she was going with this, but still said, "Okay."

"The knife—this knife"—she indicated Lena's knife on the table—"Would have made a wound with a V-shaped bottom and a squared edge at the top. A serration leaves a jagged edge in the skin. The top and bottom of the wound in Boyd Gibson's back is jagged."

He was nodding. "Based on the wound, the knife that killed Gibson was double-edged, serrated." She could hear the excitement in his voice. Statistically, most stabbing victims were killed with single-edge serrated knives because that was what was usually in the kitchen drawer. Sara had never seen a double-edged serrated knife, let alone a stab wound from one. If there was someone out there in Elawah carrying such a weapon, he was more than likely the killer.

Jeffrey tapped his fingers on the table, processing the new lead. "I'd bet it was a custom job. Maybe something off-market for the military. Definitely full tang, probably a custom handle to match the sheath… How long do you think the blade would have to be?"

"From the hilt to the point of the blade would have to be at least six inches long, then I'd guess from the wound that it's around an inch and a half wide, tops." She pointed to Gibson. "Look at how big he is. His chest is huge, his heart was enlarged. I found an entrance and exit wound through the left chamber." She indicated Lena's knife again. "This blade might have pierced the back of the heart, but there's no way it could have gone all the way through the heart and out the front. It's not long enough—the whole thing tip to handle is eight inches long."

"There's got to be a local who makes these things." He could not wipe the smile off his face. "With the handle, a six-inch knife would run close to nine, ten inches. The guy we saw outside the hospital had a big knife on his belt. He left it in his car before he got out."

"It's not unusual for men to carry knives," Sara pointed out. "My dad keeps one on his belt for work."

"Last time I checked, your dad doesn't have a big fat swastika on his arm," Jeffrey countered. "Whoever did this was trying to frame Lena. No wonder she ran."

"Or maybe he was close to his knife and didn't want to let it go." She walked over to the table where she had bagged Gibson's personal effects. "Look at Gibson's knife. It's not off-the-shelf. He paid some good money for it. This isn't something you'd easily let go of."

The door opened and Valentine appeared. He kept the door propped open with his foot, as if he didn't plan to stay long. The man was obviously furious when he told them, "That was the principal from the high school on the phone."

Jeffrey exchanged a look with Sara. "And?"

"He found some blankets and a couple of empty bags of potato chips in one of the temporary classrooms." He shook his head, his teeth clenched so tight that his jaw stood out like a carved relief. "Looks like we've found out where your detective's been sleeping." Jeffrey flashed a smile that sent Valentine straight over the edge. "My *wife* works at that school, you fuckwad."

Jeffrey offered, "Well, I wouldn't feel too bad, Jake. I'm sure Myra didn't let her sleep there on purpose."

Valentine pressed his lips together, obviously struggling to think of a cutting response. He finally settled on, "Go to hell," then turned on his heel and slammed the door shut behind him.

LENA

CHAPTER 16

TWO YEARS AGO, Jeffrey had thrown Ethan Green's arrest jacket in Lena's face, ordering her to read it.

Of course she never had.

She had pretended to skim the file, taking in every fifth or sixth word, then pushed it back in his face with a belligerent, "So?"

Jeffrey had given her the highlights, the rundown of Ethan's crimes: grand theft auto, felony assault, forcible sodomy, rape. None of his words had penetrated—Lena was still in that phase where she thought of Ethan as two different people: the one who loved her and the one who would eventually kill her. The duality was not much of a stretch; at the time, Lena thought of herself in much the same terms.

Sibyl had been dead almost a year when Lena first met Ethan. She was living at the college dorms, working campus security, struggling to get through each day without putting a gun to her head. Ethan was working on his master's degree. He had pursued Lena relentlessly, almost wearing her down.

A few months later, Lena got her job back with the police force and moved in with Nan Thomas. Ethan was still in her life; Ethan was still her life. His arrest file had stayed in her Celica the whole time, well concealed behind the CD changer in her trunk. Lena hadn't wanted Nan to accidentally come across it. Truth be told, she hadn't wanted to take it into the house where Sibyl had once lived. It was bad enough when Ethan slept over.

Lena walked across the weedy strip of land between the motel and the bar, her shoes crunching on broken glass and other debris that had been swept off the road. She passed the motel lobby on the way to her Celica. Though the night air was turning cold, Lena could still feel herself sweating as if she was sitting back in Hank's hellhole of a house.

Grand theft auto. Felony assault.

The file was exactly where she had secreted it two years ago, black tire treads marring the State of Connecticut seal on the outside of the yellowing folder. Lena took it out and for some reason felt the need to hide the file under her shirt as she bolted up the stairs to her motel room. No one was watching her. There was no need for these furtive moves. She still felt guilty, though. Still felt as if someone, somewhere was disapproving.

Maybe it would be better not to know. Ethan may have been calling Hank for money or support or perhaps he'd simply wanted to get in touch with Lena. She had moved from Nan's and had a new phone number now. Had he sent letters to Nan? Had Nan hidden them from Lena, hoping she could sever the connection?

Lena hooked the do not disturb sign on her door. She yanked the curtains closed and sat cross-legged on the bed, still holding the file to her chest. She could feel her beating heart thumping against the thick stack of pages, sweat making the manila folder stick to her skin.

Slowly, she slid the file out from under her shirt. She ran her hand along the print, tracing the circle of the seal. Her fingers found the edge and she opened the file to find exactly the thing she never wanted to see again: Ethan staring back at her.

The mug shot had been taken a few years before Lena had met Ethan, back when he was eighteen. He'd kept his hair cut short when she knew him, but in the photo, his head was shaved bald. His lips curled into a sneer as he glared at the camera, and the little sign he held in his hand was askew, as if he couldn't be bothered to keep it straight. He was wearing a short-sleeved shirt, something he never did anymore— or maybe he had stopped hiding his tattoos now that he was back in prison. They would serve him well inside.

ETHAN ALLEN GREEN a/k/a ETHAN ALLEN WHITE a/k/a ETHAN ALLEN MUELLER.

Lena could remember the time Ethan had explained the origins of his name. They were both in his dorm room, squeezed together on his single bed. He was on his back and she had wrapped herself around him so that she wouldn't fall off the narrow twin bed. Ethan was fairly short—he was only a few inches taller than Lena—but his muscles stood out from his body as if they were cut from granite. She'd had her head tucked under his arm, and the sound of his voice had vibrated in her ear.

Sometime around the American Revolution, he told her, Ethan Allen had been the leader of the Green Mountain boys, a group that had pledged its life to Vermont's independence. During the war, Allen and his crew had captured a British fort. By some accounts he was a military genius, by others an ignorant, cold-blooded killer.

She had thought then as she did now that the namesake was not far off.

Forcible sodomy. Rape.

Lena knew only a little bit about Ethan's life before he'd moved to Grant County. Ethan's father had run out on him when he was a kid. His mother, a rabid racist, had married a man named Ezekiel White, a preacher of some kind. Ethan had changed his name to Green when he dropped out of his skinhead family. Lena had no idea why he didn't go back to Mueller, his biological father's name. Ethan didn't like to talk about his dad.

When Lena had first met Ethan, he had claimed that he was working hard to change himself. Lena had accepted that, even respected it. As time passed, she had told herself there was no way he would be dating her if he still held on to his old beliefs. She was Hispanic—clearly so. She had become roommates with a lesbian—not just any lesbian, but Sibyl's lover. Ethan seemed not to care. He was more than cordial to Nan. He had said that he was in love with Lena, wanted to share the rest of his life with her. He had said that being with her was the only good thing he had ever done with his life. That his words from his mouth so sharply contrasted with the blows from his fists wasn't something she let herself think about too long.

HEIGHT: 5′6″ WEIGHT: 160 SEX: MALE HAIR COLOR: BROWN EYE COLOR: BLUE RACE: WHITE

Race. His skin privilege, he called it. His white birthright.

TATTOOS.

There were so many—some Lena had even forgotten about. The arresting officer had documented them all, making notations about their origin, what they symbolized. Lena studied the photographs, really looking at the tattoos for the first time. She had always averted her gaze or kept her eyes closed when he took off his clothes. Even then, some of the images had managed to bleed through.

A row of SS soldiers on the left side of his chest saluted an image of Hitler on the right. Below this was a large black swastika that undulated across his ripped abs. His left arm was covered with scenes of war, soldiers shouldering rifles, their hats emblazoned with the double S. The other arm had barbed wire snaking up it, faint outlines of camp barracks in the background.

How had she touched this body? How had she let this body touch hers?

Lena turned the page, found yet another photograph. Ethan's thick, brown hair had concealed more tattoos. In an arc at the base of his shaved skull were the words *Sieg Heil.* On the top of his head was another black swastika.

Beside the photo, someone had explained, *Hitler salute on back of head generally given after six years of active involvement. Swastika on head usual tag for leaders of North Conn. skinhead group.*

The last photo was a close-up of the underside of his left arm. Just at the base of his bicep was the letter A with a dash beside it. A-negative. The cop had written an explanation on the back of the picture, *Hitler's Waffen SS, the Death's Head Battalion who guarded the concentration camps, all had their blood types tattooed under their arms. Symbolizes rank of general in white power movement.*

Lena had never asked about the letter under Ethan's arm, never wanted to know the truth of his past. Now, she was confronted with the truth—overwhelmed with it. Every photo was like a slap in the face.

This was the father of the child she had left in some trashcan at the clinic in Atlanta. This was the man with whom she had shared her days, two whole years of her life.

After Ethan had been taken back to prison, Lena had tried and failed miserably to be with another man. Greg Mitchell had lived with her several years before, and it seemed like fate when he reentered her

life around the same time Ethan was leaving it. Nothing worked between them, though. She was not that same person from before, something that at first Greg took as a good thing. Later he came to be almost
frightened of her.

From the beginning, Lena had tried to hide her true self from Greg,
to cloak her darkness and rough edges. She reined in her emotions so
much that she spent most of her time with Greg feeling like a shell of
what a human being should be. Sex between them was disastrous. After
Ethan, she no longer knew how to be with a man who was gentle, how
to kiss him and hold him and take pleasure from him instead of pain.

If Angela Adams had stuck around, if she had been a mother to her
two young girls instead of abandoning them to Hank, would Lena have
ended up with Ethan? Would that defect inside of her, the one that drew
her to his violence, his ruthless control, never have been triggered? Or
would Lena have ended up like Charlotte Warren, still living in Reece,
raising a couple of kids, waiting for her husband to come home from
work so she could put supper on the table?

Ethan's rap sheet was nearly thirty pages long. Most of the notes
were written in the dry, minimalist style of a seasoned cop who knew
better than to put too much on the page so some dickhead lawyer could
later twist it all around and throw it back in his face during a trial. Lena
knew how to read between the lines, though, and as she scanned records of arrest after arrest, she started to get a sharper picture of Ethan's
life before they met.

He'd started young, his first arrest coming when he was thirteen.
He'd stolen some clothes from the local Belk. At fifteen, he was arrested for trying to steal a car. Both cases had been referred to juvenile
court. Both times, he had been given probation. That couldn't have
been it, though. You didn't go from stealing clothes to stealing cars
without something in between. Lena knew that for every one crime
you caught these guys doing, there were four more hiding in their
closet. She would have bet good money that Ethan had boosted at least
ten cars before they caught him in the act.

His record stayed clean until he reached the age of seventeen. Then,
he'd been accused of sodomizing a fifteen-year-old girl. Two weeks
later, the charges were dropped. Lena gathered from the terse language
in the report that the girl's parents hadn't wanted to put her through a
trial. This was fairly common and probably wise. The world liked to

believe differently, but any cop could tell you that there was nothing more horrible—or more likely to ruin a woman's life—than a protracted rape trial.

There was a notation on this arrest: *Suspect bears tattoos and markings associated with violent neo-Nazi sect. Suggest referral to FBI for monitoring.*

Ethan was nineteen when he was arrested for assault. He'd used a knife during a fight, which brought it to a felony charge. The victim had apparently been cut pretty badly, but he refused to cooperate with police so the charges were reduced. Again, Ethan walked away from a serious charge.

Three more years passed before the Connecticut State Police heard from Ethan Green again. Lena imagined this was during the time Ethan had finished his undergraduate degree and started his master's. That was probably the one thing about Ethan that scared people the most: he was smart, even gifted. He gave lie to the ignorant redneck racist. When Lena had first met him, he was trying to get into the PhD program at Grant Tech and probably would have made it had he not been arrested.

Oddly enough, the charge that the Connecticut State Police finally managed to make stick was for kiting checks. Ethan had written a check to A&P for twenty-eight bucks and change when his bank account showed a balance of twelve dollars. He'd put his payroll check in to cover it the next day, but it was still illegal to knowingly float a check. This was the kind of arrest that indicated the cops had just been waiting to pounce on him. Millions of people shifted around money like this every day. You didn't get caught unless somebody was watching.

Ethan *had* been caught, though. If the judge was in a bad mood, he was looking at ten years in a federal penitentiary.

Lena was turning the page to find out what happened when the phone rang. She jumped, papers scattering on the bed. Her first thought was that no one knew she was here, then she remembered Hank. She leaned over to pick up the receiver, then stopped, letting the phone keep ringing. A photograph had fallen to the floor and she bent to retrieve it, freezing in midair as she saw the image of a beaten woman lying in a pool of blood.

Lena did not move to pick up the picture. She stared at it from a distance, taking in the black bruises on the young woman's thighs, the bloody pulp of her face. The red burns around her feet and wrists indicated that she had been held spread-eagle, strong hands pulling back her arms and legs so that she would be open to any violation.

Ethan's last girlfriend.

She was black.

The phone stopped ringing as Lena stared at the photograph. The room turned deathly quiet. The air felt more stifling. The girl in the picture must have been lovely, her skin a soft milk chocolate. Like Lena, she wore her hair long, with curls that would have brushed her shoulders if her head had not been yanked back, her hair matted with blood.

Evelyn Marie Johnson, aged nineteen. College student. Soprano in the church choir. Lena thumbed through the file, looking for more pictures. She skipped past the pages of lurid crime scene photos and found what must have been the woman's school picture. It was a stunning "before." Silky black hair, bow-tie lips, big brown eyes. She could have been a model.

Lena found the crime scene report. Tire tracks had been found near her body. The impressions had been sent to the lab, which matched the tires to Ethan's 1989 GMC truck. He was out on bail for the check kiting, awaiting sentencing. He flipped for a deal that would keep him out of jail if he testified against the killers.

According to the girl's sister, Evelyn had been taken from her house by four white men in the middle of the night. The sister had hid in the closet because she had seen the swastikas on their bald heads, knew what the tattoos meant.

According to Ethan, he had been forced at gunpoint to take the men to Evelyn's house. The year before, he had tried to leave the militant neo-Nazi group calling themselves the Church of Christ's Chosen Soldiers, but they would not let him go. One of his former friends had stayed in the truck that night, holding Ethan at gunpoint, while the others went inside and abducted Evelyn. Ethan was then forced to drive them deep into the woods. His hands were tied with clothesline to the steering wheel, the keys to his truck thrown on the empty seat beside him. He sat there while he watched five men assault Evelyn and beat her to death.

Ethan claimed the men had then gotten into a Jeep that had been parked in the clearing and drove off. He further claimed that he had used his teeth to pick at the knots in the rope that tied his hands to the steering wheel, and that this had taken him at least an hour. Once he was free, he had not gotten out of the truck, not gone to his girlfriend, because he could already tell that she was dead.

Instead, he drove home.

The phone started to ring again and Lena's heart stuttered. She closed the file, her hands shaking, feeling as if she had just let something evil out—something that would stalk her like a rabid animal, not resting until she was punished. This was just how Ethan had been on the outside: relentless, savage, cunning. He had told Lena that he would never let her go and she had forced him away, pried his fingers from her life and sent him back to hell where he had come from.

Was Ethan reaching out to Hank in order to get to her?

She should just leave it be. None of this had anything to do with her. The Ethan part of her life was over. Whatever reason had compelled him to make those calls to Hank was none of her business. It did not explain who had killed Lena's father and mother. It did not explain why Hank had lied to her all of those years, or why he was pushing himself into an early grave.

Lena snatched up the phone to stop the ringing. "What?"

"It's Rod."

"Who?"

"Rod," the voice repeated. "From the desk?"

The carrot-headed idiot. "What do you want?"

"Somebody keeps calling to see if you're in."

Lena opened the file again, scattering pages and photographs as she looked for Ethan's prison intake sheet. "A man or a woman?"

"Woman," he answered. "I told her you were out. Figured when you didn't answer the phone that you didn't want to be bothered. That cool with you?"

Lena found the number she was looking for. "Can you get me an outside line?"

"I was just—"

If her stupid cell phone worked in this place, she would've already hung up. She enunciated each word clearly. "I said I need an outside line."

"Hold on." The kid heaved a pitiful sigh so she'd know that he was doing her a favor. There was a click, then she had a dial tone.

Lena dialed the long-distance number, her hands still trembling. She stood to pace, glancing at the clock by the bed. It was past midnight.

The switchboard picked up, a recorded voice told her to listen to the message because it had recently changed. She pressed the zero key and nothing happened. She pressed it a couple of more times and the phone started to ring. After twenty-three rings, a polite-sounding man answered, "Coastal State Prison."

Lena looked down at the floor, saw the photograph at her feet.

"Hello?"

"This is Detective Lena Adams with the Grant County Police Department." She gave her badge number, reciting it twice as he wrote it down. "I need to arrange a meeting with one of your prisoners for first thing in the morning." Her eyes were locked on the school photo of Evelyn again, the curly black hair, the warm smile on her perfect lips. "It's urgent."

THURSDAY AFTERNOON

CHAPTER 17

JEFFREY TAPPED HIS FINGERS on the steering wheel as Sara sat beside him talking on her cell phone. Lena's knife had not killed Boyd Gibson. Jeffrey had known deep in his gut that there was no way she had killed the man. Obviously, someone was trying to frame her for the murder. That somebody could very well be the reason Lena had left the hospital. She was a cop to her core. Lena would have taken one look at Jake Valentine and known the only way the sheriff could solve a crime is if somebody handed him the pieces. That was why she ran. She was out there trying to put together the pieces for him.

The only problem was explaining how the murderer had gotten Lena's knife. She had carried the blade for a while now. There was no way she would give it up without a fight. Whoever had taken the knife off her might have injured Lena in the process. Was that why she'd hidden out at the school? Jeffrey should have followed Valentine and examined the blankets they'd found. If there was blood on them, then Lena might be in even more trouble than he'd suspected.

"Okay." Sara had his notepad in her lap and she scribbled something down, saying, "Right, okay," into the phone. He guessed from the arrows she was scrawling that she was taking directions, and hoped she'd be able to decipher the words once they were on the road. Sara had the worst handwriting of anyone he'd ever met.

"Thanks," she finally said, closing the phone. She told Jeffrey, "There's a Holiday Inn about forty minutes from here."

Just the thought of the clean, reliable hotel chain made him smile. "We're moving up in the world."

"It's about time." Sara put on her seat belt. "I am so ready to get out of this place."

He turned the ignition key and the engine purred to life. "Tell me something," he began, indicating the glowing satellite navigation screen on the dashboard. "Does this thing have a memory on it?"

"Hank's address right?" She started to toggle through the options, looking for the address. Jeffrey shook his head as he watched her. She hated to use a cell phone, would barely touch a computer, and refused to do anything more complicated with the DVD player than press play, but somehow, she had figured out the navigation system well enough to breeze through the screens.

Jeffrey drove out of the lot and headed toward town. "It's near the school," he told her. "You could walk there pretty easily."

Sara found the directions. The tinny, woman's voice told him to prepare to take a right in three hundred feet. In Jeffrey's opinion, the engineers had made a big mistake when they chose the voice for a computer. Nothing annoyed a man more than hearing a woman tell him where to go.

Sara said, "I have that map I bought at the convenience store somewhere in the suitcase. Downtown is just a big rectangle with a forest in the middle. I'd bet you good money there are all kinds of trails through there."

Jeffrey loved the way her mind worked. "Trails Lena could have used to get from the hospital to Hank's the night she escaped."

"Or that she's been using over the last few days to get around without being seen."

Jeffrey waited for the computer to finish telling him to bear left. "You mind if we check that out after we get to Hank's?"

"Of course not."

Jeffrey followed the prompts, driving past the town dump and the high school, one looking remarkably like the other. They saw the courthouse and the Elawah County Library, which both shared the same squat, 1950s feel as the other municipal buildings in town.

He took a left onto Corcoran Court and recognized where they were. He pointed to the satellite system, asking Sara, "Can you turn that thing off?"

She pressed a button, toggled the dial, and the tinny voice stopped mid-sentence.

The silence was unbelievably welcome.

Jeffrey pulled up outside Hank's house. The cruiser he'd seen there the day before was gone. He guessed Valentine had called in the troops to search the school.

"This is it," he told Sara.

"It's..." She didn't finish the thought. There weren't a whole lot of nice things you could say about the place. Hank's house was by far the biggest dump on the block.

"His car is gone," Jeffrey told her.

She raised an eyebrow. "Did you put out an APB?"

"I left that to Jake."

"Was the mailbox like that when you were here before?"

"Yes." He saw that it was still duct-taped onto the post, the door hanging by a thread. "Cherry bomb," he said, knowing the signs.

When he'd been a kid, Jeffrey and two of his friends had cherry-bombed just about every mailbox in the neighborhood one Halloween. Unfortunately, they hadn't been smart enough to cover their tracks. The sheriff had simply knocked on the doors of the only three houses in the neighborhood that still had undamaged mailboxes in their front yards.

Jeffrey got out of the car and went around to open Sara's door.

She looked up at Hank's house as she got out, frowning. "Do you think it was always like this?"

Jeffrey took in the weeds growing in the front yard, the patches of raw wood showing where the paint had chipped off. "Looks like it."

"It makes you wonder."

"What's that?"

"If maybe somewhere," she began, her voice troubled, "the mother of our child is living like this."

He hadn't been thinking about that; the adoption was an oasis to go to when things got too overwhelming. She was right, though. People from good homes and solid families usually didn't feel compelled to give up their children. That wasn't to say they were any better than poor people, but usually the well-off were able to pay somebody else to raise their kids if they didn't want to do it themselves.

"Oh, God." Sara covered her mouth and nose with her hands. "Do you smell that?"

Jeffrey nodded, not wanting to open his mouth for fear of something coming out. Unnecessarily, he put out his hand to stop her from going up the front steps.

"Is it a body?"

He hoped to hell not. "Wait here."

The smell got worse the closer he got to the house. Jeffrey stopped, seeing that the front door had been busted open and hastily repaired with duct tape. The tape looked new.

Jeffrey glanced at Sara. "Stay there, all right?"

She nodded, and he raised his hand to knock on the door. The door shook from the impact, but the tape held. He knocked a little harder and guessed from the way the door moved that it had been taped from the inside as well.

After several knocks with no answer, he turned back to Sara. "What do you think?"

"I think if I hadn't been standing here you would have busted down that door ten minutes ago."

She was right. A good kick just under the knob sent the door flying. The jamb was busted out, the recess for the lock completely missing. Sharp metal edges jutted into the air like knives where the flashing had been ripped from the wood. Jeffrey drew his gun, giving Sara a nod to stay put before heading into the house.

He stood in Hank's living room, looking around, trying to get his bearings. The windows had probably never been opened and the fug of cigarette smoke and rotting meat made his lungs tighten in his chest. Trash was everywhere—old pizza boxes and takeout containers, soiled underclothes, stacks of papers and magazines that looked damp from the heat.

All of this was nothing compared to the smell. In his almost twenty-year law enforcement career, Jeffrey had smelled a lot of bad things, but nothing could ever compete with the stench permeating Hank Norton's house. With each step, it got worse. He couldn't tell if it was a putrid corpse or decaying trash that was making bile squirt up in the back of his throat. Sweat started pouring off his body, some kind of primal response to protect him from disease.

There were two bedrooms; one of them had obviously belonged to Lena and her sister. The second had a mattress on the floor, the bureau spilling out clothes as if it had been searched by a thief. He found the source of the smell in the bathroom. The toilet bowl was broken in two, exposing what was basically an open sewer. Black shit caked the floor. A sledgehammer leaned against the wall, and he guessed someone, maybe Hank Norton, had used it to bust open the toilet.

Jeffrey gagged, backing out into the hall. Instinctively, he took a deep breath, but there was no fresh air to clear his lungs.

A swinging door to what must have been the kitchen stood closed on the left.

"Hank?" he called. "Hank Norton or anyone in here, this is the police."

There was no answer, and Jeffrey looked down to see what his shoes were crunching. Saltine crackers, he thought.

"Hank?"

Slowly, Jeffrey put the toe of his foot against the swinging door. He pushed it open, gun aimed at the space in front of him. He could see the kitchen was the largest room in the house. The cabinets were the old metal kind, the sink rusted cast iron. He swung the kitchen door wide, thinking that the smell wasn't as bad in here, or maybe Jeffrey was just getting used to it.

"Jeff?" Sara called. From the sound of it, she was standing in the front doorway.

"Don't come in here," he warned.

Sara asked, "Are you all right?"

"I'm fine," he told her, trying to open the window over the sink. It was stuck, and he had to holster his gun and use both hands to force it up.

Jeffrey stood at the window, breathing the fresh air. The weeds in the backyard were higher than the ones in the front, but he could easily see the body lying on the ground.

It was Lena.

He ran toward the back door, yanking it open. There were boxes stacked on the back deck, blocking the path. Jeffrey kicked them aside, scattering leaflets into the air. "Sara!" he yelled. "Come to the back!"

When he got to the body he stopped. He was wrong. This wasn't Lena. It was Hank Norton. The man's body was emaciated, his face sunken. Open needle wounds pocked his arms.

"Sara!" Jeffrey yelled again, kneeling down beside the man. "In the back!"

He pressed his head to Hank's chest, trying to see if the man was breathing. Jeffrey heard nothing.

"Sara!" he tried again, but she was already pushing open the gate to the backyard. He saw her relief when she realized he was okay, then her astonished expression when she saw the body.

She dropped to her knees and pushed him aside. "Did you find him like this?"

Jeffrey nodded, taking out his cell phone to call an ambulance. "Is he alive?"

"Barely." She opened Hank's eyelids, checking his pupils. Jeffrey could see dark blood in the sclera. Streaks of dried blood flaked from his mouth and ears. "Hank?" she asked, voice raised. "It's Sara Linton, Lena's friend. Can you hear me?" She patted his face with a firm hand. "Hank? I need you to open your eyes."

Jeffrey was giving the nine-one-one operator Hank's address when Sara held up her hand for silence. She pressed her ear to Hank's chest. "He stopped breathing."

Jeffrey ended the call as Sara started chest compressions. "The ambulance should be here in ten minutes."

She nodded, then bent down to put her mouth over Hank's.

Shocked, Jeffrey pulled her away, yelling, "Sara, no! There's blood."

"I can't just sit here while he—"

"Look at him, Sara. He's an IV drug user."

"He's all Lena's got." Sara leaned over Hank again, pressing into his chest, forcing blood through his heart. Jeffrey knew she wasn't really thinking about Hank right now. She was thinking about Jimmy Powell and the other patients she had not been able to help. She was remembering what it felt like to lose them.

Jeffrey told her, "Get the CPR kit out of your trunk." She hesitated, and he said, "I'll take over here." Finally, she let him take her place. He overlapped his right hand with his left and pushed the heel of his hand into Hank's chest, counting between repetitions.

Sara jogged toward the gate, but not before saying, "Don't stop compressions."

Jeffrey felt sweat dripping down his back as he leaned over Hank, the sour odor of the man filling the air around them. He could not believe Sara had not given it a second thought before leaning down to put her mouth against Hank's bloody lips. Looking at the man, it was obvious he didn't give a shit what he put into his body. He could've infected Sara with anything, and for what? So Hank would die tomorrow instead of today?

Just as Jeffrey was thinking his effort was useless, Hank made a gurgling sound, red-tinged air bubbles popping on his lips. Jeffrey sat back on his heels, watching the old man's eyes slit open as he struggled to breathe. He saw Jeffrey and gave an almost imperceptible shake of his head, as if he could not understand why he had been brought back, why anyone would care.

Sara burst through the gate, CPR kit in hand.

"It's going to be okay," Jeffrey told Hank, taking the man's dry, waxy hand. "You're going to be fine."

LENA

CHAPTER 18

LENA HAD BEEN TO COASTAL STATE PRISON once before. Shortly after Jeffrey had arrested Ethan on the parole violation, she had driven to the prison thinking that she would confront Ethan, let him know exactly how she had set him up, betrayed him, given him the biggest "fuck you" that she could muster. She'd sat in her car in the visitors' parking lot for almost two hours, her mind cataloguing all the violence he had done to her: the split lips, the broken fingers, the sprained wrists.

Unbidden, the image of the two of them in bed came back to her. She had never thought of sex with Ethan in romantic terms, but there had been times, maybe more than a few, that she could recall clutching on to him, holding him in her arms. He had loved her just as passionately as he had hated her, and she had often returned his moods in equal measure. Sitting in the car outside the prison, her skin started to tingle from the memory of his hands, his mouth, his tongue.

She'd barely made it out of the Celica in time to keep from being sick in the car. Visiting day was popular at the prison. Women and children were lined up at the door waiting to see their men. They had all turned, staring with blank curiosity as Lena threw up onto the asphalt. So much came out that her stomach felt as if a knife had ripped it in two. When she could manage, Lena crawled back into the Celica and drove back to Grant County with her tail between her legs.

This time was different, though. It had to be different. If she couldn't face Ethan for herself, then she could do it for Hank. Ethan was calling him for a reason, and Lena would not leave Coastal without finding out what exactly had gone on between the two men. Before she'd left the motel this morning, Lena had changed into slacks, and a crisp linen shirt. She'd put on makeup and fixed her hair so that she looked like a cop who was in control instead of a terrified woman.

She went into the prison armed with lies and nothing else. Her Glock was hidden under the mattress back at the motel room and her folding knife was tucked in its hiding place under the front seat of her car. She'd even left her cell phone on the sink basin so it could charge. All she took into the prison with her was her ID and a tube of ChapStick.

Lena had told the warden that she was investigating threats made by one of Ethan's henchmen on the outside. The warden proved to be the picture of compliance. He'd given her transcripts of Ethan's phone records, his visitor log, copies of his outgoing mail. In addition, he had offered her the full services of the prison to do all they could to make a case against one of its most dangerous inmates.

The records were not going to get Ethan into trouble. The only person he'd called was Hank. He'd had no visitors. Ethan had neither written nor received any mail since the date of his incarceration. Not that any of this meant a damn thing. Lena knew Ethan was smart enough, charismatic enough, to get someone else to do his dirty work. According to the warden, his gang wasn't the biggest or the strongest, but Ethan managed to wield a psychological power that served to keep them high up in the prison food chain.

Lena had no trouble believing that. She hadn't seen Ethan in almost a year and still her heart had started pounding the minute she pulled into the prison parking lot.

One of the guards led Lena to the conference room they used for lawyer-inmate meetings. It was more like an interrogation room as far as she could see, little more than ten feet by twelve with a water-stained ceiling and heavy bars blocking the small windows. The table was bolted to the floor, a red line painted down its center as if to separate the good from the bad. The chairs were lightweight, unbreakable plastic so they wouldn't do much damage if they were thrown or used as a weapon. Guards were not allowed to hear exchanges between prisoners and their legal counsel, so there was a ring bolted to the wall where more violent inmates could be restrained.

"He's extremely dangerous," the warden had told Lena. "I'm not happy about leaving you alone in a locked room with this guy."

The man had gone on to list suspected crimes committed by Ethan within the walls of the prison: shankings in the yard, drug trafficking, inmate shakedowns, a man who'd had his face burned off in the prison laundry. None of it could be linked back to Ethan, but the warden knew who was responsible for it all.

Lena had asked that Ethan be chained to the ring in the wall. The guard had told her that with violent prisoners, that was standard procedure.

She sat at the table and waited, her ears sensitive to every noise. Finally, the bolt slid back on the door. Lena kept her place at the table, pretending to read the records in front of her, willing her hands not to shake. She could hear chains rattling, feet sliding across the floor.

"What's this spic want with me?"

Ethan's voice; a hot knife in her ears.

"Shut the fuck up and sit down." This from the guard, a beefy man who looked as if he enjoyed his job a little too much.

Lena sat back in her chair, arms folded across her chest. She kept her eyes trained on Ethan's chest, her vision blurring into the orange of his prison uniform as the guard pushed him down into the chair and linked the chains into the bolt. Ethan tested his boundaries. He could fold his hands in front of him on the table, but the restraint would prevent him from going an inch farther.

Now Lena understood what the red line was for. Ethan's chains prevented him from crossing it.

The guard told Lena, "Knock on the door when you're finished." He waited for her to nod. The warden had shown her the panic button under the table a few minutes earlier. She put her hands in her lap in easy reach of the button.

The guard left and the bolts slid back on the door. There was no window in the door, no cameras the guards could watch to make sure she was okay. Lena was on her own.

Ethan smacked his lips. "What a pleasant surprise."

Lena looked at his hands on the table. The knuckles were red, one of them cut.

She asked, "Why have you been calling Hank?"

He spoke softly, intimately. "You can't even look me in the eye."

He was right. She forced herself to meet his gaze. "Why have you been trying to call Hank?"

He pressed his lips together, leaned back in his chair. Had his eyes always been this blue? They were like ice, but colder.

He said, "I missed the old guy."

"You don't even know him."

"I thought I knew you."

Lena let the silence build—not because she was in control of the interview but because she did not know what else to say.

He asked, "You know what it's like in here?"

"I don't want to know. I'm just here to tell you to back off Hank."

Was she, though? She didn't even know where her uncle was. Hank could be facedown in a sewer right now. He could be a John Doe on someone's slab at the morgue.

Ethan's chains clunked against the table as he clasped his hands in front of him. The handcuffs around his wrist were heavy-duty reinforced steel and the chain bolting him to the wall was so thick you'd need a torch to cut it off. Still, he somehow managed to seem in control. Lena could not even hold his gaze. She looked at his arms, saw that he had embellished the prison camp tattoos. Bodies were caught in the barbed-wire fence; emaciated prisoners with their mouths open in horror.

"Do you remember Shawn Cable from school?"

She shook her head.

"He was in my class at Grant Tech. Short guy, curly hair."

She shook her head again, but she remembered the guy. They had been lab partners. Shawn had coasted by on Ethan's work.

"He's working at BASF now, in their industrial coatings division."

Lena stared at the barbed-wire on his arm.

"That could have been my job," Ethan said. "But your boss jammed me up, and now I'm in here."

Lena opened her mouth to defend Jeffrey, but stopped when she realized that she would only be implicating herself.

"I was out of it," he said, indicating the tattoos. "I was out of that life and starting a new one with you."

"A new one where you beat me."

"You hit me sometimes, too."

Lena's throat started to close, making it hard to breathe. She *had* hit him. She hadn't just rolled over and taken it. Sometimes she had even started the fights herself.

"I loved you," Ethan said. "I loved you, and this is what you did to me."

She found her voice. "Did you love Evelyn Johnson, too?"

The silence between them was different this time, and when she dared look at his face, he was looking down at his chained wrists.

She said, "You never told me she was black."

"You never asked."

They were talking like normal people now and it set Lena's teeth on edge. She tried to keep reminding herself of who he really was, but all she kept coming back to was the person sitting in front of her, his eyes down, his shoulders slouched. She had loved him. She could not get around the fact that she had loved him.

She asked, "What happened with her?"

"Are you recording this?"

"What do you think?"

He was staring at her again and Lena felt trapped in his gaze, unable to break the contact.

"Unbutton your blouse."

"Fuck you."

He raised his eyebrow. "You did, baby." The smile on his face was familiar—the old Ethan was coming out to play. "Unbutton your blouse. Let me see if you're wired."

"I told you I'm not."

"I'm supposed to take you at your word?" His lips twisted into a grin. "No dice, Lee. Last time I trusted you, I ended up in here. Show me you're not wired or I'll call the monkey back to take me to my cage."

She fumbled with the top button, trying to make her fingers work. She looked at the door as she did this, as if she was afraid the guard would come through at any moment. She'd been sweating in the small room, and the air was cool on her skin as she opened the blouse to her waist.

"No wires," she told him. "Satisfied?"

He shrugged, the smile making her blood freeze in her veins.

Lena started to button back her blouse, but he wouldn't let it go at that.

"You still look good."

She couldn't get the buttons to fasten because her hands were trembling.

"You know how many nights I've jerked myself raw thinking about fucking you?"

She gave up, clasping the blouse closed. Her voice shook. "Why have you been calling Hank?"

"Open your shirt again."

"No."

"Open it up and I'll tell you whatever you want to know."

"No."

He made to stand. "Then call the guard, because I've got nothing else to say."

"Ethan—"

"Hey!" he called, his loud voice echoing in the cramped room. "Guard!"

"Shut up," she hissed, as if she'd ever been able to stop him from doing anything.

He smiled again, that same smile he used to give before he beat the shit out of her. He pointed his finger at her, indicating that she should open her blouse.

She could barely speak. Tears blurred her vision. "Tell me why you've been calling Hank."

"You know the trade. Tit for tat."

Lena glared at him, furious with him, furious with herself. *He* was the one in chains. *He* was the one bolted to the wall. Yet, she was the one who felt imprisoned.

"Open," he coaxed.

Her hands shook as she slowly parted her blouse. She was wearing an old bra, black with lace and a clasp in the middle.

He said, "Bra, too."

"No."

He knew her so well—knew when to keep pushing and when to pull back. He said, "Spread your shoulders."

She looked at the door, put her shoulders back like he said.

"Jesus, you look so good." Ethan leaned as far forward as the chains would allow. His hands were under the table, and she kept her face turned away, staring at the metal door, trying not to listen to what he was doing.

He let out a low groan as he finished. She heard him zip himself up, sit back in the chair. She pulled her blouse closed, trying not to imagine the satisfied look on his ugly face.

"Tell me something," he said. "Just out of curiosity, when you called your boss that morning after I left, were you sitting down or standing?"

Lena shook her head.

"Come on, baby. Sitting or standing?"

She shook her head again as the day came back to her. His hand muffling the scream in her throat as he slammed her down on the bed. Forcing back her revulsion when she kissed him good-bye and told him to have a good day at work.

Lena forced herself to speak. "What does it matter?"

"I want to know," he insisted. "When you sent me into this hellhole for ten years of my life, were you sitting in the bed where I just fucked you, or were you standing beside it?"

She suppressed a shudder as his words recalled the sensation. "You got what you wanted," she told him, her hands steady now as she buttoned her blouse. "Tell me why you've been trying to get in touch with Hank."

"All right," he said, leaning forward. "Come here."

She leaned forward, waited.

The smile on his face should have been her first warning, but she was still surprised when the sound of his laughter filled the room. "You stupid bitch," he said, shaking his head as if he could not believe how hilarious the situation was. "Do you think I'm gonna tell you anything?" Abruptly, the laughter stopped. "Get the fuck out of here. You make me sick."

Lena was stunned by her own stupidity. "You said—"

He slammed his hands down on the table, the chains clanging against the steel. "I said *get the fuck out of here*, bitch."

Lena grabbed the records in front of her as she stood, backing up until she felt the wall behind her.

He looped his arm over the back of his chair, a satisfied smile on his face.

She didn't leave. She waited, wanting to hurt him, to humiliate him, as much as she had been humiliated. "You know what, Ethan?"

"What, baby?"

"I'm really glad I came here today."

"Yeah?" He reached down, grabbing himself between the legs. "Me, too, baby."

"No." She clutched the papers tighter to her chest as if they could serve as some sort of armor. "See, I was really upset about something." She paused, studying the sneer on his face, wanting to savor every moment. "Remember when I told you that I thought I was pregnant?"

He sat up in the chair. She had his full attention now.

"I told you it was a false alarm, but it wasn't."

His lips parted, but he didn't speak.

"And then I told you that I had to go to Macon for a refresher course for work," she continued. "Only, I wasn't in Macon, Ethan. I was in Atlanta." It was her turn to smile. "Do you know what I was do-ing up there, baby?"

His jaw clenched. "You shut up."

"Do you know what I was doing, Ethan? Honey?"

He lunged at her, the chains jerking him back against the wall. He screamed, "I will fucking kill you," saliva spraying from his mouth. "You goddamn whore!" Every muscle in his body shook from the ef-fort of pulling at the restraints. He was like a rabid pit bull, ready to choke himself to death rather than suppress the urge to attack.

Lena knocked on the door. "Think about what I did," she told him. "Think about what I did to your child the next time you jerk yourself raw."

The guard opened the door. He looked at Ethan, then Lena, obvi-ously sensing the tension in the room. "You finished?"

"Yeah," Lena said, glancing back at Ethan one last time. "I'm fin-ished."

✦

LENA DIDN'T BREAK DOWN until she was out of the parking lot, well on her way to the interstate. She felt disgusting from being in Ethan's presence, and like a monster for the callous way she'd spoken about their child. Leaving that room, walking down the hallway to the exit and knowing Ethan could not follow her, she had felt powerful, in-vincible. Then her words had come back to her, and the stupid way she had yet again let him talk her into doing exactly what he wanted made her feel raw inside.

By the time she made it back to the Elawah County limits, Lena was exhausted. Over and over again, she kept reviewing how she had played right into Ethan's hands. He had always taken a sick delight in mind games. She could picture him calling Hank with that smirk on his face, delighting in the prospect of torturing the old man. Ethan had always used other people to get to Lena, whether it was threatening Nan or try-ing to rile up Jeffrey. Lena wasn't even sure Hank had heard the calls on the machine. Even if he had, what the fuck did he care about Ethan Green? A couple of phone messages weren't enough to make Hank take up the needle again. There had to be something else—something Lena still wasn't seeing—and she felt in her gut that it all tied back to the drug dealer with the red swastika that she'd seen leaving Hank's house.

Hank had said that the man had killed her mother. Where had he done this? When? How?

The visit to the prison had been a waste of time. Lena had pissed away a full day tracking down a false lead when she could have been looking for information on Angela Adams. She had to find something—a birth certificate, marriage certificate, death certificate, last known address. At the very least, a Social Security number would lead to income tax information. Tax information would give an address, a place of employment—something she could use for leverage with Hank. Lena felt certain more and more that her mother was the key to all of this. Hank was spiraling out of control for a reason. If Lena knew what had really happened to her mother, why Hank had lied all those years, then she could confront him with it, make him get help. As Lena drove down the state highway leading into Reece, she started making plans.

It was time to talk to the local cops. Fuck Al Pfeiffer and his lecherous hands. Lena was no longer a cowering teenager scared of a speeding ticket. She was a detective on the Grant County Police Force. She would go to the sheriff's office first thing in the morning and demand copies of the reports in the investigation into her father's death. If Pfeiffer balked, then she would call Jeffrey and let him do the good ol' boy shuffle. If Jeffrey needed a reason for her wanting the file, she would spin him some yarn about needing closure. Since Jeffrey had married Sara again, he'd gotten enough estrogen back in his life to believe in that kind of shit.

Lena could still go to the hospital and try to track down her mother's birth certificate. If that didn't work, she would go back to Hank's and find the information on her own. She shuddered at the prospect of going up into that attic again, the smell of Deacon Simms. She had no choice, though. Hank was consistent in one respect: he never threw away anything, whether it was an electric bill from 1973 or a newspaper covering the Challenger explosion. Somewhere in that house under all the self-help pamphlets and dirty clothes and boxes of crap, there had to be information about her mother.

Lena followed the car in front of her, turning off the highway and going toward downtown Reece. She passed the motel but did not turn in, the thought of the dark, lonely room too much to handle. Without realizing it, she had made the decision to go through Hank's things tonight. She would get some big trash bags and throw out the trash as she went along.

Maybe she could find a way to dispose of Deacon's body.

As she passed the high school, the car ahead of her slammed on the brakes and Lena turned the steering wheel hard, trying to avoid an accident. Her head slammed into the steering wheel as she skidded into the oncoming lane. The Celica stopped just short of rolling into the ditch. Her heart was in her throat as her brain processed what had happened. She could feel blood trickling down the side of her head and she wiped it away as she pushed open the door.

Up ahead was a white Escalade.

Lena reached under the seat and grabbed her folding knife. She flipped the blade open and got out of the car.

The streetlights nearly blinded her, or maybe the crash had jostled her brain. She felt dizzy and sick, her head pounding like a drum. Lena squinted, trying to see inside the SUV. The rear window slid down with a mechanical whirl. Charlotte Warren sat in the backseat. Duct tape covered her mouth. Her eyes were wide with terror.

Hank's dealer got out from behind the wheel, leaving the door open. Lena clenched her fist around the pearl-handled knife, ready to use it, but the man simply grabbed her by her hair and threw her toward the Cadillac like a sack of flour.

"Get in," he said. Her knife was in his hand. She must have dropped it. He folded down the blade and tucked it into his back pocket while she was watching.

Lena pushed away from the car, but he threw her back toward the open driver's door. Charlotte gave a muffled yell and Lena saw that another man was sitting beside her. This one wore a black ski mask. Surgical gloves covered his hands. He held a gun to Charlotte's head. His smile sent a cold shiver through her body.

He said, "Get in."

Lena didn't move.

He pressed the muzzle of the gun to Charlotte's temple. "Get in or I'll kill her right now."

Lena got in.

THURSDAY EVENING

CHAPTER 19

JEFFREY SAT ON THE FRONT STEPS of Hank Norton's house as he studied the street map of downtown Reece. Sara had ridden in the ambulance with Hank so that she could manage his care on the ride to the hospital. Jeffrey knew without asking that she would want to stay with him until his condition was stabilized. Sara had cut her teeth as an ER doc. She wouldn't leave Hank's side until she was sure he was in capable hands.

That left Jeffrey with plenty of time to search the man's house. First, he had opened every window that would budge in the hopes that the place would air out. While he was waiting for this miracle to occur, he checked the shed in the backyard. Other than rat shit and about a hundred boxes full of paper so old it was starting to pulp, he found nothing. The old Chevy pickup was empty, the cab floor so rusted that the bench seat had fallen through.

The clothes Hank had worn were by the fence. Jeffrey guessed from the way the pants, shirt, and underwear trailed along the lawn that the old man had taken them off as he walked into the backyard. After the paramedics had shifted Hank to the gurney, Jeffrey had checked the grass underneath the man's body. Jeffrey took comfort in the discovery. When he'd first seen Hank lying in the grass, he'd thought Lena's uncle had lain there for days, waiting for someone to discover him. The ground underneath his emaciated frame would have been dry if he'd been there overnight.

Jeffrey was biding his time, pacing around the backyard, when his foot found the soft, wet earth over the septic tank. Obviously, the system had backed up into the house. Whoever had taken a sledgehammer to the toilet bowl had broken the natural seal and allowed raw sewage to spew out into the house. A plumber would have to suck out the septic tank, then some poor bastard would have to get a shovel and take care of the rest of it. As far as Jeffrey was concerned, the easiest thing to do would be to rent a bulldozer and push the whole damn house down.

After waiting half an hour for the odor to dissipate, he was able to go back inside without dry-heaving. Even with the windows open, rotting food and the various insects it attracted made Jeffrey gag so many times that bile had made his throat raw. He'd felt odd looking through Lena's girlhood bedroom. Like most parents, Hank had not changed much when the girls left and like most children, Lena and Sibyl had left behind the crap they didn't want to take with them. When Jeffrey found himself faced with Lena's underwear drawer, he decided to move on to Hank's room.

As he went through the man's things, Jeffrey got the distinct impression that this wasn't the first time the house had been searched. He didn't know if this was Lena's doing or someone else's. He did know that when he pulled back the duct tape from around the front door, the splintered wood around the jamb looked newly damaged.

Lena knew how to kick in a door. She also knew how to perform a thorough search. Knowing she could have done either of these things to her uncle's house did not come as a consolation. Jeffrey knew she was hiding out, sleeping at the school, or at least she had been until now, but what had she been doing in the daytime? Why was she still in Reece?

Jeffrey gave up wondering what Lena was up to as his search finally ended up in the kitchen. He supposed the stacks of Alcoholics Anonymous pamphlets on the table and the empty syringe he found under the chair was what you'd call irony, but Jeffrey wasn't in the mood to play word games with himself. He'd wiped the chair opposite Hank's and sat down at the table, wondering what would make a man do this to himself. It was suicide, plain and simple.

Finding nothing in the house but an overwhelming sadness, Jeffrey had shut the window in the kitchen and gone around the rest of the house to make sure everything was pretty much as he'd found it. He grabbed a roll of duct tape he'd seen in the kitchen and taped the bathroom door shut, sealing the edges as best he could. The window inside was wide open, but he doubted even the most desperate thief would brave the disgusting bathroom to get into the house.

For the next half hour, he wrestled with the front door. No matter how many different ways he tried, the metal flashing sticking out from the jamb kept the door from closing. Jeffrey tried to hold it down with his fingers, but all that did was end up giving him the equivalent of a metal paper cut on the tips of his fingers. Finally, he found a screwdriver in the kitchen and used the flat end to hold the metal strip flush to the door so he could close it.

His plan had been to leave the house through the kitchen door, but Jeffrey had a strange feeling as he started to pull the back door shut. He had the feeling he had missed something. Once more, he walked through the house, turning on all the lights, checking each room to see if anything jumped out at him. All that hit him was the odor. Hank must have moved from room to room, trying to outrun the decay, and finally ended up in the kitchen. Jeffrey went back to the living room. He was breathing through his mouth, trying not to gag again from the smell, when he saw the painting over the couch.

This had to be Lena's mother. She had the same olive skin and piercing eyes. She wore her hair a little shorter, but it looked almost the same as Lena's did now. Her neck had that same swan-like curve and Jeffrey could tell from looking at her that she had that same attitude that some women took as threatening and most men took as sexy. Jeffrey imagined she'd been quite the draw to the locals. It would have taken a cop's arrogance to look past that haughty tilt to the woman's chin and the wry amusement in her eyes.

Jeffrey finally left the house, turning the thumb latch on the knob to lock the kitchen door. He'd left all the lights on in hopes of discouraging burglars, or maybe it was the thought of going back into the depressing house that made him not bother.

He was finished fucking around with this. A woman had been burned alive. Jeffrey had been shot at. A man had been stabbed to death and thrown through their window. Hank Norton was on his deathbed at the hospital.

It was time to find Lena.

Jeffrey sat on the front steps and studied the map until he found the route he was looking for. Sara had been right about the town being laid out in a large rectangle with a forest in the middle. There would be trails through the forest, shortcuts that had been used for years. Maybe even a fort or some kind of hastily built shelter where kids went to smoke pot and get laid. When Jeffrey was a teenager, he'd had a similar hide-out. It wasn't a big stretch to think there was one in Reece, too.

Jeffrey had given Sara his cell phone because the battery on hers was dead. He went to the BMW and took her phone off the charger, slipping it into his pocket and locking the car before heading toward the end of the street. Given Hank's current condition, there was no way the old man had helped Lena in her escape from police custody. This left Lena on her own, which meant she had left the hospital by foot. Looking at the map, Jeffrey could see the path she might have taken from the hospital to Hank's house. He assumed she had come here first to search for money. The house had been turned upside down by some-body. That somebody could very well have been Lena.

Jeffrey doubted very seriously that the cruiser Jake Valentine had sent to the house the night of Lena's escape acted as a deterrent. Hank's backyard connected to his neighbors'. Lena could have easily gone in through the back door without anyone on the street noticing. If Deputy Don Cook was in that cruiser, he was probably doing the crossword and eating some crackers while she ransacked the house.

He was losing what little daylight was left standing there thinking about all this. Jeffrey took off his jacket and rolled up his sleeves as he walked up the street. He passed the high school, and wondered where Lena was going to sleep now that the classroom wasn't an option. Hank's bar had burned down, but he remembered Valentine telling him that the police tape on the door had been cut. Jeffrey shook his head, thinking if Lena had been staying at the bar all this time while Jeffrey and Sara were next door at the motel, he was going to kill her.

There was only one certainty in all of this, and that was that Lena would have to go somewhere for shelter. She would need food, clothes, water. Jeffrey looked up at the sun, wishing he had brought some water with him. Of course, given the state of the house, it was probably wise he hadn't ingested anything there.

At the top of the hill, he took out the map again, checking to make sure he was still on the right route. He saw skid marks on the road where two cars had almost collided and figured a couple of kids had narrowly missed getting their cars totaled.

Jeffrey could hear traffic from the highway as he took the next left. A large field on his right led into a dense forest, and he wondered if this was the same forest that backed onto the motel. Jeffrey consulted the map again and saw that it was. Lena could have walked from Hank's to the bar. The hospital was just a few streets over.

As expected, there were all kinds of trails crisscrossing the field. It was colder inside the forest and he put his jacket back on. There were no signs of secret hiding places, no trash other than some cigarette butts and more empty beer bottles than he could count. Jeffrey could still see the sun peeking through the limbs and he made sure to keep it on his right as he walked a straight line toward the motel. He kept checking his watch as he walked so that he wouldn't lose his sense of time, which always moved more slowly when you thought you were lost.

Jeffrey was starting to get a little nervous when he heard the stream that he'd seen behind Hank's bar the other night. Briefly, he had the entertaining idea that he might find whatever Boyd Gibson had dropped, but by the time he reached the bank of the stream, he'd pretty much given up on that miracle happening.

Jeffrey saw the room he and Sara had shared. Someone who wasn't exactly handy had nailed a large sheet of plywood over the broken window. The door was ajar, and Jeffrey poked his head in and checked to make sure they had gotten all of their things. The room looked exactly as they'd left it, but for some reason, Jeffrey didn't find the place as disgusting. Maybe it was because he'd spent a couple of hours in Hank's house. He didn't know how Lena had stood it.

"Shit," Jeffrey whispered. Lena *hadn't* stood it. There was no way she'd stayed in that house. She wasn't exactly a neat freak, but no sane human being would sleep in that pigsty.

Jeffrey jogged to the front office. The night clerk was gone, but an orange-haired teenager was sitting behind the counter playing video games on the computer.

The kid didn't look up from the screen as he jabbed his thumbs at the buttons. "What's up?"

"Was somebody, a woman, staying here last week about this tall." Jeffrey held up his hand to indicate Lena's height. "Brown hair, brown eyes—"

"You mean Lena?" The kid kept his eyes glued to the screen.

Jeffrey reached over the counter and ripped the controller out of his hand. "Give me the key to her room."

"The sheriff's already checked—" The kid seemed to understand this didn't matter. He quickly handed Jeffrey the passkey, saying, "Room fourteen. It's on the second floor."

Jeffrey bolted up the stairs. He jammed the key in the lock and threw open Lena's door as if he expected to find her standing there with a full explanation.

She wasn't.

He closed the door behind him and dropped the key on the plastic table. Lena's toiletries were neatly lined by the sink, her clothes still folded in her suitcase. Jeffrey couldn't begin to know what, if anything, was missing because he didn't know what she had packed. Still, he opened all the drawers, checked the nightstand, even looked under the sink.

There was nothing except a rusted flathead screwdriver that had rolled under the air conditioner by the window.

Jeffrey sat on the bed, trying to think. He had never seen Lena carry a purse, but then carrying a bag wasn't conducive to the job. He would have to ask Sara about that. Or maybe Valentine would be the person to question since the sheriff had already checked the room. On second thought, there was no need to let the sheriff know he'd gotten one up on Jeffrey.

Jeffrey stood from the bed and lifted up the mattress, finding the remnants of what he guessed had been a couple of Cheetos but nothing else. He dropped the mattress, a rush of air blowing back on him. Jeffrey's olfactory system was understandably out of whack since his time at Hank Norton's, but he could have sworn he'd gotten a whiff of gun oil. He flipped the mattress off the bed and knelt down to examine the bedskirt that covered the boxspring. Glad that no one could see him, he sniffed around the thin cotton, stopping when he heard a key sliding into the lock on the door.

Jeffrey stood up just as the door opened. The maid did a double take when she saw him, a scowl on her face.

She demanded, "What the fuck are you doing?"

"Can you come back in ten minutes?"

"Can you put that mattress back where it belongs?" Jeffrey didn't snap to, and she tucked her hands onto her hips. "I ain't got all day, mister."

He took out his badge and showed it to her.

She squinted at the tiny letters, unimpressed. "Grant County. Sounds like a real shithole. You with the mattress division, checking to see if people pulled off the tags?"

Jeffrey put the mattress back in place, hoping he could keep her talking. "Did you ever meet the woman who was staying here?"

"The one what gave Jake the slip?" She chuckled, walking into the room. "And to think I voted for that dipshit."

"Lena's a friend of mine," he told the woman. "I'm trying to help her out."

"Ain't you the gallant knight." She took a rag out of her pocket and started wiping down the phone on the bedside table, mumbling, "Must've used the phone a lot. Damn greasy fingerprints are all over it." Her head was bent, but she looked up at Jeffrey as if she was wondering why he was still here.

"Thanks for your help," he told the woman, though the opposite was the case.

Jeffrey was halfway toward the stairs when he realized the maid may have been more helpful than she'd intended. He hadn't seen Lena's cell phone in the hotel room, so it must have been in her car. Frank Wallace, his second in command, could run a records check to see who she had been talking to before the night the Escalade was torched, or maybe even after. He would also put out his own APB on Hank's Mercedes and maybe have Frank call in a few favors with the Highway Patrol to see if they could keep an eye out for Lena. As with Jeffrey's phone, Sara's couldn't get a cell signal at the hotel, so he would have to call Frank on the walk back.

Jeffrey stopped on the bottom stair. Christ, what an idiot. If he couldn't get a cell signal at the hotel, neither could Lena.

He jogged toward the front office again. This time, the kid was waiting at the counter, ready to serve. He asked, "Find anything?"

Jeffrey shot back his own question. "Did Detective Adams make any phone calls while she was here?"

"She made a long-distance one before she left."

Jeffrey knew from his own bill that the motel charged fifty cents a minute for local calls and two dollars a minute for long distance. The calls were big money and the motel would keep exact records. "Let me see all of her calls."

The teenager pulled a stack of papers off the printer. "There was only one," he explained. "Got a nine-one-two area code."

The number looked familiar. "That's Savannah."

"Yeah, I think so."

Jeffrey grabbed the phone off the counter and dialed the number.

LENA

CHAPTER 20

CHARLOTTE'S FACE WAS OBSCURED by the duct tape covering her mouth, so that all Lena could see was a pair of bright, terrified eyes. The woman trembled with fear, her sobs muffled by the tape. Lena glanced in the rearview mirror as she drove the SUV down a dark road, trying to silently communicate to Charlotte to just hold on, that Lena would find a way out of this. Though, how she would manage their escape, Lena did not know.

The tattooed man who had hit Lena was behind them, driving her Celica. She had no idea where they were going or why. She just kept driving because even though she could not see the masked face of the man in the backseat, she knew that he was not fucking around. The way he held the gun told her all that she needed to know. The weapon was like an extension of his hand. He was not afraid to use it.

Lena thought about Evelyn Johnson, Ethan driving her in his truck to that clearing in the woods where she was murdered. Had Ethan looked in his rearview mirror and seen the fear in Evelyn's eyes, knowing there was nothing that he could do? Had he been just as afraid himself? Or had he been squirming in his seat, fighting the excitement building between his legs as he thought about what was to come?

"Turn here," the man in the mask said, and Lena followed orders, turning onto Laskey Street, which ran behind the school. There was no urgency in his voice and he seemed to have no particular plan in mind.

As far as she could tell, he was making her drive in a circle around the periphery of the high school.

"Next right," he said.

Lena loooked at Charlotte again. She asked the man, "Why are you doing this?"

"Why do you think?"

"Did Ethan send you?"

"Who's Ethan?"

"If Ethan sent you, then this is between me and him. Charlotte doesn't have anything to do with this. I haven't even seen her since high school."

"Honey, I don't know what you're talking about."

She didn't know if he was telling the truth or playing with her. Had they followed her to Coastal State Prison or just waited for her to show back up in town? There was nothing in her motel room that would tell them where she had been. Ethan's arrest jacket was tucked back in its hiding place behind the CD changer in the trunk of her Celica. The only thing of value in the room was her Glock, and they obviously didn't need that.

Lena glanced over her shoulder. The man was small but well built. He sat casually with his legs spread apart, his left arm draped over the back of the seat, the gun in his hand pointing at Charlotte's neck.

He said, "What are you looking at?"

"Who are you?" Lena asked. Did the mask mean he was going to let them go? She had already seen his flunky's face, though maybe that didn't matter because his cover had been blown two days ago outside of Hank's house.

She looked around for something—anything—that could be used as a weapon. Other than the keys, there was nothing but a Styrofoam cup in one of the holders. She let her hand slide down the wheel and pressed her knuckles against the side of the cup. The contents were cold, probably water.

"Keep going," the man said. "Take another right up here."

Lena ignored him, going straight. He clicked his tongue as if she were a rebellious child, but didn't say anything else.

Rule number one when faced with an abduction was to not let the perpetrator change your location. If he jumped you in a parking lot, then you fought tooth and nail to stay in that parking lot. You didn't get in a car with him and you didn't let him drag you somewhere else.

Once he had control of you and the situation, he could do whatever he wanted. There was no going back.

Lena slowed the car, keeping her eye on the Celica behind them, wondering what she was getting herself—and Charlotte—into.

The man said, "You really like pushing your luck, don't you?"

Lena stopped the car. She turned around to face him. "What do you want from us? Why is Charlotte here?"

The back door beside Charlotte opened. The man with the red swastika stood there.

The man with the gun ordered, "Give her a little incentive so she knows we're not playing around."

The thug reached around to the back of his pants. Lena braced herself for him to pull a gun and shoot them both, but what he did instead was pull out a rolled-up plastic bag.

"What are you doing?" Lena asked, but she knew well enough when the man unrolled the bag and took out a filled syringe.

Charlotte knew what was coming before Lena did. She panicked, tucking her arms behind her back, struggling to protect herself as the thug tapped the side of the syringe, squirted some liquid out of the needle. She started to flail desperately when he grabbed her arm, then suddenly it seemed to Lena that something inside of the other woman just snapped. She simply gave up, holding out her arm, waiting for the needle to go in.

"No..." Lena said, but it was too late. The plunger was pressed. Charlotte closed her eyes, a soft sound like a sigh coming from her throat.

The man in the mask nestled the gun against Charlotte's cheek. "She likes that, don't you think?"

Lena felt tears stream down her face. How many kids did Charlotte have? She had seen one of them in the library the other day, a young girl, probably not even thirteen.

"Please," Lena said. "Just let her go."

"Why don't you drive some more?" the man suggested. He nodded to his lackey and the door was slammed shut.

Lena put the car in gear and pressed her foot to the gas. She drove aimlessly, following the circle she'd made before, the Celica close behind.

Charlotte gave a deep moan. Her eyes rolled back in her head and she slumped against the door.

Lena demanded, "What did you give her?"

"Something to take the edge off."

"I don't understand," Lena said. She was crying in earnest now. "Why is this happening? What did Charlotte ever do to you?"

"Want me to tell you a little story, Lee?"

He used her familiar name, the one reserved for close friends and family. Lena turned the rearview mirror away from Charlotte and onto her abductor.

She could see his white teeth through the hole in the mask. "You figuring it out, baby doll?"

She concentrated on his voice, desperately trying to place it. There was hardly any accent, and the tone was deep, almost as deep as Jeffrey's. Lena ran through her childhood, trying to think of the men she had known. Hank did not have friends. When he was using, he ended up screwing them or pushing them away. When he stopped using, he'd lacked the skills to make connections. There were people he knew from AA meetings and Deacon Simms, but that was it. He spent his nights at home or at the bar.

The man told her, "You know, when I saw you at Hank's place the other day, I thought, 'Now there's a good lookin' woman.'"

Had he been in the Escalade outside of Hank's house? The SUV's windows were tinted. Lena had been so focused on the man with the swastika that she hadn't bothered to look for a passenger.

"You look a lot like your mama when she was your age. Did you know that?"

"I didn't even know my mother lived to be my age."

"Oh, yeah, Angie lived a lot longer than she should have."

Hank had said that the man outside was the one who'd killed Angela Adams. Had he meant this man, the one who now held a gun to Charlotte Warren's head?

Lena asked, "Did you kill my mother?" She turned around. "Hank said that you killed her."

He laughed. "Hank says a lot of things. Not like he's gonna make it much longer doped up like he is. Tell me, honey, do you like to bet? Maybe you want to make a little wager on how long it takes for him to die?" His laughter was a dry-sounding noise devoid of any humor. "Frankly, I'd be surprised if he was still breathing after that shit Clint gave him today."

Clint, Lena thought. Now she knew the thug's name.

"Let me tell you about your mama," the man in the mask said. "Do you wanna know about your mama?"

"Yes."

"Well…" He pretended to think back. "Like I said, you're just like her. Same pretty hair, beautiful eyes. Her mouth was some kind of wonderful. I won't go into details seeing as you're her baby girl, but let's just say she could suck the leather off a baseball and swallow it whole." He cackled. "Angie wasn't always like that, of course. Tight as a damn drum in high school. Real religious, just like her mother. Would've taken a crowbar just to get her open. Up here."

"What?"

"Turn up here," he said, pointing to the grass beside the school.

"There's no road."

"I keep forgetting you're a cop," he said. "Come on, now, just turn onto the grass. Nobody's gonna arrest you."

Lena held on to the wheel as the tires dipped into the shoulder off the road. Some of the water in the cup beside her splashed onto her leg as she steered the car to even terrain.

"Keep going." He indicated that she should drive through the open gates to the football field.

Lena drove as slowly as she could without stalling the car. In the mirror, she could see the Celica pull into one of the spaces in the senior parking lot. Was this the plan, then? To kill Lena and Charlotte outside the school? She didn't understand why he was still talking if all he wanted to do was kill them.

"Little bit more," the man said. "Through the gates and onto the football field." He leaned forward, his hand brushing Lena's arm. "Give me that cup, will you? All this talking is making me thirsty."

She put her foot on the brake and did as he asked, careful not to let her hand touch his. As the cup passed between them, she got a whiff of the contents. It definitely wasn't water, but she could not place the odor. The cup felt heavier than it should've been.

"Thank you." He sat back in the seat, holding the cup at chest level. "You look like you've got a question for me."

She cut to the heart of the matter. "How did you know my mother?"

"She was just like Charlotte here," he answered. "Give them a little taste and they'll do whatever you ask."

"Taste of what?" Lena asked. "Drugs?" She looked back at Charlotte. The woman was slumped and silent, her lips slightly curled up as if she was hearing a different conversation. Had she lied about just being an alcoholic? Was she an addict, too?

"Stop on the fifty yard line," the man told her.

Lena put the car in park but left the engine running. Ahead of her, she could see Clint making his way onto the field. He strained from what looked like a heavy bucket he carried in his hand, his body listing to the side. Instead of coming to the car, he put the bucket down on the sidelines then stood there, as if waiting to be called over.

In the rearview mirror, Lena watched the masked man tuck his gun into the waistband of his jeans. He held the cup in his right hand and kept his left wrapped around the back of Charlotte's neck.

Lena could run now. She could bolt from the car. Clint was fat and out of shape. Lena could run through the woods on the side of the stadium and get lost in the darkness. She could pound on someone's door until they opened up and demand to use the phone.

"You gonna leave?" the man asked, as if he could read her mind. "Or do you want to stay put and hear what I have to say?"

Her hand had been on the door, fingers wrapped around the handle. She let it drop and turned to face him. "Tell me," she demanded.

"If I had wanted to kill you," he began, "you would already be dead. You know that."

"Yes."

"Your friend here, now she's been a pretty good girl all these years, but when it's time, it's time."

"Don't hurt her," Lena pleaded. "She's got children. Her husband—"

"Yeah, it's sad. But you make your choices."

"You call that a choice?" Lena snarled. "Having some asshole Nazi stick a needle in your arm is a *choice*?"

He was smiling again. "You sound so much like her, Lee. That same sharp tongue and quick temper. Now, Sibyl, she was more like...well, I guess you know who your sister was like. Real quiet, always caught up in her thoughts. Hell if I know where she got her brains, though. You could've knocked me over with a feather when I heard she'd gotten a full scholarship to Georgia Tech."

He seemed to know everything about their lives, yet Lena had never met him before.

What did he *really* know, though? Anyone who had followed Hank and Lena in a grocery store would know that he called her Lee. The newspaper had run a front-page story when Sibyl had gotten her scholarship. As for the details about Angela Adams's early life...those could be made up. The story she was hearing now about her mother could be just as false as the stories Hank had spun to her as a child.

"You working it out?" the man asked.

"Am I supposed to recognize you?"

"Honey, right now, all you need to do is watch and learn." He held up the cup as if to toast her. "I'm going to show you what happens to people who don't mind their own business."

He threw the contents of the cup at Charlotte, and Lena could smell it now.

Lighter fluid.

"What are you—"

He opened his door. There was a click, then a flame ignited from the silver lighter he held in his hand. He tossed the lighter at Charlotte as he left the car, and Lena lunged for it, screaming, "No—" as she tried to catch it.

She wasn't fast enough. The lighter fell onto Charlotte's lap, the flame ignited the liquid and Lena was blown back into the front seat as the woman caught fire.

Charlotte made an animal sound, her arms flailing as the flames began to consume her.

"No," Lena gasped, unable to help, unable to do anything but watch Charlotte burn. "No!" The car filled with smoke and the smell of burning meat. Lena clawed at the door, trying to get it open. Finally, she managed to find the handle and fell out of the car. She hit the ground hard, pain tearing through her shoulder as she scrambled to her feet.

Clint appeared. What she'd thought was a bucket was actually a gas can. He pushed past Lena and threw more fuel onto the SUV.

She pounced on him, flailing her arms wildly, scratching at his face, screaming gibberish as she took out her rage on him. Clint slammed his fist into the side of her head so hard that she reeled back, sick with pain. Hot bile roiled up her throat and Lena bent over, vomiting in the grass.

There was a small explosion as part of the SUV ignited. Lena rolled to her knees, trying to crawl away from the vehicle before the whole thing went up. The smoke and heat were too much. She fell onto her side, wheezing. She could hear a noise that could not be human: high-pitched screeching. Charlotte. She was still alive, still conscious of the flames that were devouring her.

Lena rolled onto her stomach, knowing it was too late for Charlotte, that she should get as far away from the car as possible. She tried to move, but her body gave out on her. Suddenly, she was scooped up by the waist of her pants, dragged toward the bleachers. The car exploded again, so loud that it must have been the gas tank. She was flung into the stands, her head banging against the metal. The thud vibrated in her ears; the gas can tumbled down beside her.

Clint was on top of her, his face inches from hers. "You still alive?"

Lena coughed, feeling like her lungs had been burned. She could barely breathe with him on top of her. "Why?" she managed. "Why are you doing this?"

He sat back on his knees, brushing debris off his arms and legs, looking at it like he had just come home from church and couldn't understand why he'd gotten so dirty.

"Why?" she insisted, her voice thick with grief.

In the light of the fire, she could see his face, the way he looked down at her with something like pity. "I can't tell you anything, Lena. You'll have to ask Hank."

THURSDAY EVENING

CHAPTER 21

SARA SAT OUTSIDE THE ELAWAH COUNTY HOSPITAL, the cold concrete of the bench penetrating her jeans. She was sick of hospitals, sick of the slow way everything moved in them. No wonder people were so furious at the healthcare industry. The tox screen, the blood work, the X-rays—everything had taken twice as long as it should have, and then a doctor had to be located, a pharmacist called in, a nurse found. All these slow machinations were designed specifically to cover everyone's ass in case a mistake was made; the wrong lab report delivered, the wrong drug administered, an incorrect diagnosis given. Meanwhile, the patient suffered in limbo. It was absolutely maddening.

The only saving grace was that Hank had not been aware of the wait; he had remained comatose during the short ride to the hospital and when they had triaged him in the ER and moved him to the ICU, not much about his condition had changed. Still, Sara did not hold out any great hope. His body was racked with infection. His heart was weakened from years of drug use and his lungs were showing mid-stage emphysema.

Sara's biggest concern was the burn marks around his wrists and feet. On first glance, they had seemed to match the other cuts and abrasions on Hank's body. Closer inspection proved that they were rope burns. She could tell from the sloping angle of the pattern on his wrists that his hands had been tied away from his body. His ankles had been bound together. What's more, he had been recently beaten. Two ribs were broken and there was a nasty bruise on his lower abdomen where someone had either punched or kicked him.

Surprisingly, the most immediate problem they'd had to deal with was drug withdrawal. For reasons of his own, Hank had stopped the meth cold turkey and his body's response had been to rebel completely. His organs were trying to shut down, to begin the cascade that would eventually lead to his death.

Working at Grady Hospital during her internship, Sara had seen her share of homeless addicts come through the emergency room doors. They were little more than the walking dead, their health so deteriorated that it was shocking that they were capable of standing upright. Pneumonia, hepatitis, scurvy, severe dehydration...Years had passed since she'd worked with these hopeless souls, and she had been so shocked to see Hank's condition when she'd first seen him lying in his backyard that for a moment, she hadn't been able to act.

The only thing she had been able to do for him tonight was help process him through the system. As long as he remained stable through the night, he would be transferred to a larger hospital first thing in the morning.

A silver car turned into the parking lot. Sara's heart sank when she saw it wasn't her BMW. Jeffrey should be here any minute now, and she was anxious to see him. He had called Sara at the hospital and told her about searching Lena's hotel room, the phone call she had made to Coastal State Prison. According to the records, Lena had visited Ethan Green the same day the SUV was burned. There had to be a connection, but Jeffrey hadn't wanted to talk about it over the phone. He told her he would wait at the motel for the warden to call him back, then he would pick up Sara at the hospital.

She could tell just by listening to him that no matter what the warden said, Jeffrey had already decided to see Ethan for himself. He thought threats and intimidation would work on the con, but Sara knew better. Men like Ethan Green did not curl up into a ball when they were threatened. They coiled like rattlesnakes and prepared to attack.

Sara had made a pact with herself the night before that no matter what Jeffrey did, she was going to stand by him. After sixteen years, she knew that her husband was never going to see a person trapped in a burning building and sit back, leaving it to someone else to save them. Sara had to accept this facet of his personality and support his choice, because it was this goodness that had drawn her to him in the first place. It was against his nature to walk away.

The glass doors to the emergency room slid open and Fred Bart walked out, patting his pockets. "Hey there, darlin'," he called, spotting Sara on the bench. He found his cigarettes, gave her a rueful grin and tucked them back in his pocket.

"Lost in your thoughts?" he asked, sitting beside her without waiting for an invitation. "Looks like rain, don't it?"

Sara looked up at the night sky, realizing that he was right. "Yes."

"My sister's here." He squared his shoulders, showed his straight, tiny teeth. "I'm an uncle!" He bumped her on the shoulder, an overfamiliar gesture, but Sara didn't protest because he looked so happy.

"Your first?"

"Third!" he told her, exuberant. "I guess you see little babies a lot what with being a pediatrician. Do you ever get over how teeny they are? I mean, just the teeniest things."

"No," Sara admitted, his happiness distracting her.

"You got any little ones in your life?"

"No."

"Well, I highly recommend it," he advised enthusiastically. "I've got four ex-wives and no kids to speak of. Don't get me wrong, it's fun spoiling my sister's little darlin's, but it's not the same as having your own." He stared out at the parking lot, his voice turning sad. "Both my parents are gone. It's just me and Sissy now."

Sara pressed her lips together, wondering when she had turned into Fred Bart's best friend.

He confided, "Jake comes from a big family, though."

"Oh?"

"Four older sisters. His baby brother, Tom, died here about six years ago. Overdose."

"I didn't know."

"Jake was awful tore up about it. I think that's why he joined the force in the first place. Then, he saw what was really going on, how nobody wanted to tackle the problem. He decided to run for sheriff so he could do something about it."

Sara wondered if he expected her to take notes. Obviously, Fred Bart was trying to deliver a message to Jeffrey. *Jake's a good guy,* she thought. *Message received.*

"Anyway," Bart said, slapping his knees as he stood. "You need a ride somewhere?"

"I'm waiting for my husband," she told him, again wondering how much longer Jeffrey was going to be.

He gave her a wink. "Lucky man."

"I'll tell him you said so."

"You do that now." Bart flashed a smile, showing her his tiny, white teeth. He walked toward a green pickup truck, and Sara waved at him before going back inside.

Ignoring the dour woman behind the reception desk, Sara walked toward the alcove where they kept the snack machines. She was suddenly hungry enough to eat a horse. That was fitting, since horse by-products were pretty much a key ingredient in most of the snacks on offer.

Jeffrey's cell phone rang and she pulled it out of her pocket, saying by way of greeting, "Where are you? I'm starving."

The line was silent, and Sara was about to hang up when Lena said, "It's me."

Shock paralyzed Sara for a moment. Foolishly, she looked around, as if she expected Jake Valentine to suddenly appear out of the woodwork and snatch away the phone.

Lena asked, "Where are you?"

"I'm at the hospital. With Hank."

She didn't respond immediately. "Is he okay?"

"No." Sara looked for somewhere more private, but in the end decided it was best to stay put in case she lost the cell signal. "We found him in his backyard. Someone tied him up, beat him. He was left there to die."

"Maybe he wants to die."

Sara could not believe the cold words she was hearing. "Some people could argue you're doing the same thing," she countered. "Jeffrey knows about Ethan."

"Ethan's not involved in this."

"Do you really think Jeffrey is going to believe you? He's going to go to the prison tomorrow. I can't stop him. If anything happens, it's all on you. Do you hear me? It's all on you."

"Tell him..." Lena began. "Tell him I went to tell Ethan that I had an abortion."

Sara felt her mouth open in surprise.

"It would've been born by now," Lena said, her voice a scratchy whisper. "Maybe you and Jeffrey could have raised it."

Sara leaned against the vending machine, feeling as if she had been stabbed in the stomach.

Lena kept talking. "I know you can't have kids, Sara. Doesn't it piss you off to know what I did? Doesn't it make you angry that I got pregnant when I wasn't even trying?"

Tears came to Sara's eyes. She shouldn't have started this game because she didn't have the heart to play it.

"Hank took me to the clinic," Lena continued. "They put this metal thing inside of me, and they cut it out."

Sara begged, "Please stop."

"I wonder what it looked like when they took it out," she asked. "You must know what it looked like, right? You're a doctor. You deal with babies all the time."

Sara felt the tears come. "How can you be so awful?"

"Tell Jeffrey everything I've said," Lena instructed. "Tell him that everything you've ever thought or said about me is true, Sara. I'm not a good person. I'm not worth saving. Go home. Take Jeffrey with you and go home."

"I know what you're trying to do." Sara wiped her eyes with the back of her hand, angry at the manipulation. She wasn't going to be Lena's unwitting accomplice again. "It's not going to work. You're not going to rope me in."

"I don't want to," Lena told her. "I don't want you here. I don't want Jeffrey here. If Hank lives or dies, I don't care. I just want you both to go back home and forget I ever existed."

Sara demanded, "Are you still trying to play me, Lena? I'm not on your level. I don't know how these games work."

Lena was quiet. Sara strained to hear if there was any background noise, anything that might give away Lena's location. All she heard was a whimpering, almost like a wounded animal. It was Lena. She was crying.

Sara made her voice firm, tried to take charge. "Where are you? Let us come get you."

She didn't answer, just kept crying.

"This has gone on long enough. You need to let us come find you."

"Did you see her?"

"See—"

Lena began to sob. "The . . . woman . . . the one in the car."

Sara tasted the same stench in the back of her throat as she had when she'd performed the autopsy.

"Did you take care of her?"

"Yes," Sara said. "Of course I took care of her."

"She suffered."

"I know."

"She suffered, and it was all because of me."

"Who was she?"

"She was somebody's mother," Lena cried. "Somebody's wife. Somebody's friend." Her voice caught. "She was somebody's lover."

"Why are you doing this?"

"Because it's what I deserve! You were right. Everything I touch turns to shit. Get out of here before it's too late."

"Too late for what?"

"Do you want the same thing to happen to Jeffrey?"

"What do you—"

"Just get out!" she screamed, cutting the line.

Sara held the phone to her chest, unable to move, her heart pounding. Jeffrey. She was scared that something—someone—would get to Jeffrey. In a split second, Sara's mind conjured up the autopsy she'd done on the burned woman, only this time, she saw Jeffrey on the table, Jeffrey burned. Tears came into her eyes. She shook uncontrollably.

"Dr. Linton?" Don Cook asked. He was wearing his deputy's uniform. His hat was in his hand.

"Yes," she answered, trying to compose herself, wondering how long the man had been standing there.

"You all right?"

"Yes," she told him, willing her voice not to shake. She closed her eyes for a moment, tried to clear her head of the awful image.

"I'm Don Cook. We met the other night?" He waited for her to nod. "Your husband asked me to come fetch you and take you to the jail."

She stared at him, skeptical. "He didn't call to tell me."

The man shrugged. "I was just told to take you to the jail. Jake and your husband are there waiting for you."

She indicated the phone in her hand. "Let me just call him first."

"All right." He stepped back into the lobby, giving her some privacy.

Sara looked at Jeffrey's phone, wondering what to do. Being a Luddite had once been a source of pride, but now she felt like a backward fool. She knew that Jeffrey's phone stored numbers, but wasn't sure whether or not dialing out would erase the last phone number received. If Lena had called from a traceable line, using the phone might erase it.

Cook poked his head from around the corner. "Everything all right?"

"I left a message on his cell phone," she lied.

"Good. Ready?"

Sara nodded. He swept his deputy's hat in the direction of the exit, indicating she should go ahead of him. Outside, she saw the ambulance parked in the bay. The paramedics who had driven Hank to the hospital were leaning against the wall, smoking. They saw Sara and gave her a friendly wave.

Cook's cruiser was parked in a handicapped space, and he walked around to open the passenger-side door for her. The seat was filled with crumpled bags of junk food and several cans of Diet Coke.

"Sorry for the mess. You mind getting in the back?"

Sara felt the hair on the back of her neck stand on end. She was either being really paranoid or really smart. "Do you mind if I get a ride in the ambulance?" She saw his surprised look and tried one of her more winning smiles. "I'll just go with them."

The ride was quickly negotiated with the paramedics. Sara had made their job a lot easier on the short trip to the hospital and the two men were more than willing to return the favor. Besides, the jail was only three minutes away. Sara felt silly as she rode between the burly paramedics, but she had learned a long time ago to listen to her instincts.

Don Cook was pulling into the parking lot as the ambulance pulled away. He scowled as Sara waved at the departing paramedics.

He got out of his car, mumbling, "Car's not that dirty."

Sara suppressed the urge to apologize. Instead, she followed him silently into the building.

"Sheriff's office is up there," he told her, indicating a set of stairs. "Unless you want someone else to tell you where it is."

"No, thank you." Sara took the stairs, feeling his eyes on her the whole time. She heard children talking as she climbed. In the lobby, three young faces looked up at her from their coloring books. They were on the floor, their legs splayed, faces intent, as they worked their crayons. A teenage girl was on the other side of the room. Her sullen posture indicated she was not pleased to be left in charge.

Sara looked around for their mother, but no one seemed to be in attendance. She was about to question them when Jeffrey opened the door.

"Back here," he said. Then, noticing her concern, he assured Sara, "They're okay."

Sara stepped over one of the children as she walked toward Jeffrey. She whispered, "I need to talk to you."

He shushed her, indicating she should hurry. He didn't give her a chance to speak as the door closed. "We've got a missing persons report."

"A woman?"

"Her husband came in about twenty minutes ago. Larry Gibson."

"Any relation?"

"Boyd Gibson's brother. Valentine says he's clean."

Sara frowned, wondering when Jeffrey had started taking Jake Valentine at his word. She asked, "How long has the woman been missing?"

"Since last Saturday."

"I didn't find a wedding ring on the body," Sara said, though she knew the metal could have melted off in the intense fire. "If his wife has been gone for six days, why did he wait so long to come forward?"

"She's gone missing before," he told her. "Had a drinking problem, dabbled in meth for a while. She's a schoolteacher. Those are her kids in the waiting room."

"Christ," Sara whispered. A schoolteacher with three kids. What had Lena said? A mother. A wife. A friend. A lover.

Jeffrey took Sara's arm, concerned. "Are you okay?"

"You got a call on your phone." She pressed his cell phone into his hand. "From an old friend."

He scrolled through the various screens, saying, "I had Frank do a trace." He meant a trace on Lena's phone. "There's only been one call made from that number since Monday night—to me at the hotel."

"She said..." Sara began, her throat going dry. "She said that the same thing that happened to the woman in the car could happen to you."

"She'd say just about anything to get us out of here." Jeffrey frowned at the phone in his hand. "Number withheld. It's probably listed on my call records, but it'll take a day or two for it to show up."

"Jeffrey..."

"Let's deal with the missing schoolteacher first," he suggested. "It'll be fine. Okay?"

She nodded, though it was far from okay. Unbidden, that same flash of Jeffrey on an autopsy table came to mind. Her stomach twisted into a knot as she preceded him down the hallway, Lena's words of warning ringing in her ears.

Do you want the same thing to happen to Jeffrey?

Back in Valentine's office, the sheriff was on the business side of his desk. He was writing on a sheet of paper, probably filling out the missing persons report, as the man in front of him gave the details.

"She's just average," the man said, sounding frightened and angry at the same time. "I don't know, Jake...describe *your* wife. I don't know her height. I don't know her weight. She's just average."

"That's okay, Larry," Valentine soothed. "Listen, I've seen her at church about a million times. I could tell you blindfolded what she looks like. No offense, buddy, but she's a good-looking woman. Am I right?"

The man gave a surprised laugh, as if he'd forgotten that detail. With a pang, Sara recalled the autopsy she'd performed on the man's brother. What if the woman in the Escalade *was* Larry Gibson's wife?

"Guy can't help but notice a good-looking woman," Valentine said. "I'd guess she's around five-six in height. For weight we'll put one-twenty. License probably says one-ten, but you know how women are." He looked up from his form, saw Sara was watching and winked at her. It wasn't a suggestive wink, more like his way of letting her know that he was just doing his job. Whatever he was doing, it was working. Larry Gibson seemed to be calming down.

Valentine asked him, "That weight okay with you?"

Larry started to nod. "Yeah, she's about one-twenty, I'd guess. And I remember now—last time I saw her was around two o'clock. She dropped off the kids at the movies, and when she came back, she got on the phone with her mama. I heard her say she needed to go check on her."

"Well," Valentine said. "Sounds like we need to check with her mama."

"She didn't go," Larry countered. "She was taking a bath, and I asked her was she going to her mama's, and she said no, that she'd told her she'd come by tomorrow."

Valentine *tsked,* shaking his head. "Can't make up her mind."

"Right, that's what I said," Larry agreed. "And then she told me she might still go for a walk and I said maybe later because there was a game on at two-thirty and did she need me to do anything before because I wanted to watch the game."

"Georgia–Alabama?" Valentine asked, probably to confirm the time. "Man, that was a good game."

"Yeah."

"Did you hear her leave?"

"Yeah," he repeated. "Just before halftime I heard the door close. I figured she was going for her walk."

"Couldn't have been the kids?"

"They were at the movies for that Halloween horror special they advertised in the paper last week."

Valentine made a note on his sheet. "Halftime, then. That'd put it at around four, don't you think?"

"Four. Yeah."

Sara looked at Jeffrey, but he was intently following the interview. She wondered if he was as impressed as she was with Valentine's ability to draw out the details from the concerned husband. The sheriff certainly liked to keep his talents hidden.

"What's that you got there?" Valentine asked.

Larry put a small metal box on the desk. It was old, the cadet blue paint chipped off, showing the gray primer underneath. A rusty lock held the top closed, but Larry easily opened it. "I wanted to show you," he said, indicating the contents. Sara leaned forward, seeing a tarnished silver spoon with the handle bent and several unused hypodermics. Tin foil, a few cigarette filters, and a butane lighter rounded out the drug kit.

Larry turned around, as if he'd just realized that Sara and Jeffrey were standing there. He explained, "She's been clean about six months now. I just brought this to show you"—he turned back to Valentine "to show *you,* Jake. If she was using again, if that's why she left, then she would'a taken this. There's a pack in here." He reached in and held up a small jeweler's bag of dirty white powder. "There's no way she would'a left this if she was using again. You know that."

Jeffrey asked, "Mr. Gibson, I don't mean to interrupt, but why did you take so long to report that she was missing?"

Larry blushed, looking down at his shoes. "I didn't want to get her into trouble. First thing I thought was she was back on the drugs. I started looking around the house, trying to see if she'd taken anything. All her clothes were still there. She'd even left her purse." He looked at Sara when he said, "She always took stuff when she ran off before— usually stuff she could sell. TVs, DVD player, iPod... she never left her purse. Women don't leave their purses."

Sara nodded, as if she could speak for the man's wife.

Larry turned back to Valentine. "I called around, talked to her mama, her aunt Lizzie. I guess I was just waiting for her to come back home. She always came back. She didn't want to leave the kids. This drug—" He indicated the bag of dope in his hand. "It does things to your brain. You don't think right. She didn't know what she was doing sometimes. That's all it was. She just needed to let it run its course and then she'd come back and everything would go back to normal."

Valentine asked, "Where's her car, Larry?"

"See, that's the other thing. Her car's still in the driveway. If she just took a walk..." He rubbed his face with his hands. "I called into the school and told them to get a sub, that she had the flu. I don't think Sue believed me." He gulped, tears filling his eyes. "It can't be her in that car on the football field, Jake. I mean, she's run off before. It can't be her. I don't know what I'd do if..." his voice was high-pitched, pleading. "We're gonna put Boyd in the ground tomorrow. I thought for sure she'd come back when she heard about him. Boyd had his problems, but he was taking care of himself. He helped Charlotte get through her bad times..."

"Mind if I look at this?" Valentine asked, but he was already picking up the box.

Carefully, the sheriff emptied the contents onto his desk blotter. He used the tip of his pen to push the hypodermics to the side, then the bag of meth and other paraphernalia. Sara didn't see anything of value unless you were a cop or an addict. Valentine obviously agreed. He tapped his finger on the inside of the box, then picked up his letter opener and used the edge to pry out the plastic lining. The box was so old that it came out in pieces.

"Well," Valentine said. "What's this?"

Sara couldn't tell what he had found until he pulled it out—two light blue sheets of paper that had been folded in two.

Valentine scanned the documents before handing them to Jeffrey, apparently unconcerned with fingerprints. Sara read the pages over Jeffrey's shoulder, recognizing them as old applications for birth certificates. Doctors handled the applications now, but back in the seventies, parents were still allowed to fill out all the pertinent information on their own. They were given six days to decide on a name, then were expected to file the application with the birth registration office at the hospital. The registrar would verify the information, then send it to the state.

Obviously, they were looking at the applications Lena's mother had filled out for her twin girls; Angela Adams had signed her name at the bottom in a feminine cursive. Everything seemed normal to Sara until she noticed the section marked "Father's Name."

The woman had listed Henry "Hank" Norton.

LENA

CHAPTER 22

LENA LAY FLAT ON HER BELLY, hidden by the grass, taking pictures of the dilapidated warehouse at the bottom of the hill. Over the last forty-eight hours, she had documented it all: the cars pulling up, the money going out the window, the dope coming back in. At night, it got downright congested. No one seemed afraid of getting caught. They kept their radios turned up, rap or country blaring from the speakers. Kids rode up on bikes. Couples strolled. One time, a sheriff's cruiser rolled by and there was a scrambling of bodies, a minuscule show of concern, but for the most part, the traffic in and out of the warehouse was pretty steady.

They might as well be printing money in there.

A white sedan pulled up and a man got out. His boots kicked up dust as he walked across the parking lot. Lena photographed every step until he went into the building, slamming the door closed behind him.

She put down the camera, checked the time and made another notation in the log.

10:15pm—CLINT arrives in white sedan. Enters building.

Lena had been lying on her back, waiting for Jeffrey to come, when she'd heard the men arguing at the end of the hallway. On the football field the night before, the man in the black ski mask had called the man

with the red swastika Clint. Now, lying in the hospital bed, she instantly recognized Clint's harsh growl echoing up the hall. Black Mask
wasn't too hard to peg down, either. His voice was soft, almost sing-
song, when he said, "Clint, listen to me. We've got to get rid of her."
Clint had disagreed, said something about needing permission to kill a
cop. In the end, nothing had been decided, though the two had gone at
it for nearly ten more minutes, according to the clock radio beside her
bed. Lena had lay there helpless, wrists chaffing from the restraints as
she used every muscle in her body to try to break free.

Finally, the two men had walked toward the elevator, their heavy
shoes scuffing the tile floor.

By then, Lena was in a full-blown sweat. What had Hank gotten
himself mixed up in? These people had burned Charlotte alive. They
had beaten Deacon Simms to death. It was only a matter of time before
they decided that letting Lena live had been a big mistake. And who else
would they take down in the process? Who else would Lena put in
harm's way because of her inability to let things go?

Sara. Poor Sara. It had been absurdly easy to escape into the bathroom next to her hospital room. Clothes Lena found downstairs in the
laundry, too-large tennis shoes in a nurse's locker. There was a wallet, a
bunch of credit cards, but she left them, taking instead a screwdriver
from a toolbox in the corner. Lena used the woods behind the hospital
as a cut-through, running as fast as she could in the ill-fitting sneakers.
She didn't know how much time she had other than very little.

The lock on her motel room door was easily jimmied with the
screwdriver, which she tossed onto the table as she eased the door shut
behind her. Lena was sweating from the run. She pulled off the scrubs
and changed into her own clothes and shoes. She grabbed her cell phone
and charger. Her Glock was under the bed where she had hidden it the
day before. The keys to Hank's bar were on the dresser. The only time
she hesitated was as she was leaving the room. Lena rushed back in before the door closed, grabbed one more thing that she needed.

She threw the scrubs and shoes into the hotel Dumpster en route to
the bar. Hank's two thousand dollars was still tucked behind the cheap
bottle of scotch. This time, she had no qualms about taking the money.

Another quick jog through the woods and she was back at Hank's
house. The spare key to the Mercedes was on the key ring she had taken
from his office. The engine cranked on the third try. An Elawah county

sheriff's cruiser was making a right onto Hank's street as Lena made a left, heading in the opposite direction. She checked the clock on the dash as she put Reece in her rearview mirror. Only twenty-eight minutes had elapsed since she'd left the hospital. She was holed up in a roadside motel on the Florida side of the border by the time the sun rose in the morning.

She had fallen into bed but was too exhausted to sleep. Everything started to sink in—what she had seen, what she had done.

That was when the demons started eating her alive.

Lena stayed in bed for almost twelve hours, only getting up when nature compelled her to. Every time she closed her eyes, she saw Charlotte sitting in the back of the Escalade again, waiting for the flames to devour her. The way the woman's arms had flailed, her feet kicking the back of Lena's seat like an animal trapped in a box... the thought of it was too much to bear.

She wanted not to *feel* anything. Wasn't that what Charlotte had said that last time they had spoken in the trailer at school? What had the woman done afterward? Probably taught her last class, then gone home to fix supper for her kids. She had kissed her husband when he got home from work. Maybe they watched a movie that night on the sofa. She would have had less than twenty-four hours left in her life by then. How had she spent them? What had Charlotte been doing that morning when the bad guys came to get her?

That was when Lena had started rereading Charlotte's letters. She had gone back into the motel for them, known that they could not be left behind. She cherished them now, these love letters that said as much about Sibyl as they did about the woman who wrote them. Charlotte had been a kind, good person. No matter what mistakes she had made in her life, she did not deserve to die in such a horrible way.

Lena should have been in the back of that car. She was the one who had made the mistakes. She was the one who deserved to be punished.

"Why didn't they kill me instead?"

That's what she had asked Jeffrey when she'd called. Lena had been so stupid to think that he would leave town. Even Sara Linton had known there was no way Jeffrey would abandon her. Hearing his voice on the phone was like a knife twisting in her gut. She had wanted to tell him everything—where she was, what had happened to Charlotte, how Hank had lied to her all these years—but she'd panicked the moment she'd heard his voice. The men who killed Charlotte could be listening in. They could somehow trace the call through the cell towers. They could kill Jeffrey for knowing too much.

They must have been watching Lena all along, following her from the minute she rolled into town. What a fool she had been. A smart person would have acted differently. A caring niece would have taken one look at her uncle and called an ambulance. A good friend would have left Charlotte Warren alone. A just person would have walked back into the fire and joined Charlotte in her violent end rather than sitting like a spectator on the sidelines.

Maybe Lena would have if the sheriff hadn't shown up. Jake Valentine. What a stupid name. He seemed to realize this, because he had ducked his head in embarrassment the first time he introduced himself, and Lena had seen something that few people had probably ever laid their eyes on: a thinning spot at the top of his head. Valentine had seen Lena notice it and had really blushed then, rubbing his hand along the spot, quickly putting his hat back on.

As if an Escalade wasn't blazing right behind him, a dead woman inside.

She hadn't talked to him, hadn't let one word cross her lips. At first, this had been because she was in shock. Lena had been sitting on the bleachers on the football field, her mind reeling, but not with the things that she would've expected. She was remembering football games, pep rallies. In school, Lena had always hung out with the bad kids and they never sat on the front row of the bleachers. They were always in the top row, hidden by the crowd so they could heckle the cheerleaders or, better yet, drop down to the ground and sneak away.

But, that night, she sat in the front row, her foot propped up on the gas can, as she watched the Escalade burn. The heat was intense, like nothing she'd ever felt before. Even sitting a hundred feet away from it, her skin prickled as if from a sunburn. Her throat hurt as if she'd swallowed acid, and when Jake Valentine had stood in front of her, trying to draw her out, she hadn't been able to make words.

"What'd he do to you?" Valentine asked, and Lena didn't know what he meant, so she just kept quiet.

He'd sat beside her on the bench, watched the car burn. "I see you've been hit. You don't get bruised like that from falling down."

Lena had stared at the flames, watched them dance along the roof of the car. The gas tank had exploded a while ago and though she could hear the man's voice, she couldn't quite process his words.

The sheriff said, "Whatever he did to you, you gotta let me know. If it was self-defense—"

Lena had looked at him, her head snapping around in surprise. She opened her mouth, felt the air hit the back of her throat, the heat from the burning SUV quickly drying the saliva.

She closed her mouth and stared at the fire.

To his credit, Jake Valentine had not handcuffed her then. Lena was thankful for that at least. Ethan had liked her handcuffs, liked sneaking up on her, wrapping his hand around her mouth and scaring the shit out of her. He had loved hitting her even more, and Lena found herself considering the irony as Jake Valentine helped her into the back of one of the squad cars on scene—the sheriff thinking Lena was an abused woman who had snapped instead of a devil who brought death to everyone around her.

Jeffrey. She had to get him out of this town before he ruined everything.

Down at the abandoned warehouse, a Harley-Davidson motorcycle pulled up, the muffler popping and roaring like an angry dragon. Lena put her eye to the camera. She had turned off the digital screen because of the light and the need to save the battery. It was hard to find a place to charge things when you didn't know where you'd be spending your nights.

She cringed as lightning illuminated the night sky. From early afternoon, the air had been heavy with the threat of rain. Lena wasn't worried so much about getting drenched as being found. These were not the kind of people who took kindly to being spied on.

The Harley revved a few times, then the engine was cut. The rider was one of the few people who went into the building but didn't come out immediately with a bag of dope. Despite the bike, he didn't dress like a Hells Angel. Of course, the bike wasn't really his—it belonged to Deacon Simms. Lena recognized the Harley the moment she saw it. The rider was around Lena's age, clean-cut, his hair neatly shaved in a military style. He wore faded jeans, but a dress shirt was usually under his leather jacket. He always left his helmet on the seat of the bike. On more than one occasion, she had seen him check his reflection in the mirror mounted on the handlebars before going inside.

She'd nicknamed him Harley for the obvious reason, but she knew he had a name and that his name probably caused fear in a lot of people. There was something about the way the others steered clear of him that made her think he was a colonel rather than a foot soldier.

Harley was Lena's suspect zero, the rat who had led her back to the nest. The first thing she'd done when she got back to Reece two days ago was look for Hank. The drive from Florida had been a long one. It was the middle of the night by the time she got into town. Lena had parked the Mercedes three streets from Hank's house and made the trek on foot. She'd nearly vomited from the smell when she first walked in through the back door. Her initial thought was that Deacon Simms, still tucked up in the attic, was the source of the odor, but a quick look in the bathroom had proven otherwise. The toilet had been shattered. The house was empty. There was no sign of anything except misery and ruin.

Lena had given up then. Hank was gone. Charlotte was dead. Lena was a fugitive. Two days ago, a couple of men had argued in the hospital corridor about whether or not to kill her, and Ethan...who knew how Ethan was involved?

Lena went outside to think. She was sitting on one of the boxes stacked on the back porch when she heard the motorcycle. The pipes must have woken up everyone on the street, but no one threw open their windows to complain. She followed the rumble as the bike came up the drive, parked in front of Hank's house. It was Deacon's bike, she knew it by sound, just like she knew there was no way Deacon was riding it.

As quietly as she could, Lena made her way toward the old Chevy in the backyard. She slid underneath, the rusted floor of the cab scraping her back as the gate creaked open.

The motion light on the side of the house tripped on. Harley blinked up at the light, clearly annoyed. Clint came behind him, closing the gate.

"He wouldn't come back here," Clint said, nervous. "Just let the dope do its work. He's not gonna go far off the needle."

Harley spoke with the clipped, nasally accent of a New Englander. "That should kill him rather too painlessly, don't you think?"

Clint was obviously nervous. "Let's just go, man. There's nothing in the house."

"I would love to talk to him, see what exactly he thought he might accomplish."

"I don't think that would be a good idea."

"I don't think you were brought into this organization to think."
Clint was much stronger than Harley, but he flinched as the younger
man grabbed him by the shoulder. "You've known Mr. Norton for a
while."

Clint shook his head, obviously seeing where this was going. "I did
my job. I did exactly what you told me to do."

"You've had a close connection to the family over the years."

"No, sir. That don't matter. I don't play favorites."

"Then why is Hank Norton's niece still alive?"

"You told us not to kill any cops." Clint spoke carefully. "You is-
sued a standing order."

"And now we've got two cops to deal with: one on the run and the
other rather curious as to why."

"I'm sorry. It was my call."

"It's good of you to accept the blame, Clint, but your lack of initiative explains your lack of progress in the organization." Harley turned
back to Hank's house. "Let's go see if you at least did this correctly."

"I can't be responsible if—"

Harley didn't say anything, but his expression must have spoken
volumes.

"I'm sorry, sir," Clint repeated, fearful, respectful. "We can go in
through the back door."

Both men went into Hank's house. Lena could hear furniture being
knocked over, glass breaking, as they moved through the rooms. There
was an old cliché that said there were two types of people: leaders and
followers. Harley was a leader, but so was Ethan. There was no way the
two of them could be working together. Neither man would take orders. Neither would put up with each other's attitudes. Put them in the
same room, and you might as well sit back for the most violent cock-
fight of your life.

The kitchen door opened. Harley came out of the house and walked
down the stairs with a spring in his step.

For his part, Clint was wiping his mouth with the back of his hand
as if he had been sick.

"Find the cops," Harley tossed over his shoulder. "Both of them.
Find out what they know, and if they give the right answers, find a way
to persuade them to go on their merry way."

"And if they give the wrong answers?"

"Initiative, Clint." Harley clapped him on the shoulder again, bowed his head as if in prayer. " 'O, God of vengeance, let your glorious justice be seen'!"

Clint seemed uneasy, but he stood there quietly until Harley raised his head. Still, he waited a few more seconds before leading Harley back toward the gate.

As soon as they were gone, Lena slid out from under the truck. She ran so fast out of the backyard that her heart felt like it was going to explode. She found the Mercedes and rolled down all four windows, listening for the motorcycle's pipes as she drove, having to backtrack a few times before she was able to find Harley stopped at a red light outside the library. A white sedan was in front of the bike, and she assumed that Clint was behind the wheel.

The light turned green and the sedan went to the left. Harley went straight, and she followed the bike. The Mercedes' headlights were off, and Lena slowed, hanging back so Harley wouldn't see her. Ideally, two cars were used in a tail, but Lena was hardly in a position to have such luxury. She just kept back as far as she could and hoped Harley wasn't the kind of driver who was constantly checking his rearview mirror. She sure as hell was checking hers. Clint could all too easily have looped around to see if Harley was being followed.

He hadn't, though, at least as far as Lena could see. The road behind her remained clear. When she saw the bike turn into what looked like an abandoned warehouse, she kept on going, steering the car up the hill and finding a spot where she could view what was going on below without being spotted.

She had spent two nights watching the warehouse, grabbing some sleep at the school before making the long journey back to the motel in Florida to regroup during the day. The second night back, she'd brought the camera. Through the lens, she'd been able to better see who was going in and out of the building—the usual suspects, plus a few surprises. It was the surprises that made her start to see her way out of this for the first time since she'd arrived in Reece. Lena just needed to get Jeffrey and Sara out of harm's way, then she would make her move.

Between the motel, the digital camera, and gas for the car, Lena had blown eleven hundred dollars of Hank's emergency cash. She figured she could find a twenty-four-hour Kinko's somewhere and make copies of the camera's flashcard. Photocopies were cheap, and her log of the comings and goings at the abandoned warehouse were meticulous.

Hank had obviously found out something about these guys and their operation. Harley had said as much that first time she had seen him at the house. He'd spoke about Hank's downward spiral in terms of vengeance, and you did not seek revenge on somebody unless they struck at you first. Hank must have tried to play the mother of all poker hands and got caught in a bluff—either that, or they had attacked him at his weakest point, his addiction. He must have fought them at first, but once he got hooked back on the dope again, the struggle was over.

Lena didn't share her uncle's weaknesses, at least not where drugs were concerned. All she wanted out of this was freedom—not justice, not money, not vengeance, though God knew Charlotte and Deacon deserved retribution. Lena couldn't think about either of them now because it was the living she had to protect. Charlotte still had a family. There was still Hank, Sara, and Jeffrey to think about. Lena couldn't afford to bluff. Whether Ethan was behind this or someone else, it didn't matter. First thing in the morning, she was going to lay all her cards on the table.

With the right hand, she might be able to win back some lives. If she lost her own in the process, so be it.

FRIDAY

CHAPTER 23

JEFFREY HAD FORGOTTEN what it felt like to wake up feeling like a human being. While he was under no illusion that the Holiday Inn of Beaulah, Georgia, was a pantheon of hygienic bliss, all he cared about was that the place *looked* clean. The sheets were crisp white, the pillows fluffed and inviting. The carpet showed tracks from the rigorous vacuuming and didn't stick to the bottom of his feet when he walked across the floor. Room service came hot and fresh. The staff seemed happy to be there—at least none of the maids had cursed at him. Best of all, the bathroom was as close to heaven as he'd been in a while: the shower had been strong enough to take the hide off an ox and the toilet flushed without an ominous gurgle.

Sara must have felt the same way. She slept so soundly he had actually woken her up to make sure she was okay. And then, since she was awake, he'd persuaded her to stay that way a little longer. Then a little longer still. By the time the sun peeked in between the gap in the curtains, she lay spent, her leg thrown over his, her head resting on his chest. Jeffrey stroked her arm, his mind unable to stay distracted without Sara's help. He couldn't quite put his finger on it, but something had changed about her lately. Sex had turned much more intense, and at one point this morning he'd felt like she was holding on to him out of fear rather than passion.

The explosion at Hank's bar had scared her. Hell, it had scared him. Jeffrey kept thinking about what Jake Valentine had told him, that his wife refused to have a child until she was certain her husband would be around to help raise it. When he was Valentine's age, Jeffrey would have laughed if someone had told him he'd be adopting a kid one day. He had always assumed that he would end up with Sara, but never that they would have a family together. Somehow, it made him feel even closer to her, like there was something greater in their lives now than just going to work during the week and staying in bed all weekend. Was that how Hank Norton had felt when he'd taken in Lena and Sibyl? Had blood made him feel an even deeper connection?

Jeffrey's cell phone was on the bedside table. He checked it again to make sure all the bars showed the strongest signal and that the battery was fully charged. It had rained all night, a hard, heavy rain that had tapped on their window like a witch trying to get in. Through the heavy curtains, he could see the sun shining. He hoped that the new day would bring some clarity. He had a decision to make: whether to go forward trying to help Lena or to take his wife and go home.

Sara had told him the details of Lena's call as they'd driven to the hotel last night. She had tried to downplay it, but the fact that Lena had cut her close to the bone was obvious. Jeffrey hadn't known about Lena's abortion. That Lena would rub it in Sara's face was enough for him to turn his back on her forever. Oddly, it was Sara who told him to see past the other woman's words. She was used to dealing with children, and she thought that Lena's hurtful words were an obvious ploy to get them to leave town. One of the last things she'd said on the subject was that maybe it would be wise to listen to Lena for a change.

Neither one of them could get over the possibility that Hank Norton might be Lena's real father. Growing up in central Alabama, Jeffrey knew several jokes that called for the phrase, "uncle-daddy," but there was nothing to laugh about now. What would Lena do if she found out? Or, did she already know? Is that why she had been mute when Valentine found her on the football field? Did the death of Charlotte Warren somehow tie into Lena's questionable parentage?

Larry Gibson had provided some background information on his wife's connection to Lena. Charlotte had been friends with Sibyl, Lena's sister, when all three girls were in high school. Like most school-time attachments, they had lost touch over the years, but they had obviously reestablished contact, otherwise there was no reason for Lena to be on that football field.

Jeffrey stared up at the shadows on the ceiling, listening to Sara breathe. His arm was going to sleep, so he slid out from under her and got out of bed. The clock read seven-sixteen, but Jeffrey felt as if he'd slept ten hours. They had asked for the highest floor in the hotel, both of them thinking but not saying it'd be nice to know that a body couldn't be thrown up to the tenth-story window. The only thing available was a small suite—a luxury, to be sure, but one that Jeffrey was willing to splurge on.

The suite wasn't the sort of lavish affair you saw on television. It was really just two hotel rooms with a connecting door. Instead of a bed in the adjacent room, there was a couch with two chairs and a television. Jeffrey turned on the TV and muted the sound. ESPN showed two talking heads who'd been on a football field for maybe ten minutes before running for the sports desk and packing on sixty pounds. He flipped the channel, watching the ticker scroll on CNN for a few minutes, then switching to MSNBC and watching the ticker there. They were both pretty much the same, so he flipped again, scrolling through all the stations until he stopped on the Discovery Channel, where a man had his arm stuck shoulder deep up a cow's ass.

Jeffrey didn't want to tie up his cell phone so he picked up the receiver by the couch and used his calling card to check their messages at home. No one had called, so he hung up and dialed the station. He entered the code and accessed his work voice mail. There were six calls, three from the mayor, who wanted to know why Jeffrey hadn't cracked down on the teenage hooligans who were kicking over trashcans up and down his street. The next two were from the county lawyer, asking details on various cases that were about to come to trial. The last call was from Frank Wallace, telling Jeffrey he'd already listened to all the messages and taken care of everything, including arresting a group of boys for kicking over trashcans up and down the mayor's street. Frank wanted his boss to know that the lead hooligan had been none other than the mayor's teenage son. Jeffrey smiled as he returned the phone to the cradle.

"Hey." Sara stood in the doorway. She had thrown on his shirt but hadn't buttoned it, and he could see just about every favorite part of her where the material fell to the side.

He made a halfhearted effort to stop the appreciative sound in his throat from coming out.

She smiled and pulled the shirt closed as she walked toward him. "You should be sleeping."

"So should you."

She sat beside him, tucking the shirt underneath her, wrinkling her nose at the television. "What is this, some kind of animal pornography?"

He turned off the set. "Wanna go back to bed?"

"I want to go back home."

"I want you to go back home, too."

Slowly, she turned to face him. She let her back rest against the arm of the couch. "Let me be the one to do it," she suggested. "He'll talk to me before he talks to you."

Ethan. She could read his mind so well sometimes it scared him. "I'm not letting my wife go to a prison."

" 'Your wife,' " she echoed, eyebrow raised. "Am I your property?"

She didn't want him to answer that. Yes, she was his property. Every part of her belonged to him.

Jeffrey put her feet in his lap and started to rub them. "You don't know what prisons are like, Sara—the filth, the level of violence."

"You think I'll set off a riot?" She laughed at the idea, but Jeffrey knew better.

He told her, "You take your life into your own hands every time you go inside. The guards only run the place because the inmates let them. That can turn on a dime, especially when there's something they want. Anything can happen, especially with a thug like Ethan who has nothing to lose."

"He's got plenty to lose," she countered. "He only has nine more years on his sentence. He's up for parole every two years. There's always the possibility he could con someone on the board and get out early. He's not going to ruin his chance in front of the parole board just to get to me."

"It's not you he wants to get to," Jeffrey reminded her.

They both knew he might as well have painted a target on his back that day he took Ethan to prison. She pressed her lips together, then said quietly, "Please don't go."

"I won't go if you promise me you'll go back to Grant County today."

She raised her eyebrow again. "And when I call tonight and you tell me that you lied to me and that you've been to the prison—what then?"

He traced his fingers down the arch of her foot.

She kept her tone calm, reasonable. "I told you that I would support you, but this is crazy. You don't even know that Ethan is linked to anything that's happening to Lena. She gave a very plausible reason for her visit."

"There are too many coincidences," he told her, wondering why she wasn't yelling at him. He knew how to ignore Sara's temper, but he'd never been able to tune her out when she was being logical. "I have to find out for myself."

"I understand," she said. "But, do you really think Ethan Green is going to sit down and spill his heart out to you? If he knows why Lena is in trouble, do you think he's going to tell you anything?" Now, she sounded as if she was pleading with him. "He hates your guts, Jeffrey. He'd just as soon kill you as look at you, and you told me not two minutes ago how violent prisons are. The guards don't control the inmates. What happens if one of them decides to look the other way while you're walking down a corridor? What happens if Ethan has a weapon on him and decides to do it himself?"

"Baby, I hate to say this as a defense, but if Ethan Green wanted me dead, I would already be in the ground." Tears welled into her eyes. He continued, "Lena isn't talking. I've got to get answers from somewhere."

"And you think Ethan Green's just going to offer up answers on a silver platter? Now who's being naïve?" Sara sat up and took his hand. "Please don't go."

Jeffrey looked at his hand in hers. Though Sara hadn't been in the operating room in years, she still had the hands of a surgeon. Her fingers were long and delicate, but there was something strong about them, too. If anyone came into their hotel room right then and asked Jeffrey to describe all the important things about Sara, he would've started with her hands.

He said, "I won't take you with me to the prison."

"So, you're just going to leave me here?"

"I'll drop you by the hospital," he told her. "I know you want to check on Hank. I can swing back by after I see Ethan and pick you up. Okay?"

Sara refused to look at him.

His cell phone started to vibrate, jumping across the coffee table. Jeffrey jumped, too, snatching up the phone, checking the number.

He answered, saying, "Tolliver."

"It's Jake," Valentine said. "Lena's here. She just turned herself in."

CHAPTER 24

SARA SPENT MOST OF THE DRIVE back to Reece on the phone, trying to locate Hank Norton. As promised, first thing that morning, the Elawah County hospital had arranged for Hank's transfer to a larger facility. The only problem was, no one knew which facility. Sara had tried every hospital she could think of in the area. Finally, she'd managed to get an actual person on the line at St. Ignatius, a regional hospital about an hour's drive away, almost in the exact opposite direction of Coastal State Prison. An ICU nurse was giving Sara the low-down on Hank's condition when Jeffrey pulled up in front of the jail.

"Thank you," Sara told the nurse. She disconnected the line, holding the phone to her chest. "He's stabilizing."

Jeffrey parked the car. "That's good, right?"

Sara nodded, though she wasn't so sure. As a doctor, she understood that a patient's recovery wasn't just down to good medicine. Family support could often energize a patient, even give them a reason to live. Hank Norton was at a crucial point right now. If he thought he was alone, if Lena didn't do her part to take care of her uncle, then he might very well give up the fight.

Jeffrey got out of the car and walked around to open Sara's door. She gave him a tight smile as she stood, but didn't let go of his hand as they walked toward the basement, where the jail was housed.

The entire trip down, she could tell that he wanted to talk to her, just as she could tell this desire came from guilt rather than a need for her to understand. For Sara's part, she didn't want to hear the excuses. Jeffrey had made up his mind that he was going to Coastal State Prison the minute he'd seen the telephone number charged to Lena's motel room. Anything he said now was just a backpedaling attempt to put a better face on the decision. Sara felt she had to support his choice, but she sure as hell wasn't going to act happy about it.

She told him, "The hospital is an hour out of your way."

Jeffrey opened the glass entrance door for her. "I know."

Don Cook was at the front desk, but unlike the first time Jeffrey had seen him, he wasn't playing the part of the relaxed old man. The deputy was sitting straight up in his chair, arms crossed, obviously furious.

Jeffrey gave him a cheery smile. "We're here to see Lena Adams."

"I know what you're here for," Cook barked.

There were footsteps on the stairs. Jake Valentine rounded the landing, stopping when he saw Jeffrey and Sara. He was dressed in his uniform again, his gun belt tight around his waist, his hat planted squarely on his head. Sara had expected the sheriff to look pleased with himself to have his prisoner back in custody, but he looked pissed as hell.

"Ma'am." He tipped his hat to Sara, then told Jeffrey, "She's being processed out."

Sara and Jeffrey both exclaimed, "What?"

Valentine narrowed his eyes, as if he didn't quite buy their reaction. "Her fancy lawyer got the judge to let her out. She's free to go until her court date on the escape charge." He instructed his deputy, "Don, you mind going to fetch her?"

Cook took his time standing, making sure everyone in the room knew he was not happy with the latest developments before he left by the steel door leading to the cells.

As soon as the man was gone, Jeffrey asked, "What happened, Jake?"

"She wasn't locked down ten minutes before the judge gives me a call, asks me to go over the warrant with him. Again." Valentine paused as if he needed to check his temper. "He dismissed all the original charges and chewed my ass out in the process. I had to beg him to bench-warrant the escape. If I hadn't spent so much money looking for her, he would've probably let that one drop, too." He rested his hand on the butt of his gun. "You wanna tell me what's going on?"

Jeffrey answered, "I'm as clueless as you are."

Valentine walked over to the front door and looked out into the parking lot. A light mist had started to fall. He glanced back at Jeffrey and Sara, then returned his attention to the BMW. "That fancy car must've set you back a pretty penny."

Sara felt herself bristle. Jeffrey told the man, "Doctors make a lot of money."

"That they do," Valentine agreed. He kept his back to them, and Sara was reminded of the sudden punch the sheriff had thrown at Jeffrey that first night outside the hospital. Jeffrey must have been thinking about this, too, because he stood in front of Sara.

"Why'd you let the judge release her?" he asked Valentine. "You could've fought the judge. You could've gone over his head, called in the GBI."

"Believe me, all those things occurred to me." Valentine turned around. "Then, I got a message."

"What message?"

He reached into his back pocket and pulled out a folded piece of paper.

Jeffrey took the note, unfolded it. Over his shoulder, Sara saw there was one sentence across the page in block print: DROP IT OR YOU WILL DIE.

Valentine took back the note, folded it. "No question about what I've gotta do. I'm not gonna end up like Al Pfeiffer, shitting in my Depends every time there's a knock on the door."

Jeffrey sounded as shocked as Sara felt. "You're just going to drop it? You're gonna let these guys get away with this? Two people are dead, Jake. Charlotte Gibson was a teacher at Myra's school."

"You're one to give me a lecture, considering your star detective is being represented by one of the biggest drug lawyers in the tri-county area." He shook his head, disgusted. "Looks like I called it right the first time we met, don't it?" He took a few steps forward, closing the gap between him and Jeffrey. "In case you're wondering, I'm questioning your integrity, hoss. You wanna go ahead and beat me to the ground now or do you wanna wait until I turn my back?"

Jeffrey ignored the challenge. "It's time to stop playing around, Jake. You need to call in the GBI."

"I did," he volunteered. "We'll call it my last official duty as sheriff."

"Wait a minute," Jeffrey said. "You resigned?"

Valentine nodded. "Next-to-last official duty, I guess. Last one was letting your detective go, and I suggest you get her out of town as soon as possible and forget you ever knew this place." He looked over Jeffrey's shoulder. "Speak of the devil."

Lena stood in the open doorway, Cook scowling behind her. Dark bruises patterned her face. Her eyes were bloodshot, but her fury was evident when she saw Jeffrey and Sara. "What are they doing here?"

Jeffrey ignored her. He told Valentine, "Let's step outside a minute and finish this conversation."

"My pleasure." The sheriff pushed open the door with a flourish.

Sara watched them through the glass door. The mist had turned into a spitting rain, but neither man seemed to care. Jeffrey stood on the curb while Valentine walked into the lot for yet another look at Sara's car. She felt shame mixing with anger that he was so focused on the damn thing. If the sheriff thought Jeffrey was on the take, he was more than welcome to look at their tax returns.

Behind her, the steel door slammed closed. Don Cook had made his exit. Lena and Sara were alone. Immediately, the walls felt as if they were closing in.

Lena's tone was clipped, cutting. "You need to get Jeffrey out of here right now."

"That's not going to be a problem," Sara returned, watching her stubborn husband standing out in the rain. "Jeffrey's going to see Ethan."

"You can't let him do that."

Sara laughed, incredulous. "I don't know if you remember your little tirade in the hospital a few days ago, Lena, but the best way to get Jeffrey to do something is to tell him *not* to do it. It helps if you make threats."

Lena muttered something under her breath.

Sara heard plenty, but still, she demanded, "What was that?"

"Nothing."

"If you're going to try to mumble, you shouldn't do it so clearly."

Lena walked toward her, stopping a few feet away. "I said he's so pussy whipped he can't see straight," she repeated. "You need to get him the fuck out of here. Now."

"How do you propose I do that?"

"Just tell him that he has to leave."

Sara shook her head. "God, you're so stupid about people."

"You think insulting me is gonna fix this?"

"Fix what?" Sara demanded. "Fix the woman who was burned alive? Fix the man who was stabbed in the back? Fix the fact that your uncle is at death's door?"

Lena pressed her lips together, stared all her hate into Sara.

"Save the theatrics. I get that same look at the clinic every time I give a toddler a shot." Sara put her hands on her hips. "Tell me, Lena, was Charlotte Gibson your friend?"

Lena kept glaring, but Sara could see the other woman's resolve was breaking.

"Was she?"

"Yes," she finally answered.

"If she was your friend, then I fear for your enemies."

Lena finally looked away, her tone softening. "I'm trying to protect both of you. I need a day—just a day. Take me at my word and get out of town."

"You've dragged us down here and gotten us mixed up in this... this... *shit*—for lack of a better word—and you think that a simple, 'because I said so,' is going to end it?" Sara looked back at the parking lot, saw that Valentine and Jeffrey were walking toward the door. "Is Ethan mixed up in any of this?"

Lena stared at Sara as if trying to divine the best response to get her way.

"Quickly," Sara snapped. Valentine was a few feet from the glass door, Jeffrey behind him. "Is Ethan involved in this?"

"I don't know." Lena shook her head and shrugged at the same time. "Probably not. I don't know."

"What will happen if Jeffrey goes to see him? What will change? Will it make anything better or worse?"

"I don't—"

Valentine opened the door. Jeffrey followed him inside.

Lena didn't waste her time. She told Jeffrey, "Stay away from Ethan."

He looked at Sara first, as if trying to decide which team she was on. Sara copied Lena's earlier gesture, shaking her head and shrugging. Maybe Lena wasn't so stupid about people after all. Of course, Sara had basically drawn her a map: the best way to make Jeffrey do something was to tell him not to do it. If Lena wanted him out of town so badly, the trip to Coastal State Prison would eat up the entire day.

Lena told him, "Ethan has nothing to do with any of this."

He gave her that cocky smile that Sara despised. "That so?"

"I'm taking care of things," Lena told him. "Just leave, Jeffrey. This is none of your business."

He was still smiling, but his tone was a warning. "Are you my boss

now, Lena? Is that how it works when you've got a big-gun drug lawyer pulling your strings?"

Lena looked at the floor. Sara tried to change Jeffrey's focus, asking
the sheriff, "Is Lena's car still at the impound lot?"

Valentine nodded.

"Do you mind driving us there to pick it up?"

Valentine was obviously surprised by the request. "I was...uh..."

Lena interrupted, "I left Hank's car at his house this morning. We
can take that. It's closer."

Sara didn't wait for Valentine to come up with an excuse. She told
Jeffrey, "Lena and I will take Hank's car to the hospital. You can pick
me up there when you're finished."

Jeffrey's jaw worked. He nodded toward the door and Sara followed him outside. The mist was back, lending a solemn mood. Silently,
he walked to the car. Her cell phone was in the glove box. He powered
it on, staring at the screen as he told her, "It'll take me a few hours to get
there, probably another hour to fill out all the paperwork." He handed
her the phone. "I'll call you when I'm on my way back, all right?"

Jeffrey wasn't one for public displays, but he kissed her cheek, then
her mouth. She grabbed him by his collar, pressed her face in his neck.

He said, "I don't know what's going on between you and Lena, but
promise me that y'all are going straight to the hospital." She nodded,
but that wasn't enough. He tilted her face up to his. "You're going to be
the mother of my child, Sara. Promise me that you're going to keep
yourself safe."

"I promise," she told him. "We'll go straight to the hospital. I'll be
there until you come to get me."

He kissed her again before letting go. "It's going to be fine, okay?"
He walked around to the driver's side of the car. "I'll see you in a few
hours. We'll be home tonight."

Sara watched him get into the car, remembering that morning six
months ago when he'd left her standing in her parents' driveway. Lena
had called minutes earlier and he was off to arrest Ethan Green on a
gun violation. Now, standing outside the jail, Sara felt the same dread
welling inside of her—the same uncontrollable fear that hovered like a
dark shadow over her heart every time she found herself thinking about
the misery of her life without Jeffrey.

As he reversed into the street, Sara prayed to God that this time would have the same ending. That tonight—just like that night—she would curl up in bed beside him and listen to the steady cadence of his breath as he fell asleep.

✦

SARA AND LENA RODE in the back of Jake Valentine's squad car. He had offered the front seat, but Lena had said no and frankly, Sara did not want to sit by the man. What little respect she'd had for Valentine in the beginning was more than cancelled out by his relinquishing his badge over the threatening letter. The irony was not lost on Sara that, had she been in Myra Valentine's shoes, she would have begged her husband to quit. Sara wondered if there would ever come a day when she would not worry about the fact that Jeffrey was good at his job.

Probably the night of his retirement party.

The brakes squeaked as Valentine pulled to a stop in front of Hank's house. Sara frowned at the Mercedes in the driveway. The car looked older than Lena.

Valentine got out of the cruiser. He opened Lena's door, then walked around to get Sara's. He seemed relieved to be leaving the job and getting on with his life. She wondered what Jeffrey had said to him out in the parking lot.

The rain had stopped, but the sky was still overcast. Lena stared at her uncle's house, asking, "Why are all the lights on?"

"What's that?" Valentine asked.

"The lights are on," Lena said, an edge to her voice. "I didn't see them on this morning."

Sara wondered why it mattered. She asked, "Are you sure?"

"Yes," she said, then, "No. I don't remember." She stared back at the house. "Hank wouldn't want all the lights left on like that."

"He's barely coherent," Sara reminded her. "I'm sure his electric bill is the last thing on his mind."

Lena started up the front walk. "I'm going to check."

"Hold on, lady." Valentine trotted up ahead of her, hand on his gun so it wouldn't slap his leg. "Let me just run in there and check things out, okay?"

Lena didn't wait with Sara. Instead, she walked around Hank's Mercedes, looking inside the windows, checking underneath, an air of paranoia surrounding her every move.

Sara followed her, asking, "What's going on?"

"We had a deal," Lena said, almost to herself.

"What deal?"

Lena stood on the far side of the car, watching Jake Valentine pull at the tape around the front door, trying to pick it open.

"What were you looking for under the car?" Sara asked, all of her senses telling her something was wrong. "Who did you make a deal with, Lena?"

"Hey," Valentine called. "Anything happens"—he gave a little chuckle—"y'all know the number for nine-one-one, right?" He didn't give them a chance to respond as he shouldered open the door.

Lena inhaled sharply as if to brace herself.

Valentine waved back at them. "It's okay," he said, holding his hand to his side. "I'm okay."

Blood seeped into the material of his shirt where the metal flashing on the doorjamb had sliced open his side. Valentine kept putting his hand to the wound then looking at the blood on his palm. Sara could tell from the bleeding that the cut was deep, but he assured them, "I'm fine. Y'all just stay here while I poke around inside."

Lena waited until the sheriff disappeared, then opened the back door of Hank's car. She reached under the driver's seat with her hand, keeping her eyes on the house the entire time.

Sara asked, "What are you doing?"

Lena closed the door quietly, locked the car. She had obviously been checking for something under the seat, but she told Sara, "That cut looked pretty bad."

The rain started up again. Sara raised her hand to shield her eyes. "You wanna tell me what the hell is going on here?"

Lena grinned, as if Sara was being foolish. "I think I just didn't notice that the lights were on this morning," she said. "There should be a first-aid kit in Jake's cruiser." She went to Valentine's car and pulled the trunk release. The lid popped open, and Sara saw a rifle bolted to the floor. Beside it was the blue metal box Charlotte Gibson's husband had brought into the station.

Sara remembered the birth certificate applications hidden under the lining, where Angela Adams had listed her brother as the father of her children. It took all Sara's effort not to push Lena aside as the other woman reached into the trunk and picked up the box.

Still, Sara tried, "That's evidence."

Lena snapped open the lid before Sara could think of a way to stop her.

Sara suppressed a sigh of relief. The box was empty. Even the liner was gone. Rain splattered the metal bottom.

Lena asked, "Where did he get this?"

"It was brought in by Charlotte Gibson's husband."

Lena shook her head. "That doesn't make sense."

"All clear," Valentine shouted from the house. He made his way down the porch, holding his side, obviously in pain. He saw the metal box, and asked Lena, "Have you ever seen that before?"

Lena shook her head and gently closed the lid.

Valentine holstered his weapon as he asked, "Any particular reason y'all are poking around in my trunk?"

The first-aid kit was strapped inside. Sara retrieved the kit, saying, "We thought you might need this."

He took his hand away from his side, showing her where the flashing had ripped the shirt, sliced apart the flesh. "I think I need more than a Band-Aid, Doc. This thing is bleeding like a mofo."

Reluctantly, Sara asked, "When was your last tetanus shot?"

"I stepped on a nail when I was twelve."

She looked at the house, dreading the thought of going inside. She didn't want to go back to the jail, either, but she couldn't very well make him stand out in the rain.

Sara headed toward the front steps, telling Valentine, "You're going to need another tetanus shot. I'll get you patched up as best as I can and then you can drive yourself to the hospital."

"Drive myself?" He seemed alarmed.

"It's two minutes away," she said, knowing she should offer to drive him.

Valentine scowled. "I hate hospitals."

"Everyone does," she said, leading him back to the kitchen. Sara was a plumber's daughter and had been exposed to her fair share of sewage, but she had never smelled anything as bad as this. "I'll clean it up and get a good look at it."

"Is it going to hurt?"

"Probably," she admitted, pushing open the swinging door to the kitchen. Trash was strewn everywhere, but the sink was empty and the light was good. Sara put the first-aid kit on top of a stack of pamphlets on the counter and asked Lena, "Can you find some clean rags?"

Lena frowned. "How clean do they have to be?" She didn't wait for an answer. She put the metal box on the table and went back into the hall, the swinging door swishing closed behind her.

Sara lowered her voice, asking Valentine, "Is there any reason I should be worried about not having gloves?"

"What?" he asked, then blushed and laughed at the same time. "Oh, no, ma'am. I'm clean as a whistle."

"Okay," she said, hoping she could trust him. Sara turned on the faucet and used the soap in the tub of Orange Glo to wash her hands. "Go ahead and take off your shirt. I can at least get the bleeding under control."

He put his gunbelt on the table and started unbuttoning his shirt. "Is this as bad as I think it is?"

"We'll have to see." Sara opened up the first-aid kit, glad when she saw large gauze pads and surgical tape instead of the usual Band-Aids.

"I hate needles," Valentine continued. Lena came in, a couple of rags in her hand. He warned them both, "Y'all don't let it get around, now, but I've been known to faint when I see a needle."

"Me, too," Sara told him. She ripped open the gauze pad and he flinched like a child. She was always amazed by how nervous cops got around anything that questioned their invincibility. The man could barely unbutton his shirt.

She asked, "Do you need help with that?"

"Aw, hell." Valentine gave up on the buttons and slipped his shirt off over his head, wincing as he stretched, the wound gaping open.

"Careful," Sara warned, a moment too late.

He looked at the blood dripping down the waist of his pants and joked, "I'm not gonna need a transfusion or anything, right?"

"Oh, I don't think so," Sara said, pressing the gauze pad to his wound. "If you do, I'm sure we can find some donors at the jail."

"I don't know about that," Valentine said. "I've got a rare blood type."

The blood was already seeping through the gauze. Sara held out her hand for the rags, but Lena did not offer them. She was just standing there, frozen in place.

"AB-negative," Lena said, her voice barely above a whisper. "His blood type is AB-negative."

CHAPTER 25

JEFFREY PASSED HIS GUN to the guard behind the metal cage at Coastal State Prison. Ever since he'd been caught unarmed with Jake Valentine in the woods, Jeffrey had kept the weapon close. He'd even slept with it on the nightstand last night instead of tucking it under the mattress like he normally did. He suddenly realized that when the adoption went through, he'd have to get a gun safe, figure out a better place to store all of his guns. The thought made him smile.

"Anything else?" the guard asked, ejecting the clip in Jeffrey's Glock and checking the chamber.

"That's it."

The man nodded, writing down the serial number from the gun and passing a claim check to Jeffrey.

Another guard opened the first of two gates, saying, "Through here."

Once they were both inside the holding pen and the first door was locked, the guard opened the second door and they walked through.

The guard, whose name tag read, "Applebaum," looked to be exactly the type of man you'd find working in a place like Coastal State Prison. Tall with broad shoulders, he walked with the kind of swagger that said he wasn't afraid of anything.

Jeffrey told him, "I think you met one of my detectives a few days ago."

"Nope," the guard told him. "Just got back from vacation." He stopped at another set of doors. These were operated from a central control station. Applebaum murmured something into his walkie-talkie and the door clicked open.

Jeffrey said, "There was nothing in Green's jacket about drugs."

Applebaum shook his head. "His boys don't touch 'em. If you're down with his crew and they catch you using or selling, you'd be better off running ass-naked through the yard than having them deal with you." He shook his head. "Had this one skinhead, must've been seventeen, eighteen, who aligned with Green's crew when he got in. He couldn't stay off the needle, though; got caught red-handed. He knew they were after him, so he made a shank out of his comb and kiestered it in the shower."

Jeffrey knew kiestering was prison slang for stowing something up your ass. "What happened?"

"They got a broom and shoved the comb up higher. The doc who did the postmortem says he found bits of plastic teeth practically in the guy's tonsils when he cut him open."

"Green did this?"

"He ordered it," Applebaum admitted as he stopped in front of another closed door. "Somebody that high up, they keep their hands real clean."

"Somebody could flip."

The guard laughed as he took out a key and opened the door, revealing the interview room. "And J-Lo could fly down to Georgia and blow me in her private plane." He turned all business as he escorted Jeffrey into the interview room. "Don't touch the prisoner. Don't get within five feet of him. See this line on the table? This is as far as he'll be able to reach with the chains, but don't trust that."

"I don't want him chained."

"Warden's orders."

"I'm not afraid of Ethan Green."

Applebaum turned around. "Listen, man, I sure as shit am, and you should be, too."

Jeffrey nodded, taking his point. "Bring him in."

Applebaum left, and Jeffrey sat at the table facing the metal ring bolted to the wall. He heard talking in the hallway and stood, not wanting to give Ethan a height advantage. Then, thinking he looked like he'd come with his hat in his hand, walked over to the wall opposite the door and leaned against it, hands in his pockets.

The door opened and Ethan shuffled in with Applebaum and three other guards. He kept his eyes trained on Jeffrey as Applebaum and the others guided him toward the chair. He sat, staring a hole through Jeffrey as he was bolted to the wall.

Applebaum said, "We'll be standing right outside the door."

The four guards left, taking all the oxygen in the room with them. The chains around Ethan's handcuffs scraped across the edge of the table as he clasped his hands in front of him.

Ethan asked, "You scared to sit across from me?"

"Where the panic button is? Not particularly."

Ethan's lips curled into a sneer, but he nodded as if Jeffrey had made a point. This was what Sara was so afraid of—some stupid pissing contest that could quickly turn deadly.

Jeffrey pushed himself away from the wall and walked over to the empty chair. He pulled it out about two feet from the table and sat, legs apart, hands resting on his thighs.

Ethan snorted, leaned back in his chair. "You just gonna stare at me all day, Chief? You got a crush on me or something?"

"I want to know what you've been doing with Lena."

He made a jerking-off motion. "Fucking around."

"I know you've been making phone calls to Hank," Jeffrey said. He'd seen them logged on Ethan's file. "Why?"

"To get Lena here." He clicked his tongue. "Worked, didn't it?"

"The only problem is, a trick like that only works once."

"I got other plans." He held out his hands, indicating the walls around them. "I'm gonna get out of here one day, and when I do, I'm gonna find her."

"She'll put a bullet in your head."

"She'll die before she gets the chance," Ethan returned. "You ever fuck her, Chief?"

Jeffrey didn't answer.

"I know you wanted to. I saw the way you looked at her sometimes."

Jeffrey did not respond.

"Let me tell you something," Ethan said, leaning forward. "She may look hard, but she's so sweet underneath all that. You know what I mean?" He smiled, satisfied. "Good stuff."

Jeffrey remained impassive. Ethan obviously thought he was pushing a button, but Jeffrey had never been attracted to Lena. He'd never had a sister, but he imagined the feelings he had for Lena were about the same.

"What you gotta do is slap her around a little bit," Ethan continued. "Bend her over and—" He thrust into the table, made a loud grunting sound.

"Bend her over, huh?" Jeffrey shook his head sadly. "I think you've been hanging out with the wrong men in here, little buddy."

He cupped his nuts, shook them. "I've got your little buddy right here, cocksucker."

"Fight or fuck," Jeffrey said. "That's what they call it in here, right? You either have to fight or fuck." He glanced at Ethan, looked at his hands. "You don't look to me like you've been fighting."

Ethan laughed. "You see these tats, bitch?" He meant the swastikas, the scenes of violence that he'd carved into his skin. "Ain't nobody gonna touch me in here, man."

"That's right," Jeffrey said. "I heard you and your little girlfriends started your own cheerleading squad in here. What's that mean, exactly? I mean, I know you wear the same uniforms, but I don't guess y'all can sit around braiding each other's hair. Do you do your nails together? Maybe give each other enemas and talk about how the white man's gonna rule the world?"

"You watch yourself, son."

"Watch what? A bunch of punk kids whose daddies never loved them? Jesus Christ, you're a fucking *Oprah* episode. Give me a break."

"Fuck that black bitch."

"Fuck this, fuck that," Jeffrey mocked, standing. "Lena was right. This is such a waste of time."

"What?" Ethan's eyes narrowed. "What did Lena say?"

"She sent me here," Jeffrey said. "She wanted me to see what a pathetic little girl you've turned into."

Ethan stared at him, obviously trying to make out the truth. Slowly, he sat back in his chair. "Nah, man. She didn't send you."

"Yeah," Jeffrey said. He was standing by the door and he leaned his shoulder against it. "She said you were hooked up with this Brotherhood."

Ethan's lips curled in distaste. "What?"

"Brotherhood of the True White Skin," Jeffrey clarified. "She said you hooked up with them in here to save your own ass."

"Shit," he said, practically spitting out the word. "Those pussies? They run meth."

Jeffrey shrugged. "And?"

"Meth is the white man's devil." Ethan leaned forward, vehement. "You don't give that shit to your own people. Fucks with your mind, makes you a slave. It's part of Darkie's conspiracy to take over America."

"You really think that?" Jeffrey asked, walking back to the table. He put his palms down on the metal surface, leaned close to the red line. "See, I've met some of those Brotherhood assholes, and they don't strike me as all that different from you."

Ethan laughed. "You stupid waste of fucking air. You think I'm up with those motherfuckers? I told you, they sell meth to their own people. They smoke that shit like the niggers with their crack. Let them all fucking kill themselves. Wipe them off the face of the fucking planet so the true race can take over."

Jeffrey kept eye contact with him, still leaning over the table. Ethan said he'd been calling Hank so Lena would come see him. If that was his plan, it had certainly worked. What connection did he have with Elawah, though? How did Ethan fit into the meth ring that the Fitzpatrick brothers were running through south Georgia and up the coast? Jeffrey knew Ethan's arrest jacket backward and forward. The other man had never been up on drug charges. All of his piss tests had come back clean from the time he was in juvenile detention to the time he'd been on parole in Grant County. Applebaum, the guard, had even said Ethan wasn't involved in drugs. Had Lena been telling the truth? Did Ethan just happen to be making the wrong phone calls at the right time?

Jeffrey pushed away from the table. "We're done here."

Ethan would not let him have the last word. "You think you're a big man carrying a gun, Tolliver, but you know what you are? You're shit on my shoe. You know Lena planted that gun in my bag. You know she set me up for a fall. You think you're Mr. Law and Order but you broke the law, man. You're just as bad as those faggots over in Iraq, those Abu Ghraib motherfuckers thinking they can toss out the Geneva Conventions because they got a hard-on to paint some Arab motherfucker in his own shit. You're just as bad as them, man, maybe worse because you're not ten thousand miles from home, eating meals out of a tin can and burying your shit in the desert. You just jammed me up in the morning and tucked right back up in your bed that same night, probably titty-fucked your wife and slept the sleep of the righteous, but you know what, motherfucker? You're just as bad as all of them."

Jeffrey did not respond because, for the most part, Ethan was right. Jeffrey had known that Lena planted that gun the minute he'd pulled it out of Ethan's backpack. The Nazi knew his way around firearms. Even the most inexperienced jackass would not throw a loaded weapon into his backpack and jog to work.

Still, knowing that, Jeffrey had arrested him, and he'd certainly slept the sleep of the just that night because Jeffrey knew—he *knew*— that Ethan Green belonged behind bars. Ethan had systematically beaten and tortured. Lena wasn't strong enough to stop him, but Jeffrey sure as hell was. He became a cop exactly because there were people like Ethan Green and Lena Adams out there in the world. It was his job to protect the weak from the strong, and he had never been more certain of anything than the moment he slapped the cuffs on Ethan's wrists.

Jeffrey raised his hand to knock on the door. "Thanks for the speech, Ethan. It's been real fun, but I need to get back home to my wife now."

"I'm gonna get you," Ethan said, his voice a low threat. "You just wait."

"When I least expect it, right?"

"I'm not going to ever leave her alone."

"You don't have much of a choice."

"I'm gonna get out of here. You wait for that, big man. I'm gonna get out of here and Lena's gonna welcome me with open arms."

"I think you're in for a big shock if you're expecting that."

"She can't live without me," Ethan said, standing as much as the chains would allow. "A part of me is inside of her."

Jeffrey smiled, then said one of the cruelest things that had ever crossed his lips. "Didn't she tell you? I thought that was why she came, Ethan. To tell you about that part of you that she had cut out."

Jeffrey had been expecting surprise, more hatred, but all he saw on the Nazi's face was sadness. Slowly, Ethan sat down in the chair. When he spoke, Jeffrey had to strain to hear him. "We're gonna go away together," he insisted. "Lena and me—we're gonna find a beach somewhere. Lay out in the sun all day, fuck all night. We're gonna be together for the rest of our lives."

"Yeah." Jeffrey knocked on the door again. "Send me a postcard, buddy."

Ethan's head jerked up. "Watch your mailbox."

Jeffrey cupped his nuts, duplicated Ethan's earlier gesture. "Watch this, you stupid asshole."

The con did not offer a parting shot. He sat at the table with his hands clasped in front of him, head down, probably dreaming of his fantasy life on a beach somewhere with Lena.

CHAPTER 26

LENA HAD SEEN THE TATTOO on the underside of Jake Valentine's left arm when he'd lifted his shirt over his head. Just at the base of the bicep was an AB followed by a dash. AB-negative. She remembered the explanation written on the back of a photo in Ethan's arrest jacket: *Symbolizes rank of general in white power movement.* Her mouth moved; words came out that she couldn't control.

"AB-negative," she said. "His blood type is AB-negative."

Sara asked, "What?"

Lena's brain had frozen, but she felt her adrenaline kick in. She lunged for Valentine's gunbelt on the table, but his reach was longer and he easily beat her to it.

Sara held up her hands as she backed toward the door.

"Stop right there," Valentine ordered, pointing the gun at her. "Lena, come around here so I can see both of you."

Lena didn't move. How had this happened? She had never seen Jake Valentine at the warehouse. He wasn't in any of her logs or photos.

"I said get over here." He grabbed Lena by the arm and shoved her toward Sara. He reached around for his belt and found his handcuffs, tossed them to Lena.

"Put one on your wrist, one on hers," he ordered. "Make 'em tight. I'm not as stupid as I look."

"No," she told him, her heart pounding in her throat. "This isn't right. Call your boss."

"Who's my boss?"

"Clint."

He laughed at the name. "That piece of shit? Clint couldn't boss a one-man army."

"I talked to him this morning. He said we had a deal."

"You're right," Valentine agreed. "*Had* a deal. You keep your mouth shut and everybody just walks away clean. But, that was before you opened your big fucking mouth and brought her into it." He meant Sara. "Now put on the handcuffs like I said while I figure out what we're gonna do here."

Lena did as she was instructed, ratcheting the cuffs down on her left wrist and Sara's right. She left only a finger's width between the metal and their skin, knowing Valentine was watching.

He pulled out a chair and told Lena, "Sit down." When she did, he told Sara, "Finish up with my side so I don't bleed to death."

"No," Sara told him. "I'm not going to help you."

"You saw what happened to Charlotte," Valentine reminded her. "You want the same thing to happen to your friend here? You can watch her burn while you wait your turn."

"Go ahead," Lena told Sara. "Stop the bleeding."

Reluctantly, Sara continued attending to the wound in his side. The cut was deep, but the bleeding had slowed to an ooze. Lena was no expert, but even she could tell what a sloppy job Sara was doing. If Lena had been able to figure out a way past the gun at her head, she would have dug her fingers into his side until she felt his organs.

"Ow," Valentine said, flinching as Sara jabbed her finger into the gauze pads. "You did that on purpose."

Sara asked, "What are you going to do to us, Jake? Are you going to hurt us? You need to think very carefully about who exactly you're trying to cross."

The flash in his eyes revealed that Sara's words had hit a nerve. Lena imagined that over the course of the last few days, the sheriff had figured out that Jeffrey wasn't someone you fucked around with. If Valentine was smart enough to pick up on that, then he certainly knew what Jeffrey would do to anyone who threatened Sara.

"Jeffrey will kill you," Sara told him. "It doesn't matter what you do, where you try to hide. He will kill you."

Valentine took his cell phone out of his pocket and dialed a number with his thumb. "I don't hurt people," he explained, putting the phone to his ear. "Clint, it's me. You know that stuff you were gonna set up for me over at the place?" He paused. "Yeah, I'm at the other place now. We're gonna do it here instead." Valentine nodded. "No, something's changed. We'll figure out another way to make that happen. I'll tell you when you get here." He looked down at Sara, almost with regret. "And tell our little buddy that his presence is required to take the edge off." He closed the phone against his leg and dropped it back into his front pocket.

"What are you going to do with us?" Sara demanded.

"Right now, I'm going to have you sit down," Valentine told her, kicking over another chair. "Go on."

Sara hesitated, but she clearly knew there was no easy way out of this. She sat in the chair, her hand on the table so that Lena's rested beside her. Her other hand was fisted in her lap, and Lena saw that she had underestimated the other woman. If Sara saw her chance, she was going to fight her way out of this or die trying.

"Does Clint work for you?" Lena asked, trying to distract him.

Valentine scooted up onto the counter, wincing as the cut in his side pulled. "Lots of people work for me."

Harley, Lena thought. Nobody worked for Harley. When she had confronted Clint at the warehouse this morning, the photos of Harley were the ones that sent him over the edge. All of the color had drained from his face, and his hand had shook as he picked up the phone, dialed the number. His voice had gone quiet as he'd explained to whoever was on the other end of the line that Lena was willing to trade the pictures and the logs for their lives. That was all she wanted—not money, not drugs, not anything but their lives. She would hold the originals for safekeeping and the swastika boys could go on their merry way.

Clint hadn't said much on the phone. Mostly, he'd nodded, his eyes locked on Lena's, his fear palpable in the empty warehouse. He'd hung up the phone and told Lena to turn herself in, that the judge was on their payroll and would let her go with a slap on the wrists. Lena had assumed that Clint had called Harley. Had he talked to Jake Valentine instead? Had the sheriff actually been pulling the strings this entire time?

"Hell, I need some aspirin." Valentine slid down from the counter and started opening the cabinets around him.

Lena knew there were all kinds of painkillers in the first-aid kit, but she wasn't about to clue him in. He had his back to them both, and out of the corner of her eye, Lena saw Sara put her hand on the metal box, move it closer.

Lena asked, "What did you mean on the phone—something to take the edge off?"

He checked the last cabinet. "You'll find out soon enough, darlin'."

Sara seemed to have the box where she wanted it. She told Valentine, "Your bandage is coming off."

He looked at her handiwork, sighed. "Fix it," he demanded, walking over to her. She lifted her hands but he stopped her, pressing the gun to her head. "I'll hold this right here so you don't feel the need to grab that metal box and hit me upside the head."

Sara taped the bandage back into place. "Jeffrey will kill you." She said the words matter-of-factly, as if it was a foregone conclusion rather than a threat.

Valentine waited until Sara was finished, then took the box, pushed open the swinging door with his foot, and tossed it into the hallway.

He leaned against the counter, asking Lena, "How'd you guess it? How'd you know about the tattoo?" She finally realized with this one question that Ethan was not involved in anything that had happened—Hank was back on dope for his own dark reasons. Charlotte and Deacon were casualties from another war. What was happening in this house right now was all about Jake Valentine and the millions of dollars worth of methamphetamine rolling through his county.

For Sara's benefit, Lena explained, "Hitler's Waffen SS had their blood types tattooed in the same spot. It means Jake is high up the ranks."

"As high as you can get," he bragged.

"It's rare to just see one," Lena commented. "Usually, they mark themselves up with swastikas and anything else they can think of." She turned to the woman, willing her to go along. "Have you ever seen a skinhead—I mean, really seen one, studied their tattoos?"

Sara's eyes locked onto hers. They both knew she had examined Ethan. "No."

Lena asked the sheriff, "Why do you have just one tattoo?"

He chuckled. "You kidding me? Myra would kill me if I came home painted up like some freak out of a carnival." He tapped his chest. "What matters is what's in here."

"Your wife knows?" Sara asked, her voice going up in surprise.

Valentine leveled her with a gaze, but he didn't answer. Instead, he addressed his words to Lena. "You were this close to getting away. You know that? And then you had to go and screw up everything. You got the wrong people mad at you, little darlin'. You should've just kept yourself to yourself."

Lena fought the urge to spit in his face. "Why did Charlotte have to die?"

"To let you know what happens to people who talk."

"She didn't say anything."

"In my experience, addicts tend to be unreliable."

"She wasn't an addict."

"Then what was she doing toking up in a meth den with your uncle last weekend?"

Lena lowered her head down so Valentine couldn't see her expression. Charlotte...poor Charlotte.

Sara asked, "What does Hank have to do with any of this?"

"He looked out his window when he shouldn't have," Valentine admitted. "Some associates and I were transacting a little business at the motel. Him and that stupid bartender of his started asking questions, thought they could ride in on their white horses and clean up this town." He shrugged. "Guess it runs in the family, not being able to take a warning."

"Al Pfeiffer," Sara continued. "Is that why he left town? Did you throw that firebomb through his window?"

Valentine just shrugged. "Things happen."

Lena asked, "Is Cook in on this, too?"

"Don?" he snorted. "Don doesn't know jack. He's just holding down that desk until his retirement kicks in."

Sara asked, "Is that why he ran for sheriff?"

Valentine smirked. "Wouldn't do for me to run unopposed, would it?" He grinned. "Poor old Cookie let it go to his head—actually thought he could win." There was a knock at the back door. Valentine called, "Who is it?"

"Me," a voice called back.

Valentine pushed away from the counter and opened the door, all the while keeping his gun trained on Sara and Lena. Clint stood at the door holding a large cardboard box.

He saw Lena and shook his head. "You're worse than your fucking uncle, you know that? Can't keep your goddamn nose out of anything."

"We had a deal."

"Yeah," Clint agreed, reaching into the cardboard box. There was a FedEx pack on top. He tossed it toward Lena. She saw her own handwriting, Frank Wallace's address at the Grant County police station. She had sent the packet to Frank from Kinko's the night before, thinking that if things went bad, Frank would have enough evidence to take down the operation. The original photos and logs were tucked up under the front seat of Hank's Mercedes. Her insurance was gone.

Clint told her, "We've been following you since you got into town. You think it's just coincidence we happened to have Charlotte with us the night we ran your car off the road?"

Lena felt her mouth open, but nothing would come out.

"You could've gone peacefully a couple of weeks from now. Needle in your arm, suicide note talking about how sad you were that your uncle was dead." He glanced at Sara, shook his head, sad. "You almost made it, too."

Valentine snapped, "Stop wasting time and get started."

Clint put the box on the counter and walked over to the stove. He pushed Hank's pamphlets off the burners and tried the knobs. None of the burners would come on, probably because Hank hadn't used the stove in twenty years. Still, Clint didn't give up. He turned one of the knobs and leaned down, sniffing for gas. Satisfied, he took out a box of matches and struck one. The flame whooshed as the gas caught. He turned off the burner and tried each one in turn. Two lighted as easily as the first, but he had to take off the grate and use his thumbnail to clean the fourth before enough gas came out of the valve to catch flame.

Sara asked Valentine, "What are you doing?"

He didn't answer as he took various items out of the box Clint had brought and lined them up on the counter. Acetone, rubbing alcohol, ammonia, lye.

"Shit," Lena hissed. "Meth. They're going to cook meth."

"Don't worry," Valentine told her, opening and closing cabinets until he found Hank's coffee mugs. They were old, handmade in Mexico—so fragile that Hank only used them on special occasions. He held up one of the cups, smiled. "It won't cook for very long."

No, it wouldn't. Once the ingredients got too hot, the ceramic would break. The liquid would explode the second it touched the open flame, burning chemicals sticking like hot wax to everything they landed on—walls, carpets, skin. Cooking meth was so dangerous that only meth-addled junkies attempted it, and the ensuing explosions could cause massive damage not just to people but to property. Most states considered meth labs weapons of mass destruction and had asked for funding to clean them up under the Homeland Security act.

"Is that the business you were doing at the motel?" Lena asked. "Hank saw you cooking meth?"

"I told you we were meeting with some associates," Valentine answered, taking small cans of Coleman fuel out of the cardboard box. "Some very important associates."

"What associates?" she pressed. "Mexicans? Skinheads?"

Valentine stopped unloading the box, annoyed. "You wanna know the story? You wanna know what happened?"

Now that she had the answer within her grasp, Lena wasn't sure whether or not she wanted to hear it.

Valentine started to turn back around, but she stopped him. "Yes. I want to know what happened."

He leaned against the counter, propping his gun hand up at the elbow. "Hank tried to go around me, hook up with some boys at the state."

"The GBI?" she asked. Why had Hank gone to the GBI instead of asking Lena for help? He hadn't wanted to get her involved, of course. He'd tried all his life to keep Lena out of the thick of things, just as she'd worked steadily to keep herself right in the middle.

Valentine said, "Fortunately, he went to somebody who was a friend of ours—somebody ready to move up north and take a long vacation." He smiled at the simplicity. "It wasn't too hard getting Hank hooked again. You know meth's only got a twenty-two percent recovery rate? And most of them never stop wanting it. Mind over matter, I guess. Clint had a couple conversations with him, shot him up a few times. Pretty soon he was paying for it."

"Did you know that I was a cop?" Lena asked. "Did you know that I would come looking for Hank?"

"Of course we knew about you," he told her. "How do you think we controlled him in the beginning? He was terrified you'd come down and get hurt. Honestly"—he shrugged—"I can't believe the dumb coot's still alive. The shit Clint was feeding him was pure enough to kill a horse—grade A Ya Ba. He should've been dead weeks ago. We figured by the time you made it down here, it'd be for his funeral."

"How can you—" Sara began, but the back door opened. Fred Bart looked just as surprised to see Sara and Lena as they were to see him. It had taken a while, but Lena had finally placed who Charlotte's killer was. Bart had been practicing in Reece since Lena was a kid. It was hard to forget a dentist who had freakishly small teeth.

"No way," Bart said, backing up. "I didn't sign up for this."

"Get your ass in here," Valentine ordered, using the gun to wave him in.

Bart said, "I only brought enough for one. Clint didn't say—"

Clint swung around aggressively. "What did I say, you stupid cock-sucker?"

Valentine ignored them, asking Lena, "You got any more questions?"

She opened her mouth to answer and he slammed his gun into the side of her head. Lena saw stars as she fell. The only thing that kept her from hitting the floor was the fact that she was handcuffed to Sara.

"Lena!" Sara struggled to pull her back into the chair.

Lena's ears were ringing. She heard Valentine say, "Do the doc. I owe it to her husband."

"No!" Sara screamed, rearing back, taking Lena with her. Clint stepped in, bear-hugging Sara from behind. Lena was dragged across the floor as Sara struggled against the man, fighting for her life. Valentine's hand clamped down on Sara's handcuffed right wrist and Lena saw Fred Bart jam a needle into her arm.

Two or three seconds later, Sara stopped struggling. She crumpled to the floor beside Lena, her eyes glassy. Lena put her fingers to Sara's neck, tried to feel for a pulse.

Bart said, "It's just a mild sedative, darlin'—something to take the edge off. She'll be fine."

Valentine fished the keys to the handcuffs out of his pocket. "Yeah, she'll be fine until she dies." He gave Bart the gun, saying, "Shoot her in the head if she moves."

Bart took the weapon, showing the same easy familiarity as that night he'd sat by Charlotte in the back of the Escalade. "What are you going to do, Jake? I didn't sign on for any of this. I don't hurt innocent people."

"You do if you have to." Valentine twisted the key in Sara's cuff and her hand fell to the ground. He told Clint, "Take her into the hall so I don't have to look at her anymore."

Clint's lips twisted up in a smile.

"Get right back in here," Valentine ordered. "Don't fiddle with her or I'll cut your goddamn cock off."

Bart had taken his eyes off Lena. She edged toward the door and he snapped the gun at her head. "Don't try it, sugar. We both know what I am capable of."

Lena sat back in the chair. The cuff was still dangling from her hand and she worked her fingers along the chain, thinking she could use it as some kind of weapon. She grabbed the cold, curved metal in her hand, fashioning it into brass knuckles. If Bart or Valentine got close enough, she would hit them as hard as she could no matter who had a gun pointed at her face. Better to die from a bullet than burn to death like Charlotte.

Clint came back, the door swinging behind him. Lena caught a glimpse of Sara lying in the hallway before the door swung closed.

Bart asked, "Jake, what are we doing here?"

Valentine reached into the cardboard box and threw out a handful of empty blister packs from a box of cold medicine. "We're making meth." He tossed more of the empty packets onto the counter, scattered some matchbooks on the kitchen table. The box had everything he needed: medical tubing, beakers, filters. He dumped the box on the table, too.

Bart asked, "Why are these girls here, Jake? I told you after Charlotte that I was finished with this kind of shit."

"You're not finished with anything until I say you are."

Bart kept the gun on Lena, but he said, "I don't want to be a part of this."

Valentine chuckled as he opened the cabinet under the sink. Years of cleaning products were stuck to the bottom but he swept them aside with his hand, saying, "Shit we could've just used this."

Bart said, "This is wrong, Jake. This is just wrong. Al never did things like this. Innocent people never got hurt."

"Al was bringing in pocket change. We got us a real organization here, Fred. We can't let our people down." Valentine reached under the sink and grabbed the drainpipe, putting his weight into his heels as he pulled on it. "That ain't moving."

Clint was just standing there. "What do you want me to do now?"

Valentine indicated the cans of solvents on the counter. "Mix 'em up. Get everything ready."

Clint started opening bottles and pouring them into Hank's ceramic mugs.

Bart tried again, "Jake—"

"Shut up your whining, Fred." Valentine groaned as he stood up, cursing, "Motherfucker, that hurts," as he held his hand to his side. "You're not even worried about me, Fred." Valentine gripped the counter, his hand leaving a bloody print. "Lookit my damn side. I ripped it open on that stupid door."

Bart glanced at the bloody bandage. "You'll live."

"Thanks for your concern." Valentine wiped his mouth with the back of his hand. He was sweating. He picked up the jug of bleach that had been under the counter and set it on the kitchen table with a thump.

Bart said, "This is crazy, man. What are you going to do?"

"What we're gonna do is handcuff her to the sink, then blow this place to hell."

Bart shook his head. "They'll find the cuffs in the—"

"Yeah, I'll be sure to make note of that when I'm filling out my scene of crime report," Valentine interrupted. "One pair of police issue handcuffs."

"What about the compound?" He glanced nervously at Lena. "Did you clear this?"

"It's all clear," Valentine told him. "They took the leash off as soon as she showed up with those pictures."

Clint said, "We're ready here," indicating the ceramic mugs on the counter. Thin plumes of smoke already drifted out of the mugs as the chemicals combined.

Valentine asked, "How long will it take?"

Clint shrugged. "The ceramic is pretty thin. I'd say it'll take ten, maybe twenty minutes tops for the heat to crack them. Once the liquid touches the flame, it'll go up like a fucking a-bomb. I'd get the hell out of here as soon as you put them on the heat, though. You never know with these things. The chemicals ain't exactly stable."

Valentine patted him on the back for a job well done. "I hear you, boy."

Bart said, "I am so sick of this shit. You think her husband's going to just let this go?" He waved the gun toward the hallway. "At least shoot her so she doesn't have to suffer through it." He glanced at Lena, though with less compassion. "Shoot them both. What harm will it do to show a little kindness?"

Valentine splashed acetone around the room. "Because that'll leave bullets in the body, Fred. I can pocket a pair of handcuffs but I can't hide a bullet in an X-ray. Even if you dig it out, you can tell when a bullet hits bone. Knives leave marks, too, so don't even think about it, Clint." He shook his head, telling Bart, "I thought you'd done enough autopsies by now to know how this shit works. We'll just cuff her to the drainpipe and get the hell out of here."

Lena finally spoke. "What are you going to tell Jeffrey?"

He smiled at Lena. "That Deacon Simms was cooking meth in Hank's kitchen and you and Sara came along at the wrong time."

She didn't even bother to act surprised that Deacon's body would be found in the ruins. It made perfect sense. "Jeffrey knows you were here."

"He'll *know* that I dropped y'all off," Valentine countered, splashing ammonia on top of the lye. "Then he'll *know* that I went home and had lunch with my wife before she had to go back to school."

"He'll put it together that you handed in your badge on the same day that his wife died."

Bart had been following the conversation closely. Lena could feel his body tense. He asked, "You resigned?"

"Yes," Lena said, gripping the handcuff in her hand, willing him to come closer. "Don Cook told me that Jake resigned this morning. Jake got a threatening letter and said he was leaving town before he ended up like Al Pfeiffer."

"She's lying," Valentine said. "I resigned, but I—"

"He said he was leaving town," Lena repeated. "Look at this stuff, Fred." She indicated the beakers, the chemicals. "They had all of this ready to go. Why do you think that is?"

"Don't listen to her," Valentine told Bart, a warning in his tone.

Lena pressed on, putting together the pieces. Valentine must have been pretty fucking pleased with himself. Lena had handed him surveillance photos. The right ones shown to the right people would paint Fred Bart as the mastermind to the whole operation. "They were going to set you up, Fred. They've been planning this all along, just waiting for the right time to bang you up." He shook his head, and she insisted, "Think about it, Fred. Look at what's going on here. Jeffrey would've needed an explanation, somebody to blame for his wife dying. Can't you see Jake is setting you up for the fall? *You* are the explanation."

"Don't listen to that crap," Valentine said, but even Lena could tell she'd struck close to home. The man was visibly nervous. He couldn't stop himself from looking at the gun. "Come on, Fred. Things were just getting a little hot and I—"

Both Lena and Valentine ducked as Bart squeezed the trigger. Instinctively, Lena put her hands over her head and the loose cuff slapped her in the face. She looked up, expecting to see Jake Valentine lying dead, but it was Clint who had been shot. Bart was an excellent marksman. The bullet had gone straight between the man's eyes.

For his part, Clint seemed the last one to realize he'd been shot. He stood there, his eyes staring blankly, body swaying to the side, at least two full seconds ticked by before he collapsed back against the door. It swung open as he fell, the chain looping his wallet to his belt clanging against the wood.

"What the fuck did you do that for?" Valentine demanded. "For the love of Christ, Fred. He was Jerry's man." He stamped his foot on the floor. "You're going to have to explain this, you stupid asshole."

Bart had the gun trained squarely at Valentine's chest. "You think I don't know what you're doing?"

"What?"

"She's right," he said. "You've never cooked meth in your life, and Clint was too far up the ladder to fool with this shit."

"That's not—"

"What were you doing with all this stuff?" he asked, indicating the chemicals, the beakers. "You were planning on leaving me holding the bag while you skipped town with that fat wife of yours."

Valentine's fists clenched. "Don't you dare bring Myra into this."

Bart said, "Al and I kept this town in line, kept the good people away from the bad, for thirty years. You didn't give a shit about right and wrong. You just offered it around like candy."

"Money is money, man."

"At what cost?"

"Them fistfuls of cash I was giving you every week didn't seem to bother you none."

"Like I had a choice," he snapped back. "You were nothing but a little pissant before you married into that family. Then all of a sudden you're the big man in town, waving your dick around like you're somebody special. All you ever were was a fuck-up."

"Like it was my bright idea to throw Boyd through the fucking hotel window!" he yelled. "What about that, Fred? Another one of your grand gestures, just like the *schoolteacher* you torched on the football field. She's what started this shitstorm in the first place." Valentine looked pleased with his point. "You and your foolish ways, thinking you'll scare people off like in the old days, and all it ends up doing is throwing gasoline on the fire. And here I am, trying to clean up your mess. Who's the fuck-up now?"

"You know why they kept me around?" Bart demanded. "You ever ask yourself why they didn't give me a one-way ticket to the swamp? It was because they didn't trust your skinny little ass as far as they could throw you."

Valentine chuckled. "If you know them so well, then you know how they feel about family."

"I think they'll be glad to get rid of you, is what I think."

"I think that I'm the only one standing between you and death right now."

"Get over by the sink," Bart ordered. "Both of you."

Valentine started, "Hold on now—"

Bart shot him in the leg.

"Shit!" Valentine screamed. "Jesus Christ, what the hell are you doing?"

Bart reached down and picked up the shell from the bullet. "I said both of you get over by the sink." When Lena didn't move, he kicked her chair. "There are worse ways to hurt you than with a bullet, darlin'."

She got up, moved toward the sink.

Valentine held his bleeding leg, fuming, "You think you can get away with this?"

"I think I'm gonna have an awful lot more bullets to dig out of your body down at the morgue if you don't get down in front of that sink and cuff your hand through that pipe."

"You think you can go back to the good old ways? There's too much money now, Fred. They're gonna put you in the ground."

"Shut up," Bart ordered, kicking Valentine in the leg right where he'd just been shot.

"Fuck!" Valentine screamed, his knees buckling as he fell down.

"You, too," Bart said, waving the gun at Lena. "Get down on the floor."

She knelt slowly. "I never told anyone it was you in the car," she said. "I kept quiet the whole time."

"I know, hon," Bart said. "That was really good of you."

"Let me go," Lena begged. "Let me and Sara go and neither one of us will say anything."

Bart flashed his nasty little teeth. "The funny thing, Lena, is if it was just you, I'd believe it. I really would. But the doctor lady out there won't lie. She may give it a good try, but no way she can keep a secret."

"She will."

He shook his head. "Jake, reach down there and pull that cuff through the pipe."

"You son of a bitch," Valentine muttered, grabbing Lena's arm and passing the cuff through the bend in the drain.

"Tight now," Bart instructed. "Tighter."

Valentine made the cuff so tight his wrist turned red. "They will find you," he warned Bart. "They will find you and rip your intestines out through your asshole."

Bart was over by the stove. He turned up the burners, as high as they would go and used the butt of the gun to knock the knobs off the stove. Satisfied they couldn't be turned down, he got the ceramic mugs and put each one over the open flame.

"You're gonna die for this," Valentine warned. "You think you can get away with killing me? I'm a fucking general in the Brotherhood of the True White Skin. Vengeance will rain down upon you like the wrath of the one white God."

"Yeah, yeah," Bart said. "And you're gonna get ass fucked by the biggest, blackest cocksucker in hell." He lifted his foot and kicked Valentine in the face. Bart's angle was off, but the bottom of the sink was right behind Valentine. His head slammed against the cast iron, an ominous crunch sounding from his skull. He slid down the sink, blood dripping from the back of his head.

Bart knelt down and checked Valentine's pockets, the gun aimed at Lena's chest.

"Don't do this," she begged. "Please don't do this."

He found Valentine's cell phone and broke it under the heel of his cheap shoe. He told Lena, "I really am sorry, darlin'."

"Yeah," Lena said, thinking if her hands were free she would choke the life out of him. "Look, no problem. I understand."

Bart shook his head, a faraway look coming into his eyes. "You're just like your mama was. You know that?"

Was. Lena felt her throat tighten, all the fight draining from her body. "What happened to her?" she asked. "Please. I've got to know."

"She was one of the good ones that crossed over, honey." Bart stood, checked the mugs on the stove. "She's in a better place now." He indicated the room, the situation. "I hope knowing that brings you some peace."

"Peace?" she echoed. "Are you fucking kidding me? You think you're doing a favor killing me?"

Bart tossed the gun onto the kitchen table. "I'm sorry, baby." He opened the door and closed it softly behind him.

"Fuck!" Lena screamed, kicking Valentine in the leg. He moaned, rolling to the side. She saw the top of his head where his skull had been caved in. The bald spot was on display now. The bottom of what could only be a red swastika was tattooed on his scalp.

"Sara!" Lena yelled, knowing there wouldn't be an answer. "Sara!" She leaned out as far as she could, looking past Clint's lifeless body. Sara was still propped up against the wall, her eyes staring vacantly back at Lena.

Lena dragged Valentine's arm through the pipe, groaning from the exertion. He was deadweight; she might as well be cuffed to a boulder. Pushing and pulling, she managed to get him inside the cabinet, his elbow looped around the bend in the pipe. He was saying something, begging her to stop, to help him, but Lena ignored his pleas, bracing her feet on the sides of the cabinet, gripping his hand in both of hers, pulling as hard as she could without dislocating her shoulders. When she'd dragged Valentine into the cabinet as far as he'd go, she reared back from the sink and kicked the pipe with all her strength.

"Help!" she yelled, kicking the pipe again and again, her foot slipping and pounding into Valentine's shoulder. "Help!"

"Lena..." Valentine whispered, his hand reaching out to her. "Please..."

Lena started coughing as a fine mist filled the room. She had bent the pipe but it held in place—it was the only fucking thing Hank had ever replaced in this falling-down piece of shit house. She screamed in fury, kicking at the pipe until her foot was so badly bruised she could hardly lift it.

"Help!" she tried again, knowing even as she yelled that no one was coming. Bart had shot the gun twice and no one had bothered to ride to their rescue. This was a working class neighborhood. No one was home in the middle of a Friday morning; at least no one who would care.

The gun. Lena saw it sitting on the table against the wall. She lunged for it, her arm nearly popping out of the socket. She couldn't reach the table. Lena rolled onto her back and kicked out her feet, trying to loop them around the leg of the table so that she could pull it over. She grazed the metal with the toe of her shoe, then stopped as she heard a bottle break. A plume of white smoke erupted over the table. The liquid dripped to the floor, sizzling like bacon as it ate through the linoleum. What was she thinking? She'd just released more chemicals into the air. And what would Lena do if she managed to get the gun? She couldn't shoot a weapon in here. Fumes were already filling the air. A spark from a gun could blow up the whole house.

"No-no-no," she panted, sitting up, trying to make herself think. "Oh, God, please." She jerked the cuff one more time and screamed in pain. Her wrist was bruised and bleeding. It hurt so bad that maybe it was broken. "No," she whispered, coughing around the word. Her lungs shook in her chest. She felt as if she'd inhaled cotton. Lena coughed to clear them, but nothing would work. She reached up and turned on the faucet, cupping her hand underneath and bringing the water to her lips, her eyes.

So many years she had sat in this house praying to God that she wouldn't die here, that she could somehow get out of this awful town and make something of herself, yet here she was, trapped in Hank's house, living out her worst nightmare.

Lena choked back a sob. Jeffrey would figure this out. He wouldn't let a fucking dentist autopsy his wife. He'd get somebody from the state to look at the bodies. They'd see Valentine's broken skull. Maybe there would be enough of Lena left for them to see the bruises on the bottom of her foot, the bloody pulp of her wrist.

Her wrist.

Lena saw it then, saw the way out.

She reached for Clint, trying to grab the leg of his pants, his shoe, anything she could hold on to. Her fingers weren't even close. She lay flat on her stomach, her arm stretched over her head as far as it would go, and kicked out her legs, trying to use her feet to pull Clint's body toward her. He was a heavy man, but she managed to clamp one of his feet between her own, inching him over until she was able to loop her shoe through the chain that connected his wallet to his belt. She tightened her abs, screaming from exertion as his body came closer. Lena sat up, reaching for him, finally able to grab the leg of his pants and drag him close enough to get to the knife on his belt.

Lena looked at Valentine. He was staring at her, fear blazing in his eyes.

She didn't give herself time to think, taking the knife and hacking it into his wrist. Valentine's mouth opened, but he didn't scream. He gave this kind of high-pitched whine that seemed to last forever. Lena tried to close her ears to it, hacking at the skin again, trying to reach the sweet spot where bone gave way to tendon. Her stomach turned as blood squirted into her face, repulsion almost overcoming her. The handcuff around his wrist was so tight that she couldn't rear back with the knife high enough for fear of dulling the blade on the metal. She stopped, trying to catch her breath, trying not to vomit. On the stove, she could hear gurgling as the liquid started to boil.

"Please..." Valentine whispered. "No, Lord, please..."

She pushed away the remains of Valentine's broken cell phone, pressed Valentine's wrist as flat to the floor as it would go and placed the knife blade against his wrist.

"No," Valentine begged, his voice rising in register as he saw what she was going to do. "Oh, God! Oh, God! No!"

Lena stood up and pressed the sole of her shoe against the knife, the double-sided blade slicing into the rubber. She leaned her forehead against the counter for balance as she put her full weight onto one leg, crunching the blade into his wrist.

"No!" Valentine screeched, his legs kicking out, animal sounds of pain echoing in the room.

She grinded the toe of her shoe into the blade, bouncing her weight until the knife cut all the way through to the floor.

The handcuff jerked up, Valentine's hand popping off his wrist like a loose tooth. The cuff was so tight that his hand wouldn't come out. Lena stood, his hand slapping against her leg. She gagged, the smoke thicker up high. Her eyes stung and she couldn't get her bearings.

The mugs on the stove were white-hot, liquid boiling up. She tried to turn off the knobs but just the stems remained and she couldn't get them to budge. Smoke filled the room with rolling black clouds. In the distance, Lena could see Sara had managed to sit up. As Lena watched, Sara's mouth moved, but she made no attempt to stand, no motion to leave the burning house.

Lena stumbled toward her, slamming against the table, knocking the matchbooks onto the floor. She looked down, saw that the red strike pads had all been peeled off, the matches unused. Her arm started throbbing and she realized she had put her hand in broken glass. There was a strange odor, then blinding pain. Acid. She had put her hand in the broken bottle of acid. Her mouth opened, but there was no breath in her lungs to scream as she jerked her hand away from the table.

"Lena..." Valentine called from behind her. "Please..."

Lena moved forward, away from his voice. She felt as if her own skin was dripping off the bones of her hand, but she pushed herself on, made her legs move toward Sara, even though every ounce of sense left in her body was screaming for her to go the other way.

She coughed, gagging from the smoke, the heat of the enclosed room boiling her skin. He had set it all up so perfectly. The kitchen was a mad scientist's dream and every cop's nightmare.

Lithium batteries. Iodine. Paint thinner. Lye.

Some of the same ingredients used to make crystal meth were used in the bomb that brought down the Murrah Building in Oklahoma City.

She had to reach Sara before the house exploded, had to get them both out of here and into the open air.

"Sara!" Lena screamed, lurching down the hallway. She squatted in front of her, grabbing Sara under the arms and trying to pull them both to standing. "Help!" she yelled, her legs cramping as she forced them both up the wall. The smoke was so thick now that Lena couldn't see. She felt tears running down her cheeks from the stinging chemicals. Something popped in the kitchen, like a champagne cork or a popgun. Lena swung Sara's arm over her shoulders, dragging her toward the front door. She could see the crack of sunlight coming through where the door hadn't quite shut.

"Please, Sara," Lena begged. "Please help me. I can't lift you."

Sara's legs started to move in an awkward walk. Lena pulled her forward, yanked open the door. The sunlight was blinding. She could feel the handcuff and what was still in it banging against the door as she pushed Sara outside.

They both fell in a heap at the foot of the stairs, but Lena did not let herself stay down. She grabbed Sara underneath her arms and walked backward, dragging her across the yard and into the street. They had reached the neighbor's sidewalk when the air changed. There was something almost like a vacuum sucking all the oxygen toward the house, then a violent pushing out as a blast of hot air shot past them. Lena did not hear the explosion until she was diving to the ground, using her body to cover Sara's. Then came the heat, an intense, horrible heat that burned her skin.

Lena lay on top of Sara. Her body was out of adrenaline or whatever it was that had made Lena capable of getting them both out of the house. Somehow, she forced herself to roll to the side, falling onto her back.

In the distance, a siren announced that help was finally on its way. Lena closed her eyes, let herself feel relief, then joy that she had gotten away. She struggled, sitting up, coughing up a spray of blood. Her hand was hurting so badly that she could barely breathe. She tried not to look at it, tried not to see the melted skin where the acid had eaten into her flesh. That was when she noticed the empty handcuff dangling from her wrist. She looked around her, traced their footsteps across the street. Nothing.

Sara tried to sit up but fell back against the lawn. Up the street, Lena saw an Elawah County sheriff's cruiser take the turn on two wheels.

"What happened?" Sara mumbled, pressing her fingers into her eyes. "Lena, what happened?"

"It's okay," Lena told her. "It's all over."

"Are you okay?" Sara asked, still a doctor even though she was flat on her back.

The cruiser screeched to a halt in front of them. Lena struggled to stand as Don Cook got out of the car. Her legs wouldn't work, and her hand felt as if it was on fire.

"What the hell is going on here?" the deputy demanded.

Lena tasted blood in her mouth. Her stomach clenched and she could barely speak. "Fred Bart," she told Cook. "You need to find Fred Bart."

Sara had managed to sit up. She put her hand to Lena's back, told her to take deep breaths. Lena tried to do this but the blood caught in her throat. She coughed, her body tensing from the effort.

The last thing she heard was Sara screaming, "Call an ambulance!"

Then she passed out.

MONDAY

CHAPTER 27

NICK SHELTON HAD NOT BEEN entirely forthcoming when he'd told Jeffrey the Georgia Bureau of Investigation could only step in when the local law enforcement agency asked them to. There was one exception to this rule: when the local law enforcement was so corrupt that there was no other choice but for the state agency to come in and clean house. You didn't get more corrupt than trying to blow up a cop and a police chief's wife in a meth lab, and the state agency had swarmed into Elawah County like a pack of angry hornets.

Jeffrey had been halfway between Coastal State Prison and Reece when his cell phone rang. He hadn't recognized the number, but knew the voice as soon as he picked up.

"I'm okay," Sara told him, not even bothering with the formalities. Her words had stopped his heart in his chest, because you didn't say you were okay unless you'd been decidedly un-okay before.

Sara was calling him from the back of an ambulance; the siren in the background competed with her voice. She had laid out everything she could remember, from Valentine pulling the gun to Bart injecting her with something that had knocked her out. By the time she'd finished the story, Jeffrey's jaw was so tight that he could barely form words. He had been blowing smoke up Ethan Green's ass while Sara had been in mortal danger. He would never forgive himself for leaving her alone with Valentine. If the man was not already dead, Jeffrey would have found him and done the deed himself.

Two hours later, when he had finally reached the hospital, Sara seemed more concerned about Lena than herself. She was worried about the plastic surgeon being good enough to fix the burn on her hand, scared an infection would set up in her lungs, sure that the pulmonologist didn't know what he was doing. She'd been almost manic, pacing back and forth as she spouted her concerns until Jeffrey had physically stopped her.

"I'm okay," she kept telling him, long after he figured out the words were more for her own benefit than his. Even when he drove her back to Grant County, she kept telling him that she was fine. It wasn't until last night that she'd finally broken down. He'd told her he was returning to Reece to help Nick Shelton interrogate Fred Bart. She hadn't told him not to go, but this morning, he'd felt like a criminal as he sneaked out of the house before she woke up.

Jeffrey pulled up in front of the Elawah County jail, vowing that this really would be the last time he laid eyes on the place. There was a HAZMAT truck parked in the lot, a couple of government types milling around and drinking coffee. After the explosion at Hank's house, they had evacuated his neighborhood within half a square mile so they could clean up the toxic waste. The only things left of the sheriff were bits of DNA they'd found in the yard and the man's severed hand.

Jake Valentine. Jeffrey felt sick every time he thought about the man. Now that Valentine was dead, they'd found out all sorts of interesting things about him. His modest house in town was obviously his idea of slumming. He owned a large cabin at the lake with two power-boats docked outside. His arrest jacket was pretty clean, but his brother's was another matter. David Valentine had been stabbed to death in a knife fight with a rival skinhead gang, but judging from his rap sheet, he'd been pretty high up in the Brotherhood. Arson, rape, assault with a deadly weapon, attempted murder.

Valentine must have learned from his brother's mistakes; he'd kept a low profile. Except for a misdemeanor arrest for public drunkeness back in college, there was nothing on Jake Valentine's record that would tell you he was a skinhead drug trafficker running millions of dollars worth of meth. The missing piece of the puzzle was Myra, his wife. Myra Valentine, nee Fitzpatrick, was the baby sister of Jerry and Carl Fitzpatrick, the leaders of the Brotherhood of the True White Race. Their parents had moved to Elawah after their hometown in New Hampshire had made it clear that they didn't want the family of a cop killer living in their midst. Myra had liked it in Reece well enough to stay. Jake Valentine had married into a powerful family, and like most powerful families, they had found a way to employ their shiftless brother-in-law.

Nick had sent out a request to the Brotherhood's New Hampshire compound, asking to interview Myra. The compound had not replied.

Jeffrey had never entirely trusted Jake Valentine, but he'd been so damn hot on putting Ethan in the middle of everything that he'd let Sara and Lena go off alone with the man. Jeffrey didn't know whether to feel angry or ashamed at his own blindness. He remembered Grover Gibson's words that day Jeffrey and Valentine had gone to the man's shack in the woods to tell him that his son was dead.

"You did this to him!" Grover had screamed, fists flying as he jumped the sheriff. "You killed him!"

Valentine had set it up so well, warning Jeffrey ahead of time that Grover blamed him for his dead son's drug dependency. Jeffrey had actually helped defend the sheriff.

He couldn't dwell on that now, because it only made him furious. Fred Bart had to be his focus now. The slimy dentist was the only one left to punish, and he seemed intent on fighting it every step of the way. He'd been in his office filling a cavity when Don Cook finally got around to looking for him. Bart insisted it was sheer coincidence that the patient in his chair also happened to be his lawyer. Nick was sure that Jeffrey could help him break the man. Jeffrey didn't share the state agent's optimism. Elawah County was built on secrets that went back decades. The town thrived on looking the other way. Jeffrey doubted very seriously anyone was about to change that, especially Fred Bart.

The jail lobby was even more claustrophobic than Jeffrey remembered. Don Cook was probably in the sheriff's office upstairs, measuring for new furniture. Nick was seated at the man's desk, thumbing through one of the deputy's hunting magazines. He glanced up when he saw Jeffrey. "You look like hell, man."

"Sara's not too happy about me being here."

"She'll get over it," Nick said, but Jeffrey wasn't too sure. "I'm real tore up about Bob Burg, man. They picked him up last night."

Jeffrey felt the same way. He'd assumed Burg was one of the good guys, but the GBI agent had apparently been taking money for years. "Is he saying anything?"

"Not a peep," Nick answered. "Bob's not stupid. He knows he's not going to see daylight for a while, and he's not about to rat out a damn skinhead."

"You didn't find anything about Hank contacting him?"

"Bob didn't write down jack, man. Even if he did, we'd need him to testify, and there's no way he'll flip. Those Nazi fuckwads are everywhere. Bob's gonna be sleeping with one eye open for the rest of his life."

Jeffrey guessed that was some kind of payback.

"How's Lena doing?"

"Fine," he answered, glad to be talking about something else. "She's gonna need therapy for her lungs, but she should be ready to go back home by the middle of next week." He added, "They moved her to the same hospital as Hank last night."

"How's he doing?"

"Better. Still not out of the woods yet. What about Bart—he doing any talking yet?"

"Shit," Nick mumbled, standing from the desk. "He's doing nothin' *but* talking. That jackass thinks he can squirm his way out of anything. Claims Lena must've been high from the chemicals, that she's remembering it all wrong. His lawyer says Bart will tell us everything he knows about Valentine if the charges are reduced to reckless endangerment."

Jeffrey laughed for the first time in days. "He really thinks he's gonna walk away from this?"

"His lawyer indicated he'd be open to probation with time served."

Jeffrey laughed again. He was suddenly looking forward to seeing Fred Bart.

Nick turned serious. "I want your read on the lawyer. Something's going on there."

"All right," Jeffrey agreed. "You got the goods?"

Nick handed him a folder, then reached under the desk and buzzed the door open. Jeffrey followed him to the back, thinking that even though only a few days had passed, the building had an air of neglect to it. Don Cook wasn't exactly a leader, and it was going to take someone with a strong personality and a lot of experience to help the town recover from Valentine's betrayal. Jeffrey gave the man two months before he stepped down, took his retirement and went fishing for the rest of his life.

A tripod with a digital camera on top stood outside the small conference room. Nick rapped his knuckles on the door as he opened it.

"Finally," Bart said, as if he was glad to see them.

Jeffrey threw the file Nick had given him on the table, then he held out his hand, introducing himself to Bart's lawyer. The man didn't offer his name, and Jeffrey guessed from his expensive suit and fancy haircut that he was more at home in Atlanta than Elawah County.

Nick indicated the camera. "Just let me get this set up." He whistled under his breath as he placed the tripod at the head of the table, moving it just so, acting like he had all the time in the world. Jeffrey knew he was just trying to make the dentist antsy, but the technique was working on Jeffrey, too. By the time Nick was finished, Jeffrey was almost squirming in his chair.

Nick sat down beside Jeffrey, opposite Fred Bart and his lawyer. For the sake of the camera, he said, "I'm Nick Shelton with the Georgia Bureau of Investigation. Beside me is Grant County Chief of Police Jeffrey Tolliver, who will be leading this interview. That okay with you boys?"

The lawyer nodded. He was a burly man, his hair shaved close to his head. Jeffrey wondered if he had something tattooed on his scalp.

Bart said, "Can we get this over with?"

Jeffrey opened the file on the table. He fanned out the photographs they had found in a folder on Jake Valentine's desk. Judging from the charred debris in his wastebasket, there had been more photographs, but Valentine had taken care to make sure it was only Fred Bart and Boyd Gibson implicated in the surveillance photos. The sheriff had been telling Jeffrey the truth when he said he'd called the GBI. Nick's office had logged a call on his voice mail about an hour before Jeffrey and Sara had gotten to the jail. Valentine had sounded giddy as he laid out the case of the drug-pin dentist.

Fred Bart barely glanced at the photographs. The pictures were grainy, but they still managed to tell a story. Jeffrey tapped his finger on the top one, which showed Fred Bart with Boyd Gibson smoking cigarettes outside an abandoned-looking warehouse. Behind them, a drug transaction was taking place. Another photo showed Bart in his Jag passing off a stack of money to Boyd Gibson. All the photos pointed the finger at Fred Bart as being the meth mastermind in town with Gibson as his muscle.

Bart blustered, "Obviously, those have been doctored."

"I'm sure you can find an expert to tell that to a jury," Jeffrey admitted. Jake Valentine had done a good job setting up the dentist. If Lena hadn't seen the tattoo under the sheriff's arm, no one would have questioned Valentine's evidence—or Bart's death in his own home-grown meth lab, courtesy of Clint Jones.

Jeffrey told him, "Your bank account shows a cash deposit of over two hundred thousand dollars Friday morning."

"I was in my office with patients. I have no idea what you're talking about."

"You mean your office where they found enough meth to powder a ski slope?" He paused. "Jake was ready to hand the GBI the bust of a lifetime."

Bart shook his head slowly side to side. "I have no idea what you're talking about."

Jeffrey laid it out for the man. "You're looking at the death penalty."

The lawyer interjected, "My client is cooperating in every way he knows how."

"He shot a man in cold blood in front of a police detective."

"She was high," Bart protested, much as Nick had predicted. "With the amount of chemicals in that room, I'm surprised she even remembers she was there. You know what she did to Jake. She cut off his hand! That's not the action of a thinking person."

Jeffrey thought it was the action of somebody who didn't want to die. "You injected my wife with a sedative."

"Jake would've hurt her if I hadn't knocked her out. Mark my words. He was a violent man."

The lawyer stiffened. Jeffrey would have missed it if he hadn't been watching.

Jeffrey asked Bart, "How were you protecting Charlotte Gibson in the back of that Escalade?"

"I've already told your friend here that wasn't me," Bart insisted. "I was at home watching TV that night."

"Lena's willing to make a positive ID."

Bart flashed a smile. "It's my understanding that the perpetrator of that crime was masked."

"Yeah," Jeffrey agreed. "But it's hard to hide behind a mask when you've got little ferret teeth."

Bart covered his mouth with his hand before he could stop himself.

Jeffrey said, "Tell me about Boyd Gibson."

The lawyer seemed to perk up at the sound of Gibson's name. Was Fred Bart the only person in the room who didn't realize the guy was working the other side? Jeffrey would've loved to roll up the man's sleeves, look for any tattoos he might have.

Jeffrey repeated, "Boyd Gibson?"

Bart talked slowly, moving his lips as little as possible as if he could hide his teeth. "Jake told me what happened," he said. "Clint and Boyd never got along, but Jake kept them in line. He told them to burn down Hank's bar. Lena had spent some time there and Jake didn't like her poking around. He was trying to scare her off."

"So?" Jeffrey prompted.

"So, Jake said that they poured gasoline around the outside of the bar. Clint threw a match on it, but then Boyd started yelling about how Hank kept some money inside, stuffed under a floorboard or something."

"He ran into a burning building to get cash?" Jeffrey asked, thinking that if Bart was telling the truth, Jeffrey had risked his life to save one of the stupidest bastards on earth.

Bart nodded. "At that point, you came along. Boyd got away and he met up with Clint in the woods. They had some kind of argument. I told you these men were hotheaded." Bart paused for effect. "At any rate, Clint ended up stabbing Boyd."

"And then what?"

"And then he had to tell Jake."

"What about the knife?"

"Clint didn't want to lose his knife—it was expensive—so he used one he'd...found." The man held out his hands in an open shrug. "Mind you, I got this story second-hand from Jake, so I can't confirm the veracity."

"Yeah," Jeffrey said. "I understand that." He crossed his arms. "Did Jake say whose idea it was to throw Boyd's body into my hotel room?"

"His. Jake thought if your wife got scared enough, you'd leave town."

Jeffrey asked, "What about Charlotte Gibson?"

"Jake got worried because she was talking to Lena."

"So Jake torched her?"

"Yes. Jake liked to send messages."

"Is that right?"

"Yes."

Jeffrey remembered what Lena had said about Bart's last words to Valentine, the anger that had boiled up between the two men. The dentist had been supplementing his income with meth since Valentine was in diapers. He'd been the big man in town until Myra had married her college sweetheart.

"Lemme get this straight." Jeffrey summarized, counting off the dead bodies on his fingers as he said, "Clint Jones killed Boyd Gibson, Jake killed Charlotte and of course you were kind enough to shoot Clint in—what—self-defense? I guess leaving Lena and Sara in the house to die was some kind of oversight on your part?"

"I know I shouldn't have left those women there, but I was terrified. Jake has some powerful friends. I ran away because I was frightened. I take full responsibility for that."

"I'm happy to hear you take responsibility for something."

He tried to defend himself, saying, "I called the sheriff's office and gave an anonymous tip."

Nick had obviously heard this before. "We listened to the nine-one-one tapes from Friday, Fred. We haven't found anything."

"Then you need to keep looking," Bart insisted. "I called from a pay phone at the Stop 'n' Save. It should have my fingerprints on it."

Jeffrey didn't doubt the phone had Bart's prints on it. He'd had plenty of time to think up an alibi while Lena and Sara were fighting for their lives.

"What about the other body?" Jeffrey asked.

"Other body?" Bart echoed. "What other body?"

He seemed as surprised as Sara and Lena had been. Both women swore they hadn't seen anyone else in Hank's house, but the remains of a man's body had been found somewhere in the vicinity of the back bedroom.

Jeffrey told him, "There was another set of bones in Hank Norton's house. The state coroner says he was an older man, maybe in his sixties."

Bart looked at his hands. "I don't know anything about that."

"You don't know anything about a lot of things," Jeffrey challenged. "I think you're just sitting there with your little mind spinning, trying to come up with quick answers for every question, but the thing is you've got no idea how deep this hole is you're standing in."

"I don't know what you mean."

Jeffrey looked at Nick. Both men knew that Bart was either too arrogant or too stupid to see that his life was pretty much over the minute he shot Clint Jones and told Jake Valentine to get under the sink.

"All righty." Nick sighed, pressing his palms against the table as he stood up.

Bart yelped, "What are you doing?"

"Packing up," Nick told him, collapsing the tripod. "You don't know doodly squat, Tonto, and I have a feeling any second now the Lone Ranger there's gonna be heading back up to the corral to get along with his little doggies."

The lawyer chuckled. "Well put."

Nick told him, "No offense, buddy, but we're really hoping none of this goes any farther than it has to."

"I think we've had enough collateral damage to last us for a while." The lawyer pushed Valentine's photos of Fred Bart across the table. "It seems to me you have an overwhelming amount of evidence here. Surely enough to charge the guilty party." He stood, telling Jeffrey. "I'm very sorry that your wife was in harm's way." As an afterthought, he added, "And your detective, too, of course."

Jeffrey took the man's meaning, but he wanted to be clear. "Just so long as they're safe now."

"They are."

The lawyer turned to leave, but Bart clawed his arm, screaming, "You said they'd work a deal! You said they would—"

"Get your hands off me," he barked, jerking his arm away.

Bart finally seemed to understand that the lawyer wasn't on his side, that the only reason the man was here was so he could make sure Bart wasn't a threat to the people who were really paying his fees.

For his part, the lawyer seemed relieved that the masquerade was over. He gave Nick a nod, then Jeffrey. "Gentlemen, if you'll excuse me."

"What are you doing?" Bart demanded. "You're my lawyer! Where are you going?"

The man left the room without looking back.

Bart stood by the table, wringing his hands like a woman.

Nick told him, "Sit down, Fred."

Bart sagged into his chair. "I want to cut a deal," he muttered. "I need to cut a deal."

"Welcome to the State of Getting Your Head Out of Your Ass." Nick clapped his hands in mock congratulations. "What kind of deal you think you can make, Freddy boy?"

"Any kind," Bart pleaded. "Just tell me what you want me to say."

Nick shook his head. "We want you to say some names, Fred. Only problem is, you don't know 'em."

"I know them!" Bart screeched. "I know all of them!"

"Like?"

"Like…" His mouth worked as he tried to come up with something. "Just tell me. Tell me who you want and I'll say it!"

"Rhymes with Spitzpatrick."

He paled. "No," he said. "I can't do that."

Nick shrugged. "Lookit, hoss, we're giving you enough rope here to hang a snake. Not my fault you can't tie the knot."

"They'll kill me," Bart said. "They'll… worse than that. They don't just kill people…they…" His words stopped as he gulped for air. "Please…" he cried.

Jeffrey stood up and Nick opened the door.

"No!" Bart begged. "You can't just leave me here."

Nick couldn't help himself. "Don't worry, hoss. We'll go by the Stop 'n' Save and call nine-one-one on our way out of town."

✦

JEFFREY HAD A BAD TASTE in his mouth as he drove past the Elawah County High School. He should feel good about leaving Fred Bart to the wolves, but instead he felt dirty. Fred Bart had left Sara to burn, and Jeffrey was a firm believer in an eye for an eye. He was also a cop, and he knew the state had a process for taking care of its most deserving criminals. What was the difference between waiting ten years for appeals to fall through and letting the Brotherhood take care of him?

The difference was that the Brotherhood got stronger with every life they took. They wouldn't roll Bart into a sterile room and slip a needle in his arm. They would make him beg for his life. They would beat him, torture him—make it so that death was the only thing he had to look forward to. Fred Bart would be a lesson for every other thug and moron out there: you did not cross the Brotherhood without paying the ultimate price.

Still, Ethan Green's words kept coming back into his head, and Jeffrey couldn't help but wonder if the young man had seen the real Jeffrey, the one who hid behind his badge while he looked the other way. Jeffrey had taken an oath to protect and defend everybody, not just the people he thought deserved it. He was supposed to work within the system, not make up the rules as he went along.

He was supposed to take care of the weak and protect them from the strong. Fred Bart sure hadn't looked strong when Jeffrey and Nick had left him crying in the interrogation room. He had fallen to the floor on his knees, begging for help.

Jeffrey realized he'd passed the motel and made a U-turn. He pulled up in front of the office as the maid was coming out of one of the rooms. She stood there, watching him get out of the car.

Jeffrey told her, "I need to get the things out of room fourteen."

"They're packed up," the woman said, walking away.

Jeffrey guessed he was expected to follow her. He caught the office door before she let it slam in his face.

"Thanks," he said.

She went behind the front counter, scratching her arms through her long-sleeved shirt. She told him, "There's a balance on the room."

Jeffrey glanced at the keys hanging on the board behind her and figured maybe three rooms were checked out. "Been busy lately?"

"Listen, asshole. I don't make the rules."

He laughed, taking out his wallet. "How much is it?"

She scratched her neck, calculating how much she could get off him. "A hundred bucks."

"How about twenty?"

"How about fifty?"

Jeffrey paid her the money, though he seriously doubted the cash would ever make its way into the register. Judging by the woman's appearance, he guessed he was looking at one of those rare things: a meth addict who had made it past her thirties.

The woman asked, "How's the girl doing?"

"Lena?"

"Yeah, her."

"She's okay."

"Right," the woman said. She took out a bag from under the counter and pushed it toward Jeffrey. "Here's her shit. Go on and get the fuck out of here."

He studied her face for a moment, the arrogant tilt of her chin. Slowly, he said, "She's at St. Ignatius for a few more days."

"Great. My tax dollars at work."

"You pay taxes?" She gave him an eat-shit look that he should have been used to by now. "You know, your daughter looks at me the same way sometimes."

"I ain't got a daughter."

"Lena looks just like you."

Angela Adams grunted, giving up. She had fifty bucks in her pocket and a need in her veins. "Got her head up her ass just like me. Didn't recognize her own mother standing right in front of her."

Jeffrey had barely made the connection himself between the oil painting that he'd seen hanging over Hank Norton's living room couch and the woman standing in front of him. Something about the tilt of her chin had given it away—even after all these years, she had that arrogant challenge in her eyes. Angela had been beautiful once, but meth had taken that from her, just like it had taken her away from her young daughters.

Still, Jeffrey tried to be kind. "Sometimes you don't see what you're not looking for."

"You think I don't know what I look like?" She picked at the edge of the laminate. "Hank doing okay?"

Jeffrey felt another piece of the puzzle click into place. "Hank was with you the whole time he was missing. Wasn't he?"

"Stupid fucker should've known better. Didn't last no more than a coupl'er three days before we were ready to kill each other." She picked at the sore on her neck. "Bastard just walked off one morning. I guess he turned up at his house."

"He's cleaning up," Jeffrey told the woman. "All the meth is out of his system."

"He's always looked after them." She caught herself. "Her."

"We found the birth certificate you filled out with Hank's name on it."

"Did she see it?"

"No," Jeffrey said. "It got lost in the shuffle."

She gave a rueful laugh. "Dumb fuck that I was—I figured it'd make it easier for him to take the girls, keep them safe. I nearly got him arrested." She started picking at the sore again. Blood trickled out. "I was the one who got Hank hooked. Did he tell you that?"

"We've never really talked about it."

"When Cal was killed—that's their father—I just couldn't take it. Pregnant, fat, miserable, alone. Then, I had a toothache on top of everything else. I went to that stupid bald fuck Fred Bart. He told me he had something that could take the edge off." She glared at Jeffrey as if he'd challenged her. "I made my choice."

"Lena would want to see you."

"I been in and out of jail the last twenty years. You think a cop wants a con for a mother?"

Jeffrey certainly hadn't wanted his own father, but then you didn't get to choose your parents. "I've known Lena a long time. She'd want to see you."

"You think she wants to see this?" Angela demanded, rolling up her sleeve.

Jeffrey winced at the damage the needles had done to her skin over the years.

"I work here," Angela said. "I make just enough money to keep myself going. I don't need nothing in my life that makes it complicated."

"I'm not sure Lena would agree."

"Yeah, well..." She pushed her sleeve back down. "I don't really give a fuck what you think, asshole. Get the hell out of my face."

She walked around the counter, heading toward the door. Jeffrey expected her to leave, but she stopped.

He tried, "You're her mother. Nothing will ever change that."

She kept her back to him, her hand on the glass door. "You wanna know what kind of mother I am?" She shook her head, disgusted. "I promised I'd leave them alone, but I was broke, twitching so bad it hurt. I went over to the house, begged Hank for some money. He gave it to me, and I—" she took a deep breath. "I was backing up the car, not looking where I was going, and I ran right over her, right in front of her sister and that pudgy little girl from up the street. You know about that? You know I blinded my own daughter?"

Jeffrey couldn't fathom that kind of guilt.

"Cops banged me up the next day for holding. There was some other stuff on my sheet—some bad checks, a couple of priors. The judge came down on me hard. Me and Hank, we figured the girls would be better off thinking I was dead instead of knowing what I really was."

"Still—"

"Mister, giving up those babies was the only good thing I ever did in my life. Don't take that away from me."

She pushed open the door and walked out, leaving Jeffrey alone with Lena's things.

CHAPTER 28

LENA SAT IN A WHEELCHAIR beside Hank's bed, holding his hand with her good one. His skin was dry, his fingers like sticks that wouldn't bend. He wouldn't look at her, wouldn't return her grip. At first, she thought he was mad, but she was slowly beginning to realize that he was ashamed. If he was talking to her, he would've said something about his own pride ruining him. He had been almost arrogant about his recovery from addiction, but it had only taken one needle to get him hooked again. His body was ravaged from the drugs he had taken. The ones the doctors had prescribed were doing their best to counteract the withdrawal, but there was nothing they could really do for his depression.

Mostly, the two of them just stayed like this, Lena holding his hand, Hank staring out the window, until the nurses came and told them both to get some rest. Lena didn't talk much because there wasn't really anything to say.

"Doing okay?" the nurse asked, coming in to check all the tubes and machines Hank was hooked up to. She was a nice woman, but her cheerfulness grated and her voice was loud enough to wake the dead.

"Fine," Lena told her, coughing.

The nurse shot her a look of concern. "Did you do your breathing exercises this morning?"

"Yes, ma'am," Lena answered.

She smiled, patting Hank's hand. "See how good your niece is being, Mr. Norton?" Her voice was even louder when she talked to Hank, probably because he never responded.

She asked Lena, "How's your hand doing?"

Lena held up her right hand, which was tightly bandaged. "Doing okay. The doctors say I should be able to get full movement back."

"Of course you will," the nurse said, relentlessly positive. "Just a few more minutes with your uncle, okay? You both need to get some rest." She wagged her finger in warning. "I'll check up on you!"

The door snicked closed, and Hank mumbled, "Sure is damn loud enough."

Lena felt so relieved to hear him speak that she couldn't respond.

His voice was rough when he asked, "You really doing those exercises, girl?"

"Yes."

"I never could tell when you were lying."

"Me, either."

Hank took a deep breath and let it go slowly.

She said, "Tell me about my mother."

He smiled. "Which story do you want to hear?" He thought she was playing the old game Sibyl and Lena had made up when they were little.

"The true one, Hank. The one where she lived."

His eyes watered all the time now, so she couldn't tell if he was crying. "She always loved you girls. That never stopped."

"She blinded Sibyl."

If he was surprised, she could not tell. His face was still turned away from her. "She came to the house looking for money. She was out of her mind with grief when it happened. I got her out of there, took the blame when the cops rolled up, said it was all my fault. I couldn't let you hate your own mother like that. I wanted you to love her, love the memory of her."

"What happened to her?" Lena asked. "How did she die?"

His head jerked around. He was obviously shocked by the question. There was almost panic in his eyes, as if he could not decide what to tell her.

"It's okay," she soothed. "I'm not blaming you. I'm not angry. I just need to know the truth. Just tell me the truth."

Hank's throat visibly tightened. He pressed his lips together as if to force back the words that wanted to come. He had never been a man to dwell on memories, maybe because none of his were good.

"Hank, tell me," Lena coaxed. "Tell me this one time and I'll never ask you again. I think after all this time I deserve to know how my mother died."

He stared back at the ceiling as if to collect himself. When he finally answered, he spoke so quietly she could barely hear him. "Car accident."

"Fred Bart told me that she's in a better place."

Hank was quiet again, thinking it over. "Losing your daddy, and then hurting your sister like that…" He swallowed, obviously fighting with his emotions. "I'm a selfish man, Lee. You're all I have left and I can't…" His voice caught. "I can't lose you."

Lena tightened her grip on his hand, willing him to understand that she would never leave him again. "When I saw you at the house, you told me that man, Clint Jones, killed my mother."

"He dealt to her," Hank said. "He dealt to both of us."

Lena sat back, trying to reconcile the image she'd had in her head for all these years of Angela the angel with this new one of Angela the drug addict. Had her mother been as bad as Hank? Had her arms been as marked, her features as ravaged? Lena shuddered at the thought, almost wishing she'd never been told.

"Meth is just…" Hank shook his head. "You die the minute you take it. The person you are, the person you were gonna be—that's gone the second the liquid hits your veins. You're dead from that moment on."

"How did it happen? How did she die?"

He closed his eyes, chest rising and falling with each breath. He would not look at her when he said, "She went over Taylor Bridge too fast and hit a telephone pole. Snapped her neck. The doctor said it must have been instant."

Lena had been called out on her share of single-car accidents. Invariably, there was a dark story behind them.

His fingers wrapped around her hand. "She would've never left you if she'd known how sorry I'd turn out to be. She thought I would take care of you."

"You did," Lena told him. "You did the best you could."

"Don't forgive me," he said. His hand was weak but he held on to her as tight as he could. "Don't ever forgive me."

Lena couldn't stop herself. Not after all that had happened, all he had done for her and Sibyl.

He glanced at her, then looked away quickly. "Better get now before that nurse comes back. Makes me wish I was back in a damn coma."

"All right," she said, letting his hand slip from hers. Neither one of them had ever been good at talking about their feelings. "Call me if you need me, okay?"

Lena shuffled out of the room, feeling more tired than she'd thought herself capable. The doctors had told her the reason was because she wasn't getting enough oxygen. Lena thought it was because all she did was lie around the hospital all day with nothing to do but feel sorry for herself.

Her room was right next door to Hank's and she could hear the phone ringing from the hall. Lena hastened her step, snatching up the receiver mid-ring.

"This is a collect call from an inmate in Coastal State Prison," an automated voice informed her. Lena didn't sit on the bed so much as fall. She waited for the recorded voice, her heart thumping against her ribs as she heard, "Ethan Green."

Lena crooked the receiver between her shoulder and ear, pressing the button on the phone to accept the call.

There was silence, nothing but a soft beep every three seconds to remind them that time was passing.

He said, "How you doing?"

Lena glanced around the room, feeling like someone was watching her. "Why are you calling me?" she demanded. "I don't want to talk to you."

"That why you accepted the call?"

"I'm hanging up right now."

"I heard about what happened."

Her hand had been hovering over the phone, ready to hang up, but she stopped at his words. Of course Ethan had heard about what happened. His network would have fed him the news before the media even knew about it.

"That toothache I had when you saw me?" She knew he wasn't expecting an answer. "Don't worry about it," he told her. "I got some medicine. It doesn't hurt anymore."

She thought about Fred Bart, the way the dentist had smiled with his nasty little teeth before he set Charlotte on fire. She spoke before she could stop herself. "Good."

"Nobody hurts my girl. You got me?"

"Nobody but you," she reminded him.

He chuckled lightly. "That's right, Lee. Nobody but me."

Her breath was coming up short. Her hand was still inches from the hook, ready to hang up, but she couldn't make herself do anything but listen.

"I'm gonna write to you," he told her, his voice soft, coaxing. "I'm gonna write to you and you need to write back, okay, baby?"

"No," she said, a begging quality to her voice. She tried to be stronger. "I don't want you in my life anymore."

"You think it's that easy? You think you're ever going to get away from me?" He laughed again, humoring her. "I'm gonna be out of here before you know it, Lee. Then we can start over. Just you and me. Okay?"

She shook her head, words failing her.

"Sleep tight, baby. I'll be thinking about you."

Lena hung up the phone, still hearing his voice, sensing his presence in the room. Who would get to her first—Ethan or Harley? Both men always settled their scores. Neither let anyone get the upper hand. Would she be beaten to death or wake up a couple of weeks from now with some stranger sticking a needle in her arm, telling her not to struggle, that it would be easier if she just gave in? Lena hoped it was the needle; hoped to God that she would never have to see Ethan Green ever again.

She looked up at the ceiling where shadows danced against the white tiles. Ethan was still there—filling every part of the room, every part of her soul. She lay back in bed, his dark presence hanging over her, until exhaustion won out and she finally fell into a deep, dreamless sleep.

CHAPTER 29

SARA SAT ON THE FRONT PORCH, talking on the phone to her mother. Jeffrey had called half an hour ago and said he was just crossing the Grant County line, but she wasn't going to feel safe until he was home. He had told her he needed to talk to her about something, and Sara guessed it was the same thing that had been bothering her for the last few days. She couldn't keep going on like this. Something had to give.

Her mother sounded exasperated. "Are you listening to me?"

"Yes, Mama," Sara lied.

"He told me that he'd fixed the automatic sprinkler. Half the plants are dead."

"I'm sure he didn't do it on purpose."

"We've been home less than a week and he still hasn't offered a credible explanation."

"I'm sure he meant to fix the sprinkler."

"Sara," Cathy began, and Sara braced herself for a lecture. Surprisingly, her mother offered, "Do you want me to come back over? I can be there in five minutes."

Sara loved her mother, but Cathy had been with her practically twenty-four hours a day over the last week. She needed time alone to think. "Jeffrey will be home soon."

"You sound so distant. Is it the lawsuit?"

"No," Sara answered, but the word brought a sour taste to her mouth. Buddy Conford had called two days ago to tell Sara that Global Indemnity was settling with the Powells. The parents would get two million dollars for their son's death, barely enough to cover Jimmy's hospital and lab fees. Buddy had tried to make a joke about how rare it was that an insurance company was actually paying off somebody's medical bills, but Sara hadn't been in the mood for humor.

"If it's not the lawsuit, what is it?"

"Mama…"

Obviously, she'd had enough. "Sara Ann Linton, I am your mother, and I know when something is bothering you."

Sara let out a stream of breath between her teeth.

Cathy cut straight to the heart of the matter. "Did you hear from the adoption agency?"

"Yes," she said. The social worker had left a message on the machine that morning while Sara was at her parents' house. She'd come home to find the red button flashing, but had let three hours pass before she pressed play. It was the same thing that kept her from checking the mailbox or listening to the voice mail on her cell phone. Sara had waited so long to hear that there was a child out there for them, but now that the moment was at hand, she could not bring herself to reach out.

"And?" Cathy prompted. "What did she say?"

"She said that they have a nine-month-old boy," Sara answered. "He's mixed race, Asian and African-American."

"Oh, honey, that's wonderful!"

"Is it?" Sara asked, feeling like her heart was going to break. Just saying the words had conjured up the creamy skin and wiry hair—the way his little feet would curve into the palm of her hand. "What am I going to do, Mama, stay up with a baby all night while I wait for the phone to ring so some stranger can tell me my husband's dead?"

"Stop being ridiculous," Cathy snapped. "Cops have families, Sara. *Plumbers* have families. You take a risk every time you get behind the wheel of a car or go to the post office. You can't put your life on hold because you're scared of something that *might* happen."

"Jeffrey's so stubborn," she argued. "He never listens."

"Welcome to marriage, honey. I'm sorry we can't organize you a parade."

Sara put her hand to her neck, tried to coax the words that needed to come. "What if…" she tried. "What if…" She dropped her head in her hand, finally voicing her darkest concern. "What if I can't take care of him, Mama? What if he gets sick or injured and I can't..."

Her mother was gentle, but stern. "It is not your fault that Jimmy Powell died of leukemia."

"What if my baby gets sick?"

"I know you pretend you don't believe in these things, but you'll know the first time you hold your child that he is a gift on loan from God. For however long that gift lasts, you cherish it, you hold it to your heart, and you do the best you can to never let go."

"I just can't..." Sara thought about Jimmy Powell the last time she had seen him alive. His eyes had lit up when Sara entered his hospital room. He'd always had such a crush on her. She was as close as he would ever come to having a girlfriend. He would never steal a kiss from a girl after school or make out in the back of his father's car. He would never have a wife or a child. His mother would never have grandchildren. For the rest of her life, Beckey Powell would have nothing but lost milestones to remind her of her dead son. Other children would go to school. Other families would take holidays together. Beckey would only have an empty calendar, days without Jimmy stretching before her like a bottomless pit.

Cathy's tone softened. "What did you tell the social worker?"

"That I would need to talk to Jeffrey."

"You call her back right now and tell them you want that baby."

"Mama, I don't know."

"I do," Cathy interrupted. "I'm hanging up the phone so you can call her." She paused. "Call me right back, okay? I want to hear all about my first grandbaby."

The line went dead, but Sara didn't make the call. Now that she had time alone, she found herself incapable of putting together any logical thoughts. Her mind kept jumping from Jimmy Powell, to Jeffrey, to the baby that was waiting for them. She sat motionless, staring at the street until her BMW pulled up in front of the house.

Jeffrey waved at her through the windshield, giving a half-smile. He had told her there was something he needed to tell her, something important. This wasn't just her decision. Maybe he was having second thoughts, too.

Sara put the phone down on the steps and walked toward the car.

He opened the door, saying, "Man, I'm sick of driving." He saw her face, asked, "What's wrong?"

"The adoption agency called."

He closed the distance between them, scooping her up into his arms. "A baby!" he yelled. "Oh, God, Sara." He spun her around. "I can't believe it. I can't believe—" He was laughing, trying to catch his breath. "Is it a girl or a boy?"

"A boy."

"Ha!" he said, spinning her around again.

Sara laughed, too, caught up in his excitement. "You'll make me dizzy."

He put her down, cupped her face in his hands. "I've got a boy!" He kissed her. "This is it, Sara. This is the beginning of our lives." He kissed her again, deeper this time. "God, I love you."

She could see tears in his eyes, the absolute joy he felt at the news. Suddenly, all of her doubts fell away, meaningless distractions. She wanted a child with this man, wanted nothing more in her life than to raise their baby together.

He asked, "Can we pick him up tonight? Right now?"

"Tomorrow," she said, laughing at his eagerness. "We have to meet at the agency and start the foster care procedures."

"Paperwork," he groaned, but he was still smiling. "Oh, God, Sara. I love you so much."

She put her hand to his cheek. "I know."

He laughed again, almost a whoop. "What do we do now?"

"They said they already sent the forms," she told him. "Check the mailbox. I'll get the phone."

She was halfway up the front walk when he yelled at her. "Hey, foxy mama!"

Sara turned around, her face blushing red. "Hush," she warned him. "The neighbors."

"Call them all!" he yelled. "We're gonna be parents!"

He opened the mailbox. There was a flash of light. Jeffrey flew up and back, his body twisting as the air cracked from the explosion.

Sara was running toward him before her mind processed what she had seen.

A bomb. Somebody had put a bomb in the mailbox.

"Jeffrey!" she gasped, falling down on her knees beside him. Chunks of metal were everywhere, mail flying all around them. She saw his open chest—bone, muscle, beating heart.

"Help!" she screamed. "Somebody help me!"

He opened his mouth and blood pooled out. His right arm lay on the asphalt a few feet away, torn from his shoulder. She pressed her hands to the open wound, desperate to stop the bleeding. Blood poured between her fingers, soaked her hands.

"No," she whispered. "No."

"You..." he said, his teeth chattering.

She pressed her lips to his, kissed him on his mouth, his face. "Oh, my love... my love...."

"You..." he whispered, blindly reaching for her. She could see the pain in his eyes, knew that his life was slipping away.

"Don't leave me," she pleaded, squeezing his hand. "Oh, God, Jeffrey—please don't leave me."

"You..."

"No," she begged, willing him to hold on. "Please! I love you. I love you." Why had she always teased him, never telling him the words? "Jeffrey, I love you."

"Only..."

She kissed him again, tasting his blood in her mouth. This couldn't be happening. He could not leave her.

"Only..." he tried, blood gurgling in his throat. "Only... ever..."

"Only ever what, baby? Only what?"

"You..." He gasped, choking. "...Only... ever... you..."

His body relaxed. The blood stopped spurting from his shoulder. Sara realized that their neighbors had come. They stood in a circle around her, not knowing what to do. She screamed, ordering them to go away. She didn't want them to see him like this, didn't want anyone to touch him. The ambulance came, then the police; his men, his friends. She railed against them all, begging them to leave. She lifted Jeffrey up, holding him in her arms, refusing to let them near. She held on to him like this, keening like a child, until her mother came and made Sara let them take him away.

ACKNOWLEDGMENTS

There are many people to thank for helping me with this novel. My agent, Victoria Sanders, has been there from the beginning. Susan Sandon, Kate Elton and Kate Miciak – as always – were invaluable. I would also like to single out Rina Gill; my champion, my Bossy Sheila, the best publicist and friend a gal could hope for. Richard Cable belongs in here somewhere: thank you so much for all you do. Claire Round, Adam Humphrey and Rob Waddington deserve special praise as well. It's so brilliant to work with people whose company you really enjoy. Dave Parrish and Simon Littlewood, you are both international superstars. Richard Ogle again did a great job on design. Georgina Hawtrey-Woore, thanks for keeping the wheels turning. Speaking of which – Gail Rebuck, you have my undying gratitude for putting together the most well-oiled machine in publishing. And speaking of well oiled . . . Simon Master, you are most certainly missed.

Sue Kurylowicz was the winner of the "Get Slaughtered!" contest, granting her the dubious honor of having her name appear in this book. Sue, honey, you *did* ask to be bad . . .

On the medical side of things, David Harper, MD, was again a huge help. It's not many people who will keep listening when you begin a conversation with, "So, I want to burn someone alive . . ." Family-wise, I want to thank my daddy for teaching me the important things early on, and to DA, as always, you are my heart.

I've written a little note for my readers that can be found at karinslaughter.com/letter. Please note that this letter contains major spoilers for this novel, so don't ruin it for youself and save it for after you've read the book.